Absolution: Winner of the 2013 Holt Medallion
award for paranormal romance

"Fast paced and filled with well-developed characters. *Redemption* is the first book of The Penton Legacy, and readers will anxiously await the sequels!"

—*RT Book Reviews*, 4 ½ stars for *Redemption*

"This is a must read for vampire fans. Fans of authors like Kresley Cole and Jeaniene Frost should really enjoy."

—Parajunkee Reviews on *Redemption*

"*Absolution* is a fun and fast-paced read loaded with well-developed characters and believable, fully realized settings. This is one of those rare sequels that almost outshines its predecessor."

—*RT Book Reviews*, 4 ½ stars for *Absolution*

"I loved this book. *Absolution* has officially cemented Sandlin's Penton Legacy as one of my favorite new series this year."

—She Wolf Reads on *Absolution*

"This series continues to ratchet up the drama and this reader hopes that Hollywood will take notice."

—*RT Book Reviews*, Top Pick, 4 ½ stars for *Omega*

"I love when an author gets me so caught up in the tale and characters that reality slips away, and Sandlin manages this every time. I cannot wait to see where she takes this series next!"

—The Caffeinated Book Reviewer on *Omega*

ALLEGIANCE

ALLEGIANCE
THE PENTON LEGACY

SUSANNAH SANDLIN

Montlake
Romance

Text copyright © 2014 Susannah Sandlin
All rights reserved.

Published by Montlake Romance, Seattle

www.apub.com

ISBN-13: 9781477823316
ISBN-10: 147782331X

Cover design by Kerrie Robertson

Library of Congress Control Number: 2014900301

Printed in the United States of America

Dedication

To Dianne, who, as always, reins in the melodrama.
Cage thanks you.

❧ PROLOGUE ❧

Movement from above. Unfamiliar voices. The dreams always began this way.

A shaft of light would pierce the darkness. Heavy boots would descend the steps. The gleam of a sharpened sword would rivet his attention until his gaze rose to the face of the man who bore it. The Slayer, Mirren Kincaid. The man who'd come to kill him.

In the dreams, Matthias Ludlam always met his final moments not with brave defiance but with humiliation, pleading for mercy from the man whose life he'd tried to destroy.

Each day at dusk, as Matthias came out of another daysleep, the dream would reach the same end. Kincaid would smile, and the blade would fall.

He had spent the past three months thinking of little else. Tonight, finally, could be the night the dream became real. The muffled thumps that drifted down from above were real enough, sounding as if an army were marching heavy jackboots across Matthias's kitchen at the top of the stairs. His meticulous marking of time on the wall of his cell told him he still had one day before his execution, and he felt absurdly resentful that they'd even rob him of an extra day in which to brood about his fate.

His sluggish vampire heart sped up at the sound of keys rattling in the locked door at the top of the stairs. Every two weeks, always on a Wednesday, a silent brute of a vampire guard would accompany a human in and allow Matthias to feed—enough to keep him conscious and aware of his surroundings, but never enough to satisfy. Never enough to kill the gnawing hunger that burned his gut and further frayed his nerves.

But today was not Wednesday, nor was it his week to feed.

The voices were not familiar—but then again, his keepers rarely spoke. Never answered questions. Never responded to taunts or threats or pleas.

The last words he'd heard spoken to him—"Your death sentence has been issued, you sonofabitch"—had come three months ago, delivered by that British turncoat Cage Reynolds. He'd taken Reynolds into his inner circle and paid for it dearly. With a cadre of human soldiers, Reynolds had shoved Matthias down the narrow staircase into the basement of his own Virginia estate. He'd thrown him into the silver-lined cell Matthias had constructed for his own enemies. And Reynolds had pronounced the Tribunal's sentence for Matthias's so-called crimes.

Since then, Matthias had spent his nights in darkness, and during daysleep he dreamed. Oh, how he dreamed. Of killing Reynolds. Of dying at the hand of Kincaid.

A shaft of light penetrated the eternal, damnable darkness of the basement, followed by the click of the overhead light switch. Squinting against the harsh glare, Matthias held his breath, waiting for Kincaid's heavy boots to come into view. Then the sword. Then the smile.

But it was a stone-faced behemoth with a clean-shaven head and a diamond embedded in one of his fangs. Matthias had never seen him before. Nor did he know his companion, a big, ugly, lethal-looking vampire; knives hung in scabbards on each hip and a rifle had been slung by a strap over his shoulder. A nice match to the big automatic that Stoneface wore in a shoulder holster. They expected trouble.

"Stand away from the door." Stoneface pulled a set of keys from his pocket and dangled them from one finger. "We have a field trip planned."

So they weren't going to kill him here. Matthias stepped back, relieved that if he had to die, at least it wouldn't be in this dungeon of his own making. He'd locked up his son, William, here throughout the boy's early days as a vampire, hoping to starve or beat or whip him into submission, for all the good it had done. He'd kept that bastard Kincaid prisoner here for a month, starving him and keeping him locked in silver chains that burned his skin, hoping to coerce him into joining Matthias's organization. Until William rode to the rescue on his proverbial white horse and took Kincaid back to that backwater town of theirs in Alabama.

Penton. Matthias wished he'd never heard of the accursed place.

"Where are you taking me?" Matthias didn't struggle when Stoneface pulled his arms behind him and snapped his wrists into cuffs—silver, judging by the sting on his skin. They wouldn't hurt him; just burn like hell and render him as weak as a human.

"Shut up and walk."

Matthias paused, causing Big and Ugly to lower the rifle.

"You could at least tell me where you're taking me. It's my execution, after all. Is it Kincaid? Are you taking me to that godforsaken rat's nest in Alabama? Has the Tribunal hired Kincaid to perform one last execution for them?"

Bad enough to die looking at Kincaid's smirk. Worse if his own son William stood by and watched.

Faster than Matthias could track the movement from behind, Stoneface jerked a cloth bag of some kind over his head and shoved him toward the stairs. A shoulder-first crash into the side of the stairway was the only thing that kept him from hitting the floor.

"I can't breathe." The overwhelming fear that had haunted him since his arrest kicked into hyperventilation territory. "I'm going to pass out. Take off the hood. Please."

Rough hands took his shoulders and pushed him forward until his toes bumped the bottom stair. "Keep moving. I don't give a shit if you ride to your final destination conscious or unconscious. Either climb out or we'll carry you out."

Weakened from hunger and with his hands cuffed behind him, Matthias took the stairs slowly in order to keep his balance. Once he'd calmed, he realized he could breathe. In fact, he could see the area around his feet, and some light permeated his hood, which had probably begun its life as a pillowcase.

At the top of the stairs, the air-conditioned cool of the kitchen stroked his body, offering such relief he wanted to cry. It also made him more aware of the sweat that coated him under the once-white silk shirt that now stuck to his chest like cheap gray paper, and of the grime and stench of three months spent in the same clothes.

The air-conditioned relief lasted less than a minute. He might not have been able to see his surroundings, but Matthias knew this house well. This estate outside Fredericksburg, Virginia, had been his favorite among the half-dozen properties he held around the world—properties that, ironically, would be inherited by his ingrate of a son as soon as he died. He hoped William would choke with guilt every time he spent as much as a penny of the money he'd rejected for most of his life.

Stoneface and Ugly guided him out the west entrance of the house, through the door nearest the basement cell. Matthias could still visualize it perfectly. Once he'd stumbled off the step and regained his balance on the smooth pavement, he gasped rich lungfuls of fresh air that smelled of recently mown grass. The hint of coolness told him autumn would soon end the humidity of another long Southern summer. This one had seemed longer than most.

"Stop here." Ugly's hand remained on Matthias's shoulder, but Stoneface stepped away. A jangle of keys preceded the unmistakable click of a car trunk being unlocked.

By God, enough was enough. If they thought he'd go quietly into the dark again—into a coffin on wheels—they had the wrong vampire.

"Fuck. You." Matthias twisted away from Ugly and aimed his head in the solid mass of muscle somewhere to the north of Stoneface's feet—all he could see—and butted him with the rage he'd kept bottled up for months. Stoneface fell with a grunt and Matthias propelled himself on top, scraping the man's cheek open with his fangs—the only weapon at his disposal.

He spat out the blood. "Fuck you if you think you'll lock me in there. Grow some balls and just kill me here."

A sharp, sudden pain in his upper back riveted his attention away long enough for Stoneface to shove him aside and Ugly to jerk him to his feet. Ugly had stabbed him, the sonofabitch. During the scuffle the pillowcase had come off Matthias's head, and he swayed, the floodlights of the driveway blinding him for a few seconds before dulling to gray as if they shone through a filmy screen.

He scarcely had time to think "silver blade" before one of his tormenters shoved him from the side; he had no option but to roll into the trunk. He'd barely jerked his feet inside before the trunk lid slammed shut and he was again in darkness.

The next couple of hours, or maybe it was three or four, passed in a series of jolts as the vehicle—a rough-riding sedan—bounced his head against a wheel well and sent a dull, throbbing ache skittering through his nerve endings. Rolling to his side helped the pain from the stab wound, but it put his nose in closer proximity to the reek of old oil and the car's rubber tires rolling on asphalt that was still warm from the day's sun.

Matthias had drifted into a dull-witted stupor—the state in which he'd spent most of his waking hours, the last three months—when the vehicle jolted to a stop. It sent him rolling face first, a rug burn from the industrial-grade carpet scraping his right cheek.

Before he could roll onto his back and put his legs up in anticipation of taking a healthy kick at his tormenters, the trunk lid popped open. He had a brief view of a clear black sky dotted with stars before Big and Ugly leaned in, stuck meaty hands under his armpits, and dragged him out of the vehicle.

Matthias looked around him at the black mounds of starlit hillsides. "Where are we?" It was too mountainous for Penton, but it had that same earthy smell of pine and moldering leaves.

"Where you end your life," Stoneface said, and Matthias was pleased to see that the results of his fang work, the man's bloody new trench of skin and tissue, had yet to heal. "Or start a new one."

The headlights of an approaching car shone from below their stopping place several seconds before it crested the hill into view and came to a stop in front of the sedan. Matthias squinted to see inside the silver SUV, his heart speeding up as Stoneface's words sank in. "What do you mean, start a new life?"

"You'll see." Stoneface threw the keys to the handcuffs in a clump of leaves to Matthias's right and walked to the passenger-side door of the sedan. Ugly had already slid behind the wheel. Stoneface looked back. "You have fucked things up for a lot of people, Matthias Ludlam. Tonight was just a job, but if I ever lay eyes on you when I'm not on the company payroll, I will tear out your fucking throat."

He got in the vehicle with a slam, Ugly cranked it up, and they pulled away, leaving Matthias to face the mysteries ahead.

Perhaps by "start a new life," Stoneface had meant a rebirth in the heavenly realm, or whatever afterlife one believed in. But Matthias suspected that maybe, just maybe, he'd gotten a reprieve.

And where there was a reprieve, there was the chance for revenge.

❧ CHAPTER 1 ❧

Cage Reynolds sighed in relief when the 727 began its descent to Atlanta's Hartsfield-Jackson International Airport. Vampires and long red-eye flights made bad companions, even if the vampire in question wasn't claustrophobic. An unexpected delay that trapped a plane on a runway after sunrise would lead to a very public frying.

Frying publicly in the midst of a planeload of humans would truly suck.

Now that he'd arrived on American soil, Cage let his thoughts travel to Penton, Alabama, his ultimate destination. He'd gone there six months ago to gauge if master vampire Aidan Murphy's idea of a scathe community that could weather the current "vampire apocalypse" could work in Cage's native London.

He'd fled like a coward three months later with way more baggage than he'd bargained for, including friends—a scarce commodity for a nomad—and a woman who'd awakened in him a compassion so alien he thought he'd lost it a century earlier.

Penton had gotten complicated.

If Cage had learned anything in his seventy-five years as a vampire, it was this: keep things simple. Caring hurt. Loving killed. The fight—that was what filled the empty spaces of a life that stretched on too long. The adrenaline rush of besting an enemy, of taking down a despot, of feeling a power so strong it filled those voids in his deadened heart.

Now? Melissa Calvert, a human turned vampire barely three months ago, held his future in her small, fragile palm.

When Aidan had called and asked him to return and help shore up security before the upcoming Tribunal elections, Cage had leapt at the chance, even though the idea of facing Melissa again set his heart thumping—whether out of fear or guilt, he wasn't sure.

All he knew was that he'd found her being held captive, had saved her, had let her transfer all of her gratitude to him, had let her call it love. He'd planned to fuck her and flee; that was his MO, after all.

He'd fled, all right, his reawakened conscience bristling after having done no more than kiss her. Somehow she'd reached inside and touched him. Appealed to the part of him that had been a psychiatrist in his human life. Burrowed past the thick outer shell of the soldier of fortune he'd become since being turned. Brushed gentle fingers against the nerve endings still raw after Paris.

He wouldn't think about Paris.

So here he was again, moving toward Penton—only this time he hoped to stay. To finally make a home for himself. If Melissa could forgive him. If she accepted his admission that he'd fucked up by letting her care for him, for allowing her to think they had a future. He loved her, but not in that stay-with-me-forever kind of bond that vampires instinctively formed when they met their intended mate.

Cage Reynolds was not a bond-mate type of vampire. And Melissa Calvert was not a casual fuck-buddy kind of woman.

If she accepted the truth and didn't poison the rest of the town against him, then maybe Cage the Wandering Boy could finally stop roaming. God knew there was enough drama in the vampire world these days to keep even the most jaded adrenaline junkie happy. Starvation. Civil unrest. Political intrigue. Penton was a veritable oasis in that desert of chaos, now that Matthias Ludlam was out of the picture; once Aidan took a seat on the Tribunal, maybe other places could follow Penton's example.

Then again, the people of Penton might only see Cage as the selfish bastard who ruined Mark and Melissa Calvert's perfect marriage.

The lights of Atlanta fanned out below him, growing from twinkles to dots to streetlights as the plane lowered its landing gear and approached the runway.

The pilot welcomed them to the United States and advised them on Customs requirements, prompting Cage to dig in the interior pocket of his leather jacket for his brilliantly faked passport. It identified him as Cage Reynolds, age thirty-two, resident of London, citizen of the UK. The face in the passport photo was the same one he'd had since 1942, after Paris. After the pit.

Everything had changed since then, and yet nothing had changed. His hair was longer, sweeping his shoulders when it wasn't pulled back, but it was the same light caramel brown. He had fangs rather than canines and lived on the ultimate low-carb diet, but he'd never eaten his veggies like a good boy even as a human. His eyes lightened to a silvery green when he was hungry, or angry, or aroused, or stressed out—which seemed about 90 percent of the time. The rest of the time, they were the same mossy color they'd always been. The face that looked back at him from the passport had a cocky, self-sure expression that didn't show the arsewipe who lived inside the shell.

A chickenshit arsewipe as well, or he'd have told Melissa Calvert before he left that he didn't return her feelings, not in the way she wanted. Or he should've fucked her as planned, scratched that itch, and at least not left both horny and guilty.

Cage dallied toward the back of the Customs line, and then dawdled in gift shops on his way to baggage claim. Aidan had said whoever picked Cage up would probably be a bit late. Cage hoped it would be Aidan himself, so he could get the rundown on the situation in Penton. Last time he was there the town had lain in ruins, more than half of its citizens dead or gone, and he was leaving to inform Matthias Ludlam, who'd started the whole mess, of his pending execution.

Tomorrow, the date Matthias was due to meet whatever was the opposite of a heavenly reward, would be a lovely day to celebrate.

Of course, if he were picked up by Aidan's massive second-in-command, Mirren Kincaid, Cage also would get a report, only it would be much less pleasant and filled with many more expletives.

No such luck. It was Melissa Calvert's face he zeroed in on as soon as he rounded the last corner into the baggage-claim area. His breath caught at the rush of memories and feelings, some good, some bad. Most a perplexing cocktail of both.

Stop overthinking, Reynolds. He hadn't practiced psychiatry in more than seven decades, but overanalyzing was a hard habit to break.

Melissa gave him a shy wave, and he felt an annoying blossom of warmth open in his chest. He ignored the spinning carousel of luggage, elbowed his way among a dozen tourists chattering in German, and pulled her into a hug. The pressure of her arms around his waist, her sweet cinnamon smell, and the warm stroke of her fingers on his back grounded him more than the wheel of the plane thumping onto the runway had done. Now, he was home.

He just hoped he could talk Aidan and the rest of the good people of Penton into letting him stay after he hurt this woman who was so intrinsically one of them.

Cage might have spent most of his human and vampire years in London, but Penton was where he fit. Where he felt whole again—something he'd thought was out of his reach.

Melissa's curly, strawberry-blonde hair brushed across Cage's cheek like floral-scented whispers as he stepped back and held her at arm's length. She'd grown thinner, her rounded face taking on the paler, more honed look of a vampire, but her hazel eyes sparkled. New vampires often had a hard transition, and hers had been traumatic. She'd publicly had her throat slashed and then been spirited away and secretly turned vampire just before the point of death. Matthias Ludlam couldn't die too soon. Cage's only regret was that Ludlam's executioners would probably be humane.

"You look lovely, Mel. I . . ." He frowned at her suddenly pained expression, her mouth thinned, brows scrunched together. "What's wrong?"

She spoke through lips compressed so tightly they'd turned white. "I'm trying not to grin at you. Aidan says if I can't stop showing my fangs, he's going to lock me in the old clinic subbasement again and tie me down with silver-laced rope."

Cage laughed before he could stop himself. He'd forgotten the singsong lilt of her Southern accent and her penchant for saying exactly what she thought. "See. Watch my technique." He grinned at her. "Push your lower lip up on the sides."

She tried a lopsided grin that made her look like a grimacing Halloween monster before she gave up and collapsed against his chest in laughter. When the giggles faded, she wrapped her arms around him again, tighter this time. "I missed you, Cage."

"Me too, love." And he had. He'd forgotten how easy they were together, and in this time of turmoil, comfort was a rare commodity. When was the last time he'd laughed?

It certainly hadn't been in London. The city's starving vampire community had split into radical fringe groups, some even supporting the idea of revealing their existence to the unwitting human population. They believed vampires could rely on human mercy to save them.

Cage didn't agree. He'd seen genocide and unspeakable behavior both in his human life and afterward. Mercy was a gift, not a given.

Starving vampires didn't respond well to political rhetoric, however, so his Tribunal leader, Edward Simmons, had a boatload of work ahead to prevent his desperate people from committing the vampire version of seppuku. Things were slightly better in the States, he'd heard, but only because the vampire population was waiting to see how the blood banks would work.

"You got a lot of luggage?" Melissa pulled away from him and looked at the thinning crowd around the edges of the baggage carousel. "Aidan wanted to come himself, but he just got back from Washington and had a conference call with Colonel Thomas." The human Army colonel, whose daughter was a member of the Penton scathe, had helped them put the old sadist Matthias away.

In exchange, the US vampires had agreed to stay hidden while banks of unvaccinated blood were set up. Starting with the Penton scathe, they'd also be providing vampire operatives to work side by side with human Army Rangers on national security cases. They'd taken the name Omega Force, after the underground bunker the Pentonites had lived in while their town was under siege.

Cage wanted to ask how the Omega Force units were doing, but Melissa wasn't the right person. She'd not likely be privy to Tribunal or security issues.

For now, they'd keep the subject easy. "I travel light—one bag. Pull the car around, and I'll meet you outside."

Cage watched her leave, her navy sweater disappearing from view as she blended with the travelers piling in and out of taxis and shuttle buses. He quelled his instinctive rise of worry. She'd survived—maybe even thrived—away from him for the past three months. It would be too easy to fall back into protective mode, and they'd be right back where they were before, with her needing something he wasn't capable of giving.

He turned back to the carousel and waited for his heavy trunk to roll round again; it was all he had to show from his life in London. He'd cleared out the flat he'd leased for the past five years. Longer than that in one place and the neighbors might wonder why the bloke down the corridor hadn't aged. Not that he was there much. Soldiers of fortune went where they were hired and fought for whoever offered the most payoff in adrenaline and cash.

That life had grown old, however, and he had grown tired. Living in Penton and feeling part of a community had shown him how tired.

He'd donated most of his meager belongings to a local shelter, packed up the rest, and mailed the flat's owner two months' rent and the key. He'd broken the news to Edward Simmons—the UK Tribunal representative and his scathe master—that he wouldn't be returning.

He just wanted Penton.

He rolled his trunk outside. The midnight-blue BMW idling in front of the baggage-claim exit belonged to Aidan—another reminder that it was not Cage's job to be Melissa's protector.

Aidan took care of his people. He didn't need Cage Reynolds to do it for him.

Melissa popped the trunk for him but got out and walked around, helping move some of Aidan's papers aside to make room. His shoulder brushed hers, whisper light, but neither of them moved away. An accident or a test?

This time, when she turned and looked up at him, the lights from the taxis and other vehicles seemed to move like a carousel around their still little world, where nothing could touch them. Her lips parted slightly, but her expression was troubled, not aroused.

They spoke at the same time.

"We need to—"

"Now's not the time, but—"

They smiled, and Melissa slammed the trunk. "You want to drive?"

Oh, hell no. "Love, the last thing I drove was a 1941 Peugeot, in Paris. You do not want me behind the wheel."

She cocked her head. "I never knew you lived in Paris. Or were you visiting? This was before you were turned?"

"Before, yes." He had no more to say on that subject. "Not a happy subject with me, though."

Understatement. He hoped she'd let it go, and after studying him a second, she nodded and climbed behind the wheel. He strapped himself into the passenger seat.

They remained silent while she pulled the car away from the loading area and circled the terminal via the byzantine airport roadways. Well, this was damned awkward. Time to turn on the Reynolds charm. It wouldn't do to get into relationship matters before they reached Penton. For one thing, he didn't want her turning him out on the highway.

"How did the fam situation sort itself out?" Cage kept his voice casual, but he saw Melissa's fingers tense around the leather steering wheel. Not a good sign. She didn't answer until she'd gotten the car out of the airport traffic glut and reached the freeway feeder road.

"We're short on fams." Melissa had been Aidan's familiar—a bonded human feeder and also a close friend—before being turned by Matthias and his lackeys, who'd hoped to use her against Aidan.

"When you say you're short, how short? Has Aidan begun recruiting in Atlanta again?" Their Irish-born master vampire had a clever system, taking unvaccinated addicts or abuse cases and rehabbing them with enthrallment and counseling. Once they were clean and sober, they could move to Penton as a familiar, or he'd alter their memories and help fund a new start for them wherever they wanted. "How many of the fams left?"

"It wasn't just fams; scathe members left, too." Melissa took the exit for I-85 South and settled back as they left Atlanta traffic behind and cruised through the suburbs toward Penton, about eighty miles to the southwest and just across the Georgia-Alabama line. "We're down to about twenty-five scathe members and ten humans, so fams are doing double and triple duty."

She glanced over at him. "I think there are some new people coming tomorrow night who can be feeders, but until then you've been assigned to Max. He was the only one in the town's inner circle without three to feed."

"Bloody hell." Max Jeffries was one of Penton's resident Army Rangers. He'd joined the Penton Omega Force team and had butted heads with Cage from the day he arrived until the night Cage left. "Does he still think he can best a vampire in a fistfight?" Because Cage might have to refresh Max on a few facts of life.

Melissa laughed. "Judging by the cuts and bruises he's always covered with, I'd say he's still trying. Mirren will have to fill you in on that. He's going to help with the training."

They'd moved out of suburban traffic, and the interstate highway stretched before them like a gray ribbon illuminated by the sedan's headlights. The dark outlines of pine forests buffeted each side of the highway, deserted at 2:30 a.m. except for the occasional big-rig truck hightailing it toward Montgomery and points west.

The headlights' high beams caught a flash of white in the woods to their right, and then a second flash.

Cage leaned forward. "What the hell was that?"

Mel hit a switch on the driver's-side door, and all the locks clicked shut. "Open the glove box. Mirren sent you a present."

Cage opened the compartment cautiously—the big Scotsman distrusted Cage on a number of levels. One, Mirren had been a Scottish gallowglass warrior living in Ireland when he was turned vampire four centuries earlier, and he considered Englishmen high on the satanic scale. Two, Cage had been the newest, and thus least trusted, of Aidan's lieutenants in Penton. And three, Cage had been, in Mirren's colorful phraseology, a "fucking brain-shrinker." Never mind that he hadn't shrunk a brain professionally in decades.

On the other hand, Mirren Kincaid would be any psychiatrist's dream study—except Cage figured there was a high probability at any given moment that the oversized oaf would wield his circa-1600 sword and start lopping off heads, starting with the brain-shrinker's.

So he stuck his fingers in the compartment with a delicate touch lest something cut, latch onto, or bite them. Instead, they brushed across the cold, polished steel of a shape he recognized: a Colt .45 semiautomatic, both Mirren's and Aidan's weapon of choice. He approved; the gun was big and heavy, and it fit well in a man's hand.

Not comforting that he needed a weapon for a ninety-minute automobile ride, however. "So, what exactly did I see in the woods out there?"

"We call them vampabonds. Vampire vagabonds. The numbers have really picked up in the last month." She gave a halfhearted laugh. "It's gotten worse since some yahoo in Montgomery got the bright idea of offering one-dollar bus fare from Atlanta. Now, they blend in with all the humans on the late bus and can get here cheap, with air conditioning and Wi-Fi along the way."

Cage confirmed that the gun had a full cartridge and scanned the woods and fields they sped past. "These vampabonds—are they looking for food or for Penton?"

"Both. Some are heading for Penton, hoping Aidan will take them in and let them stay, thinking it's an easy way to get unvaccinated blood. Some are just moving farther into the rural areas, hoping to find humans they can feed from."

Neither of those would necessitate a gun. After all, someone wanting to move to Penton would want to cooperate, and the ones looking for humans would avoid other vampires so they could keep unvaccinated feeders to themselves.

There had to be more. "What part are you not telling me?"

"The vampabonds are increasing," Melissa said, disgust clear in her tone. "Word travels, and they know there are unvaccinated people in Penton. We've had a few coming into town thinking if they get lucky and kill Aidan or Mirren or Will, some of those humans would be free for the taking."

Every vampire and human in Penton had to be bonded to one of the three master vampires: Aidan, Mirren, or Will Ludlam, Matthias's much-abused son. No one outside the scathe could feed from a bonded human—unless the master vampire who held their bond got killed.

"That's inconvenient." Cage had hoped his fellow vamps would see Penton as an idea to emulate, not a feeding buffet. "We shouldn't be surprised, I suppose. Some humans are bad people. When they become vampires, they don't suddenly develop morals." Like he was any judge of morality.

He stared out the window as they whizzed past the black shadows of pine forest. "Any chance some of our old enemies from the Tribunal are behind this influx, and how many are we talking about?"

"There's been nothing to make us think it's Tribunal related." Melissa shook her head. "Numbers . . . I don't know, maybe six or seven coming into Penton every week or two? Enough that Mirren's got the patrols going around town again."

So much for easing back into Penton life and training leisurely for whatever the Army Rangers had in mind for the special unit. Cage fought back a smile, his blood moving faster. He might be looking for a place to settle down, but he still got off on the rush.

The one good piece of news was that Matthias Ludlam was about to be truly and finally dead. "How's Will doing? I mean, Matthias is his father, as well as being a right evil bastard."

Melissa shrugged. "Randa says he's either ignoring talk about Matthias or making wisecracks. Typical Will, in other words— bottling everything up inside." She flipped on the turn signal as they approached an exit where the lights of a convenience mart shone through the trees. "I need to get some gas."

"What about his—"

"Damn!" Melissa stomped on the brake at the flash of movement in front of the car, holding the vehicle steady while its back end decided whether to shimmy left or right. Cage braced his boots hard against the floor and was glad he had buckled his seat belt.

They lurched to a stop less than ten yards from a gaunt man who'd careened onto the pavement of the feeder road in front of them, arms waving.

"Good reflexes, love. Pull off the roadway and stay in the car."

Once the sedan was safely off the pavement, Cage studied the man for a couple of seconds and then slowly opened his door and slid out. He held the Colt in his left hand, hidden at a slight angle behind his back.

"Oh God," the man said, "so sorry. I thought you were somebody else." The man's dark hair was cut short on the sides, longer on top—a modern, fit-in-with-the-humans style that complemented his high cheekbones, square jaw, and the ball cap he wore. "Hope the car's okay."

What was this man's game? Finding unvaccinated humans, or finding someone driving Aidan Murphy's car? Cage might not be a master vampire, but his senses were keen and he recognized another vampire when he saw one.

Especially this one.

❧ CHAPTER 2 ☙

Melissa had expected Cage to shoot the skinny guy who'd jumped in front of the car and almost given her heart failure. Well, not that she could actually have heart failure. Probably. Another thing to add to her endless list of vampire questions for Aidan's mate, Krys, who had the patience of a saint.

Not a quality Melissa possessed. Never had. And instead of shooting the guy or running him off, Cage stood there talking to him. She'd forgotten how much Cage talked. Well, how much Cage asked questions without ever saying much about himself—a trait Melissa had always attributed to his human occupation as a psychiatrist. That comment about Paris had slipped out unintentionally; she'd seen it on Cage's face.

If Cage and the vampabond planned on having a set-to, as her grampa used to call it, here at exit 42 next to I-85, she might as well join them.

Melissa opened the door and took a deep, appreciative breath of night air. Her favorite season was imminent, with cooler days, longer nights, and the leaves turning brilliant colors in the soft autumn sunlight. Not that she'd see them unless she set up a spotlight under a tree. Living in darkness, plus the weirdness of feeding, were the worst parts of becoming vampire.

Forget autumn. Winter would be her new favorite season; it had the longest nights of the year.

She walked up behind Cage, appreciating his slim hips in their tight jeans and his broad shoulders filling out the black sweater. A few months ago, he'd intentionally starved himself to infiltrate Matthias's camp and pass himself off as a stray, but he'd obviously been feeding steadily in London and again had the muscled, hard-planed body admired by most of the women in Penton when he'd first arrived in town last spring. He'd been unofficially voted as having the best ass in Penton, something she doubted he'd ever know and would be mortified by if he did.

Cage turned and smiled, beckoning her alongside him. "Mel, this is Fen Patrick. Fen, Melissa Calvert."

"It's Fenton Patrick, technically, but everyone calls me Fen—unless they call me something that can't be repeated in front of a lady." Fen Patrick's accent was a bit like Aidan's, only much heavier. Irish, then, maybe. And despite the nylon jacket and Atlanta Braves baseball cap that screamed rural Georgia, he was a vampire.

Make that a hungry vampire with a smarmy gift of gab. The lights of the sedan created blue glints on his short, dark hair as he leaned forward to shake her hand. "And always trust Cage to have the prettiest ladies with him, vampire or not."

"You two already know each other, then?" Melissa thought Fenton Patrick had a hungry, desperate look that fit a starving vampabond, but he also had a glimmer of arrogance that set off her fraud radar. Plus, what were the odds of someone Cage knew appearing on the road just as they were passing? "That's quite a coincidence—or is it?"

Fen paused a moment, a smile playing on his lips in an expression she couldn't decipher. Or maybe she'd imagined it, because it was gone in a heartbeat.

"It's a tremendous coincidence, perhaps an act of God Himself, if He still hears the prayers of those who live in the dark." Fen's accent grew more florid as he talked. "Of course, I'd heard my old mate Cage was in Penton, so I hoped he might put in a word for me with Aidan Murphy—a fellow Irishman, I understand."

If Fen thought an acquaintance with Cage and an Irish accent would get him in good stead with Aidan, he might be surprised. Melissa knew Aidan probably better than anyone in Penton besides his mate and Mirren, and he was tougher than most gave him credit for.

"Fen wasn't a vampire when I knew him." Cage's frown had deepened the longer Fen talked—or had Melissa imagined that, too? "We did a lot of missions together in the '80s and '90s, mostly in Central America. He was the only human who'd voluntarily sign up for the hazardous night jobs. He knew what I was and kept his word that he wouldn't tell anyone. As far as I know, he kept his promise."

"Always." Fen grinned. "Hell, I even let you feed from me, and I don't ever want to get that feeling from another man again. Nothing personal."

An eighteen-wheeler rumbled past them and then slowed with a flash of brake lights.

"Damn it, go on." Cage stepped onto the edge of the pavement and watched the truck slow further, its brakes high-pitched and loud in the still night air. "He's stopping. Probably thinks we need help. Let me send him on his way."

He strode toward the truck, which had finally come to a stop a couple hundred yards down, near where the exit lane ended at a state highway running east-west. The truck driver, a heavyset guy wearing a baseball cap, climbed down from the cab, stretching his back with his hands on his hips before walking to meet Cage.

Fen blocked Melissa's view of Cage, forcing her to look at him. "The two of you been together long?" he asked her. "Perhaps you can give me some insight into Aidan Murphy; I'm rather desperate to stay in Penton and get away from all the Tribunal politics and starving vampires in Atlanta. Any tips on how to win him over?"

She didn't like him, but she tried to shake off the dislike. He'd done nothing suspicious other than simply being there, and there was no way Fen could have known his former colleague would be in Aidan's car heading for Penton at what had to be almost 3:00 a.m.

Plus, at least some of her dislike stemmed from the fact that she'd hoped to spend this time alone with Cage, figuring out how they felt about each other. These months away from him had given her some perspective. She suspected that her love for him had been born out of fear, insecurity, and gratitude, but she needed some time around him to be sure—and to see how he felt about her. The last thing she wanted to do was hurt him.

She did some quick mental calculations. "I've known Cage for about six or seven months." Penton had been a real, whole place then instead of a burned-out shell they were trying to rebuild.

"Practically newlyweds then. Or mates, as the vampires call wedded bliss." Fen cocked his head, glancing at her left hand. "Or perhaps you're just friends, I might hope?"

Seriously? "Look, I don't mean to be rude, but we don't know each other well enough to be having this conversation. What's taking Cage so long?"

Melissa frowned and glanced around Fen's shoulder, relieved to see the trucker climbing back into his cab and Cage heading their way.

"Sorry, no offense meant." Fen held up his hands in surrender, turning to Cage when he finally reached them. "Feisty mate you have here."

Cage raised an eyebrow, and Melissa shrugged. He could trust this guy all he wanted. Didn't mean she had to. And she'd ignore the "mate" assumption. What she and Cage were, or weren't, could in no way be considered his business. "I was just about to ask Fen how long he'd been turned."

"I'd like to know that as well, but we need to get back in the car, get our petrol, and move along toward Penton." Cage glanced down the exit ramp where the truck driver was pulling his rig onto the road, heading away from the lights of the convenience store. Two other eighteen-wheelers had passed by on the interstate, and there were more oncoming in the distance. "Otherwise, we'll get more well-meaning freight drivers stopping to help."

Cage walked toward the sedan with Fen on his heels.

"You're going to take him to Penton?" Melissa didn't want to hear Mirren's tirade when Cage arrived with a stranger an hour before daysleep. "We could drop him off in Opelika and let Aidan talk to him tomorrow night when there's more time."

Cage stopped and turned, looking from her to Fen and back. "I'm pretty sure Aidan got rid of all our safe spaces in Opelika and Auburn after the dustup with the Tribunal. He thought they'd all been compromised."

What? Where would Cage get such a stupid idea, unless . . . Melissa gave herself a mental slap on the head. Cage didn't trust Fen, either. He wanted him close at hand until they found out whether he was trustworthy.

"Right." Melissa shook her head. "Sorry I'm such a ditz tonight. Driving in Atlanta traffic always shorts out my brain."

"Understandable, although it's not half as bad as any large city in Europe," Fen said, hesitating when Cage opened the front passenger-side door and motioned him in. "Dublin is a nightmare. I sincerely believe Irishmen weren't meant to operate automobiles."

Damn it. It was bad enough this guy had interrupted what might be her only chance to talk to Cage alone. Now, he was going to sit next to her the rest of the way into Penton while Cage sat in back?

She shot Cage a look to convey her annoyance over the whole Fen Patrick situation and got behind the wheel again. Cage sat in the backseat behind her, where he could keep an eye on Fen. Good sense from a security standpoint; bad timing from a sorry-but-we'll-always-have-Omega relationship standpoint.

As soon as they got to Penton she'd lose him to Mirren and the Army guys, and no telling how long she might be left wondering how he felt about her—and examining her own feelings for him.

Cage leaned forward and put a hand on her shoulder. "Wait a second, Mel. I need to make something clear to Fen before we take him to Penton. My apologies, mate, but the only advantage our old acquaintance will get you is a foot in the door. Aidan Murphy will make the call as to whether or not you can stay. Our security chief, Mirren Kincaid, will have a say in it as well."

Melissa looked for any glimmer of irritation to cross Fen's face, but she found none. He turned a wide smile toward Cage. "No problem. Can't be too careful these days given what all happened in Penton, from what I've heard. And would that be *the* Mirren Kincaid, the Slayer? I'd heard he was around, but one never knows which rumors are true and which ones are sheer fabrications."

Cage relaxed against the seat back. "The one and the same Kincaid. Only I wouldn't call him 'Slayer' to his face. He can be a bit surly."

Melissa had to smile. Surly was the Mirren Kincaid version of jovial.

Once they'd bought gas and gotten back on the interstate, the final forty minutes of the drive into Penton told Melissa more about Cage's life than she'd ever heard. Not so much from what he said—he was as unforthcoming as ever—but from Fen's easy reminiscences that shone a small bit of light on Cage's shadowy pre-Penton days.

She knew he'd spent a lot of time in military duty; she had wondered how he'd managed that as a vampire. He couldn't exactly operate in the normal armed forces and be unaccounted for during daylight hours. A willingness to take night duty would only carry a soldier so far.

Fen kept mentioning night raids and forays into foreign villages, however, all of which had apparently been filled with free-flowing alcohol and available women. Finally, Melissa couldn't stand it any longer. "Exactly whose army were you in?"

Of course, it was Fen, not Cage, who answered: "Our own army, darlin'. Cage and I were what you'd call soldiers of fortune. We had dozens of names, dozens of passports, and for a price you could hire us to do the dirty work you didn't want to be associated with. Guess I'd still be at it if regular meals weren't so scarce."

Mercenaries, then. Melissa raised her gaze to the rearview mirror and caught Cage giving Fen a narrow-eyed look through green eyes that shone silver with annoyance.

"Sounds like perfect work for an adrenaline junkie like Cage." She smiled into the mirror, hoping it told him that his past didn't matter. People changed. Mirren was proof of that. Good grief, she herself was proof of that. A year ago, with Mark at her side and as Aidan's familiar, she couldn't have imagined being a vampire herself. After she'd been turned she became afraid of hurting Mark, rejecting him because she knew he'd ultimately reject her. "Well, an adrenaline junkie psychiatrist."

Fen laughed. "Well, I think he gave up head-shrinking after the POW camp, right, Cage? Something about learning what evil lurks in the hearts of men, or some rubbish as that?"

Cage had been in a POW camp? Melissa glanced in the rearview mirror again and found Cage looking out the window, his face set into rigid lines, the occasional lights of an oncoming vehicle flashing across a countenance both grim and haunted.

Fen seemed to realize he'd crossed a line and changed the subject to the weather, and then to how living in the States—first Wilmington, North Carolina, and then Savannah and Atlanta—had compared to Dublin. He chattered so much Melissa wanted to scream. On the other hand, he required little response and had filled up that horrible silence following his gaffe.

Melissa had always thought of Cage as compassionate but invincible. But the man she'd glimpsed in the mirror just now had been set upon by ghosts, and they weren't friendly ones.

While her thoughts wandered, Fen had moved on to babbling about a raid into a jungle encampment in Nicaragua, during which Cage had been stabbed and had, apparently, ripped out several rebels' throats with his fangs—thus the necessity of explaining his true identity to Fen. Cage contributed a few details to embellish the tale, but Melissa thought his facial expressions were revealing: amused at first, but when Fen got to the throat-ripping part, annoyed again.

Maybe Fen would be fun to keep around Penton after all. It might be the only way she'd ever learn about the man Cage had been before arriving in town with his worn old traveling trunk plus box after box of his favorite small cigars. Even if, as she suspected, they didn't have a future as a couple, she really, really wanted him as a friend.

All conversation ceased when the few working streetlights of Penton came into view. She tried to imagine how it must look to a stranger. Burned-out shells of buildings, heaps of construction rubble, and, overseeing it all like a dying god of industry, the hulk of the long-closed cotton mill.

Melissa stopped the car in front of the new communal house where Aidan and Mirren were supposed to be waiting. She'd resigned herself to the loss of any remaining chance to talk to Cage alone before dawn.

She popped the trunk and Cage got his luggage out. Mirren's bulk filled the doorway, waiting on them. The hostility practically rolled off him in visible waves when Fen bustled over to introduce himself. Mirren and Aidan had wanted to bring Cage up to date on Omega Force before daysleep, but not in front of a stranger.

Before joining them, Cage leaned in the car window. "I'm sorry we didn't get the chance to talk, Mel. We need to . . ."

His voice trailed off, but she knew what the rest of that sentence should be. We need to settle things between us. "I know. Tomorrow night, maybe." She looked back at Mirren and Fen. "I don't know why, but I have a bad feeling about that guy. I'm not sure we should trust him."

Cage looked past her at his old acquaintance, whose nonstop prattle was likely putting Mirren in a homicidal mood. "Don't worry, love. I never fully trusted my old pal Fen when he was human. I surely don't trust him now."

☙ CHAPTER 3 ❧

R ob Thomas scratched his head, causing the bright late-afternoon sunlight and shadows to create the effect of a golden halo above his red hair. "What's this say? Who taught Mirren Kincaid how to write, anyway?"

"Probably somebody who died about four centuries ago and didn't speak any version of a language we'd recognize." Mark Calvert took the notebook from Rob and blew out a frustrated breath. He bought and sold stocks, calculated investment risks, and monitored trending start-ups. He didn't build military training facilities. Well, not in normal times.

Penton had blown way past normal almost a year ago.

The chicken scratches on the notebook made no sense whatsoever. How Mirren could be such a talented artist and yet write in gibberish, he didn't know.

But Mirren Kincaid and the rest of the vampires were snoring happily away in daysleep while the Penton business manager stood in the broiling sun, trying to wrangle enough warm bodies to build the new Omega Force training center to Slayer standards.

Mark shoved the notebook back at Rob. "Damned if I know. Call Glory at the Chow House, and see if she can decipher it for us."

Rob stuck the clipboard under his arm. "I'll just go down there and ask her in person. Maybe you and Max can finish putting up that wall while I grab something to eat before she packs it all away for the day."

Mark nodded. "When are Will and Randa coming home?"

"In a week if everything goes as planned. Never thought I'd say this, but I'm ready for Will to take over this project, big mouth and all." Rob was the human brother of Penton lieutenant Randa Thomas. Randa's mate, Will Ludlam, thrived on this type of planning-and-construction project, leaving the humans who toiled through daylight hours with neat printed instructions, diagrams, and explanations.

"So he's definitely having the surgery?" Mark asked. Will's left leg had been mangled in one of his father's attacks on Penton and had healed badly. Using a little admittedly unethical enthrallment, Aidan had managed to get an Atlanta orthopedic surgeon to take a look at Will after-hours.

"If the doctor thinks he's a good candidate," said Rob. "All they're doing tonight is shooting X-rays and hoping the doctor doesn't see anything weird. You know, like fangs.

"Randa says Will is being one pain in the ass because he can't start training with us." Rob laughed. "Wait. Will is always a pain in the ass, so let me rephrase that: he's being a bigger pain in the ass than usual."

Mark smiled. "Yeah, but he's a lot better than Mirren at this construction stuff. Not that I'll be sharing that opinion with the big guy."

"No shit. He won't hear it from me, either. The man's like a bad attitude with feet."

Mark had expected a combat-tough Army Ranger like Rob to be a total hard-ass like his father. Colonel Rick Thomas, who headed up the Omega Force project, could out-grouch Mirren.

Rob was cool, though—a lot easier to get along with than their other Ranger-turned-Penton-resident Max Jeffries. Max constantly tried to prove himself bigger and badder than any vampire; as Mark could tell him from long experience as one of Aidan's closest friends, he was wasting his time. The only way for a human to outfight a vampire was to cheat.

If a human wanted to live among vampires, he had to capitalize on his few advantages—like walking around in sunlight and conducting business during daylight hours.

Something Melissa would never be able to do again.

Mark tried to brush away the thought, but as usual when it came to the subject of his wife, he lost the battle as surely as if he'd been trying to fistfight a vamp.

He hadn't given up on Melissa; he still loved her, fangs and all. But he had given up on begging for any attention she might toss his way like a stray bread crumb.

His supply of pity and empathy for her situation had expired. After all, he was the one who'd been dumped on and avoided like a walking cancer. He'd been willing to give her space and try to win her back, until he heard Cage Reynolds was returning to Penton, possibly for good.

No more Mr. Nice Mark. If she wanted that smug English sonofabitch, she could have him.

"Earth to Mark." Rob slapped him on the arm with the clipboard.

"Sorry, what'd you say?"

"Got anything else that needs to go to the Chow House?"

Mark looked around the job site and took a quick inventory. "We could use a few more bottles of water. Max sweats it out faster than he can drink it."

"Fuck you." A disembodied voice rumbled from the other side of the wall, within the wooden framework of the building in progress. "Forget the water. Bring me a six-pack and one of Glory's subs."

Rob saluted the brick wall and grinned at Mark. "Got it. Be back in a half hour or so, unless Glory's too busy to interpret Mirren's secret code and I have to wait on her."

Mark watched him descend the hill into downtown Penton, where a long wooden building had been erected at the site of the old barbecue place that had been bombed earlier in the year by Aidan's psycho brother. His late psycho brother.

All that mess seemed like a million years ago, not nine months.

The Chow House had been Will's idea, as had the communal houses that gave them all places to live while rebuilding the rest of the town.

Eventually, if they could get Penton back up and running, they'd all reestablish their own homes. For now, those doing the rebuilding needed places to live and eat. Six communal houses with lighttight spaces beneath them sat at the site of the old mill village.

A block away was the Chow House, where Glory oversaw the preparation of three meals a day for any among the few remaining humans who wanted to stop by—at least until an hour before dusk, when she went to greet her rising vampire. And here, at the site of the former community center, the new Omega Force training facility would overlook it all.

"We taking a break?" Max rounded the corner from the other side of the wall, wiping sweat off his face with the front of his camo-patterned Army Rangers T-shirt.

Mark handed him a bottle of water and took the last one for himself. "Yeah, might as well. We just need to finish this wall, and it's all ladder work. Going to be a slow go. We need to get Mirren's instructions deciphered before we work on the back wall."

Max looked at the red bricks stacked neatly on the concrete pad inside the building's framework. "Be easier if we could bring some real brick masons in here. One of us could oversee things and they'd never have to know about the"—he fluttered his arms in a poor imitation of bat wings—"big bad vampires."

"We talked about it." Mark stepped over a couple of extra two-by-fours and sat on the nearest pile of bricks, stretching his sore back muscles. Old back injuries and construction made unhappy bedfellows.

At least there was shade inside the rectangular framework. "Too risky to bring in brick masons, though. Even if they didn't find out about the vamps, they might be curious about the town."

"I guess." Max took a swig of water. "Now that you mention it, I'm not sure I'd know what to say when they asked why the town looks like an atomic bomb went off on Main Street. Or who lives here in this heap of destruction. Or how it is that a guy named Aidan Murphy, who no one outside Penton has ever seen, owns everything."

Mark knew that answer; he'd brokered every last real-estate deal. Aidan owned Penton outright, down to the last pinecone and cracked sidewalk.

Max sat on the concrete slab and stretched out six-feet-three-inches of muscle and alpha male. Mark had never considered himself a slouch in the physique department, but Max and Rob both made him feel like an eighth-grader in remedial gym class. Max's dark hair had grown out a little from the buzz cut he'd had when he and Rob had first arrived in Penton—but not much. He still looked like an Army Ranger.

Three months ago, Max and Rob had slipped into town at night with the colonel, trying to figure out how this combined Ranger-vampire antiterrorism team might work. Max currently sported only one fading bruise, on his left cheek—but with Cage back in Penton their sparring would probably pick up where it had left off.

The thought of Cage Reynolds gave Mark a headache.

"Where are things with the Omega Force?" Mark took a sip of water and screwed the cap back onto the bottle. "I heard there are some new team members coming in. Does that mean you guys will get to do something besides build houses and training facilities? That's gotta be frustrating." As frustrating as it was for an investment analyst to be building houses and training facilities.

Max finished off his water and rolled the plastic bottle between his palms. Fidgeting. The guy always needed to be moving. "The colonel was so anxious to get the project rolling he put a team together in Texas back in July. They've already handled a case— that bombing last month in Houston. Their team leader and a couple of others are out of commission for a while, so two of them are coming here."

"How'd they get up and moving so fast?" The whole vampire-Ranger thing had been dreamed up here as a way for the human special-ops people to help the vampires survive the pandemic crisis without outing them to other humans. In return, the Penton vampires would train to help on counterterrorism maneuvers. Only the Houston team had already wrapped up a case while Penton's team was, well, laying brick.

Max shrugged. "They had people in Houston already trained and available. I had to be moved off active duty, plus we have all that vampire political shit to deal with. Vamps can't train during the day, and I think most of that Houston team were shape-shifters, so it was easier."

He groaned and flopped on his back, pouring the rest of the bottle of water on his face. "Who even knew there were such things as fucking shape-shifters? How does that work? If one bites me, will I turn into a duck or a weasel or something?"

"Hell if I know." Mark hoped at least one of the new Omega Force members was human. Being a feeder for three vampires sucked—pun intended. Aidan fed first thing after sunset; his mate, Krys, fed before Mark went to bed; Britta Eriksen, a woman who'd moved to Penton a few weeks after the big showdown with Matthias, fed before sunrise, as soon as Mark woke in the morning. He'd filled the top of his dresser with bottles of iron supplements purchased on his last supply run to Opelika.

Penton needed fresh blood, literally. "Reckon shape-shifters can feed vampires?" He thought about Max's "duck or weasel" comment. "What kind of shape-shifters are they?"

"One is a human, a Ranger. The other is . . . Hell, I don't know what he is except a shifter of some kind. I guess it could be any kind of animal. Mirren just read us the memo up to a certain point and stomped off, cussing." Max laughed. "Hard to believe that of Mirren, I know."

They sat in silence a few moments before Max sat up. "You know, I've been thinking. What other monsters are living out there that we don't know about? The more I think about it, the freakier it is."

Mark shook his head. "Nothing would surprise me anymore."

If vampires and shape-shifters were real, other myths and legends could be real as well. After all, Glory was telekinetic, and Hannah, the Penton lieutenant who'd been turned vampire at age eleven or twelve, had visions. Premonitions, he guessed they'd be called. "Well, whatever the other guy is, I hope he can feed vampires. After a while, even orgasmic sensations get old."

"I hear you. I have to feed Cage Fucking Reynolds, and if ever I didn't want anybody giving me a happy hard-on, it's that British asshat. My only consolation is that he hates it as much as I do."

Mark's laugh sounded bitter, even to himself. "Better you than me."

"Ah, yeah. Sorry."

How much did Max know? He was Hannah's feeder, too, and Aidan did his best to keep Hannah away from the uglier sides of life in Penton—like when a man's wife got turned vampire by a sociopath and decided she no longer wanted her human husband. Judging by the apology, Max knew plenty.

Great. Everyone probably considered him a pathetic loser. Or maybe they blamed Melissa, which would be appropriate. And he felt like a pathetic loser, which pissed him off even more. Thank God Aidan had the good sense not to ask him to be a feeder for Cage Reynolds. He'd have to just drain his own blood into a glass and let the man drink the old-fashioned way.

Mark sighed. This line of thought was depressing. He climbed to his feet and set the half-empty water bottle aside. "Let's finish off that wall. You want top of the ladder or bottom?"

"Better give me bottom." Max looked up at the wall, which had grown to about ten feet in height; Mirren wanted twelve. "I have longer arms to hand stuff up."

"Yeah, make the shorter guy do the dangerous work." Mark headed around the wall and positioned the ladder and makeshift scaffolding at the corner. Last night they'd checked all the places where the brick veneer was anchored to the building's frame, so it should be quick work to finish off the wall.

He might even have time for a shower before Aidan got up and wanted his dinner, so to speak.

Rob's voice sounded from down the hill. "I think it's a rule for short guys to take the worst jobs." He crested the rise and walked across the leveled-off construction site, waving the clipboard with one hand and holding a six-pack of Coors and a white paper bag in the other. "I got Glory's interpretation of the specs. We can go over them tonight—we'll need more supplies. Let's get that wall finished and help Max drink his beer and eat a sandwich before Mirren gets up and bitches about what all we did wrong."

"Sounds like a plan." Mark climbed to the top of the extension ladder while Rob and Max piled bricks on a pallet and raised them via a pulley system—something Will had rigged up when constructing the Chow House and the living spaces. Digging a trowel into the concrete mix, Mark plopped a pile on the top layer of the wall, spread it evenly, and wedged a brick into place.

The work was hot and slow, but mindlessly relaxing. By the time they reached the midpoint of the wall, he found he could release that knot of gnawing pain in his chest that had resulted from too much thought about Melissa and too much talk about Cage.

Finally, Mark placed the next-to-last brick in place. One more in the middle section, and he'd have to move the ladder to do the south end. "Wait, I think something's gotten mixed in the concrete; this one's not squaring up." Something about the brick hadn't set right. He looked down at Max and Rob. "Did you notice any irregularities in the last bunch of bricks we picked up?"

Rob shook his head. "We checked them when they came in."

"Pull that one off," Max said, "and I'll hand you one from the new shipment stacked on the other side." He disappeared around the corner.

Mark removed the brick and set it back on the scaffolding. "Pull the platform back down, and see if you can tell what's wrong with that one. If one's bad, there's probably more."

"Got it." Rob grasped the rope and untied it from its mooring, lowering the scaffolding platform.

A wave of dizziness almost made Mark lose his balance. Too much heat, physical work, and being up on the ladder. Everything swayed.

"Move! You gotta move! It's coming down!" Max's voice seemed to come from far away, and Mark had only a fleeting moment to think *the whole fucking wall is collapsing* before he was thrown off the ladder, watching his world literally turn upside down before going black.

❦CHAPTER 4❧

Something wasn't right. Just past dusk, the air around Penton should smell of warm pine clinging to the last rays of sunlight, nocturnal animals creeping from beneath rocks and brush, pungent night-blooming plants opening their petals to welcome the cooling air.

Mirren Kincaid paused outside the communal house he shared with his mate, Glory, and Melissa Calvert. The air was soaked with unease, as if something bad were about to happen. Everyone should have been celebrating, after the news spread that Matthias Ludlam would finally be going to meet his maker. Yet the streets lay quiet and deserted.

Whatever had happened, he needed to deal with it instead of babysitting the new Omega team members due to arrive within the hour. Mirren had a bad feeling about them, too. The colonel had been cagey about Ashton and Dimitrou, only saying that Mirren and Aidan should keep an open mind and let themselves be pleasantly surprised.

Mirren hated fucking surprises. In his experience, they were rarely pleasant.

He had a feeling what he scented in the night air wouldn't yield any pleasant surprises, either. Mortar. Dust. Blood. Nothing pleasant about it.

"Something's wrong at the job site." Aidan Murphy took two steps at a time as he descended the staircase of the communal house across the street. Krys trailed behind him, pulling the large rolling suitcase that had served as her medical kit while they'd been stuck in the underground bunker Omega during the siege.

She'd been a human doctor before being turned earlier this year; unfortunately, her skills had been needed to treat a lot of vampires, too, including Aidan.

Aidan nodded toward Mirren's old Bronco. "Better take that. All I got from Mark's thought patterns was that something went down at the construction site. Mostly, it's a muddle. There's blood scent on the air, though."

"That there is." Mirren looked at the sky and wouldn't have been surprised to see a scroll roll back and the Four Horsemen come riding through, spreading pestilence and death before them like floodwaters.

Penton couldn't get a fucking break—and they were supposed to be the good guys. Though Mirren hadn't grown used to thinking of himself as a good guy; he'd spent too many years wallowing in self-recrimination and guilt. He'd reached peace with his past, though. Glory had made him understand that his history could only haunt him if he let it.

But damn, Penton needed a stretch of heaven, not more apocalypse.

They all climbed in the Bronco, and Mirren drove up Cotton Street past the half-burned husk of the old textile mill. Mark's blood bond to Aidan had given them a heads-up to disaster before, reinforcing their policy of bonding all residents to one of the master vampires. It was damned helpful. "You got a zing from Mark, but what about Rob and Max the Asshole? Aren't they with him?"

"They're both bonded to Will, and he's out of range, so I don't know." Aidan ran his hands through his hair—an old habit that didn't work quite as well since he'd cut it shorter, to better fit in with the puffed-up bureaucrats on the Vampire Tribunal. Meg Lindstrom, the US vampire rep, planned to step down and had nominated Aidan to take her place.

Aidan didn't want the job, but as usual, he was putting his overdeveloped sense of responsibility before his desires. In nine days, it would be official—as long as the Penton supporters on the Tribunal continued to outnumber the haters. Aidan thought he could help the vampire population weather the pandemic vaccine that had made human blood poisonous to them. He had a lot of ideas; a Tribunal seat would give him the influence he needed to put them into action.

"Think this has anything to do with the vote coming up?" Mirren asked. "I mean, that old Austrian sonofabitch Frank Greisser is not going to just sit back and welcome you onto the Tribunal without doing something to hurt you or keep you in Penton or skew the vote." Or all of the above.

"We definitely can't rule it out." Aidan stared out the window at the burned ruins that constituted pretty much all that remained of downtown Penton. "Whether it's the Tribunal or just buzzard's luck, we need to find out what's wrong and do damage control so people don't freak out. Then we've gotta speed up the rebuilding efforts, even if it means hiring human crews. We need places for people to live and work before this town can really recover."

The idea of bringing in humans made Mirren's muscles twitch, but Aidan was right. They'd been licking their wounds for three months. It was past time to get Penton on track. No reason Mark couldn't supervise human crews, especially with the Rangers helping.

He pulled the Bronco in front of the last community house before the turn to the job site and leaned on his horn. Might as well have a little more muscle. Plus, their resident psychiatrist probably knew all kinds of damage-control mind games.

"Good idea." Aidan motioned to Cage, who had stepped into the doorway of the house he'd moved into with Hannah and Max— and now, Fen Patrick. "Might be nothing, or it might be another Penton clusterfuck. In which case we'll need him."

Before Cage cleared the porch, Fen followed him out. Mirren's first instinct last night had been to lock the guy in their silver-lined room back in the old Omega underground facility. He'd suggested it, in fact, and had even gone to retrieve the key. Glory had guilt-tripped him until he reluctantly agreed to have Cage babysit the guy instead.

But some long-lost buddy, suddenly turned vampire, shows up in town at the same time Cage happens to be returning? Rotten fish weren't the only thing that smelled like shit.

Cage turned and spoke to Fen, who shrugged his shoulders, flashed his smarmy grin, and went back inside. Mirren got the sense that Cage didn't trust the man, either, which made Mirren think more of the shrink, even if he was an Englishman. Aidan wanted Fen under surveillance, though, which was easier to do if they let him stay in town, under their noses.

"What's up?" Cage slid into the backseat and gave Krys a hug. "The air smells like open house at the blood bank."

Aidan filled him in on what he knew. "It might not be serious, but any bad news at this point can shake people's confidence. Everyone's nervous."

"I think people are wondering if we should've come back and tried to rebuild this soon," Krys said. "If we lose any more feeders or familiars, we'll have to start recruiting again. We probably shouldn't have let Shawn and Britta come in, although I like both of them. And now, Cage is back, and Fen."

Cage nodded. "Yeah, two more sets of fangs to feed. Pity I couldn't have brought a feeder or two with me from London, but Edward wouldn't allow it. Things are worse there than here. Who are Shawn and Britta?"

Mirren hadn't formed an opinion on the Penton scathe's two newest members. They'd come together, both newish vampires who'd tracked Aidan down at the Atlanta community clinic where he volunteered and scouted for fams.

"Both of them moved to Atlanta from Mobile, thinking it would be easier to find feeders there, but it wasn't," Aidan said. "They seem okay. Still too early to tell."

The two new women were under surveillance, too, although they'd relaxed it in the last week or two. There wasn't enough manpower to watch everybody.

As badly as he wanted Penton to be the way it had been before the siege, Mirren had wondered if they should even try to rebuild before the whole pandemic vaccine crisis was resolved. No one trusted the Tribunal members to keep the vampire population calm and at peace in exchange for the humans setting up the blood bank and keeping their mouths shut.

Colonel Rick Thomas didn't trust the Tribunal members who weren't Penton allies, either, or he wouldn't have parked this many of his Ranger operatives in town. Rob and Max, and the two new guys due in tonight, were now full-time Pentonites, whether they liked it or not.

Aidan filled Cage in on the rebuilding status, and Mirren had to admit he was glad to have the man back in Penton—as long as he kept his psychoanalysis bullshit to himself. They needed every experienced fighter they could get, and Cage had a cool head under pressure. They might not be at war since they'd defeated Matthias and forced the Tribunal bullies to back down by bringing in the Rangers, but he wouldn't exactly call it peacetime, either.

"Aw, fuck." Mirren spotted the construction site at the top of the hill and sped up. The work site was illuminated by three floodlights, and a heap of brick-filled rubble was visible even from a distance. "Looks like the whole east wall came down. They'd almost finished bricking that one."

He slammed the truck to a halt, slinging white nuggets of loose gravel across the parking lot. Aidan, Krys, and Cage jumped out before he had the key out of the ignition.

Mirren popped the hatch to retrieve Krys's medical kit, stopping to study the site and the woods behind it. Max stood upright and looked uninjured, judging by the way he waved his arms around as he talked to Aidan. Fucking drama queen. Mark sat off to one side with his head propped on his bent knees.

Pausing beside the Bronco, Mirren scanned the wooded area behind the job site, looking for anything out of place. It had become habit to suspect Matthias of being behind anything bad that happened here, but Penton had other enemies on the Tribunal—not the least of whom was Director Frank Greisser. He wanted both Aidan and Mirren dead. They'd challenged his ability to lead and had "fomented rebellion" by advocating a partnership with bonded humans as a way to survive the pandemic crisis. After Aidan's power play of bringing human military personnel into vampire affairs, Greisser had been forced to throw Matthias to the wolves and pretend an alliance with the Penton scathe. But things weren't over. Mirren could feel it.

He sensed no unbonded vampires lurking around, however, so he walked up to the site where Aidan, Krys, and Cage knelt next to the pile of collapsed brick.

Aw, fuck.

From the parking lot, the heap of bricks had camouflaged the body lying underneath. Rob Thomas looked like he'd been at ground zero when the wall collapsed, and Mirren could tell by one look at the guy that he was dead or dying. That much weight didn't land on your head without breaking something unfixable.

He skirted around where Krys knelt next to Rob, trying to talk to him, and approached Max and Mark. "Mark, you okay?"

"Just had the wind knocked out of me. Give me a minute and I'm good." His blond hair was caked with blood around his right temple, but it had already dried. "Rob's in bad shape, though."

"Yeah, he is. Start talking, Max."

Max looked back to where Cage and Aidan were trying to talk to Rob while Krys ripped away clothing to assess the wounds. If Mirren knew he was dying, Krys knew it, too. He guessed that as a doctor she had to at least go through the motions.

Max and Rob had been best buddies since college and throughout their Army tours, so he would cut the guy some slack—as long as he didn't revert to smartassery. "What happened?"

"Hell, I don't know." Max stuck shaky hands in his pockets. "Mark was having trouble with one of the last bricks, so I went over to get a new one off the stack that came in yesterday. When I turned around, the whole wall was coming down on them." He looked down, but not before Mirren saw tears.

Aw, fuck me. He was not the Mother Teresa of vampirehood, by a long shot. He didn't know what to say to a guy watching his best friend die. "Focus," he said. "The anchors holding the wall to the frame must have come loose."

As soon as he said the words, Mirren realized how ridiculous that scenario was. One anchor could come loose. Two? Not outside the realm of possibility, although unlikely. But not all of them. "You sure all the anchors on the construction plans got put in? No shortcuts?"

"No way." Max took a deep breath and turned back to Mirren. "We even checked them before we left the site last night, Rob and me both, 'cause we knew we'd be adding that last section today. They were solid. No way fifteen anchors came loose." He looked around again. Aidan and Cage were talking to Krys, who held her hands to her face. Max's voice softened to a whisper. "No fucking way."

Which meant sabotage—and Mirren didn't have a clue who the saboteur might be, although his first thought went to Fen Patrick. Everyone else, even Britta and Shawn, had gone through one of Will's background checks. They'd all turned up clean. He should've locked Fen up himself. Although he couldn't imagine Cage would have left the newcomer unguarded long enough to be able to come to the job site and screw with the anchors. How could Fen even have known about the construction project when Cage didn't know himself?

Mirren helped Mark to his feet, and once he was sure the man wasn't going to tumble over, he walked back to the others. "He's gone, isn't he?"

Aidan rose and wiped his blood-covered hands on a shop towel lying nearby. Krys had walked several yards away, where she stood next to a portion of the wall that was still intact.

"Yes." Aidan picked up a brick and threw it as hard as he could down the hill, then hung his head. When he spoke again, his voice was subdued but under control. Aidan could suck down anger and grief better than any vampire Mirren had known in his long years—himself included. "How's Mark?"

"Head wound, but he's lucid." Mirren looked at where Mark had been sitting in relation to the broken ladder. "I think he was on the ladder and got thrown free of the wall. Probably the only thing that saved him."

Krys rejoined them, her face white as chalk in the harsh floodlight, her cheeks wet with tears. Her transition to vampire had been so smooth, Mirren tended to forget she'd been turned less than a year. She could still cry.

"I'm going to take Mark to the house instead of the clinic. I want him close tonight in case anything goes wrong. Maybe Max can stay with him during daysleep." Krys rubbed her hands up and down her arms and looked at Rob. "I hate that the blood gets to me this way. I feel like some kind of monster—it's obscene."

Yeah, the blood scent was strong enough to make Mirren lightheaded, and he had about four hundred years' more vampire experience than Krys. He grabbed a tarp from atop a pile of lumber and spread it over the body. Poor guy deserved at least that much dignity.

Krys's eyes widened. "Oh my God. I just realized—we have to tell the colonel. And Randa's going to blame herself for bringing Robbie into this."

Aidan drew Krys into his arms, but he turned his gaze to Mirren. His light-blue eyes had gone winter white, and Mirren figured his own were an equally frigid shade of gray. Fury tended to have that effect.

"It was somebody's fault, all right," Mirren said. "But not Randa's."

"What do you mean?" Krys turned to look at Mirren, rubbing her eyes. Behind her, Aidan gave a slight shake of his head.

"Nothing, darlin'. All of this can be laid right at the feet of Matthias Ludlam, may he rot in hell by this time tomorrow." Mirren dug his keys from the pocket of his black combat pants and held them out to Krys. "Take Max home with you; he doesn't need to be here right now. Keep him busy. Hell, give them both something that'll knock them out."

"What about . . ." Krys took a deep breath. "Do we call an ambulance for Rob?"

"No. We'll take care of it." What a bad, bad idea: three vampires, sitting around waiting for human EMTs to show up and take away a body from a town that, by design, barely registered on human maps. Plus, the nearest emergency room was in Opelika, thirty miles away, which meant the Chambers County sheriff would have to get involved.

If Rob had still been alive, Mirren would've taken the risk. Calling them now wouldn't help him, though, and probably would bring more trouble to their doorstep. They already had plenty.

Aidan kissed Krys before she got in Mirren's Bronco. Max helped Mark into the backseat and then climbed in the passenger seat. He gave them a halfhearted wave as they drove away, and Mirren thought he'd never seen a more brokenhearted man.

Cage joined them, giving wide berth to Rob's body. "I was looking at the structure from the back side. At least half of the anchors between the brick wall and the frame are missing."

Not loose. Missing.

"Damn it. See anything else out of place? Don't guess our visitor left a calling card." Mirren led the others around to examine the building frame, which remained sturdy and solid. Even illuminated only by the floodlights, the holes in the wood were visible. He scraped a finger across one and turned his finger toward the light. "Mortar dust. Max insists the anchors were there when he and Rob checked the site last night; now, they're gone."

Cage squatted and felt around on the concrete foundation. "Wish we had a better light to see whether they're still here or our saboteur took them."

"Will this help?"

Mirren turned to see a man walking up the hill toward them, apparently leaving his recent-model white SUV on the shoulder of the road near the turnoff to the construction site. The newcomer was about six feet tall, human, and a stranger. Black shaggy hair, dark eyes, olive complexion, very white teeth, no fangs. Probably one of the new Rangers, but Mirren was making no assumptions.

"Who the hell are you?"

"A man with a light." The man held up a key chain with a small flashlight hanging from it. "It's not very big, but brighter than you might think. Depends on what you're looking for."

Mirren stared a second at the proffered hand before taking the key chain and tossing it to Cage. "Can't hurt. If you're one of our new Rangers, welcome to fuckin' paradise. If you aren't, you're lost."

The guy smiled. "You must be Mirren Kincaid. You'll be pleased to know Colonel Thomas described you as a grizzly bear, only bigger. I'm Sergeant Nikolas Dimitrou—Nik—from the Texas Omega Force team. I'm supposed to check in with either Rob Thomas or Aidan Murphy."

"I'm Murphy." Aidan had been watching the exchange with narrowed eyes, sizing up the new guy. "Unfortunately, Captain Thomas was killed tonight. We were just about to discuss whether or not to call an ambulance. What do you think?"

Mirren didn't know if Zorba the Greek realized he was getting his first test in vampire politics, but he crossed his arms and waited for the newcomer's response. If he said that, of course, they needed an ambulance because the law required it, then he wasn't ready to work with vampires. And if he thought Aidan sounded cold and dispassionate, he was a poor judge of character.

Nik introduced himself to Cage and shook hands with Aidan. "Normally you'd call an ambulance, but this isn't a normal situation, is it?" He gave Aidan a steady, unflinching look and then shifted the same intense gaze over to Mirren. "Your eyes tell me how upset you are about this—both of you. The colonel put us through vampire basic training, you might call it.

"But this is Colonel Thomas's son." He looked down at the tarp. "I'd say if you have a place in town where the body can be preserved, it should be the colonel's call on how to handle it. His sister lives here, too—Randa, right? The family should make the final decision. I can't imagine the colonel would do anything to jeopardize Penton."

The guy had balls, Mirren would give him that much. If he was uncomfortable standing around with three vampires who could all tell with a single sniff that he was unvaccinated, he didn't show it. And he'd clearly done his homework on his new fellow citizens.

Mirren had been trying to place Zorba's accent, which was sort of Southern but with an odd turn to it. Finally, it hit him. "You from New Orleans?"

Nik grinned. "First generation Yat. Grew up in Broadmoor. And now, I guess I live in Penton."

Aidan's smile was slight, but genuine. "Welcome to town, Nik—wish the circumstances were better. I'm guessing the colonel will need to reassess things here before deciding your chain of command. One other Ranger is here—Max Jeffries—although he and Rob were tight. I don't know how he's going to react. Another guy from your unit is due in tonight. Mirren's in charge of training unless we hear differently, and we'll wait to see if the colonel has a mission for you."

"Penton is our mission for now, as I understand it." Nik cocked his head and looked at Aidan with a bemused smile. "So my Omega team member isn't here yet?"

"Guy named Ashton," Mirren said. "The dickhead's already late."

"No he isn't. His timing is perfect."

Mirren swiveled at the voice coming from somewhere behind him and scowled as a girl approached them from the woods behind the construction site. No, not a girl, but a woman. A tiny woman who couldn't be a hair over five feet. She was slender, with short spiky hair that glinted auburn in the floodlights, big dark eyes, jeans, and a tight T-shirt that revealed an inch of tanned skin and the glint of a navel ring.

What the hell was a human woman doing out here, in the woods?

He looked back at Dimitrou, who stood next to Cage, their arms crossed over their chests and smiles on their faces. Aidan, at least, looked properly concerned, unlike Tweedle-dee and Zorba.

Sometimes a little fright therapy was a valid psychiatric treatment, as he was sure the shrink would know if he hadn't been standing there like a fucktard.

"Who the hell are you?" Mirren took a step toward the woman. "You need a ride back to the sorority house?"

She grinned and walked to within a foot of him; he had an inexplicable urge to take a step back. He'd be damned if that was going to happen.

He pinned her with his Slayer expression, which alone had driven many lesser men to their knees, including vampires. She frowned at him and didn't answer.

Mirren took another step toward her. "I'll talk slower so you can understand, lady. Who. The. Hell. Are. You?"

The woman's chin didn't even reach Mirren's sternum, so from her close vantage point she had to crane her neck to look him squarely in the eye—which she did.

"I'm Ashton, a.k.a. the dickhead," she said in a drawl that had "smartass" written all over it. "And I am your worst fucking nightmare."

❧CHAPTER 5❧

Cage coughed in an unsuccessful attempt to camouflage the laugh that started deep in his gut and bubbled out before he could stop it. Mirren's expression morphed in quick succession from intimidation to disbelief to outrage. Bloody priceless.

The laughter faded fast, however, when Krys returned with the Bronco, backing it up to the edge of the job site. It was a sobering reminder of why they were standing there, and what—or who— lay under that blue tarp. Cage was surprised at his own reaction. He hadn't known Rob well, but he'd been a genuinely good man. The people of Penton were good people, whether human or vampire. None of them deserved this.

If Cage could find the saboteur, he'd kill him. If it turned out to be his old "friend" Fen Patrick, he'd kill him slowly. While Fen had given him no cause to be suspicious, the man had been a very good operative as a human soldier of fortune. Good enough for Cage to have shared his own identity with Fen all those years ago instead of killing him, so he could keep him as a partner. And good enough for Cage to not quite trust him now.

Rob was a serious loss. Cage had met a lot of battle veterans but never one more able to fit in with anyone—vampire or human—so he couldn't imagine Rob being the target. Besides, everybody in town had worked on the site at one time or another, so no one could've known he'd be there, standing at that place, at that time.

The tableau at the construction site remained static during the somber business of death. Krys and Aidan wrapped Rob's body in a heavy utility blanket from the back of Mirren's Bronco, and Aidan gently carried him to the truck and placed his body in the back. They'd likely be taking him to the Penton Clinic, where the town's minuscule morgue thankfully lay in the half of the building that still had electricity.

The newcomer, Ashton—was that a first or last name?—had remained in her face-off with Mirren, although she'd taken a couple of steps back and kept her mouth shut while they moved Rob's body. Cage was pretty sure she hadn't moved away from Mirren out of fear. More likely, she wanted the ability to glare at him without craning her neck. Her fierce expression hadn't relaxed one iota. This little spitfire soldier was like a mini-Slayer, and watching the two together would be worthy of an expensive ringside seat.

Mirren Kincaid was six feet eight inches of muscle and bad attitude, and Cage would wager few had ever spoken to him the way the girl had. At least not and lived to tell about it.

Cage glanced at Nik, who was biting his lower lip and not doing a very good job of hiding his own amusement, despite the fact that Aidan and Krys hadn't even reached the bottom of the hill with their solemn cargo. "Is she always like this?"

Nik gave a slow shake of the head. "Negative. Not at all." He paused. "Sometimes she's worse."

This time, Cage couldn't stop the smile that spread across his face. "This is going to be fun, as long as we stay out of the way."

"I can fucking hear you, Reynolds." Mirren growled at Cage over his shoulder, but kept his eyes pinned on the girl. Woman, Cage should say, although she was so diminutive next to the Scottish behemoth, it was hard not to see her as a waif. Probably accounted for her Mirren-like attitude. Short-man syndrome, so to speak.

Mirren's hands balled into fists, and if the man had still been human, his face would have turned about six ugly shades of pissed off. Cage couldn't see the big guy's face, but he'd bet those gray eyes had gone from thunderstorm to snowstorm.

"The colonel has lost his fucking mind." Mirren's voice dropped about an octave. "What could you possibly do to help us here?"

She propped her hands on her hips, gave Mirren a slow, sultry once-over with more than a little come-hither in her expression, and lowered her voice—but not so low that Cage couldn't hear. "I can do things to you that are beyond your wildest dreams, vampire."

"Uh-oh," Nik muttered under his breath. "She's gonna blow."

If Cage hadn't been afraid Mirren would turn his wrath on the nearest safe target—him, in other words—he would've explained to Nik that Mirren was showing uncharacteristic restraint, and if anyone was going to violently break the stalemate it would be the big guy. He figured the only reason Mirren had held his temper in check so far was that he'd gotten used to mouthy women. His mate, Glory, was a talker. She also wasn't the least bit intimidated by her big vampire and, in fact, had him pretty well tamed. Cage would not be sharing that opinion with the Slayer, however.

"Little girl, I suggest you walk back into whatever hole in the woods you crawled out of." Mirren's voice dropped even lower and softer. Funny how, on some people, a soft voice was more menacing than a shout. "In the morning, the colonel can reassign you to a more fitting place. I don't care what you turn into—squirrel, otter . . ." He gave her a head-to-toe once-over and waved his hand in a dismissive gesture. "Chipmunk."

Nik groaned and looked at the ground. "Oh man."

Ashton took a step toward Mirren, craning her neck again. "And where might that more fitting place be, Mirren Kincaid? Oh, don't look surprised. I did my homework. Where is it you think I belong in this man's army? On my back?"

Mirren shrugged. "Probably, but don't spread your legs on my account, honey."

The air around them crackled with tension, and even Cage thought Mirren had gone a step too far. He opened his mouth to suggest that Nik take Ashton far, far away for the evening and start fresh at dusk tomorrow, maybe with a referee. He froze at her expression, though. She was grinning, dark eyes alight with mirth and a look Cage recognized all too well. The undeniable, addictive power of the adrenaline rush. Ashton was having fun.

Clearly, the woman was insane. She was suicidal. She was . . . superb.

With a screech that would do a banshee proud, she ran at Mirren headfirst. If Cage hadn't heard the man's *oof* and been knocked off-balance himself when Mirren fell ass over teakettle, he'd have sworn he'd hallucinated the whole thing.

"Told ya," mumbled Nik, who'd stepped out of the way with nimble speed.

A burst of pain erupted on Cage's cheek, followed by the trickle of blood streaming toward his neck. Damn, but that little woman could throw a punch. Unfortunately, she was throwing them so hard and fast, she'd clocked him as well as Mirren.

Cage rolled out of the line of fire and took the outstretched hand Nik offered. "That woman is barking mad." Cage rubbed his jaw, amazed that Mirren was fending off blows but not striking back.

Nik nodded. "As a hatter."

Finally, breathing hard from either fists or fury, or both, the woman stopped her assault. She sat astride Mirren, looking down at him with a frown. "Why the fuck won't you fight back? Afraid of being beat by a sorority girl? It's no fun if you don't fight back."

Cage waited for it. The name-calling. Maybe a backhand to show Ashton what the Slayer was made of—which, even from his prone position, would send her flying. The lesson-teaching that was sure to follow.

Instead, the choked noise Mirren uttered was one it took a moment for Cage to recognize because he'd never heard it from the man. Didn't think it was possible. Mirren Kincaid was laughing.

His voice even sounded different—lighter, amused. "What the hell are you, Ashton?"

She climbed off him and rose to her full height, which wasn't much. "Eagle shifter. And a damn good tracker. And stronger than you fang-faces can imagine. Plus, I can fly. So don't fuckin' mess with me."

Mirren rolled to his feet with surprising grace for a man his size and rubbed his face. The fingers he drew from his mouth were covered in blood from multiple scratches, and there appeared to be tooth marks along his jawline. "You got a first name?"

Ashton squinted up at Mirren a few heartbeats. "It's Robin."

An eagle named Robin. Bloody brilliant. Cage opened his mouth to comment but caught an elbow in the ribs from Nik, who gave a slight shake of his head.

Right. Don't tease the eagle about her name.

Mirren seemed to have reached the same conclusion, since he bypassed any comment about ironic names. "Guess you'll work out after all, Ashton. Gonna have to find a new place for you to crash, though. Since the colonel didn't say you were a girl"—Cage saw Robin's eyebrow take a dangerous spike at that, but Mirren was oblivious—"I'd planned to put you and Zorba in a room together."

"That's fine." Robin ran her fingers through her short, spiky hair, and Cage tracked the movement. Such delicate fingers in hands that held such power. "We sleep together half the time anyway."

"Aw, shit," Nik huffed out under his breath. "I swear that woman has no filter."

Interesting. "And where do you sleep the other half of the time, little bird?"

The words came out before Cage could stop them, which he instantly regretted. Talk about no filters; his were usually a mile high, but they seemed to have suddenly vaporized.

He'd been off Robin Ashton's radar during her preoccupation with Mirren. Now, however, she stepped away from Mirren and looked at him. Really looked. Cage felt naked, as if she could see way more than he'd ever intended to share. When had he developed such a big mouth?

"You asking me to sleep with you the rest of the time, vampire?"

Oh yeah, Robin definitely had him on her radar. She edged past Mirren and approached Cage with a gait more feline than avian, and he was aware of Mirren crossing his arms over his chest, probably relieved to have her focused on someone else. "What's your name, Brit Boy? You're kind of pretty, and I've never done a vampire."

Cage opened his mouth to suggest she give doing him a try, and then closed it again. He had a feeling Robin Ashton could complicate his life way more than he wanted. And maybe kill him in the process. Plus, he was swearing off romantic entanglements. He still had one to wrangle his way out of.

"Congratulations, Ashton." Mirren suddenly seemed to be enjoying himself. "You managed to shut up our resident shrink, something no one else in Penton has ever been able to do. Cage Reynolds is his name, and I do think he's afraid of you."

"Don't be daft." Cage's bravado didn't sound very convincing, even to himself. She did scare the hell out of him, and not for any reasons he cared to examine.

"A shrink, huh? You're interesting, Cage Reynolds." Robin smiled at him—not the predatory show of teeth she'd given Mirren while threatening to eat him alive, but something almost sweet, a touch tentative. The edges of his mouth rose in an involuntary response.

Shit. What was he doing? Whatever, it was time to stop. "If you and Nik are a couple, we shouldn't have to change the living arrangements."

Awkward transition, but it broke the moment. Robin felt it, too, judging by her startled blink. "Right. We're not . . . we're just . . . convenient. Niko?" She frowned at something past Cage's shoulder, and he looked behind him.

Nik had left them to kneel next to the pile of bricks from the collapsed wall. He clutched one in his hand, his dark eyes looking at something a million miles away, not unlike the million-yard stare soldiers developed after too much combat.

Mirren joined them, the three of them standing in a row like see-no-evil monkeys, watching Nik as he looked at . . . what?

"Don't tell me he's a head case," Mirren said. "What the hell's wrong with him?"

"Hush." Robin's voice was soft and her expression worried. "Give him a couple of minutes. The faster he does this, the less painful it is for him."

Whatever "it" was. But Cage had seen that kind of unfocused stare before, on the face of their little child vampire Hannah, when she was having one of her visions. If he had to guess, their new friend Nik might not be as much of a plain-vanilla human as he'd originally thought.

God knows Robin Ashton wasn't plain-vanilla anything— though her protectiveness of her "convenient" bedmate Nik was another sign of the sweetness he'd glimpsed earlier. They might not be a couple, but she cared about him. It showed in the softened lines of her face, the worry that darkened her eyes.

A few more seconds passed before Nik began picking up bricks one at a time, holding each one for a few seconds and then tossing it aside. He still hadn't spoken.

Robin knelt next to him and looked over her shoulder. "Help us. He needs to touch as many of the bricks as he can. Don't talk to him. Anybody got a sheet of paper and a pencil?"

Cage glanced over at Mirren, who wore that uneasy expression he only got around Hannah. Mirren was all about what he could see and touch and punch the shit out of. Stuff like visions totally freaked him out. If anybody in Penton scared Mirren, it was little Hannah in the midst of a premonition.

He flinched when Cage touched his arm. "I can help them here. Maybe you could check in with Aidan and Krys. On the off chance the colonel wants to talk security, you probably need to be there." It was doubtful that Colonel Rick Thomas would want to do anything more tonight than mourn the loss of his son, but the possibility gave Mirren a graceful way out if things were about to get weird with Nik. Make that *weirder.* "You could probably take Nik's SUV and we can walk back."

Mirren glanced down the hill at the vehicle, no doubt wondering whether he might get psychic germs from driving it. "Good thinking, but I'll walk to the clinic and take Aidan and Krys home in the Bronco."

He didn't waste time, his long legs eating up the distance down the hill before Cage could respond.

With Mirren making his way north toward the clinic, Cage walked to the back side of the wall structure. Earlier he'd spotted the clipboard from the job site on the ground near the extra bricks, and, sure enough, there was a pen attached. He flipped the pages to turn blank sides up, clipped them back in, and handed it to Robin.

"Thanks." She touched Nik's arm and held the clipboard in front of him. He nodded and tossed another brick aside.

They worked another thirty minutes. Robin would hand a brick to Nik; he'd hold it for two seconds, or four, or half a minute, sometimes with his eyes closed. Then he'd hand the brick to Cage, who'd set it aside and wait for the next one while Nik took the clipboard and sketched furiously.

Finally, Nik stared at the last sketch a few seconds before thrusting the clipboard at Robin, struggling to his feet and lurching behind the building. Where, by the sound of it, he was retching his guts out.

"You need to help him?" Cage asked Robin. Whatever kind of abilities Nik had, he paid a physical price for them.

"No, he'll need to sleep it off. He hasn't done this in a while." She scooted next to Cage and held out the clipboard. "You might need more light to study these, but he gets images off things he touches—things that happened in the past. Here's what he got from your bricks."

The top drawing was an amazing likeness of Max Jeffries, laughing. "This is Max," Cage said, "the other Ranger living in Penton. Rob was his best mate."

Several drawings appeared to be from the brick manufacturer. Another one showed Mark, and another showed Rob himself, looking happy and very much alive. There was a scathe member Cage didn't know well, but the guy was bonded to Mirren.

He flipped to the last drawing, an image of a wild feline—a mountain lion, maybe, or a jaguar. There was no context, so it was hard to tell how large it was.

He held it up to Robin. "What does this mean?"

Before she could answer, Nik stepped back around the corner, looking like death's last victim. "If you don't recognize it, I'd say it means Penton has a shape-shifter you don't know about."

⚘CHAPTER 6⚘

Melissa sat hunched on the sofa of the community house she shared with Mirren and Glory—and, after tonight, a couple of new Ranger members from the Omega Force project. They needed people, especially feeders, but she was tired of new faces.

The noise of a car engine reached her from the street, and she tugged back the ugly light-blocking black curtains that Will had installed in all the community houses. He claimed it was to prevent the vampires from frying in case any of them got stuck upstairs, away from the safe spaces, during daylight hours—but she'd overheard him assuring Mirren the fabric was both fireproof and bulletproof. So much for rebuilding without the shadow of danger hovering over them.

The car passed without stopping; she recognized the driver as Shawn Nicholls, one of the vampires who'd come into Penton just before everything fell apart. Both Shawn and Britta Eriksen had been bonded to Will, but Melissa knew virtually nothing about them except that both she and Shawn fed from Glory because Mirren wouldn't let another man near his mate.

Damn it. There had been a time when no one moved to Penton without Melissa Calvert taking the time to invite them to lunch or introduce them around town so they'd feel at home. Aidan teased her about "snooping," but she'd always thought of it as friendly interrogation. She knew everybody, and everybody knew her. She had enjoyed being seen as a direct link to Aidan. She liked it that people would come to her in order to get an issue or problem in front of him. And she liked helping people settle into life in Penton, especially the new human familiars.

She'd learned a lot about people in those lunches at the no-longer-standing Penton café, and she thought she'd been a big part of why Penton worked so well. People were friendly and open, and it started with her.

No more lunches for her now. At least not unless they involved a vein at 3:00 a.m. She didn't want to feel bitter about what had happened to her, but she didn't know where she fit in anymore. She was no longer Aidan's fam. No longer Krys's daytime help at the clinic.

No longer Mark's wife, at least not technically.

Where are they? Krys had called from the clinic to tell her about Mark's injury and assure her it wasn't life-threatening. Still, Melissa wanted to see him for herself. She knew him better than anyone; just by watching him get out of the car and walk to the community house across the street, she'd be able to tell where he hurt and how badly. She knew his facial expressions better than her own: the way he'd grit his teeth, suck in a breath, and turn his head to the side with his eyes closed if something hurt; the way his mouth would quirk up on the left side two times—never once, never more than twice—just before he burst into laughter.

Old habits, and all that.

From her perch, she could also see the community house at the head of Cotton Street. She'd know when Cage came home from the accident site and know that he, too, was safe. Melissa no longer took a single day for granted. She'd learned the hard way that monumental change could take place in a heartbeat.

She thought she'd seen Cage earlier, but it had been Fen coming out of the house. He'd sat on the porch for a while, then walked down Cotton Street toward the old mill. She watched him until he turned the corner, and she thought about calling Aidan.

She was probably being paranoid, but Fen was one more person she didn't know. And after the last nine months, that meant more people she didn't trust. In Penton, trust was now a rare commodity. She resented like hell what had been done to her town; she resented all the bad things that kept happening to people she cared about.

And she, Melissa Calvert, former familiar of Aidan Murphy and wife of Mark Calvert, sat here with fangs, at midnight, afraid, not sure who she was anymore. Cage, Aidan, Krys—they all kept telling her she wasn't a monster, that she was still the woman she'd always been.

They were right on one count; she wasn't a monster. She'd been around too many kind and honorable vampires to believe that lie.

But she had changed. She'd turned from a naively fearless human into a cowardly, fanged night crawler, like those big, stretchy worms she'd dug up as a kid to use as fishing bait.

The worms were slow, rubbery creatures that instinctively hid from anything that came too near, seeking out the comfort of earthy darkness in which to burrow and hide. That was her. What Melissa Calvert had become. Or had reverted back to—just like when she'd been Melissa Williamson, before meeting Aidan. The young woman who had gravitated to abusive relationships like iron filings to a magnet. The woman who sank so deeply into her mother's trap of depression that she couldn't climb out and thought a bottle of pills was her only escape.

Aidan had saved her that time. Turned her into a new person. And Mark had completed her.

Now, she felt the depression threatening to take her down again, and damn it, she didn't want to resurrect Melissa Williamson. She didn't want to wallow in a paralysis of sadness and fear. She didn't want to be a blind, light-fearing night crawler that could function only in mental darkness.

Cage had been the light that tried to lead her out of it after Matthias took her, but she didn't want to rely on him again. Or on anybody but herself.

Another hour passed, and finally, just before midnight, Mirren's Bronco stopped in front of Aidan and Krys's house. A wave of relief washed through Melissa when Mark slid out of the backseat; her tense shoulders released, a shaky breath escaped. He had a bandage on his left temple, but no other visible injuries.

Her relief died a quick death, though, as she watched Mark walk up the sidewalk. His movements were slow and stiff, and he half-pulled himself up the short set of steps to the porch by grasping the side rail.

She recognized the gait. Chronic back pain had turned him into a heavy user of oxy 80, which led to a string of petty thefts when the doctors cut him off and he needed money for black-market buys. Then heroin, cheap and plentiful on the streets of Atlanta, had claimed him. None of it helped him move any better; it simply made him care less.

Melissa swallowed down the dark thoughts that threatened to overwhelm her. She stood up once she saw Aidan, Mirren, and Max getting back into the Bronco, leaving Krys behind. Krys was a doctor, but she might not know all of Mark's history. Melissa could help.

She walked out of the house without stopping to think about what she was doing. Otherwise, she'd chicken out. Since she'd been turned, Mark had made her feel guilty with his need, his love, his patience. He would wait for her, he said. He'd love her when she was ready. They'd try again, as soon as she felt comfortable feeding from him.

Instead, she had turned away. She'd turned to Cage out of fear. She'd broken Mark's heart, even though she'd done it for both of them.

Oh, Mark would be honorable. He'd try to make it work. She loved him so much her heart felt big and ungainly behind her ribcage, as if it might swell and burst whenever she saw him. But eventually he'd reject her, and as selfish as it would seem to everyone else, she had to protect her own heart and walk away before he had the chance. She couldn't survive his rejection.

Krys stepped out the front door and onto the porch, closing the door behind her before Melissa cleared the stairs. "I'm glad you're here. Mark needs sleep, but his medical records were stored in the part of the clinic that burned." She sat on the top step and slid over for Melissa to sit beside her. "I know about his problem with heroin, but it started with painkillers, didn't it? He injured his back again. Wasn't that his problem before—his back?"

Melissa stared out at the street. She knew Mark's story as well as she knew her own. "He was a financial analyst—did you know that?"

Krys nodded. "He told me a little of his story when I first came to Penton. There was an accident, right?"

"Multiple spinal fractures, courtesy of a drunk driver." Melissa traced the edge of the step with the toe of her sandal, stopping when she remembered Mark had surprised her with those sandals one time after a business trip to Birmingham for Aidan. He'd thought they were sexy. She should take them off before going inside. If she went inside. "The doctors couldn't do much for him, and they were afraid surgery would make it worse."

"So he tried to kill the pain instead. It happens a lot." Krys sighed. "I just shot him up with enough morphine to take off the worst edge of the pain; I was afraid to give him more. Maybe he'll be able to sleep, though. I'll see if Glory can stay with him during the daytime and get someone else to run the kitchen. Aidan's finding a substitute feeder in the meantime. We'll reassess tomorrow night."

Melissa slipped out of the sandals and set them aside. "What about Max? He's just got Cage and Hannah to feed, and he could stay here during the day."

"He's also got the new guy, Fen." Krys looked at Melissa's bare feet and started to say something. Finally, she just shook her head. "Plus, I think Max will want to take Rob's body home, so we're going to be short on feeders. How are you doing?"

Krys had always been too perceptive for her own good, but she was Melissa's best friend now that Mark no longer held that title. "I'm fine."

Her friend didn't answer, and again Melissa could practically hear her biting her tongue. "Go ahead. Say whatever you want to."

"Why are you here, Mel?"

Talk about a loaded question. Why was she saddled with this strange new life? Why was she still in Penton? Or why was she sitting here on the porch of the house where Mark lived, unable to stay away from him?

Melissa figured she knew which "why" Krys was after. "I thought you might need Mark's medical history, and I could tell you what you needed to know. Probably more than he can."

"Uh-huh."

Melissa sighed. When Krys had been agonizing over her relationship with Aidan, Melissa had given her friend a lot of tough love; she suspected she was about to get a shot of her own treatment handed back to her. She waved her hand in a rolling motion. "Go ahead."

"Here's what I think." Krys turned sideways on the step to face Melissa. "Deep inside, you still love Mark, but you don't know your limits yet and he scares you. Cage, on the other hand, is safe."

Melissa laughed; talk about being off base. "Cage Reynolds is not safe. The man was a soldier for hire, for God's sake. You should hear some of the stories Fen was telling last night about their years as mercenaries in Nicaragua." She paused, hesitant to say what she hadn't even told Cage. "Besides, I'm not with Cage. I'm not going to be."

Krys smiled. "You have no idea how glad I am to hear you say that." She leaned back against the top step, propping on her elbows. "Don't get me wrong. I like Cage a lot, and I know Aidan does, too. Even Mirren. But . . ."

"I know." Melissa stared down the block at Cage's house, wondering when she'd get to tell him all of this and how he would take it. Wondering if she'd be disappointed if he didn't care. She had no idea how the man felt. "I've watched you and Aidan together, and Mirren and Glory. I just don't have that kind of connection with Cage.

"I held onto him after I was turned for the exact reason you said, out of fear. But whatever that bond-mate reaction is that vampires get? I don't have it, and I don't think he does, either."

"Have you told Mark that?"

Melissa shook her head, opened her mouth to respond, but realized she didn't know what to say.

"You'll figure it out." Krys threw an arm around her shoulders and hugged her. "Speaking of Cage, I'm going down the block to meet his Irish buddy. Aidan wants my take on Fen."

"I'm not sure they're buddies at all. I am sure Fen Patrick is kind of a sleazoid with the one-liners." Melissa was relieved to veer the subject away from her love life. "I don't much like him, but it might just be because he tries so hard to be charming. It feels desperate."

Krys nodded. "Yeah, but if he's starving—and Aidan said he was really thin—he probably is desperate. He wants to find a place here."

Maybe, but Melissa still didn't like his vibe. "Meet him and see what you think. He left the house a while back, walking down toward the old mill. I don't know if he's back yet, so you might have to wait."

At the mention of the old Southern Mills building, a shadow crossed Krys's face, visible even in the dim light of the porch. She'd almost died at that old hulk of a rotting building—more than once. Shame filled Melissa's chest at the bolt of jealousy that shot through her. Krys had been turned vampire, but Krys's and Aidan's love for each other had survived it. Of course, Krys had mated with Aidan when she was still human. That choice hadn't been forced on her.

"I haven't been down there since . . ." Krys didn't need to finish that sentence.

"If he's not at the community house, come back here and catch up with him later." Melissa couldn't imagine going back into that building where so much fear and hurt had taken place. Most of the clinic subsuites had collapsed, and there was no need for her to revisit the place where Matthias had held her captive. "No need to put yourself through seeing it again."

"Nope." Krys got that determined look, and there was no point arguing with her once her jaw had clenched into that firm set. "I need to go back there and face it. Besides, I want to meet this guy. What happened to Mark and Robbie was no accident, and he's the newest person in town."

A familiar and unwelcome tingle of fear streaked across Melissa's scalp. "It was deliberate? Are you sure? Who would want to hurt Rob? Or Mark or Max, for that matter?"

"Mirren's sure of it, and that's good enough for me." Krys had walked a good half-block toward the mill before she called out over her shoulder, "By the way, stay with Mark until he falls asleep, would you? Sure you would. Thanks!"

Damn it. Melissa hadn't even decided whether or not to go inside, much less babysit Mark until he fell asleep. But she climbed to her feet and walked onto the porch. Her hand wavered over the knob to the heavy front door; it felt like some kind of stone that, if rolled away, would let all of her guilt and fear come spilling out.

But Mark had been hurt, and she had failed him. Two facts. If he needed to lay a little guilt on her tonight to feel better, she could suck it up and take it. She owed him that much.

❧CHAPTER 7❧

Krys meant well with her little morphine shot, delivered in a low dose as a nod to Mark's history of addiction. What she didn't realize was that his junkie days were recent enough that he wasn't likely to keel over into unconsciousness from anything other than enough morphine to fell a rampaging rhino. He'd probably always have a high tolerance to any kind of opioid.

Opioid. A good vocabulary word. Maybe if he ever had a kid, that would be its name. Melissa couldn't have children, but deep inside, he'd thought they would leave Penton someday and adopt kids—although they'd need Aidan's help, given their shaky personal histories. He doubted any adoption agent had ever uttered, "Sure, we'll be happy to turn over this child to the depressive with suicidal tendencies and the overeducated junkie."

Didn't matter now. He could kiss that little domestic daydream good-bye.

He'd told Krys not to give him anything for pain, said he could tolerate the clench of muscles in his back and the pain that knifed in sharp bursts all the way to his knees. But when he broke into a cold sweat after the twenty or so steps from the car to the house, she knew he'd been lying. He couldn't tolerate that much pain, not gracefully. It sliced through his back like a heated blade.

After the shot, it still hurt like a sorry bastard, but the tentacles of agony stayed rooted in his lower back instead of racing up and down all the nerve endings in his hips and legs.

Better living through chemistry. It had been the only motto he'd lived by for most of his late twenties, years whose details had blended into a big, drug-addled fog.

Krys had left a few minutes earlier, but Mark still heard her soft voice outside. He pulled the dark curtain aside a fraction to see her on the porch, talking to someone.

He moved the curtain farther. Not someone. Melissa.

Mark waited for the familiar twinge of heartache the sound of Mel's voice usually brought, but it didn't come. Maybe he was over her.

Or maybe he'd had enough morphine to kill the heartache kind of pain.

Whatever the cause, the rise and fall of her voice made him angry instead of sad, and he welcomed the anger like a beloved friend. He deserved to be angry, damn it. He should've been angry a long time ago. Ever since Melissa had been rescued from Matthias and attached herself to Cage Reynolds as if he were a six-foot security blanket with abs, Mark had turned into a pathetic sap.

Anger was a welcome change.

Hopefully, Krys was telling her to get lost. Maybe he'd climb into bed and feign unconsciousness in case she came in anyway, because Melissa usually did what she wanted. He doubted becoming a vampire had curbed her pigheadedness. Once she decided to do something, changing her mind took an act of God Himself. Or, at the very least, Aidan Murphy.

Yep, faking unconsciousness was an excellent idea.

Mark turned in a slow, stooped swivel, stopped a few seconds to see if the pain worsened or sent him to his knees, and shuffled like an old geezer toward his bedroom. He'd toed off his shoes when he came in the house, so his socks slid across the dark bamboo flooring. One small slip and he'd be on his ass again. If that happened, he probably wouldn't get up this time, opioids or no opioids.

The flooring had cost a small fortune; Mark knew because he'd organized the purchase. Will had gone high-end on designing these houses, trying to make them feel like real homes instead of barracks.

And barracks reminded him of Rob.

Damn it, they'd been careful with that construction. He'd gone over and over the scene in his mind, wondering if he'd be dead had Rob not shouted out a warning. It had prompted him to turn, and then instinctively throw himself clear. If Rob had been on the ladder instead of him, Mark would have died and Rob would have been spared. The world would no doubt be better off with a live Rob Thomas, war hero and all-around good guy, instead of a live Mark Calvert, former junkie whose vampire wife wouldn't get her fangs anywhere near him.

And who'd apparently stepped off the abyss into a deep chasm of pathetic self-pity.

Mark grabbed the edge of a table when his left foot skated a few unplanned inches on the shiny dark wood. Enough already, idiot. Pay attention. By God, this wallowing would not continue. He was even sick of himself. From now on, he'd live in a no-wallow zone if it killed him.

He turned too fast going into the bedroom, twisted the back he'd been trying to hold rigid, and held tight to the door facing for a few seconds, waiting for the pain to settle back into a dull throb.

"Here, let me help." A strong arm wrapped around his waist, and he closed his eyes at the scent of vanilla and cinnamon. Melissa's scent. Her warm touch. Her . . . muscles?

"Damn, Mel. When did you get so strong?" She could probably pick him up. And he hadn't heard her come in. Sneaky vampire.

She took more of his weight than she had to as she eased him toward the bed—just to prove a point, no doubt. "I got that strong when I died, Mark. Because I look the same, you keep thinking I am the same. But vampires are strong, remember?"

"Oh, believe me, I haven't forgotten. I haven't forgotten any-thing." He turned with more help from her than he wanted, and sat gingerly on the edge of the bed. Maybe the morphine was doing a better job than he'd thought, because his back felt as if only a match had been set to it and not a blowtorch.

While he gauged his ability to lie down without help—because he'd be damned if she was going to put him to bed like a baby—Ms. Strong and Mighty Vampire stacked pillows against the headboard.

Then she reached for him. "Let me help you—"

"No." Mark pushed her hands away. "I can do it." He used his arms to lift himself, slowly pivoting his hips into the middle of the bed and lifting one leg at a time. Finally, he eased back against the pillows. He'd feel a lot prouder of his independence if he weren't sweating like a pig under a heat lamp. He might also be breathing like a water buffalo after a two-mile stampede. He could probably keep going with the wildlife metaphors if he tried hard enough.

Melissa had watched his slow descent with a deepening frown line between her eyebrows. He knew that look. That particular crease said she had an opinion and wouldn't rest until she shared it.

"Krys said she gave you a shot of morphine but was worried about giving you too much. She shorted you, didn't she? It didn't work."

"Sure it did. Pain's not bad at all." Especially if he kept his teeth clenched.

"Pants on fire." She smiled when she said it, her hazel eyes lighting up like they used to before all the shit happened. Then they both froze in awkward silence.

Liar, Liar, Pants on Fire. It had been a silly little game with them. She'd say it, and he'd answer with a suggestive comment on what actually would set his pants on fire, and they'd eventually end up in bed. Maybe they'd tease it out for hours, flirting and verbally sparring, but they always ended up between the sheets.

Whose fault was it that the tease no longer worked? Not his.

No wallowing. Right. Too bad, because he was really good at it.

"Thanks for your help. I'm going to sleep now." Mark rested his head against the pillows and closed his eyes. Her scent was everywhere, inviting him back into the pity party he'd promised to boycott.

He opened his eyes at the sound of a chair being dragged across the floor. "I thought you left."

"I'm going to stay until you fall asleep." Melissa reached across the foot of the bed and tugged off his socks before moving to fiddle with the drawstring of the loose pants Krys had brought to the clinic and helped him climb into. "I'll help you get undressed. You'll be more comfortable. You never like sleeping with anything around your legs."

The idea of her undressing him led to all kinds of mental images. She'd ease the loose pants over his hips, and her arm would brush across his bared skin. He'd inhale the scent of her as she leaned over to tug his shirt over his head. Maybe her beautiful breasts would be within reach of where his mouth . . . would never go again.

Mark closed his eyes and flayed his flaring libido into submission with the only thing he could come up with that was guaranteed to push her away. "I guess it's time we talked about getting a divorce."

Melissa stopped fussing with his pants and sat hard on the chair. He'd laugh at her stricken expression if he didn't feel like crying himself.

She looked at the floor for ten seconds, then twenty. Mark knew because he was counting, waiting for the eruption of glee or horror or acceptance—some kind of reaction. He honestly wasn't sure what to expect, but he steeled himself. If she was going to look relieved that he was moving aside for her to be with that pompous British shrink, he wouldn't want to show how much it hurt.

No wallowing.

"Mark, you can't mean that." When she finally looked up at him, one of the tears that had pooled in her hazel eyes spilled down her cheek.

Yes. Something fierce and gleeful unfurled in his gut, something that whispered *she still loves you* in his mind before he slammed that mental door shut. He wasn't rolling over that easily. "How is Cage, by the way?"

Melissa's posture stiffened, and she wiped away the telltale tear. "This isn't about Cage. It's about—"

"Stop it." Oh, hell no. She wasn't going to start spouting that crap about special vampire chemistry and mating bonds and how her heart didn't remember him. He'd seen that look on her face at the mention of divorce. She loved him. Her mind might not acknowledge it, but her heart remembered.

"But you just don't understand. I'm not—"

"I understand plenty, Mel. I understand that you're a vampire. I understand things have changed for you." Mark shifted on his pillows, ignoring the threatening shard of heat that shot into his hip. "I understand that you want Cage Reynolds to keep you warm at night while I hang around in the wings hoping for a crumb of kindness or a shred of attention."

He paused briefly at the stricken look on her face, the wide eyes, the hurt. But he'd held it in too long, and once he'd begun, he had to finish. "But I'm done with the drama, Mel. I can't do it anymore. I love you, but I won't beg you to love me back. You want your vampire version of Dr. Phil? Go for it. Be happy. I don't have to watch it."

He should feel better now that he'd said his piece, but the way her knuckles had turned white as they twisted in her lap, the slight quiver of her lips, the way she swallowed hard to audibly bury her grief—all it did was make him feel like he'd kicked his dog. Or stuck a knife in the woman he loved, and then twisted it hard.

Mark closed his eyes again, suddenly drained. Whatever burst of energy had fueled his rant, it was spent. "Just go, Mel. I can't do this anymore tonight."

He didn't open his eyes when the bed dipped to his right, or when her hand came to rest on his.

"You've changed." Her fingers twined with his, and damned if they didn't feel as if that's where they should be. "Have you met someone else?"

Huh? Mark opened his eyes and searched Melissa's face for some sign that she was joking. But she looked as miserable as he felt, and some spiteful, petty part of him wanted to hurt her just a little more.

"Not really. I've been a feeder for Britta Eriksen since we split into the community houses. It's been . . ." He paused for effect and bit back a smile at the way her eyes narrowed and the vertical "opinion line" etched itself between her brows. "It's been nice."

Nice was a good, utilitarian, all-purpose word. It could mean nice like a sister, which was an accurate description of his relationship with Britta. Or it could mean nice like a man and a woman engaging in a meaningful bit of blood-fueled foreplay.

"Nice." Melissa frowned harder, and Mark's inner demon-child danced again. She might not admit it, but she was jealous. "What do you know about that woman?"

Quite a lot, actually. Britta had been in Penton only a month, and he'd been her feeder from the outset. "I know she's got a great sense of humor and can make me laugh. She likes movies. And she's sexy."

"That hair's dyed, I can tell." Melissa stood up and pushed the chair back against the wall next to the closet door, looking around the room. Her gaze paused on each piece of furniture as if it might reveal secrets about what went on here when he and Britta were alone. If his dresser could talk, the tales it'd tell would be boring as hell.

She turned back to him, the flash of anger gone now, her features relaxed into the face he'd loved, only maybe a sadder version. "Guess I'll go back to Mirren's and see if there's any update on Rob. Aidan was going to call the colonel and break the news to him. "

"Send word if you hear anything." Suddenly, Mark's games seemed childish to him. Their friend lay in the clinic morgue, and because of Penton's fucked-up politics, they probably wouldn't even be able to give him a proper funeral with military honors and folded American flags. "It should have been me, not him. He deserved better."

"I'm sorry about Robbie. But I'm glad it wasn't you." Melissa paused at the door and looked back. "And for the record, I'm not with Cage."

❧CHAPTER 8❧

Robin Ashton couldn't remember when she'd had quite as much fun as in her first few hours in Penton. Who'd guess a bunch of old vampire dudes in Alabama could prove so entertaining?

Mirren Kincaid was a big, ancient, grumpy—and did she mention big?—piece of work. She couldn't wait to yank his dick a little more. Maybe a lot more.

Knocking alpha males off their pedestals made for delicious fun. It was tiring, though, especially after a six-hour flight . . . without an airplane. Thankfully, Nik had arrived early and stashed some clothes for her in the woods. Mirren really would have freaked out if she'd emerged from the piney backwoods naked. She had the distinct impression that in the dictionary of life, Mirren Kincaid's photo would not illustrate the entry for "enlightened male."

Curling up in the backseat of Nik's SUV, Robin left Nik and Cage to get acquainted while she pretended to nap. Through her shuttered eyelids, she looked out the window at the few details she could see of Penton, illuminated either by moonlight or from one of the infrequent bursts of working streetlights. She saw lots of rubble, charred support beams, skeletons of buildings with bits of wood and masonry stretching into the dark sky like clutching fingers.

That Matthias guy had done a number on Penton; there wasn't much left. It hadn't occurred to her that she wouldn't be able to buy clothes here. Until she could get to a shopping center, maybe she could borrow something from the little vampire girl Hannah, whose psychic abilities Cage had been discussing with Nik when they left the construction site.

And if she ever ran into him, she'd string up the nutjob who'd thought it appropriate to turn a little girl into a vampire, psychic skills notwithstanding. She wouldn't just string him up; she'd hang him by his nuts from a tall building and leave him to dangle in a stiff breeze until something fell off. Even bloodsuckers should have some standards.

She'd already known about Hannah, of course. The colonel had given both Nik and her dossiers on the major players in Penton. Nik had been cautiously excited—only Nik could be both cautious and excited at the same time—about meeting another person with psychic powers, even a young vampire girl.

Thanks to the dossiers, Robin also knew that humans and vampires alike had been brought here by Aidan Murphy, who'd begun buying up the property in this little half-horse abandoned mill town even before the pandemic vaccine had made the blood of vaccinated humans deadly to him and his followers. Aidan had amassed too many acolytes, their reports said, giving the Vampire Tribunal—a bunch of predatory old farts, from the sound of it—an excuse to hunt him down. There was also some kind of personal vendetta involving one of Aidan's senior people and the guy's father, who happened to be on the Tribunal. Will Ludlam, son of Matthias the Lunatic.

Messy stuff. Then again, families usually were. She knew that all too well.

On paper, Aidan Murphy looked like a saint, rehabbing addicts and forming a little commune out in the wilderness—not so different from what her hippie parents had done back in Texas. Those would be the tie-dye-wearing parents who thought it would be funny to name their two eagle-shifter kids Robin and Wren. In the flesh, though, Aidan Murphy had been inscrutable. Frosty-eyed and silent, that one. Kind of the way she'd expected all the fangaroos to be. She'd been pleasantly surprised to find Mirren lived up to his grizzly-bear rep. But Robin had the distinct impression, from the way those intense blue eyes followed her movements, that not much escaped Aidan Murphy's notice. He might be a saint, or he might be dangerous. She'd withhold judgment. The colonel liked him, and she liked the colonel. For now, that was enough.

Which brought her back to the only other vamp she'd met so far. Cage Reynolds was intriguing; his dossier had hinted at broad military experience but mostly off-the-grid stuff, which probably meant he'd been fangs for hire. His human military service, back in World War II, was sealed so tightly within the archives of the British Army, even the colonel's connections hadn't been able to get at it. What kind of guy had sealed records seven decades after his supposed death?

He was magnetic, for sure. Hell, all the vamps she'd seen so far were fuckworthy, even the grizzly. Their physical beauty probably helped them lure unsuspecting humans into offering up veins. Would her blood taste different from that of a non-shifter? She'd like to experience feeding a vampire at least once. Of course, she might feel differently after she'd actually seen the fangs; so far, they'd all proven skilled at hiding them.

Still, Cage managed to come across as calm and competent without being arrogant. Maybe his training as a psy-fucking-chiatrist helped. He probably overanalyzed everything. He'd stood back and smiled as she sparred with Mirren, and he definitely gave off a sexual vibe when she talked to him. She could tell when a guy wanted her, and he wanted her whether he knew it yet or not. Cage was cool like Aidan; she couldn't imagine him getting over-the-top excited about anything. Yet his face revealed more emotion than that of his boss, or scathe master, or whatever the vamps called their alpha.

Yep, Cage Reynolds had a certain *je ne sais quoi*, as her latte-drinking friends back in New Orleans would say.

Make that former friends. Or, rather, current friends living in her former city. She'd been injured during her first and only Omega Force mission when a psychotic wolf-shifter threw her out a third-floor window down in Galveston, Texas. The off-kilter fall had broken her wing.

Which meant she'd been forced to seek out her family's healer.

Which meant he'd ratted her out to her family and they'd managed to discover where she lived.

Which meant she had to literally fly the coop again.

When the colonel asked who'd be willing to transfer to the Penton team, she'd volunteered in a wingbeat—even if it meant working with blood-sucking freaks.

Still, Cage Reynolds was an intriguing freak.

In the front seat, he and Nik had been doing that odd, circular bonding dance that straight men did. Guys never said what they thought—human guys, shifter guys, and, apparently, fanged guys. They'd never say, *Hey, you're cool. I like you. Let's hang out.* Or *Hey, you suck ditch-water. Get out of my face or I'll rip your balls off.*

No, they'd do exactly as Nik and Cage were doing, making small talk to see what they could read into the other's answers. Jumping to conclusions. Never saying what they meant.

"How'd you end up in Penton?" Nik asked, which Robin translated as "Where are your loyalties and what are you looking for?"

"It started as a way to scout out Aidan's idea of a human-vampire community, to see if we could replicate it in the UK," Cage said, establishing himself as a team player. Then he parried back a question to Nik: "Why would you volunteer to get mixed up in this project?"

Nik hesitated at this one, and Robin knew he was grappling with how honest he should be. His answer would set the tone for this friendship—and whether he'd admit it or not, Nik needed friends who wouldn't judge him or try to use his gift. Robin's gut told her Cage could be one of those kinds of friends, so it was her duty to nudge Nik along.

"He can't read stuff off us," she said, catching Nik's frown in the rearview mirror as she sat up and leaned between the front seats. "If he touches a person, he—"

"Robin, zip it," Nik snapped. "You have the brain-to-mouth filter of a parrot."

"Parrots are highly intelligent birds." She reached up and squeezed his shoulder. He was a good guy, her Nik. Too bad they didn't have more sexual chemistry—but then again, she'd learned that lovers were a hell of a lot easier to find than friends, and Nik was her best friend.

She patted his shoulder. "What I was saying before I was interrupted is that Nik can do the same thing with people that he does with stuff like the bricks back there. He can touch somebody and get strong flashes of their history—like bad or embarrassing things. The shit people try to repress. And he doesn't have control over it; he can't decide who he can and can't pull stuff from."

"That would be . . . horrid," Cage said, frowning. "What about with shifters and vampires?"

"He can only read shifters if we're really upset or emotional, or have completely let our guard down and let him in." Robin thumped Nik on the ear when he shot her another glare over his shoulder.

"What about vampires, Niko?" Robin asked. She thought Nik was going to break his jaw one of these days from grinding those pretty white teeth together.

"How the hell would I know?"

"Exactly."

She might as well annoy Cage too. Robin pulled the ponytail he'd tied his hair into, then grabbed the leather cord and jerked it off. Unbound, his hair fell to his shoulders and was the color of her lightest feathers when she shifted into her golden eagle form. Most of her feathers were dark reddish-brown, the color of her hair, but her wings had tips of golden brown like Cage's mane, which was soft and fine as silk, but thick, with just a touch of curl.

He shifted around to face her. "Have a hair fetish, do you, little bird?"

"Ooh, flirty." And sexy as hell. Maybe this one was more dangerous than Aidan Murphy, at least for her. "So, even in this light, I can tell your eyes have gone kind of silvery green. That means you're pissed off at me?"

Anger and hunger, the Vampires 101 dossiers had said. That's what would cause their eyes to lighten. "Or do you need a blood transfusion?"

Cage shifted to look at her more closely, and she had a foreign urge to squirm under his examination. His eyes had lightened even more, and she couldn't decide if it made her want to fuck him or fly away.

"Guess it's not too soon to start your lessons in the ways of the vampire," he said, his deep voice taking on a silky quality that caused her heart to do a stutter step. "Three things will cause a vampire's irises to lighten."

Well, she knew two. "Yeah, yeah, anger and hunger. What's the third one?"

He reached back and stroked a finger along her jawline. "Arousal, little bird." Then he turned back around and laughed. "You'll have to decide which one applies to the present situation."

She didn't hear Nik laughing, but his shoulders were moving up and down suspiciously, so she thumped him on the ear again for good measure. "Well, never mind about me; back to Nik. Let him touch you—unless you have secrets you want to keep."

Cage swept his fingers through that silky hair, which gave him a kind of reckless-rogue look. Then he held his arm out in front of Nik. "There's some ugly shit hiding inside this skin, but go for it."

"Is 'go for it' secret vampire code for 'get that predatory eagle-girl away from me'?" Nik glanced back at her with a look that said they'd be discussing all of this later. Good. He was awfully fun to fight with.

"Oh no, I can handle the eagle girl." Cage, on the other hand, didn't look at her at all, and she considered that comment a challenge. "I was offering to let you touch me—on a purely professional basis, of course—to see if you can read anything off vampires. Oh, and take the next left, third house on the right."

Nik brought the SUV to a stop in front of a long, narrow building that reminded Robin of the modified shotgun houses back in New Orleans, especially the new rows of buildings erected after Hurricane Katrina. But this was bigger, and obviously a new construction, identical to a half-dozen other houses scattered along the block, all painted white. Bo-ring. At least in New Orleans the houses were all painted different colors, from pastel to garish.

Nik hadn't moved, so she squeezed his shoulder again, gently this time. "Go ahead and try. It's just us here, and you need to know what to expect before you meet more fangeroos."

Cage twisted in his seat, and she wished the light were better out here so she could see his expression. "Fangeroos?" He laughed, which transformed his features from hard planes to drool-worthy, and—oh, holy pelicans—she saw fangs. She'd known he had them, of course, but it had been theoretical up to this point.

"How sharp are those things?" She leaned over the back of the seats to get a better look and stretched a hand toward Cage's face. He caught her wrist in his grasp, forcing it toward his mouth slowly as she tried to pull it away, his gaze fixing her like a butterfly on a pinboard.

Damn, but he was strong. She wondered what it would feel like if he punctured her finger. She relaxed the muscles in her arm. *Do it, vampire.*

"Stop that, you two. Seriously." Nik gave her another dirty look and held out his hand to Cage. "Let's see what I can pull from your past—although I have to tell you I don't hold hands with just anyone on the first date."

"And there won't be a second, mate. I think we both play for the other team." He slid his gaze to Robin and gave her a slow smile, sans fang, before grasping Nik's hand.

Nik closed his eyes and lowered his head, concentrating. Good sign. Robin had never seen him strain to capture the images; they either came or they didn't.

"Are you trying to block me?" Nik dropped Cage's hand and looked at him with such relief that it made Robin want to dance.

Cage shook his head. "Negative. And believe me, I've had at least sixty years of deplorable behavior you could be enjoying vicariously right now."

"Oh, thank God. I was praying for this." Nik took a deep breath and released it. "To go way back to your question before Robin hijacked the conversation, I took this assignment hoping I couldn't get images off vampires. You're an even bigger blank than shifters. It's just . . . peaceful."

"Maybe you can find a nice vampire girl. Do vampire girls have sex with human boys?" Robin opened the car door and took in a lungful of clean night air. She sure didn't miss the pollution of the city or the scent of exhaust fumes. It smelled like an open bottle of pine cleaner out here, only fresher, without the chemicals.

Cage and Nik followed her out, and Nik went to the hatch to retrieve his duffel bag.

Robin stood with her eyes closed, taking in the feel of the cool air, the scents, the chirping of crickets and frogs.

"Do shifter girls have sex with vampire boys, little bird?"

She jolted back to awareness at the feeling of Cage standing close behind her, speaking so softly she doubted Nik could hear. Adrenaline pumped through her veins, tingling her fingertips and scalp, and her heart took off at a gallop. The heat from his body seeped into her back through her thin top. Why had she assumed vampires would have cold skin? Too many bad movies.

"What's between you and Nik anyway?" Again that soft voice. He wasn't touching her anywhere, but he was close, so very close.

"He's my best friend." Robin swallowed hard, stepped away from Cage, and turned to face him.

"And she's one of mine, even if she does have a big mouth, the manners of a guttersnipe, and an utter lack of willingness to observe social niceties. So don't even think about hurting her." Nik handed her a white plastic bag and hefted his duffel over his shoulder. "I picked up some clothes for you when I stopped for lunch in Mobile. They might not fit, but I wasn't sure you'd be able to find anything here. They'll last a day or two."

Robin laughed. "I was going to see if I could borrow something from—what's her name, Hannah?"

"Oh, that would be interesting." Cage crossed his arms over his chest. "Hannah's style is, well, let's say it lies somewhere between Hello Kitty and Sesame Street."

Nik made a grab for the bag. "Give me back the clothes. I want to see you in something fuzzy and pink."

"Forget it." Robin tucked the bag under her arm and started toward the house. "Who all is going to be living here with us?"

Cage and Nik followed her up the sidewalk and onto the porch, and Cage knocked on the front door. "Among others, your favorite sparring partner."

The door opened and almost seven feet of vampire blocked the light from inside. "Well, if it isn't Zorba and the little lost girl. What's your sorority name—I Ate-a Pie?"

Robin opened her mouth to respond, but shut it when Nik rested a hand on the back of her neck and tickled her. "Not fair," she mumbled. How could you get a good temper brewing if someone was tickling you?

It might not happen now, but soon, someone needed to knock down that big oaf Mirren Kincaid—again. And she knew just the sorority girl to do it.

❧ C H A P T E R 9 ❧

Frank Greisser arrived at the hotel in Innsbruck five minutes before midnight, the collar of his long black raincoat pulled up to ward off the cold drizzle, a black hat hiding the blond curls that made him look more like a thirtysomething playboy than the most powerful man in the vast world of vampire politics.

"Close the door before someone sees us." He strode in as if he owned the place—which for all Matthias knew, he might—and tossed the hat on the dark-green duvet folded across the foot of the narrow bed. "I trust your accommodations are sufficient?"

Matthias looked around the small, simply appointed room. The view of the Alps out the window during daylight hours was likely spectacular, but he'd never be able to see it. So the hotel room's greatest asset was the owner's willingness to cover that alpine view with a dark blackout curtain and make the south wing of the hotel inaccessible during daylight hours. It was a service for which Frank no doubt paid a premium.

"I would prefer to be at home, in New York or Virginia." Matthias poured a brandy for himself and the man who'd saved him—although Matthias, too, had paid a premium. He'd be allowed to live as long as he followed the orders of the officious Austrian, remained isolated, and kept the information flowing. Frank had told him one misstep and no matter where Matthias went, he'd be found. Once found, he'd wish in vain for a merciful execution.

Matthias did not doubt him. He'd met only two men by whom he was truly intimidated. Mirren Kincaid was one, and the other sat across the room from him now, polishing a scuff off his expensive Italian leather shoes.

"All things considered, I'm quite comfortable in these rooms. *Danke.*" Matthias raised his glass in salute.

"*Bitte.*" Frank settled into the chair nearest the covered window and sipped his brandy. "I thought you would enjoy an update from your friends in Penton. I'm sorry to say there has been a most unfortunate accident."

The rush of anticipation heated Matthias's nerve endings more than the brandy. He tried not to sound too eager. "Is it too much to hope one of the Penton Five is no longer among us?"

Aidan Murphy. Mirren Kincaid. Cage Reynolds. Gloriana Cummings. Melissa Calvert. They needed to die. And Matthias's own son, William, was number six, the one who needed to suffer most. He'd been promised the opportunity to deal with his rebellious, traitorous son himself, in whatever manner he chose, as soon as the others were dead. He anticipated years of breaking the boy, again and again.

"Sadly, no. Not yet, anyway. But the stupid human soldier who helped lead the charge against us this summer is dead," Frank said. "I'm told morale is low, and many of those who moved back into town are again considering defection."

"Let me go after them personally." Matthias rose and paced the length of the room. "Give me three or four good fighters, and we can take them out. After all, after today they'll think I'm dead. Their guard will be down."

Frank gave him an assessing look, but ultimately shook his head. "It's too risky. One of the guards who arranged for your escape has disappeared. We're looking for him, but there's no way to guarantee his silence until we find him. Hunger drives even vampires to make strange alliances, yes?"

Matthias hated inaction. "So we just arrange for a run of bad luck and hope we manage to take out Murphy? If he's gone, the others will crumble, but it's a slow tactic, especially with him having the votes to ascend to the Tribunal next week."

Matthias bristled at the notion that Murphy, no more than a brawling Irish farm boy, would be seated at the Tribunal meeting table while he, one of the vampire elite, was a fugitive.

Frank got up and poured himself another brandy. "It's not that simple. You forget Mirren Kincaid. The others will follow Kincaid if something happens to Murphy. They all have to be taken out—but especially those two."

Matthias laughed. "They'd follow if Kincaid would lead, but he won't. It's not in his nature. The only other person in Penton capable of taking over if something happened to Murphy was Cage Reynolds, and that sorry backstabbing sonofabitch went back to London." He'd also like being the one to kill Reynolds. Slowly.

"Not any more. He returned to Penton last evening." Frank smiled at Matthias's look of astonishment. "Murphy asked and he didn't hesitate, or that's the word in London. Edward Simmons released him from his bond."

"More reason to let me go after them. After all, it keeps your hands clean."

"I said no." Frank's tone turned sharp. "You're where I need you. I have help on the inside, and our plan will work. You have the unfortunate American trait of impatience. Your way led to failure. Mine will take longer, but it will succeed."

Greisser had managed to place someone inside Murphy's organization? "Who is your plant? What is the plan?"

Pulling out a sheet of paper from his coat pocket, Frank rose and handed it to Matthias. "The plan is my concern. Yours is to tell me the strengths and weaknesses of everyone on that list."

Matthias scanned the short column of names. Most of them he recognized from his own research into Penton.

"Fine." He returned to his seat. "Where do you want me to start?"

Frank sipped his brandy and smiled. "Start with your friend Cage Reynolds."

☙ CHAPTER 10 ❧

Cage followed Robin and Nik into the big common room of the community house the new Pentonites would be sharing with Mirren, Glory, and Melissa, at least for now.

The idea of seeing Melissa filled him with guilt. What the hell was wrong with him? He'd spent the whole ride back from the job site acting like a sex-starved horndog with the fierce little shapeshifter, not thinking about their lost team member, or about how he might help Max cope with losing his best friend, or about the woman he wanted to let down gently and keep as a friend.

Cage suspected he wouldn't recognize friendship if it bit him on his horny arse.

The scent of vanilla candles made the big, warm room of the comm-house soothing, even relaxing. The sweetness blended with the pungent scent of new wood and the rich, velvety aroma of overstuffed leather furniture. This felt like a home, or what Cage imagined a real home might be like. A fire burned low in the stone fireplace, its flames crackling enough to add ambience without making the room too hot, casting soothing shadows on the arched tray ceiling. A crimson rug stretched across the bamboo floor.

Who'd ever have imagined that the Slayer, once the Tribunal's most feared executioner, would end up with the most domestic setup in Penton?

Must be the result of having two women in the house who both had an interest in nesting. Cage hadn't seen the insides of Aidan's or Will's houses yet, but neither Krys nor Randa struck him as domestic types. Although he'd lay odds that their community houses looked a hell of a lot better than the spartan digs he and Fen had moved into last night, where Max and Hannah lived. If GI Joe moved in with Barbie, their place would resemble the Max and Hannah house, all camo and pink. Unsettling, that.

He'd planned to spend tonight making sure Fen wasn't up to anything more than he claimed, but nothing about this evening had gone as planned. He'd halfway expected to find Fen here, sucking up to Mirren for a permanent spot in the scathe—but Aidan was here instead, standing in the doorway with an expression that hovered somewhere between shell-shocked and furious.

No sign of Fen, though, nor of Melissa. And Aidan's look meant trouble. He was the most even-tempered man Cage had ever met, but when he finally lost it, everyone had better get out of the line of fire. He was as close to losing it as Cage had seen since the worst days of the Omega siege.

Krys spoke. "Mel went to see Mark, if that's who you're looking for, Cage." Cage looked behind him, to where she had curled up in one of the corner armchairs with a glass of wine. Thank God vampires could still drink, although it would take an enormous volume to create any kind of real buzz. Maybe he'd start an experiment to find out.

He sank into the buttery leather seat of the adjacent sofa and poured himself some wine from the bottle on the end table. He looked at his half-filled wine glass for a second, then finished filling it up to the top.

Melissa had rushed to see Mark; he wondered how much, or little, to read into it. "That's understandable. She'd want to reassure herself that he was going to recover."

"I think the two of you need to talk." Krys's expression was unreadable, but Cage recognized a knowing comment when he heard one.

"That we do." He sipped his wine, looked at the bottle, and topped off his glass. "Nice vintage. You weren't happy to see me return, I imagine."

Krys's dark-brown eyes were somber. "I don't think you and Mel are right for each other, but you're wrong about the rest. I was really glad to hear you were coming back to Penton. We need you. Especially . . ." She trailed off and looked at Aidan with worry etched into every feature.

An adrenaline spike sent a rush of heat through Cage's limbs, and he sat forward and put down his glass. "What else has happened?" Had he missed something while his brain had been preoccupied with the feisty little shifter? "What is it? Did Aidan talk to the colonel?"

Krys locked gazes with Aidan and gave a slow nod in response to some unspoken communication between them. Aidan was a strong master vampire—the strongest Cage had ever encountered—so he and Krys, as his bond-mate, probably had the ability to communicate telepathically. Which was damned inconvenient for everyone else.

Krys set down her glass and uncurled herself from the chair. "Time for me to go. Glory and I will be across the street with

Melissa; Mark's asleep for the night, I hope. Aidan wants to meet with the lieutenants and Omega Force team, and we're not invited." She looked up as Glory returned with Nik and Robin, talking nonstop about the high points of the kitchen. "Speaking of which, what do you think of the new people?"

"I like them," Cage said without hesitation. He'd been surprised at how much he did like them and how quickly they'd won him over. He didn't usually trust easily, but Nik, especially, had impressed him. So had Robin, but he wasn't sure which part of his anatomy was more intrigued with the shifter, and one head's opinion didn't count as much as the other's. "Nik's kind of reserved, but comes across as very competent and serious and in control. Robin's . . ." Sexy as hell. Scarier than Satan himself. "Robin's interesting."

"I didn't know shape-shifters existed. Of course, a year ago I didn't know vampires existed, and now, I am one." Krys's laughter sounded forced. "Robin seems, I don't know, kind of confrontational."

Cage followed Krys's gaze to the kitchen doorway, where Robin stared up at Mirren with her fists propped on her hips and daggers shooting from her eyes. "You have no idea."

Her tour-guide duty done, Glory sat next to Cage and wrapped her arms around him, and he kissed her cheek. She had filled out again after getting sick in Omega, and it was a good look for her with her strong Native American features. She had a wide sweet streak and was genuinely kind. Glory Cummings was way too good for Mirren—but fortunately, the big guy knew it.

Only now, she looked worried, too. "I'm glad you're home, Cage. Mirren was afraid you'd stay in London, and he wanted you back here. We all did."

Her words lit a warm fire in Cage's chest. When was the last time so many people had been happy to see him, the eternal loner both by choice and by occupation? That would be never. Still, one thing about Glory's statement didn't ring true, so he raised an eyebrow. "Let me get some clarification here. Mirren said those actual words? He said, 'I miss Cage and want him to come home'?"

Glory looked over at her preoccupied mate in the next room and grinned. He was now mimicking Robin, standing with his hands stuck on his hips, scowling down at the shifter with his should-be-patented Slayer expression. "Well, not those exact words, but I knew what he meant." She shook her head. "Those two are going to be entertaining. I don't think Robin knows what she's up against."

Yeah, well, Cage had felt that way earlier. Now, he had a feeling Mirren might have met his match. "I'm giving them even odds. It could go either way."

Glory patted his knee before standing up. "Krys, you ready to leave and let the big dogs make their plans?"

"Guess so." Krys stood up and turned back to Cage. "By the way, I had a talk with your friend Fen Patrick earlier tonight. He was exploring the old cotton mill. Seems like a nice guy if you don't mind the cheese factor. He's trying awfully hard to be charming."

Cage had worked with Fen. He'd lived alongside him in close quarters. He'd seen the ugly side of the man, and Fen had seen Cage's ugliness in return. They were both capable of brutality, both got a rush from danger, both were wandering souls. But friends? "I'd call us acquaintances. I didn't even know he'd been turned vampire until last night. Hadn't seen him in more than a decade, and suddenly there he is, on the side of the highway. He's trying hard to win everyone over here, but he needs to prove himself."

"Exactly what Aidan said." Krys looked at her mate and nodded. "Fen told me he was turned about five years ago. I can fill you in later or he can tell you himself, but Aidan's giving me the look. We've gotta go."

As Krys and Glory headed out the front door, Aidan and Mirren joined Cage in the common area near the fireplace. Nik and Robin remained in the doorway to the kitchen as if unsure whether to join in. Cage was surprised that Robin had the self-restraint to wait and see if they were invited to this party—until she elbowed Nik in the ribs. When they moved apart, Cage saw that Nik had a firm grip on the back of her shirt collar, holding her in place.

Brave man, Nik.

"We have some stuff to talk about." At Aidan's voice, everyone stilled, even Robin. "We have some decisions to make. But I have to first remind everyone that what's said here tonight stays here."

Mirren had bypassed the chairs and leaned against the wall next to the fireplace, his arms crossed over his chest. Standing in his favorite Mirren position, in other words. "What about them?" He didn't have to say who "them" was.

"Colonel Thomas speaks very highly of both of you." Aidan nodded at Nik and Robin. "And God knows we need you here, desperately. But before we go any further, you need to be bonded to either Mirren or me. I require it of everyone who lives in Penton, and the colonel has agreed to it. It's safer for all of us. Cage, we never broke our bond before you went back to London and I can still feel it, so you're good to go. Any questions, Nik or Robin?"

They exchanged glances. "We were told a little about the bonding requirement, but not the specifics," Nik said. "Like, you can draw strength from us, right? And know where we are? But how does it work, exactly?"

Aidan nodded. "If I'm within range of you, I'll know if you're in danger. I can pull physical strength from you if I'm injured, but again, only within a certain range. You can't be fed from by any vampire who is not also bonded to me—either directly, or indirectly through Mirren or Will."

"Okay." Nik shrugged. "What do we do?"

"You exchange blood with a master vampire." Mirren pushed himself away from the wall with one foot and stalked toward them, coming to a stop in front of Robin. She looked up at him with narrowed eyes. "Afterward, whoever you're bonded to will know if you're being dishonest or disloyal."

"I got no problem with that." Robin turned to look at Cage. "But I want to do it with him, with Cage."

Mirren hiked one dark eyebrow northward. "Oh, you would, would you?"

Thank God vampires couldn't blush; otherwise, Cage might have to slink back to London in humiliation at the speculative look Mirren was laying on him. He could swear the man was almost smiling—except that, of course, it was Mirren.

"I don't give a fuck what you and Reynolds do with each other in your own time, but he's not a master vampire. You got me, or you got Aidan."

"Let's just get it over with." Nik wedged himself between Robin and Mirren. "How do we do this?"

"Better to do it sitting, so I'll show you." Aidan moved to the end of the sofa, and Nik sat about a foot away from him, back rigid, jaw clenched. "Relax. Roll up your sleeve and hold out your arm."

No man bound for the gallows ever had a more grim expression than the one on Nik's face as he shoved up the right sleeve of his olive-green shirt and stuck his arm out toward Aidan. "It's not like feeding," Cage said, hoping to reassure him. "It doesn't last long, and it'll be easier if you relax your posture a little."

Nik shot an irate look in Cage's direction, but took a deep breath and relaxed his shoulder muscles—until Aidan grasped

Nik's wrist firmly in one hand and pulled out his pocketknife. Nik struggled to pull away but couldn't; it was his first taste of vampire strength. "What's the knife for?"

Aidan's smile was faint. "You'd rather I bit?"

"Uh, no. The knife's fine." To Nik's credit, he only flinched slightly when Aidan made a small horizontal cut across the soft underside of his forearm, swept his tongue across the cut, and quickly placed his mouth over it. Before the first draw of blood, Nik closed his eyes and visibly relaxed. A vampire's saliva numbed the cut and sent nice, orgasmic waves of pleasure through the feeder. The longer the feed, the more intense the feeling.

Most likely, Nik barely had a buzz before Aidan licked the wound to seal it. He quickly flicked the knife across his own forearm and held it out. "Now, you."

"Seriously? Man, this is so gross—nothing personal." Nik grasped Aidan's arm, raising it toward his mouth. Cage missed the rest of the exchange, though, because Robin had turned around slightly to watch, her lips parted and a rapt look on her face. Bloody hell. She was turned on just by watching it.

Cage had never wanted to be a master vampire. It was a pain in the ass, seemed to him. Sure, you developed some nifty psychic skills, but with power came responsibility and all that claptrap. He didn't want more responsibility.

But he also found he didn't want Robin Ashton's mouth on Aidan or Mirren—or any other vampire. And he didn't want anyone else's mouth on her. Somehow, her friends-with-benefits relationship with Nik hadn't bothered him. But this did. It shouldn't, but it did.

You're being a fool, Reynolds. He hadn't gotten laid in a while, that was all. And the self-sabotaging part of his personality probably thought fucking Robin Ashton would be the surest way of hurting Melissa so she'd end things with him before he had to do the dirty work himself.

Still, when Robin insisted Mirren be the one to bond her, saying it was the only way she'd truly win his trust, Cage felt that shot of adrenaline burst into his bloodstream again. He looked at the painting of a forest scene on the wall, focusing on that instead. *I wonder if Glory finally got Mirren to use the art supplies she bought him after the shit with Matthias settled down? Maybe that cold weather will move in next week. Wonder what Americans are watching on the telly these days?*

Except Robin kept talking, which made it pretty hard to ignore her and focus on inane internal chatter. Especially when he could follow the sounds of their movements as they took the seats where Aidan and Nik had been.

"What did it feel like?" Robin asked Nik, and then didn't give him a chance to answer. "Put the knife away, big boy. I want you to bite me."

Oh, hell no! Cage caught himself before he said it aloud, but he couldn't stop himself from looking.

Mirren flicked open his blade, grabbed her arm, and cut it before she could react. "These fangs go in no one but my mate. Deal with it."

"But—Oh . . ." Robin's voice drained away as Mirren raised her arm to his lips and latched onto the cut, drawing deeply. Her eyes closed, and a small sigh escaped.

Enough already. Cage waited for Mirren to stop, but he drew from her a second time—a big draw, way more than was necessary. Then all thought left Cage as she turned a hooded gaze to look at him. His head spun from the force of the desire on her face. Her pupils had dilated to black pools, her lips trembled slightly, and she shivered.

"Holy fuck." Mirren shoved Robin's arm away from him with enough force to jostle her on the adjoining sofa cushion, and Cage caught her. He didn't remember moving, but he had his arm around her before Mirren cleared the end of the couch.

Mirren started to walk away, but Aidan spoke with more force than Cage had ever heard from him, especially directed at his second-in-command. "Mirren, finish it."

After a long pause, Mirren did as he was told, drawing out his knife again and making the cut on his own arm. He sat as far from Robin on the sofa as he could and still get his arm in the vicinity of her face. He never turned to look at her.

She shook her head. "I can't. I don't . . . I can't."

Cage tightened his arm around her shoulders and leaned close, taking in her scent of pine and sunshine and warmth. She felt so fragile, so small, and yet so alive. Her heart raced, and his head swam at the scent of her blood. Mirren hadn't sealed the wound, and a trickle of it trailed down her arm. He forced his gaze away from the tantalizing path of red. "It doesn't taste like you think it will, love. Just a little. I'm here with you."

She swallowed hard and nodded, but didn't move.

Cage reached out and took hold of Mirren's beefy arm, guiding it toward her face. "Just do it quickly and be done, little bird," he murmured.

Again, Robin nodded. This time, she dipped her head and pressed her lips to Mirren's skin, taking in a small bit of blood. She began to shiver, and Cage pulled her close as Mirren, his duty done, propelled himself off the sofa like he'd been burned with silver. He took his position against the wall next to the fireplace, looking at the floor.

"Well, that was interesting." Aidan looked from Mirren to Robin and back again, then settled his gaze on Cage. "Looks like feeding from a shape-shifter is going to be a whole new adventure. I'd suggest Robin not be in rotation as a feeder until we can learn more about it. Cage, why don't you research that for us?"

"Right." Cage stroked his fingers up and down Robin's arm, shoulder to elbow and back, until she finally stilled. He had no intention of letting another vampire anywhere near her.

❧CHAPTER 11❧

Mirren leaned against the wall of the common room and studied the looped fibers at the edge of the crimson rug. The stupid thing looked black to him, but Glory assured him it was red.

He might be color-blind, but he knew a fucked-up scene when he got in the middle of one—and bonding with the little shifter had been one fucked-up scene.

It hadn't occurred to him—or to Aidan, either, obviously—that bonding a shifter would be any different from bonding a human. But this bonding had blown his mind. It hadn't been sexual, exactly. Mirren had no desire to fuck Robin's brains out like he did when he fed from Glory, not that this had been a real feeding. It had been two sips—one more than he should have taken. He couldn't help himself.

A full feeding might have killed him.

Ashton, too, from the looks of it. She was holding on to Reynolds like he was a life raft and she was about to go under for the third time.

No, it hadn't been sexual. It had been powerful. Addictive, even. Harnessing that kind of power for an extended period? Hell, you'd either conquer the world or self-combust and smile as your heart stopped beating.

Something was going on between Ashton and Cage Reynolds, and Mirren couldn't help but wonder what would happen if Reynolds mated with her, or worse, just took her as a regular feeder. Did they know the guy well enough to entrust him with that much power?

Then again, it might kill him, and Penton couldn't afford to lose him.

"Mirren." Aidan's voice cut through the mental fog, and Mirren looked up. "We've only got a couple of hours until sunrise and we need to talk. You with us?"

More with them by the second. The afterglow of whatever had happened was fading fast, thank God. He sat heavily on the chair opposite Aidan. "Yeah, I'm good."

"Robin? Nik?"

Robin still hadn't said anything, but she'd quit shaking. She nodded and pulled away from Reynolds, who didn't look like he wanted to let her go. In fact, he had that look on his face—the one a vampire got after being flattened by a dose of mating hormones.

Poor fucker; he probably didn't even know it yet. And Mirren wasn't going to be the one to share it with him.

He shifted his focus back to Aidan. The man had been on edge all evening, waiting for all this other shit to get done. Now, he leaned forward in his chair and repeated his warning: "What's said in this room stays between us until I say otherwise. Everyone agree?"

No one spoke until Reynolds finally asked, "What about Hannah?"

With Will Ludlam out of town, their resident child vampire psychic was the only one of Aidan's lieutenants unaccounted for. "She's been having too many issues adjusting," Aidan said. "I want to keep this stuff away from her as long as I can."

Which meant something bad. Something else bad. Some days, Mirren wanted to drive Glory out of here, go somewhere in the mountains where they could live alone, and never look back. The only things keeping him here were his loyalty to Aidan, his respect for Glory's need to be around other people, and his own refusal to let the Tribunal assholes win.

"First, I talked to Colonel Thomas tonight." Aidan took a sip of his whiskey. "He's devastated; no surprise there. Tough as old boots, of course, so he tried to cover, but I could tell. He wanted to call Randa himself, but I thought Will needed to tell her. He's the one she'll need to rely on."

Cage leaned forward with his elbows on his knees, his posture mirroring Aidan's. "Are they still in Atlanta?"

Aidan nodded. "The surgeon told Will pretty much what Krys told him, and what Mirren has said from the beginning. The leg he broke in the Omega cave-in is not going to improve without going in and rebreaking it in at least two places. Even then, there's no guarantee he'll regain his full range of motion. He's probably done as far as Omega Force goes, and it goes without saying that he's pissed as hell."

No shit. Junior wanted to be in the thick of everything and was usually damned good at whatever he tackled, not that Mirren would ever say that aloud. Will had a big-enough ego without Mirren's input.

"He's not necessarily out of Omega Force." Nik stood in the doorway to the kitchen. "Our background on you guys says he's a computer whiz, right?"

"He is," Aidan said. "Mostly self-taught, but he's probably the smartest guy I've ever met. Why?"

Nik came back into the sitting area and snagged the chair next to Cage. "Our Omega team in Houston had a tech guy— also crazy smart. He figured out ways to get us around security systems, tracked Internet chatter, monitored surveillance footage, conducted background intel, that kind of thing. He's good with a weapon, but doesn't do the fieldwork unless it's an emergency. I don't know Will, of course, but it sounds like a perfect role for him. I'm sure Gadget—our Texas techie—would talk to him if he's interested. We did Ranger School together."

Mirren looked at Zorba with renewed interest. He'd stayed in the background up until now, but he seemed like a straight-up guy. In fact, he reminded Mirren of Rob Thomas, which was a good thing.

Aidan seemed to be reaching the same conclusion. "Thanks, that sounds perfect for him, and I think he'd like doing it. I'll take you up on that conversation with your Gadget guy as soon as Will gets back. It'll be a relief for him to know he has a role, and an important one."

At least it was another warm body. The Penton Omega Force team might finally get off the ground now. Nik, Robin, Cage, Will, and Mirren himself made a good start. Mirren wanted them all training together in order to earn the kind of trust they'd need in fieldwork. There was one other option. "What about Jeffries?" Mirren asked.

Max was a pain in the ass, but he was a good fighter.

"Gone." Aidan set his glass down and leaned back in the chair. "He's taking Rob's body back to Columbus, where the family buries its dead. I don't know how the colonel will pull it off, but he wants Rob buried next to his mother and Randa's twin brother."

Mirren thought Colonel Rick Thomas could pretty much get around any law that needed circumventing, even explaining away an unofficial death. "When's he coming back?"

Aidan shook his head. "Don't know—that's between him and the colonel. But we don't want him back until his head's in the right place."

Mirren hated to lose anyone at this point. "Things are better now that Reynolds is back, but we still need to get our numbers up." The restless, itchy feeling between his shoulder blades—the drugged aftermath of the shape-shifter bonding—was long gone, and Mirren got to his feet. "What happened at that job site was no accident."

"No, it wasn't." Aidan took a deep breath. "And while we're trying to figure out who might be sabotaging us, ponder this: Matthias Ludlam is still alive. He escaped, or was helped to escape. No one knows where he is."

No one spoke. The crackle of a log in the fireplace reverberated like a gunshot through the room, and Mirren would swear the temperature dropped several degrees. "How the fuck is that possible? We were told—"

Aidan held up a hand. "I know. The Tribunal members who sided with Penton in the standoff this summer all got messages from Frank Greisser's office in Vienna that Matthias had been executed in Virginia. We all thought it was true."

Mirren hated Greisser. The man looked like a fucking angel and had the integrity of a pit viper. "Greisser lied." It was more statement than question.

"That would be my guess, although his people are claiming a miscommunication." Aidan turned to Nik and Robin and gave them a quick rundown of the vampire political structure and its major players—Greisser, the Tribunal head; Meg Lindstrom, the

US representative; and UK rep Edward Simmons—and which countries sided with Penton and which didn't.

"Edward Simmons found out from an American vampire who applied for a transfer into his territory that someone—he doesn't know who—hired this American and a colleague to take Matthias from his cell at the Virginia estate and leave him in a wooded area in rural West Virginia, where he was picked up—again, we don't know by whom."

Mirren had been in his favorite spot against the wall, but the itchy feeling came back, only worse. Time to pace instead. "What are the chances this guy knows more than he's saying?"

Aidan shrugged. "I heard it thirdhand from Meg, but she says Edward believes him and that the guy was bothered by his part in Matthias's escape. He knew if he talked, he'd be dead before he left the States. Edward has given him the equivalent of a witness protection agreement in the UK."

"Which begs the obvious questions." Cage's voice was quiet, but tight with coiled anger. "Where is the bastard? And is Frank Greisser behind it?" He paused. "My vote would be yes on the second question."

"Mine as well," Aidan said. "Frank was furious that we one-upped him by going to the colonel and getting humans involved in our affairs. Plus, he and Matthias are longtime allies. But we can't prove he was behind it, not yet. And wherever Matthias is, he's staying under the radar for now."

"We should go after him." Robin spoke for the first time since the bonding, and Mirren was glad to see the usual fire back in her expression. "They don't know Nik or me. We could be the main team, and a couple of you guys could be our shadow team. You'll draw the attention, feed us information, and we can take him out. He has to surface."

What a perfectly fucked-up idea. "You have no—"

"Wait, Mirren." Aidan steepled his fingers in front of his face and looked at Robin, his brows drawn down in thought. "That's not a bad idea."

Had the man lost his mind? "But—"

Aidan held up a hand. "Mirren, let me finish. I think it's a good idea, but not until you've worked together enough to know each other well. You need to communicate easily. You have to trust each other. Nik and Robin, you have to get used to working around vampires. That means we have to trust you with our secrets—how to kill us, what our weakness are as well as our strengths. And we need to learn more about shifters. Obviously, something happened here tonight that we hadn't anticipated."

Aidan looked up at Mirren, who nodded grudgingly.

"There's something else you need to know, but Nik should be the one to tell you." Cage Reynolds's voice carried quiet authority.

Nik closed his eyes a moment, and for just a flash, before his jaw tightened and he looked up at Aidan, Mirren thought Zorba looked like one tired Greek. Not like a guy who was tired after a hard day, but like a guy who carried around a bone-deep weariness that had taken a while to accumulate. Mirren had been there, and it wasn't a happy place to live.

"I have an ability to read history from objects or people." Nik paused and, when no one spoke, continued. "I picked up a brick at the job site, not thinking about it, but when I got a flash of history from it—just something from the brickworks or factory—I decided to go through all of the bricks that had fallen on Rob and the other guy. Cage and Robin helped me sort through them, and I sketched any scene I caught that had specific faces in it, or anything unusual."

"The other guy was Mark Calvert." Mirren wondered if Nik Dimitrou might have the same trouble controlling his visions of the past as little Hannah had with her future visions. Between the two, it could be a powerful combination of abilities. Or a couple of head cases.

"Yeah, Mark." Nik finished off the glass of whiskey Mirren could've sworn had been full only a couple of minutes ago. Hell, if he saw visions every time he touched something, he'd carry a bottle in his pocket.

"Sounds like Cage thinks you saw something interesting," Aidan said.

Robin reached inside the plastic bag she'd come in with, extracting some folded sheets of construction diagrams. She looked at Nik; when he nodded, she held out the papers to Cage.

Cage pulled the sheets from her fingers, glanced through them, and handed them across the table to Aidan. Mirren walked behind him and leaned over Aidan's shoulder as he unfolded them.

He was no art critic, but his eye told him these drawings were first-rate. There was Max, laughing. Mark and Rob, talking. And on the last sheet . . . "What the fuck is that? A stray cat that wandered in from the woods?"

Except, come to think of it, he'd never seen any cats around here. Dogs, either, except for Hannah's ugly-ass bloodhound.

"Don't think so." Nik leaned forward. "I think it's a shapeshifter."

Aidan had been frowning at the drawing, his eyes lightening as he examined it. "It's too goddamned big to be a domestic cat. If the Tribunal is working with shifters, they're taking this battle to a whole new level. It's a leopard?"

"Jaguar," Cage said.

Once again, Mirren leaned over the back of Aidan's chair and looked at the drawing. They were right; now that he sized it against the pile of bricks Nik had drawn for scale, he saw that the animal was too big to be a house cat. "This area's surrounded by heavy pine forest. What makes you think it isn't a wild cat?"

"Melanistic jaguars—what people call black panthers—aren't native to the United States," Nik said. "Two of our Omega Force team members in Houston were jag-shifters, and even in shifter form they're rare."

Aidan was silent for a few moments, staring into the fireplace as if he'd like to pick up a smoking log and heft it at something. Finally, he turned that angry gaze on the only shifter in the room. "Robin, do your people have any type of central governing body— like the vampires have the Tribunal?"

If Robin had been in eagle form, Mirren imagined her feathers would have ruffled. "By 'my people,' do you mean eagle-shifters? Or are you lumping all shifters into one big homogeneous population group?"

Aidan simply looked at her.

She sighed and shook her head, and Mirren felt some tension ease from his shoulders. He kind of liked Robin, despite the weirdness of the bonding, and didn't want to see her alienate Aidan over semantics.

"Sorry," she said. "It was a fair question. The answer's no. Each species of shifter has its own independent governing body or leader—what you'd call an alpha, although different species have different names. For golden eagles, it's the Goia. But there's not one group that sets rules for all shifters. We don't get along well enough."

"Thanks." Aidan gave a tight smile and rubbed his temples. "Okay, so we probably have a shifter either acting independently, which isn't likely—shifters and vampires don't generally inhabit the same areas—or we have a shifter working for a vampire."

"Or the Tribunal. Or Frank Greisser. Or Matthias," Mirren added. "There's a whole fucking list of options."

"Not much we can do about it tonight." Aidan finished off his whiskey. "But training starts in earnest tomorrow. Mirren's in charge. Robin and Nik, sorry, but you'll have to get acclimated to training at night. Welcome to the world of vampires."

"What about Fen?" Cage asked. "I'm not endorsing him, mind you. Under normal circumstances I'd keep him away from our plans, but he is a good fighter."

Aidan shook his head. "Not yet. If he's here honestly, he'll understand it's too soon to be in the middle of our scathe's business. If he acts put out by it, that's a red flag—let me know. Be careful what you say around him in general, all of you. Same with Shawn Nichols and Britta Eriksen."

Cage lit one of the little cigars he was so fond of, and managed to get two puffs out before Robin's glare and less-than-subtle coughs led him to snuff it out. "Bloody hell. Can't a man keep one bad habit?"

Robin frowned. "I don't get it about the women; their bios were in our dossiers. They're both vampires that joined up in Atlanta, right? I thought you usually recruited humans from that Atlanta free clinic, from the addicts who hadn't been vaccinated."

Aidan smiled faintly. "Shawn was strung out before she was turned vampire, and was still getting juiced from feeding off junkies. She's clean now. Britta actually came looking for me at the clinic and asked to be allowed to move here. She's a fairly new vamp—two or three years—and wanted to be part of a community. Like many of us, she didn't enjoy the hunt for feeders."

Mirren didn't like the idea of bringing any of the newcomers into their training plans, but they did need extra bodies. "What about some basic grunt work for them? We need people to patrol."

Aidan rubbed his temples again. "Just the very basics. Put them on basic security details and have them report anything that looks unusual. Not a word about Matthias or sabotage or extra shape-shifters."

"Aidan, what's wrong?" Cage slid to the edge of his seat, frowning. "If you weren't vampire, I'd say you had a headache."

"Someone's trying to reach me through a bond." He jerked his head from side to side, as if trying to shake something out. "I think it's Hannah, but . . ."

Voices reached them from the street, shouting, and Mirren recognized Glory's among them. He ran toward the door and threw it open in time to see her in the street with Krys and Melissa. More people were running to join them from both sides of Cotton Street. When Glory saw Mirren, she veered toward the house while the others raced toward the old mill.

"Hannah's house is on fire!" Glory yelled.

✣CHAPTER 12✣

Nik leaned against the community house three doors down from the fire and checked the clip on his Army-issue Beretta. He'd been ducking in and out of cover near the buildings that lay between Mirren's house and the fire.

The whole street was a combination of new houses and burned-out shells of houses that had been partially demolished. Nik shook his head and surveyed both sides of the street and farther down, toward the old mill. If he'd been a sniper, wanting to lure out the Penton leaders and then take them out like ducks in a shooting gallery, a fire would make effective bait. Even Aidan and Mirren and Cage had run toward the flames, which was stupid. They weren't thinking of their own safety—and from what he'd seen so far, their survival was the key to Penton's survival.

Nik scanned the scene again, looking for anyone who might be watching from a distance or running away from the fire instead of toward it. He didn't know the people here, damn it. No way he could spot who didn't belong.

He'd lost sight of Robin as soon as they followed Mirren out of the house, but she could take care of herself. She'd probably shifted so she could fly above the scene and spot anyone skulking, running away, or driving like they were in a hurry.

When he reached the second house from the fire, the heat pressed against him with warm, gentle pulses. Another few yards and he discovered why—sparks from the hot mass of burning wood had been picked up in the southerly breeze and had spread to the roof of the second house. It was old construction, though—probably an original mill house—and Nik didn't think anyone lived there.

He grabbed the arm of a woman running past, and she turned to him, blue eyes wide, blonde hair reflecting the blaze like a golden halo. She jerked away from him, then grabbed his arm and wrenched it behind his back before he could react. She twisted it higher, and it felt as if it might snap off.

"What the hell are you doing?" Nik struggled to free his arm, but stilled when she reached from behind him and pressed against his neck what felt like a knife blade. Besides, she was seriously strong. Since he got no psychic flashes from her touch, as he normally would a human, she was likely a vampire. Which meant she could slit his throat and twist his arm off at the same time, and there wasn't much he could do about it.

She pressed her mouth next to his left ear, her hair tickling the sensitive skin of his earlobe. The blade pressed more tightly against his neck. "Who are you? I don't know you."

"Sergeant Nik Dimitrou. US Army. Came in tonight for the Omega team."

She relaxed the blade for a second, and then pressed it again. "How do I know you're telling the truth?"

"Lady, we could be doing a lot more to help put out that fire if we could actually get to it." What would convince her? "Okay, I was just in Mirren Kincaid's house. He has a red rug in his living room, leather sofa. There are three bedrooms along the back hallway. His wife, Glory, is Native American and she likes to cook. And she talks—a lot."

Finally, she pulled away from him. "Yeah, Glory's a real chatterbox. And vampires have mates, not husbands and wives. I'm Shawn, by the way."

Nik rubbed his neck, and his fingers came away bloody. His vampire Valkyrie noticed, too; her gaze locked on his hand like a laser target, and her eyes took on a silvery glaze.

"You can suck on my fingers if you can tell me whether there's a water source nearby." Nik looked down the street and spotted an old-fashioned red-and-white hydrant near the old mill. "Does that hydrant work?"

Shawn jerked her gaze away from his hand and looked down the street at the mill and then back at the burning house. "There's an emergency fire hose in each of the new community houses. Why didn't I think of that? Come on."

Fortunately, someone else had thought of it. By the time they reached the house adjacent to the corner lot, Cage was on his way down the steps hauling the heavy coiled gray hose. "Shawn, take this over and hook it up to the hydrant."

The man's voice was hoarse, and it was no wonder. The roof on the house was blazing now, and the smoke had grown as thick as the blinding fog they'd get during training in the woods and hills near Fort Benning.

Nik squelched his first instinct to be the man—take the hose from Shawn and drag it to the hydrant. If he'd learned anything from working with Robin and the big-cat shifters, it was that paranormal beings needed no muscle from him. Far from it.

He walked alongside Cage toward the main blaze. "What can I do?"

"We can make—"

Whatever he'd planned to say was lost when a thin, tall guy with a soot-blackened face yelled at them from the adjacent sidewalk. "Cage, she's inside! Hannah ran back inside after that goddamned dog. I'm going in after her."

"Bloody hell." He clapped Nik on the shoulder. "Next lesson in Vampires 101, mate. We burn up just like humans. Let's go."

They ran across the lawns, following the skinny guy. Judging by his accent, Nik assumed it was Cage's old acquaintance Fen Patrick.

Shawn pulled the heavy hose across the street, but lost control of it when two women—Nik recognized Aidan's mate and the other was a strawberry blonde he'd never seen—turned on the hydrant. The hose uncoiled like a malevolent, awakening serpent, flipping and flopping in myriad directions while spraying a heavy blast of water at everything except the fire.

Shawn raced after the end of the flailing hose, moving with a blur of speed, and pinned it down with one good stomp of her boots. She lifted it without so much as a grimace, even though Nik knew it was heavy and hard to control, and directed the spray toward the house.

Cage waved to get Shawn's attention, then pointed at himself and at the house. "Cover us!"

Shawn nodded, adjusting the stream of water to douse the doorway and make sure it was clear.

Fen ran ahead of them. "Let's each take a room," he shouted. "The dog is probably hiding under furniture. We find the dog and we find Hannah."

Nik took the rear, pulling his shirt over his nose and mouth, thankful for the Ranger survival training that had forced them to maneuver burning buildings. His shirt was woven cotton, which was good. He assessed Cage's and Fen's clothing as they edged their way through the front door. Cage's black shirt was lightweight but also looked like cotton. Fen wore some kind of light sweater Nik suspected was synthetic; he'd be in trouble if he hit the flames. Synthetics didn't burn; they melted.

Cage took point, motioning Fen to one side of the common room area and Nik to the other. He disappeared into the kitchen. Nik would follow as long as Cage made good decisions. He trusted his own training a hell of a lot more than the vampire's.

The smoke didn't just make seeing difficult; it distorted everything, resizing objects like a fun-house mirror. Everything was smaller or larger than his logical mind could accept. A chair-back loomed like a mountain he needed to circumvent. One table became three. A rug could be a rug, or its dark shadow could be mean a disastrous drop off a collapsed floor into the crawl space below—or one of those basement spaces where the vampires spent the daylight hours.

Nik crouched low where the air was clearer and ran his fingertips along the wall, trying to block out the images that came to him unbidden. Mostly, he saw faces—the men and women who'd built the house, some of whom he recognized. Mirren, pressing against a wall to test its strength. The guy Rob, the one who'd been killed, wielding a hammer. Aidan, painting. A sawmill, probably where the lumber had been cut. Nothing traumatic, thank God.

The toe of his boot hit something hard, and he crashed to his hands and knees, taking down a stool along the way. Hell, as long as the floor was nearby, he might as well crawl.

He edged along the wall, reaching out blindly in the choking gray smoke to grasp at anything whose thickness made it look solid. Lots of furniture. No little girls, though, and no dogs.

When he reached the end of the room, he rose to a crouch again and saw Cage pointing Fen toward the back hallway. They'd come up empty, too.

Nik's eyes watered so heavily that the image of Cage standing upright seemed to shift, going in and out of focus. One sharp Cage; two fuzzy Cages. He grabbed the hem of his shirt and rubbed his eyes, nodding when Cage pointed him toward the second bedroom along the hallway.

Halfway there, Fen emerged from the last bedroom. "I think I heard the dog somewhere back here," he shouted. "What's his name?"

Cage hesitated, looking unsure, and jumped out of the way as a bit of the ceiling fell, pushing Nik clear.

Thank God for the colonel and his anal-retentive mission notes. "The dog's name is Barnabas," Nik shouted. He struggled to see through the smoke. They had to find the girl, and fast.

"Barnabas, like the vampire in *Dark Shadows*? Brilliant." Fen's face broke into a lopsided grin for a split second before he turned and bellowed, "Barnabas, you sonofabitch—where are you? C'mere, you cursed hellhound!"

They paused to listen, but all Nik could hear was crackling wood and the whoosh of flames. Fires bellowed like angry beasts.

A dark smudge had appeared on the hallway ceiling above them when the drywall fell. Cage pointed at it, but then cocked his head and listened a moment. "I heard him, too! Middle bedroom on the right."

Fen was closest. He crouched and disappeared through the doorway. Damn it, he was only three feet ahead of them, but Nik groped blindly as he reached where he thought the door should be. "Watch it!"

Nik turned in the direction where he thought Cage stood, but his outstretched hands clutched nothing but smoke. Then the room spun; no, it was him. Spinning. Falling amid a rain of singed Sheetrock that sparked on his shirt in hot pinpricks.

His cheek slammed into the smooth wood of the floor, and he had just enough time to think it was oddly cool against his skin before a splinter pierced his cheek and something heavy fell on him, knocking out what little breath he had left.

Things went black for an instant. Maybe several instants. Maybe he was dead, because he seemed to be moving independently of his arms and legs.

Something hard cracked his head and jarred him out of his stupor. "Sorry, mate. Door facing." The voice came from above him, and finally he realized Cage Reynolds was hauling him out of the burning house in a classic fireman's carry. Yeah, he might trust the man from now on.

"Down." His voice came out somewhere between rooster and chain-smoker, but Cage got the message, setting him down as soon as they'd cleared the front door. He kept a firm grasp on Nik's arm, though, and hauled him down the stairs at what the colonel might call triple-time.

But he could breathe now. Nice thing, breathing. To hell with dignity; Nik gasped in big lungfuls of cool night air. Out here, it might smell like smoke, but it inhaled like oxygen.

"You're all right, mate? Gotta go and check on Fen." Cage leaned over him, soot smudged across both cheeks and part of his shirt missing.

"Yeah." Nik coughed up half a lung. "M'okay. Go."

The pressure on his arm disappeared, and the world tumbled again. He landed face-first—again. This time it was on wet, cold mud, though, which felt pretty damned good. He thought he might just lie in the mud puddle for a few seconds. Then he'd be ready to help.

He closed his eyes, thinking he might need a few minutes instead of seconds, but cracked them open when feet came to a stop a few inches in front of his nose, splashing mud on his face and in his mouth. He craned his neck, looking up and up and up.

Tall woman, Aidan's wife. Mate. Whatever.

"Take Hannah to our house, and Fen, too," she yelled, and Mirren answered . . . something. Nik groaned and closed his eyes again. Just a little nap and he'd get up.

At least they'd gotten the girl out. Nobody had mentioned the dog. He liked dogs. This dog had sure caused a lot of drama, though. He might like to get a dog when he—

"Hey, Nik. Nik. Wake up." It was Krys again. Mrs. Aidan.

"M'awake." He sort of opened his eyes.

"Uh-huh, sure you are. Mel, sit here with him, will you? He's not burned, but he needs to keep this on until he's able to stand up by himself."

This what? Nik raised his head an instant before Mrs. Aidan shoved him onto his back and smacked something over his nose and mouth. The mud didn't feel as good oozing down his ass as it had on his face.

He opened his mouth to tell her he didn't appreciate her bossy attitude but, in doing so, he took in a breath of air. No, not air, but real oxygen. He raised his hand and felt the mask over his face, the tube stretching toward . . .

"Leave it on."

Damn, but his eyes burned. The woman leaning over him was the strawberry blonde he'd seen helping bossy Mrs. Aidan turn on the fire hydrant.

Nik tried to sit up. His shoulders hovered about two inches off the ground for a couple of excruciating seconds before he gave up, flopping back into the mud.

The woman laughed. "You are one dirty boy."

Yeah, well. She had a big black smudge across her nose that qualified her for Barnum & Bailey's clown act.

"Oh, stop glaring at me. I'm Melissa Calvert." She frowned. "You're one of the new Rangers?"

He slipped a hand up and edged the oxygen mask away from his mouth. "Yeah." He didn't recognize his own voice. Sounded kinda sexy. "How are the others?"

She reached out and slapped the mask back over his mouth. All the women in this freaking town were bossy. Robin would fit right in.

"Hannah's unconscious, but her burns weren't bad. Krys thinks it was smoke inhalation and she'll get it out of her system during daysleep. Fen got burned bringing her out, though. The whole ceiling came down just after Cage got you."

Yeah, he owed Cage Reynolds a big cigar.

Melissa looked up at the house. "Damn it. This is gonna make even more people leave Penton. It's like God doesn't want us to rebuild."

Nik suspected God had nothing to do with it. He'd be interested in digging around in the ruins after daylight to see what he could find. He was no fire investigator, but Ranger duty had honed his powers of observation pretty sharply—plus, he could use his Touch on whatever was left.

The fact that he remembered he was a Ranger meant the oxygen had finally revived his smoke-saturated neurons. This time, when he tried to sit up, he only wavered once. Might as well be really reckless and pull off the mask.

"How do your lungs feel? You breathing okay?" Melissa turned the wheel atop the small oxygen tank to the "Off" position. "If you get light-headed, tell me and I'll give you some more."

"Thanks. I'm Nik Dimitrou, by the way. One of the new Rangers, as you guessed. You're a nurse?"

No, that wasn't right. Melissa Calvert. Her dossier had identified her as Aidan Murphy's human familiar, at least until she was turned vampire by the nutcase who'd tried to destroy the town.

"I had a year of nursing school, so I help Krys out when I can—that's Aidan's mate."

Nik nodded. "The bossy redhead."

Melissa laughed, and Nik felt badly for comparing her to a circus clown. He just hoped he hadn't said it aloud. She was pretty, even with the black nose and fangs.

"Krys wouldn't disagree with you, and neither would Aidan." Her voice softened. "And here comes your rescuer, who seems to make a habit out of saving people."

Cage walked toward them from the direction of Aidan's house. He looked as wiped as Nik felt. "Guess I owe him a . . ." What did one give a vampire as a thank-you gift? "A pint of blood or something."

Melissa grinned. She was the first vampire in Penton that Nik had seen flash a fang so openly. Maybe she hadn't figured out how to keep them hidden yet, being a newbie and all. "Better hurry,

Cage," she said. "He's still kinda delirious and is offering to repay you in blood."

"Good thing, because my feeder left town tonight." Cage looked down at the muddy ground, shrugged, and sat down in the spreading mud puddle alongside Nik. "Hannah's and Fen's feeder, too, although neither of them will be needing anything until tomorrow night."

"She's gonna be okay?" Melissa reached out and smoothed Cage's hair away from his face. Interesting. The man had been all hot over Robin—and, Nik had to admit, she'd been all hot over him—but Melissa's gesture seemed awfully intimate. Then again, Cage had saved her from being tortured by Matthias Ludlam. Made sense that they'd be tight.

Still, he'd want some reassurances. Robin wasn't Nik's great romance. Hell, he wasn't even sure he believed that fairy tale anymore. But if Cage Reynolds hurt one piece of her surprisingly vulnerable little heart, the vampire would find out what Rangers could do during daylight hours.

Nik liked Cage, but Robin came first. Besides Kell, his Ranger buddy back in Houston, she was his best friend. Sure, they occasionally had benefits, but not as often as she'd made it sound. The friendship came first.

"I guess I should go and help Krys." Melissa dragged the toe of her sandal in the mud. "I wonder where Aidan will want Fen to take his daysleep? And you, Cage? Hannah already goes with Aidan and Krys to . . . wherever they go."

Which brought up an interesting question Nik wasn't sure anyone would answer, at least not until they got to know him better. Where did the vampires of Penton take their daily naps? He knew there were spaces underneath the community houses, but those were too obvious. Their enemies could send in humans to knock them all off in one big vampire slaughter if they were that easy to find.

"Yeah, it's going to take some sorting out," Cage said. "I think Mirren wants all of us, including you and Nik here, at his place before dawn to figure it out."

Melissa looked down at Cage. "So we could be bunk mates?" She didn't exactly look happy.

"Looks like." Cage didn't look too elated about it, either. Interesting.

What he did look was as tired and grubby as Nik. He scrubbed his palms over his cheeks and flicked off dried flakes of mud. More like iron-rich clay, Nik decided. In the harsh glare of the portable floodlights someone had set up, it looked more orange than brown.

Behind them, the fire continued to burn, but it had already done its worst. The adjacent house had been soaked enough to prevent the flames from consuming it.

"I'll see you later at Mirren's, then," Melissa said, picking up the portable oxygen tank. "You too, Nik."

"Right," he said. "Thanks for the O."

Cage watched Melissa leave, and Nik watched Cage. Couldn't read his expression, though. "She seems nice—well, in a bossy sort of way."

"She is." Cage laughed. "Both nice and bossy. She's had a rough few months, that one."

Maybe he'd counseled her in his psychiatrist role. Or maybe that intimate touch she'd given him meant more. "You're good friends, then?" At Cage's sharp look, he added, "I'm just trying to suss out the local dynamics. Friendships."

Cage shrugged, tugging what was left of his shirt over his head and tossing it in the mud in a heap. "We're all friends, all the lieutenants and fams—those are feeders that are bonded to one vampire, but you probably knew that already."

"Yeah, the colonel's pretty thorough in his dossiers."

"Then you know Mel used to be Aidan's fam—had been for a long time. So it upset the balance of things when she was turned vampire." Cage had been scanning the block while he talked. "I just realized Robin wasn't here. Is she okay? Have you seen her?" He climbed to his feet, looking farther down the block toward the old mill.

"I haven't seen her since we first heard about the fire and left Mirren's." Nik wasn't sure if that meant Robin had found something, or if she hadn't. He rolled to his hands and knees, willing his wobbly legs to propel him upright. Cage held out a hand, and Nik hesitated before taking it. Habit and hard experience had taught him to touch with caution, but he grasped Cage's hand and accepted the help. It felt good to be standing upright.

"Thanks for that—and for getting me out of there when the ceiling started coming down."

"No problem. Shouldn't we look for Robin? She doesn't know the area and no way that fire was an accident."

Cage hadn't quite gotten the big picture on Robin yet, if he still thought of her as a frail flower in need of saving. "She's a— oh no."

"What? What's wrong? Is something wrong with Robin? Oh . . ." Cage's voice trailed off, but his mouth didn't close.

Nik waved at the vision of a wood nymph walking toward them from the old mill. "I was about to say, Robin will show up when she's good and ready."

And probably naked, he didn't add, since that was now obvious. She had a beautiful, tight little body and no qualms at all about uncovering it. The moonlight made her fair skin glow, and even when the glare of the floodlights hit her, she looked pretty damned good.

Shaking his head, Nik grinned and took a step back. There was no controlling this particular drama, so he might as well enjoy the show. He didn't know what would come out of her mouth, but it was bound to be highly entertaining.

Nik pulled his own singed shirt over his head and held it out to her when she got within reach. "You might want to put this on before ashes fly into Cage's open mouth."

She snatched it out of his hand and held it up. There were more holes left than shirt, so she tied the sleeves around her waist in a smoky approximation of an apron. "I thought I might see something if I flew over the area, but it was too late. Whoever set it was already tucked out of sight. You two all right?"

Cage's expression had gone from open-mouthed gape to appreciative astonishment, and he seemed incapable of speech.

Which Robin noticed as well. She walked to within a foot of him and reached up to flick more mud off his cheek. "Is the little girl okay?"

Cage nodded and cleared his throat with some effort. "She's fine. You're, uh . . . fine as well, I see."

Robin laughed, a surprisingly sweet sound that always took Nik by surprise. "Get over it, vampire. I'm naked. If you haven't seen a naked woman in your, what, seventy or eighty years of life, then it's time you did."

She huffed out a frustrated breath and edged around Cage close enough for her breast to brush against his arm. Not an action he missed. He opened his mouth to say something, then closed it.

"Any female body parts I need to explain to you?" She stared at him until he shook his head in a quick negative. "No? Good. I'm hungry, then. Let's go."

❦CHAPTER 13❦

A pang of longing swept through Melissa as soon as she opened the door to the community house. Soft music, something vaguely Celtic, filled the dimly lit room. The banked embers of the fire flickered in orange and gold shadows on the polished floor.

Mirren sprawled on one of the plush leather sofas with Glory curled up next to him, her hand resting underneath the hem of his black T-shirt, his arm around her both possessive and protective.

Melissa recognized the signs of post-feeding euphoria mixed with love. She'd had enough brushes with violence to know that the experience left you desperate for the warmth of another, desperate to hold the most important people close, desperate to be held.

If you hadn't run away from Mark after you were turned, you could've had that.

She put on a bright face that belied the thoughts buffeting her inside, as thick and heavy and choking as the smoke from the house fire. It was the internal storm of a woman who'd thought she knew her own heart, only to fear she might have been wrong.

"Hey guys, sorry to interrupt."

Glory answered without looking around. "You're not interrupting. We'd have to actually be doing something for you to interrupt, and we're too tired to do anything except sit here."

She sat up and yawned, which set off another unexpected wave of longing in Melissa. Vampires didn't yawn; they simply had a slight fading of power as dawn approached. Her arms and legs were already growing heavy in anticipation of daysleep, still two hours away. She envied Glory her humanity and the sureness of her heart.

Glory settled back, propped against Mirren's shoulder. "Krys says a couple of other scathe members—Shawn and that guy who's running the gas station—are gonna spend their daysleep in the space beneath the house across the street, along with Fen and Hannah. There's nothing else anyone can do tonight."

Melissa scratched her nose and a sprinkle of dried Alabama clay flaked off, settling to the front of her shirt like a red snowflake. "I need a shower before daysleep, for sure. What about Cage? He staying to keep an eye on Fen again?"

Except for Cage, all the lieutenants and their mates were spending their daysleeps in an underground bunker somewhere in Penton; even Melissa didn't know its location. The rest of the scathe had an elaborate setup west of town. Cage had spent his first daysleep under the now-burned community house so he could keep an eye on Fen until the newcomer had convinced everyone, particularly Mirren, to trust him.

Mirren leaned forward. Shadows from the firelight danced across his face, but not so much that Melissa couldn't read his somber expression. "We need Cage to move in with the lieutenants tonight," Mirren said. "Aidan wants you there, too. Both of you. From now on."

Melissa's heart sped up. "Why?" Not that she didn't welcome the news that she would be spending her daysleep near Cage.

Maybe if she could spend more time with him, she could finally get the chance to put things to rest between them. Plus, he should stay with the lieutenants since he was one of them. She, however, wasn't. "I get why he wants Cage there, but why me?"

Mirren glanced at Glory before he turned those searing gray eyes her way again. "Matthias escaped. We have to assume he's alive, and you're pretty high on his hit list—even more than Glory and Krys. You're the one he turned and kidnapped. And Cage not only helped you escape but played Matthias for a fool by infiltrating his organization."

Old fears and weighty dread settled on Melissa's shoulders like a yoke. She was so tired of being afraid, so ready to move on, so sick of being a victim.

A new thought poked a tender root into her fear and gradually took hold. Why was she afraid? Matthias had killed her once. She'd been through the worst. If he came after her again, as a vampire she could fight back. Maybe even be the one to finally kill him.

The firelight grew warmer and brighter with her epiphany. She had options. She was not weak. She lived in fear only if she chose to, and she chose not to. Not anymore.

"Let me train with you, and then let Matthias try coming after me again." Melissa's voice came out stronger and more sure than it had in months. "It's time we stop hiding and rebuild our lives."

"Don't even think that—you know better than anybody what Matthias is capable of, and you don't want him coming after you." Glory's brows met in a frown, but Mirren nodded slowly—once down, once up.

"Mel's right," he said, laying a hand on Glory's knee. "And it's just the thing our old friend Melissa Calvert would've said. I was beginning to wonder if that fire was ever gonna return. Welcome back."

Melissa stared at him. Mirren had considered her fiery? Aidan had used that word for her, too. When Matthias's hired hand had cut her throat, and then she had turned, she'd lost herself. Until now, she hadn't realized how much.

She'd been wandering around in confusion and self-pity long enough. Too long.

"Will you let me train with you?" Determination replaced doubt, and it felt damned good.

Mirren nodded. "Not with the lieutenants, not yet. But I'll work with you tomorrow night." He looked down at his mate. "You need some training, too, Glory. Even though you have the telekinesis, you need basic self-defense training—whatever humans are taught. Dimitrou should be able to help with that."

"One more thing." Melissa wasn't the only Calvert Matthias might go after. "You need to warn Mark. Getting at him is a good way to get to the rest of us, and he's vulnerable during the day."

Matthias might have to spend his days as zonked out as the rest of them, but he likely had humans on his payroll.

"That's Ashton's job," Mirren said, and paused a moment before adding, "In the meantime, I want you and Cage with the lieutenants. Tomorrow night we'll figure out how to find Matthias, and how to rebuild our city."

Melissa nodded. "Does Cage know where to go?"

Mirren shook his head. "Didn't get a chance to tell him, so we'll wait till he gets back."

That, she could handle. "Tell me, and I'll wait on him. I need to talk to him anyway."

She wanted to see Cage alone, to see if her newfound backbone made her consider him in a different light.

One thing was for sure. Penton's recent string of bad luck made more sense now that she knew Matthias was out there, pulling strings like some evil puppet master.

Mirren handed her a napkin, on the back of which he'd sketched out a simple map. "Memorize that, and then throw it in the fire."

Taking a deep breath, Melissa studied the drawing. "The lieutenants' daysleep space is under the old Quik Mart between here and LaFayette?"

At Mirren's nod, she tore the napkin in shreds and threw the pieces into the fireplace, watching as they blackened and disappeared into soot.

"There's a four-digit lock that gets you into both the first and second levels. The combinations are different." Mirren gave her the numbers and made her repeat them back to him until she'd mastered them. "We change the numbers every day. Find me or Aidan to get them. You sure you want to wait for Cage?"

Almost as badly as she wanted to take a shower. "Sure. He should be here soon—I left him sitting in a mud puddle in front of the burned house with that Nikolas guy. They can't stay there forever."

"I like Nik," Glory said. "He seems quiet but, I don't know, competent. And then, of course, there's—"

"Ro-bin Ash-ton." Mirren drawled out the name, and Melissa would swear he almost smiled. "What a fucking menace."

"F-word. Show me the money." Glory held out a hand and Mirren, grumbling, pulled a roll of bills out of his pocket and handed her a five. "That leaves me with four credits. Fuck-fuck-fuck-fuck."

"Funny, foul mouth; this is buying me a car." Which was ridiculous, because Mirren had as much money as God. He and Aidan both did, thanks to Mark's investment genius. He could buy her a dozen cars—but Glory wouldn't take what she hadn't earned.

"Mel, I'm guessing you haven't met our other new Omega team member yet?" Glory smiled, too.

No, but now she was intrigued. "Not yet, why?" Melissa reclaimed the corner of the adjacent sofa. "Something about him I need to know? Or, wait, Robin, you said? The other Army person is a woman?"

"Not Army," Glory said. "She's a shape-shifter recruited to be part of the Omega Force team in Houston, although I think the colonel made them go through a special version of Ranger training, right?" She looked at Mirren, who nodded with that unsettling half smile.

Mirren distrusted newcomers on principle; Melissa had never known him to find one vaguely amusing. In fact, only Glory—and Will Ludlam, although Mirren probably wouldn't admit it— consistently amused him. "She's some kind of eagle," Glory said. "Weird, huh?"

Not as weird as they were acting. "What are you not telling me? Mirren Kincaid, come clean." Melissa had seen through the big guy's rough exterior a long time ago, and thanks to being Aidan's familiar, had mostly gotten to know him through Aidan's eyes. He didn't intimidate her for a minute. "What's so funny about Robin Ashton?"

Mirren made a big show of stretching before standing up, a broad spread of long arms and packed muscle beneath his short-sleeved T-shirt—there was a lot of him to stretch. "She'll show up here soon enough and you can draw your own conclusions. Maybe you can train with her." He held out a hand to Glory. "Come on, woman."

Glory's face came alive when she looked at Mirren, and Melissa's sense of emptiness returned as if on cue. She missed the easy intimacy she'd had with Mark before she was turned. Funny how she had forgotten it until now, when he wanted to move on. Now that she'd pushed him away until she no longer had to push, it came back to her.

Glory wished Melissa a good daysleep before heading down the hallway to the back door, but Mirren remained a second longer, looking at her with an expression she couldn't interpret.

"What is it, Mirren? I swear, you've been acting weird since I got here. Weird even for you."

One side of his mouth quirked up—the normal version of the Kincaid smile. "Decide what you want, Mel. And that's all I got to say on the subject." He turned and disappeared down the hallway. In a couple of seconds, Melissa heard the back door open and then click shut again.

Well, that was oblique.

Except the more she thought about it, the more sense his comment made. She hadn't discussed with them the conclusions she'd reached about her relationships, so Mirren and Glory probably thought she still was torn between Cage and Mark.

That question, she'd finally answered. The one that remained was whether she could get over Mark. Until tonight, when he'd hinted that he and Britta were getting close, the possibility that he might love someone else hadn't occurred to her. Until tonight, she'd taken for granted that if she ever decided to try again with him, he'd be there. It had been unfair to him and naive of her.

Until tonight, she'd thought she could walk away from Mark first to spare herself the agony of his eventual rejection. Now, she wasn't so sure. The thought of him with someone else tangled her heart in knots. He was still a part of her; she'd just been too fearful to admit it.

Melissa shuffled down the hall into the back bedroom on the left, pulled out clean jeans and a sweater, and stopped at the drawer of lingerie. She usually didn't bother with the sexy stuff anymore; it wasn't like anyone saw them. But tonight . . . well, tonight everyone was tired, but at dusk tomorrow, maybe she and Cage could figure things out and lingerie might help.

She wanted him to see her as a woman, not a pathetic newbie vampire who needed him as a security blanket. Unless he saw her as a woman, whole and healthy, neither of them would know if they were together because of natural attraction or because she was needy and he had a savior complex.

And women who wanted to attract a man didn't wear old university sweatshirts to bed.

Opening the drawer of the utilitarian wooden chest, identical to the one in every community house on the block, Melissa fingered the sheer dark-blue fabric of a negligee, closing her eyes as she remembered the first time she'd worn it. She'd liked the black one better, or even the red one, but she'd bought this color because Mark loved the way she looked in it. She'd worn it no more than fifteen minutes before he had slid the straps off her shoulders and left it in a heap on the bedroom floor.

The memory was enough to give her an empty, aching feeling that only a man could fill. Or love.

Oh no, you're not trotting down that corner of memory lane tonight. Melissa shoved the negligee back in the drawer and slammed it. In the adjacent drawer were T-shirts, and she picked out a paint-stained dark-green crewneck that had been stretched into shapeless comfort. The only memories associated with that shirt were the long hours of painting community house bedrooms. Just thinking about it made her shoulders ache.

She stuffed the sweatshirt into a small bag with a couple of days' changes of clothes to keep in the daysleep spaces, and then walked down the hall to the nearest of the three bathrooms they all shared.

Pig-Pen—the dirty guy in the *Peanuts* cartoons who was perpetually surrounded by a cloud of dirt—had nothing on her. She stripped off her mud-spattered clothes and threw them away; washing wouldn't get out the red-clay stains. Turning on the shower, she let the water pelt her fingers until it was as hot as she could stand it.

She stood under the spray with her face turned up, wishing the rivulets of hot water could wash away not just the iron-red mud but most of the last year.

At least she started out thinking that. But without the last year, Melissa would never have met Krys or Glory—and Aidan and Mirren had found such happiness with them. She wouldn't wish them the loss of that happiness; plus, she'd made the best friends of her life. She would never have met Cage if he hadn't come to study Penton for Edward Simmons.

But Hannah would still have her fam-parents, whose deaths at Matthias's hands had sent her into a tailspin none of them knew how to handle. Without the last year, Will would still be whole. Penton would still be a peaceful place to live. She wouldn't be a vampire.

She'd still be with Mark.

By the time she climbed out of the shower, dried off, and dressed, she'd taken the circumspect view. No way to change the last year, so she might as well appreciate the good things that had happened and not dwell on the bad.

A low rumble of voices reached her as soon as she opened the bathroom door into the hallway. "Cage, is that you?"

"In the common room," he called out.

She ran her fingers through her towel-dried hair, all the primping she had time for.

"Mirren said you need to—"

She'd glanced in the kitchen doorway in passing, and now backed up to look in again. A young woman stood in front of the open refrigerator, eating a chicken leg and staring at the shelves.

She wasn't completely naked. A grimy garment that looked like a man's shirt was tied around her waist, but her small firm breasts were standing at attention from the chill of the fridge.

"What, you've never seen a naked woman before, either? How does that work when you're in the shower?" The woman reached in and pulled an apple from the crisper, and turned to Melissa, apple in one hand, drumstick held up like a club. "I'm Robin. You must be Melissa. Thanks for helping Niko, in case he didn't think to say so."

Robin edged past Melissa and sat on the nearest sofa next to a bare-chested Nik, whose shirt had apparently been donated. She held the apple out to Nik. "Here. Eat. Man can't live by bourbon alone."

Cage sat on the opposite sofa, facing them. He'd watched Robin cross the room and seemed to pull his gaze from her—or her perky little mammaries—way too slowly. "Hi, Mel." Finally, he looked at her, blinked, and smiled. "A shower sounds like a grand idea."

Well, wasn't that just . . . impersonal. "Wish I'd known you were coming so soon, I'd have waited to shower with you."

Cage's eyes widened to mossy green orbs, and his focus shot over to Robin, chewing on her chicken leg and staring right back at him.

"You're doing her?" Robin leaned back and gave Melissa a slow head-to-toe visual inspection.

Melissa felt like the tall, fat, and gawky wallflower at the prom. She propped her hands on her hips and waited for Cage's answer.

He looked from one to the other, and then to Nik, as if his new best buddy could provide an answer. Nik shrugged and bit into his apple.

Cage ran a soot-covered hand through his hair. Melissa didn't think she'd ever seen him wear it down, but it was a good look for him. Better than the one he wore on his face, which she would describe as deer-in-headlights. "I, ah . . ."

Melissa had never seen her calm British lieutenant this rattled, so she put an extra swivel in her hips as she crossed the room, sat next to him, and slid a hand from his knee to the top of his thigh, where an interesting bulge rested. And stirred. "Cage and I are very good friends," she told Robin, adding a sugary smile to emphasize just how good.

Nik bit into the apple again, its crisp crunch filling the awkward silence of the room. Melissa stared at Robin with a "you can flaunt your tits all night but he's leaving with me" look.

Robin just grinned. "Fang-girl's getting territorial, Cage. And back in the car, you practically promised to introduce me to shifter-vampire sex."

Nik choked on his apple and collapsed in a fit of coughing.

"I'll get you some water, mate." Cage practically leapt off the sofa and propelled himself into the kitchen. When he returned, he handed the glass to Nik but remained standing.

Robin laughed. "You okay, Niko?"

"Go to bed, Robin." Nik wiped tears from his eyes, and Melissa wasn't sure if it was from choking or laughing or the aftereffects of the fire.

"You coming with me? I had my heart set on not sleeping alone tonight."

Nik closed his eyes and seemed to be counting to ten. "Go to bed, Robin."

Okay, this girl was way over the top. Melissa began to understand Mirren's amusement by her—except she was a loon, not an eagle. And Cage was acting like a bashful tween boy seeing breasts for the first time since infancy.

"I, uh, think I'll go and take a shower." He looked at Melissa, at Robin, at the floor. His voice sounded strained and oh-so-British. "Right, then. Off I go."

"You'll need to come with me afterward, to daysleep," Melissa called after him. "Aidan wants us in the lieutenants' space from now on." She looked at Robin. "Both of us."

Was that a look of irritation flashing across Robin's face for a split-second? If so, it was replaced soon enough with a smile. "I don't want him when he's sleeping. I want him wide awake. So sweet dreams, my fangy friends."

With that, she finished off the last bite of her chicken leg, tossed it into the kitchen trash, and ran her fingers across Cage's ass on her way past him down the hallway, where he remained frozen halfway between the common room and the bathroom.

The door to one of the back bedrooms closed with a firm click, which seemed to bring Cage out of his stupor. "Right," he mumbled, turning to walk down the hallway. "Shower."

Melissa turned to Nik, who watched her with narrowed eyes such a dark, liquid brown they looked almost as black as his hair.

"What?" she asked him. "You have something to say?"

He studied her a few seconds. "Only that this could get really messy and I don't want to see Robin get hurt."

Like that was possible. "I think Robin can take care of herself." Melissa studied him in return. Were he and that naked little jaybird involved? "You seem possessive of Robin, protective even. But not quite jealous. I can't quite figure you guys out."

He wrapped his apple core in a napkin and threw it in the trash. "I could say the same about you and Cage Reynolds."

☙CHAPTER 14❧

Matthias slammed the cheap hotel phone receiver back onto its base. Another accident in Penton, but only a partial success. The real target, Cage Reynolds, had survived.

"It was not a total failure, *mein Freund*," Frank had told him in that oily politician's voice that got on Matthias's last nerve. By God, when all this was over, he'd add Frank Greisser to his elimination list. It was a long list.

Not a total failure, no. The little girl Aidan Murphy kept with him like a mascot had been injured, as well as at least one other scathe member. Frank had yet to get more than a cursory report from whomever he had on the inside.

That person wasn't doing a very good job, if Frank's only requests of Matthias this time were to explain the relationship between Melissa Calvert and Cage Reynolds and provide background on Mark Calvert.

Why did anybody care who fucked whose wife?

Matthias startled at the loud knock on the door. No one knew he was here except Frank, and the Tribunal director—as he'd so smugly boasted on the phone—was lounging in a posh New York hotel suite, awaiting the Tribunal vote on Aidan Murphy's nomination in only a week.

The knock sounded again, followed by a rough, deep voice. "Herr Ludlam? It is Wolfgang, the hotel manager. I have something for you, a gift sent by Herr Greisser."

Matthias considered not answering. He hated to be paranoid, but better paranoid than dead. Still, while Wolfgang did bring a bag of unvaccinated blood for him after each daysleep, however much Frank paid for that service, it was not the same as feeding from a live human. Perhaps this was a human feeder.

Matthias opened the door a crack and then pulled it open wider. Wolfgang was not alone, and the person next to him was definitely human—disappointingly, a man. But Matthias wasn't in a position to be choosy.

"I hope that is my gift." Matthias sized up the human: a young man in his mid twenties, with the classic Austrian chiseled features, blond hair, and clear blue eyes. Yes, he would do nicely.

"Herr Greisser wished to reward you for being such a good friend and helping in his business ventures," Wolfgang said, smiling. "Peter here will be at your disposal for the next half hour, at which time I will come and collect him. Is he satisfactory?"

Matthias wondered if Peter had a sister; then again, he was so anxious for blood that didn't come in a plastic container, he'd have fed from small, balding Wolfgang himself. "Of course."

When Wolfgang had gone and the door closed on his footsteps, Matthias gestured Peter to a sofa.

He looked at the chair, then at the bed. "You do not wish me to undress?"

Interesting thought. He was quite a pretty man and Matthias grew hard at the thought of that young, firm flesh under his hand.

But a half hour limited his options. He'd rather have a warm vein than a blowjob. "Just your sweater, please."

Peter nodded and pulled the white wool sweater over his head, giving him a tousled look that became even more tousled as he reclined on the bed.

Matthias's fangs ached at the thought of sinking into that lovely spot on the inside of the groin, but time had become his enemy. He unbuttoned his own shirt and removed it before climbing on the bed and lowering himself on top of Peter.

The young man's warm skin was as silky and firm as he'd imagined, and Matthias grew harder still at the idea of flipping him over and taking him. But the bloodsong was too loud, too enticing.

He kissed Peter's firm lips and then turned the young man's head to the right and bit.

Peter jerked beneath him, then relaxed with a sigh. Matthias moved with the rhythm of his feed, rocking his hips against Peter with each draw of blood. The young man's cock was a hard, solid ridge against Matthias's, and he rocked his hips harder, fed more deeply.

He didn't feel the needle going into his skin. Only when the pain began searing through his veins did he pull back and look stupidly at his arm, the syringe emptying its yellow liquid into his body. The horrific burn spread from his arm and traveled like liquid fire through his bloodstream.

He was so sated from feeding that his reactions were sluggish. "What was that? What the hell?" He rolled off Peter, no longer aroused but angry, and more than a little frightened. The syringe still hung from his arm; he pulled it out and threw it on the floor. "What did you give me?"

Peter smiled. "I do not get paid to ask questions." He got off the bed, retrieved his shirt, and headed toward the door. "I get paid to let you feed from me, and to give you the injection." He looked back on his way into the hallway, where Matthias could see Wolfgang leaning against the opposite wall—waiting, no doubt, in case there had been trouble. "The hard cock, you did not have to pay for."

He slammed the door behind him, and before Matthias could pull it open, the lock clicked.

He turned the knob, fury rising inside him like a storm surge, red and hot. "Let me out!" Surely Frank Greisser had not ordered this done. Hadn't Matthias given him every last bit of information he'd requested?

No answer came from the hall, and Matthias learned quickly that the door had some type of reinforced steel or other fortification. He couldn't break it. Couldn't pull it from its frame. He charged to the window and found a fine grid of silver bars across it. Added during his daysleep, no doubt.

Fury turned to panic as Matthias paced the room, his gaze finally landing on the syringe that lay in the floor. The burn that had followed the injection had calmed; he was aware of it if he tried to sense it, but it was no longer painful.

What was Frank up to? And what the hell was in that injection?

❦CHAPTER 15❧

Robin sat on the front stoop of Mirren's community house on Cotton Street, drinking strong black coffee that Glory had brewed before leaving for the dining hall everyone called the Chow House.

She didn't know how Glory managed. Stayed up until dawn with her vampire, stuck with him until he was asleep, went to make breakfast and lunch for the humans at the Chow House, and then, finally, slept a few hours before cooking an early Chow House dinner and greeting Mirren again when he woke up at sunset.

Seemed like it would be easier to always keep vampire hours. Except the whole missing-the-sun thing would suck.

Sucking reminded her of vampire feeding, which reminded her of that whole freakball scene with Mirren last night. It had scared the crap out of her, not that she'd admit it aloud. Although the way she'd wimped out, she wouldn't have to. They already knew.

It had felt good. Way too good. And she wanted to try it again, for real this time, with fangs, in private, and not with Mirren Kincaid.

Not this morning, either. Her head ached from lack of sleep. A throbbing pain had settled behind her eyeballs, where it would stay until she either napped or drank enough caffeine to fuel a battleship. She was already on cup number three.

"Figured you'd still be zonked out." Nik came outside and sat next to her, holding his usual cup of sweetened creamer laced with just enough coffee to make it a light golden brown. Take away the man's sugar and he'd die. "I heard you leave last night after Cage and Melissa headed out. You followed them?"

"Jeez, why don't you announce it over a fucking loudspeaker, Niko?" Robin looked up and down the street for any sign of eavesdroppers.

"Got a tip for you," he whispered, leaning close enough so she could smell the spearmint of his toothpaste and that caramel macchiato creamer he liked. "The vamps are asleep when the sun's up. They can't overhear us."

"Smartass." She took another sip of coffee and was about to get up for more when Nik held up the whole carafe—he'd brought it with him and set it beside him where she couldn't see it. "Figured you'd be bitchy and needy."

"Damn straight. That's why I love you." She topped off her cup and set the carafe beside her. She'd probably end up drinking the whole thing. "Yeah, I followed them."

"I don't want you to tell me where they went, just if you found out what you needed to know."

Robin respected that need-to-know thing the Rangers preached. A compromised soldier, they'd told her, couldn't tell secrets he didn't know, even if tortured—although he'd probably die before letting himself be taken if that option were available.

But *need to know* had all kinds of meanings. "What I needed to know was where the big vamps spend their days. I might need to find them someday, and I don't like surprises."

"Bullshit." Nik laughed and sucked down the rest of his cup full of creamer. "What you needed to know was whether or not Cage Reynolds is screwing the curvy redhead and, if so, whether or not it means anything."

"That would be the curvy *married* redhead, and she's really more of a strawberry blonde." Might as well not deny it. Nik knew her too well. "And no, I didn't learn much since the vamps have an annoying habit of disappearing underground before daylight."

"What, you want them to stay outside and fry in the sunrise?" She looked at him with interest. "Do they really do that? Fry? What does happen if one of the fangaroos goes sunbathing?"

"I honestly have no idea except our dossiers said it's fatal." Nik shook his head. "You are one warped little bird."

She took that as a compliment and kept her mouth shut when Nik pulled a silver flask out of the pocket of his jeans and tipped a measure of amber liquid into his coffee cup. He replaced the flask and held up his cup in salute. "Breakfast of champions."

He only drank his Black Jack bourbon at breakfast when he'd been having nightmares—or was planning to use his Touch to learn something. "Looks like we had the same idea for today." She looked toward the end of Cotton Street, where wisps of smoke still rose from the burnt-out ruins that lay catty-corner from the old mill.

"Yep." Nik sipped his drink, his dark-brown eyes fixed on the blackened brick chimney that, along with the concrete steps and porch, was the only part of the house still fully intact. "I figure between my abilities and your shifter sensibilities, we can learn more than anyone else from that fire scene."

"My gut tells me it was no more an accident than the construction-site wall collapse." Robin studied the hulk of the old mill. "There's a million places to hide in there. We should check it out as well."

"I think we're meeting Mirren and the others there at nine tonight, to set up a training schedule. Maybe we can poke around afterward. Now that the psycho vampire's on the loose again and we know the construction site was sabotaged, people have to be on alert."

"They should never have not been on alert." Robin didn't understand why they thought the war was over just because one particularly evil combatant had been locked up. Except maybe wishful thinking. "It's not like that Ludlam guy was the only one after them. He was the scapegoat."

"Yeah, but part of the appeal of Penton was that it could be a kind of utopian society where they didn't always have to be looking over their shoulders. Most people came here to avoid fighting, not to wage a war—that was forced on them. You can't really blame them for hoping it was over." Nik finished his drink, set it aside, and picked up the sketchbook he'd brought with him. "You ready?"

Robin looked up at the sun and gauged the time at noon or a bit later. "Let's do it."

She tugged at the fabric of the sweater Nik had bought for her; she had to make a trip to a place with a store, and soon. The warm brown color looked good on her, but it was too big and had a boatneck that kept slipping off her shoulder. The jeans were rolled up at the hem, so she was rocking the homeless waif look big-time.

She still hadn't seen Hannah, but the Hello Kitty ensemble was off the table—everything in that house had likely burned or had smoke damage.

"Leave the neck down." Nik held out a hand, and when she grasped it, hoisted her to her feet. "It's sexy."

"Sexy-schmexy." Robin slapped at his hand as he tugged the brown sweater off her shoulder again. "You don't know sexy. Wasn't it you who told me—who's told me on numerous occasions, in fact—that you've seen better figures than mine on twelve-year-old boys?"

"Aw, you know I just say it because it annoys you so much."

True, but it chafed all the same. She was short, wafer-thin, and while not precisely flat-chested, could easily get by with training bras. What she wouldn't do to have one of those soft, curvy figures men liked so much. Like Glory. Or that damned Melissa Calvert, whose curves Nik had obviously noticed, the jackass. At least Krys was built more like Robin, only about twice as tall.

They walked the length of the block and stood on the sidewalk in front of the burned house. It wasn't down to ashes, at least—the back rooms of the house weren't habitable by any stretch of the imagination, but they still had outside walls, and Robin thought one might have part of a ceiling.

"Why don't you walk it first, before I start touching things?" Nik pulled out his flask and sipped his bourbon straight this time, sans coffee creamer.

Robin nodded and left him to his crutch. She never preached at him; she understood why he drank, and she knew he could stop if he were ever in a situation where he wasn't in danger of being blindsided by a bunch of memories. She hardly ever saw him drink when they were away from other people.

What Nik needed was a brand-new start in a town filled with vampires. Penton was perfect for him—except for the little sabotage problem.

She walked carefully, not touching anything with her bare skin lest she leave signatures that would throw Nik off. He couldn't read shifters for the most part but would get flashes that didn't make a lot of sense. Shifters lived long lives, and part of their ancestors' DNA lived through them even more strongly than in humans, so he might pick up a shifter memory flash that was centuries old.

The front rooms of the house had a couple of side walls still standing, but the roof overhead had caved, so Robin toed aside stray bits of building materials, charred support beams, and what had probably at one time been pieces of furniture. She tested each step to make sure she didn't crash through twenty or thirty feet into the daysleep spaces built beneath each house.

A mass of debris to the right was probably the remains of the dining table Nik remembered passing in the smoke.

The thick odor of charred wood, smoke, and ash overwhelmed her senses until she wasn't sure she'd be able to scent a can of gasoline or another accelerant, even if it were sitting in the middle of the house with flashing lights and a signpost on it.

This house had the same layout as Glory and Mirren's, so she picked a route to the kitchen, looking for any scent or evidence of an electrical fire. It was too early in the fall to need heat and too late in the summer to need air conditioning, so the kitchen would be the most likely source of electrical malfunction.

She leaned in toward some exposed wiring and sniffed. Nothing out of the ordinary, but she'd better warn Nik to be careful in what he Touched in case no one had had the forethought to turn off the electricity.

The biggest pile of ceiling materials lay in the hallway near the middle bedrooms. This must be where Nik had fallen, and where Cage had saved him.

According to his dossier, Cage had also saved curvy old Melissa Calvert from the evil Matthias, at considerable risk to himself. Even took a bullet getting her out.

A man who made a habit of saving other people was a man with problems, at least in the Robin Ashton lexicon of life. He might save others because by focusing on their problems he could ignore his own and look like a hero doing it. Or he might get a rush from being the savior. She suspected Cage Reynolds wasn't hooked on saving people; he was too damn reserved. Which meant he was avoiding something in his own life.

Something to think about later, or as soon as she got a chance to fly.

The worst damage lay in the center of the house, particularly the middle room on the right. The outside wall had even tumbled. Although Hannah slept in the lieutenants' daysleep space, she kept her stuff in one of the back bedrooms, if Robin remembered Mirren's explanation clearly. The other back room and the room on the left—where Hannah and the dog had been found—belonged to the two Rangers, Rob and Max.

Which meant the room on the right, where the fire seemed to have started, was the one in which Cage was staying, with Fen and Shawn in the front bedrooms.

If the fire began in Cage's room, was he the target?

That genuinely sucked, since he seemed to always be running into danger with his Superman cape swirling behind him anyway. He'd make it easy for them. Create havoc anywhere nearby, and Cage would run right into it, looking for someone to save.

Nik needed to start here.

When Robin got back to the front of the house, Nik had taken a seat on the concrete stoop—now separated slightly from the house it was supposed to anchor. She didn't have to see his face to know he was getting in touch with that inner psychic he spent most of his time trying to tamp down.

Nik's father had had the Touch, too. That's what Nik's dad had called it, so Nik had picked up the name as well. It seemed to fit. But his father hadn't learned to control it, and the visions had driven him mad. Nik had found his father's body hanging from a purple-and-green Mardi Gras flagpole off the courtyard balcony of the family home in New Orleans's Garden District. He'd been sixteen, and since he'd inherited his father's Touch, everyone began treating him like a fragile freak who'd probably be hanging from the Crescent City Connection bridge over the Mississippi River at any moment.

Families were so fucking hard.

If her Niko wanted to drink to keep his demons at bay, so be it. Whatever it took.

She sat beside him, quiet and still.

Finally, he took a deep breath, let it out, and opened his eyes. His smile was sweet and sad, and she wrapped her arms around him. Robin didn't have many friends, and Nik was special. The gentle warrior who didn't judge what he didn't understand. She thought she might be willing to die for him. She knew she'd be willing to kill for him.

He hugged her back and gave her a kiss on the cheek. "Okay, eaglet. What do I need to know?"

She pulled her arms from around him and twisted to look back into the grimy ruins. "Begin at the center bedroom on the right. I think that's the origination point."

Nik frowned and followed her gaze with his own. "Cage's room? You think he was the target?"

"Dunno. Maybe he was the main target and killing the others would be gravy. I didn't catch any scents that would make me think there was an electrical problem. I also didn't scent an accelerant, but anything that was there would be camouflaged by fire scents." Scent and sight were her gifts; now, it was time for Nik to use his.

He stood up and flipped his sketch pad open to a blank sheet. Two of his drawing pens were clipped to the top.

"You want me to go in with you, hold the pad?"

He shook his head. "Run interference and keep anybody out who happens to come by. And wish me luck."

"Always," she said softly, watching him pick his way through the rubble toward the central hallway.

For fifteen minutes, she entertained herself by considering the issue of Cage Reynolds and Melissa Calvert, and why after watching them as much as she could the night before without being obvious, she didn't think they were involved. Or at least they weren't screwing like bunnies at every opportunity.

For one thing, Cage was too damned uptight; he was like a coiled spring in a tight casing. Having a fuckfest with a married woman, especially a married woman who'd been Aidan's familiar and was married to the city's business manager? She couldn't see it.

Yet Melissa had been jealous last night, annoyed at how *verklempt* Cage had been around Robin. The woman had been amused, yes, but also jealous. Robin got the impression she'd staged all that "showering together" trash talk just to make Cage more uncomfortable and punish him for paying attention to Robin.

Still, however they started out, Robin thought Cage and his curvy companion were probably just friends now. Maybe friends who cared a lot about each other, but not in love, or love as Robin thought of it, the capital-L kind that meant forever and exclusive.

She'd never experienced it, but she knew how it should go. Racing hearts, violent passion, blinding love so fierce it was on the borderline of insanity. People who couldn't live without each other. Consuming.

That's how it should be, anyway. It was too late for Robin; when she'd killed a man and gone on the run, she'd ruined any hope of settling down for a lifetime with a capital-L Love, even if she'd been suited to it personalitywise.

But her parents had come close to having it. Before the whole mess with Robin and Wren and that sonofabitch husband of hers, Robin's parents had still cuddled on the sofa and kissed in front of their eye-rolling grown children. They used stupid pet names and held hands in public. Part of Robin thought she was unsuited for that kind of relationship; another part of her was almost desperate to find it.

No way Cage and Melissa had it, which meant he was fair game. Capital-L Love might be out of Robin's reach now, but a really consuming case of capital-L Lust would do, and she thought Cage Reynolds would be quite lusty once she knocked that stuffy Brit reserve out of him—maybe literally.

"Need any help?"

Deep in her plot to overthrow the tower of stodginess that surrounded the Vampire Reynolds, Robin startled at the voice and then the man it belonged to. She didn't know who the hell he was, and she'd let him slip up on her like she was still a nested chick. *Stupid.*

"No thanks. Who are you?"

The man was medium height and almost pretty, with tousled blond hair and bright eyes the color of cobalt. He wore running pants and a T-shirt, but what gave him away was the cane. As in, he was leaning on one.

"Never mind, I know who you are. Mark Calvert, right? You got hurt at the job site."

"Yep, that's me." He walked with some effort to the steps, and Robin moved over to make room for him. When he finally sat down, the pain lines on his face smoothed out. "Gonna tell me who you are?"

She stuck a hand out to shake. "Robin Ashton. I'm one of the Omega Force team members from Texas."

He nodded. "You the Army Ranger or the shape-shifter? I heard there was one of each." Leaning back slightly, he took in her oversized sweater and rolled-up jeans. "I'm guessing shape-shifter. You're too short for Army. Nice fashion sense, by the way."

"A man wearing dark-green track pants and a gray T-shirt shouldn't be casting fashion stones."

He placed a hand over his heart. "I'm wounded." Then he grinned. "Seriously, I'm wounded. You're lucky I have on pants at all. You ever tried to get dressed with a back injury?"

She laughed, then cut it off. She didn't want to like Mark Calvert. If he'd kept his wife sufficiently occupied, she wouldn't be hanging around being friends with Cage Reynolds.

"I met your wife last night. She's"—annoying, suspicious, and distracting the guy I want to play with—"nice."

"Yeah, well, we're getting a divorce, so don't feel you have to talk her up." Mark fidgeted on the step. "Damn it, I can't get comfortable."

Robin was only half listening. She'd spotted a jagged row of scars on the inside of Mark's left arm. "What are those from?"

Mark glanced down, then back up at her. "You don't mind asking questions, do you?"

Robin shrugged. "I'm told I have no brain-to-mouth filter, so you'll have to get used to it. They look like—"

"Track marks." He held out both arms, scored with a criss-cross of scars. "I was one of Aidan's first rehab successes. Been his business manager for almost six years since he scraped me off the highway to heroin."

Interesting. "So you were with him before he bought up Penton?"

Mark laughed. "Who do you think carried out all the transactions? Aidan and daytime business meetings? Not happening."

"Right." Fangeroos. They were too high-maintenance. Cage might have to be a one-night stand. Nothing wrong with that. It would be a really good night.

A crash sounded from behind them, followed by an "I'm okay" from the back of the house. "Nik Dimitrou, the Ranger half of Penton's new dynamic duo," Robin explained. "He's got some experience in fire dynamics and accelerants."

She had no idea what the hell that meant, but it sounded good. Cage had needed to know about the Touch so Nik could find out if he could read vampires. Nik could tell Mark Calvert about the Touch if he wanted; that was his secret to tell.

"Good—I hope he can find something," Mark said. "Probably the same jackass that sabotaged the job site."

"Or maybe a different jackass." Nik came out the front door, shoved the notebook at Robin, and introduced himself to Mark. "I'm driving to the Chow House to get a late lunch. Want to go with me?"

"'Driving' is the magic word." Mark struggled to his feet. "Can you make a stop by the power station down the hill from the old Baptist church? I want to make sure the power's been cut to this building and the one adjacent. I was planning to walk, but that was"—he held up the cane—"insanely ambitious."

"Let's go, then. Robin, I would invite you, but I know you have a book you're anxious to dig into." Nik looked pointedly at the sketch pad.

Got it. Look at sketch pad. Don't tell Mark. "Yep, a great new romance novel. It has a whole platoon of lusty Army Rangers in it." Nik laughed. "Whatever it says, it's all true. Mark, hang out here and I'll pick you up."

They watched Nik walk down the block to the white SUV parked in front of Mirren's comm-house. "Ah, so that's how you met Mel last night; you guys are staying with Glory and Mirren. I'm across the street with Aidan and Krys."

As Robin recalled from the dossiers, he was the feeder for both of them and another vampire—but not for his wife. And asking for a divorce. Curiouser and curiouser.

Only Nik's untimely arrival prevented her from asking Mark outright why Melissa didn't feed from him instead of from Glory. But as she said her goodbyes and watched them drive off, she put that on her growing list of Rude Questions to Ask. Amazing what info people would give up if one just had the balls to ask.

In the meantime, she had pictures to look at. There were lots of smoky gray scenes. One of Cage standing outside the kitchen door, pointing through the inferno, Fen just ahead of him. Several sketches of a young dark-haired girl that must be Hannah, holding onto a plug-ugly bloodhound. *Barnabas is a bloodhound?* Good Lord. A vampire with a bloodhound. Oh well, probably no more bizarre than eagle-shifters named Wren and Robin.

A couple of drawings showed a pretty blonde Robin didn't know, but from Nik's description of running toward the fire, it must be the vampire named Shawn something-or-other.

Robin stopped at the next drawing, confused. She'd been waiting for an image of a person who didn't belong in the house, or of the black jaguar Nik had seen from Touching the job site. This drawing wasn't of a feline, but of a canine of some sort. Not quite big enough for a wolf, but the shape of its head didn't quite look like a dog. Could be an ugly mixed-breed, though.

In its mouth, it carried a bottle of liquid.

It was the accelerant. Had to be. The fire would break the glass, the accelerant would feed the fire and help it spread, and the broken glass would look like any other fire debris.

But the dog. What had Nik said? Maybe another person had set the fire. Could the dog be another shifter?

She stashed the drawings under the edge of a piece of Sheetrock laying on the porch and walked back into the house, picking her way to the room that had been Cage's—not that he'd spent more than a few hours there at the most.

The floor had burned through, and she could see metal about a foot beneath the subflooring. Kneeling, she tapped on it; it sounded solid. It hadn't occurred to her that the underground vampire nap rooms were steel-lined, but that had to be what this was. Which explained why the floor didn't collapse; it got as far as the top of the oversized fireproof vampire coffins and had nowhere to go.

Robin shuddered. She'd last about an hour in one of those before going berserk.

For the next hour she crawled the floor, inch by sooty inch, using her sharp vision to examine every solid thing that remained in the ash. Rough splinters of wood pierced her fingers, but she ignored the welling up of blood. No fangs around to take notice, and her shifter DNA would heal her quickly.

Anything she couldn't immediately disqualify as important, she shoved in the pockets of her oversized jeans. Then she took her haul back to Mirren's house, to her room, where she could study them without interruption.

Spreading everything out on the soft quilt that covered the heavy oak bed, she sat cross-legged against the headboard and picked up each piece, using what was left of Nik's borrowed, soot-blackened shirt to gently wipe it clean. A brass buckle and a few frayed strips of a leather strap like one might find on a trunk. The sole of a boot—Cage's? She set it aside in case Nik wanted to Touch it.

Finally, she wiped off an irregular, sharp thing the size of a quarter. Glass. Blue glass. Impossible to tell if the bottle being carried by the dog was blue in Nik's black-and-white drawing, but it looked about the right thickness. She set it aside as well and, by the time she finished, had found two more pieces and an intact ring of the glass—the rim of a bottle.

Robin felt her headache returning. She needed food, a nap, and some flight time, in that order. When Nik returned, they could talk it out.

A few hours and a nap later, Robin shifted. The sun had just slipped behind the tree line. She'd tucked her clothes underneath a bush at the edge of the woods behind the community house, spread her wings wide to test the temperature of the air and velocity of the currents, and then she flew.

She might not be as physically menacing as the jaguar shifters she'd gone through military training with, but by all that was holy, she could fly. Away from the dirt and decay and death of the earth, she saw things more clearly, healed both body and spirit, solved problems, and hunted.

Her Omega Force team leader in Houston used to tease her by saying she hunted rats and ate them. She hunted rats, all right, but she didn't kill or eat her prey. She gave them a chance to do penance.

Police reports gave her the kind of rats she hunted. Fine things, police reports, part of the public record. She'd find the accounts of abusers and bullies online at a local library, make note of the address, stake out the place, and catch her target.

Then the guy would suffer a visit from something he didn't know existed: a vengeful woman who could turn into a ruthless bird of prey. After all, who would believe him if he told?

A frightened bully responded well to threats, she'd learned—meaning she'd never had to kill any of them. But she would if she had to.

She'd done it before, killed a rat, and it had cost her the life she knew. And she'd do it again.

The higher she soared into the pine-rich air, the cooler it grew and the swifter the currents. She let herself coast, catching the gusts under her wings to lift her higher, and then letting herself plummet until she was forced to right her course.

There was a rat somewhere in Penton, and Robin was ready to hunt.

❧CHAPTER 16❧

With twilight's approach came Cage's gradual awakening. For most vampires it was sudden, that magical moment when the sun dropped below the horizon and awareness dawned. It was a gentle nudge to awaken you from a deep sleep, and you'd blink, groggy and disoriented for only a split second before sentience returned. That's how it had been with Cage at first. But after he'd been turned about two decades, he'd begun awakening more gradually, and he considered it a gift. Edward had told him his powers were growing and he might one day reach that master vampire strength. A real mixed bag, that. Responsibility was a burden as well as a gift, and if one had the powers that came with master status, one had an obligation to use them.

Still, it was a deliciously human experience, burrowing under one's duvet for the odd half hour to enjoy the peace and quiet while other vampires slept on.

When one wasn't alone, the sensation was especially nice. Not that he'd enjoyed company in his daysleep for quite a few years. Well, decades. And never consistently.

The thought of waking next to a woman made him think of sex, a subject his cock found of extreme interest.

The thought of sex made him think of Robin Ashton. What a bad idea sex with his little bird would be. The woman was insane. And dangerous. His cock thought that was even more interesting.

The thought of not having sex with Robin made him think of Melissa, which woke him fully, persuaded his cock that no further encouragement would be forthcoming, and ruined the enjoyment of even solitary duvet burrowing.

They had to talk. Tonight. Now. Well, as soon as she woke. Wouldn't do much good to let her down gently if she wasn't conscious, although it would be considerably less stressful for him.

Cage sat up and threw off the thick, soft cover, his limbs still heavy with the last dregs of daysleep. They should've talked last night, but by the time he and Melissa had gotten her car, and she'd shared Mirren's theories about the order in which Matthias probably wanted them to die—with both of them near the top of the list—they'd had to hoof it to get settled before sunrise.

Once they'd maneuvered the locks, the subbasement spaces beneath the abandoned Quik Mart weren't so different from the ones Will had designed under the old clinic. Big rooms, thick walls, and luxury furnishings Aidan must've had brought in by the truckload.

Mirren had left them an envelope taped to the hallway wall, with keys inside to adjacent rooms. They'd each taken a key and stood in the corridor like bloody idiots for a good thirty seconds, dithering. He didn't know whether to shake her hand or kiss her. If he shook her hand, it might feel like a brush-off. He might not see a future for them as lovers, but he did want her as a friend. Last thing he wanted to do was hurt her.

If he kissed her good night, or good morning in this instance, it sent a signal he couldn't follow up on. Not and live with himself. Awkward as hell, the whole thing. First with Melissa and Robin squawking at each other like hens at the communal house, and then arriving here.

So they'd each paused between the respective doors whose keys they'd claimed, finally ending the indecisive stalemate in an awkward hug.

"We need to talk at dusk," he'd said.

Ominously, she'd answered, "Yes, we certainly do."

Fortunately, albeit for all the wrong reasons, his head had been abuzz with so many details he hadn't been able to dwell on the pending conversation before daysleep claimed him. The job site sabotage. Matthias's escape. The fire. Unidentified shifters mucking about.

Robin.

The annoying, fascinating little shifter was a complication Cage hadn't expected. A complication he sure as hell hadn't gone looking for, nor did he want. Now that she wasn't nearby, filling his head with her colorful, unpredictable bluntness or searing his retinas with the sight of her breasts, forcing him to think about how they were the perfectly sized fruits, ripe for plucking or nibbling on. Well, now that they weren't right in front of him, he could think.

He'd come to Penton with the notion of settling down, finding a home, and not following every adventurous road that beckoned him. Robin Ashton was an adventurous road, and he needed to remain on the off-ramp.

Cage walked across the room and held up the clothes he'd been forced to wear last night, after exiting the shower and suddenly realizing all his belongings had been incinerated. Mirren's clothing was the right style—one could never go wrong with black—but he wasn't comfortable stealing any of them, plus they'd make him feel rather like a child playing dress up.

Nik had rescued him with a pair of jeans that were a couple of inches too short and a button-front shirt that stretched too tight across his shoulders and wouldn't button. Not a look he'd ever try to achieve intentionally. Robin would wind him up mercilessly.

And since when did you dress for any woman, Reynolds? Take a reality pill.

The sound of the adjacent door opening, then softly closing, preceded the knock by a few seconds, long enough for Cage's heart to speed up. Fuck, but he hated dealing with feelings. Analyzing everyone else's made a great hobby, but putting his own into words?

It wasn't akin to being back in Paris—the standard by which he judged horrific experiences—but it was bad enough.

Time to man up, as the Americans liked to say.

Melissa had ditched the paint-spattered T-shirt from last night and wore a pale-green sweater that gave her hazel eyes an extra shot of sage. They were dark and serious when she nodded at him from the doorway. "I'm sorry this is so awkward; I wish we'd had a chance to talk the night you flew in."

He stepped aside, closing the door behind her. She sat on the sofa and he wavered. Sofa or armchair? Too intimate or not? Why did every damn decision have to carry so much weight?

Melissa laughed. "You look like your dog just died and you might be blamed for it. Come and sit in the chair. That way you won't be too close in case I decide to bite you."

He smiled and relaxed his posture. This is Melissa. Whatever else she was or wasn't, *friend* applied. "Sorry, I seem to be better at listening to others' problems than discussing my own."

"Well, duh." She patted the arm of the chair next to the end of the sofa where she sat and waited for him to get settled. "Whatever you might have done in your human occupation, you're a guy first. We women don't expect you to talk about feelings without hemorrhaging."

"Right." Cage crossed his legs. Uncrossed them. Cleared his throat in order to launch into why things wouldn't work between them. "Speaking of dogs, do you know if they ever found Barnabas?"

So sue him, he was a right bloody chicken as well as the bastard who'd originally planned to screw Melissa Calvert but never had plans to love her.

Melissa bunched her brows together in a look of disbelief and answered in the tone people reserved for addressing the slow-witted. "The dog is fine. Britta found him hiding under a bush two doors down, scared but not hurt, and took him to Hannah. Changing the subject much?"

"Right." He seemed to be saying that a lot lately. "Okay, I'll just jump in here." Talk, don't think. "The way we left things in June, you know, I wasn't sure. And then you were sure and I was . . ." Bloody hell, he should have rehearsed. Why hadn't he rehearsed?

She held up a hand. "You aren't very good at this, so why don't I start?" She took a deep breath. "You were right. About me, in June."

Cage settled against the chair back and pursed his lips, trying to look intelligent but with no clue what she meant. He decided he couldn't fake it. "Well, I do enjoy being right, but what was I right about, precisely?"

"That I was using you . . . oh, Cage, I'm so sorry. I was scared, and you made me feel safe. I put you in a horrible position."

Fucking hellfire and brimstone, she was going to cry.

"You're wrong." He leaned forward and grabbed her hand, clarity finally slapping him in the face. They'd been so awkward together because each was trying to keep from hurting the other. "I knew you didn't love me, that you'd find your way back to Mark eventually. But I was a bastard to let you get close, knowing I didn't . . . to make you think . . ." He ran out of steam, his verbal locomotive chugging to a halt under a dearth of power.

Melissa looked at the floor, and Cage steeled himself for the tears, but when she looked up, she was laughing. "We were gonna tell each other the same thing, weren't we?"

He smiled, and all of a sudden his body felt almost weightless. The unsettled questions between them had weighed on him more than he'd realized—whether or not she'd hate him, or blame him, and knowing he deserved it. "I do love you, you know.

She looked him square in the eye, with a touch of the old playfulness he hadn't seen since his early days in Penton. "I love you, too, Cage Reynolds. I think we're going to be great friends—already are. I'm just not 'in love' with you." She formed little quote marks with her fingers. "Just like you're not 'in love' with me. Truth?"

Cage looked at the ceiling, examining a pattern of rough paintbrush marks that crisscrossed one corner of the rectangular space. He was so out of his element.

"I don't think I've ever been in love." What a pathetic thing to admit—but, hell, loving was hard enough without the "in love" part, if it even existed. "Never stayed anywhere long enough, I guess. But, really, at the heart of it, is there a difference? Isn't 'in love' just love mixed with infatuation? And when the infatuation cools, isn't love what's left over?"

Melissa laughed and shook her head. "You really are such a guy. Yes, there's a difference between loving and being in love. There really is."

Her words brought a grudging smile. "I haven't heard you laugh like that in . . . maybe ever." Things hadn't exactly been cheery since he'd come to Penton.

She tucked her feet underneath her on the sofa and propped on the upholstered arm. "I realized something last night when Mirren told me about Matthias being alive. If I let myself get lost because of what he did to me, he wins. That's true for all of us. If we let Matthias, or the fear of Matthias, tear us apart, he wins, and Penton dies. We deserve better than that."

Cage smiled. "You're a wise woman. Penton is one of the reasons I came back." He took a deep breath. "You were the other. To set things right between us."

She reached over and squeezed his knee. "I don't know if I have a future with Mark. In the long run, I don't think he'll want me. But here's something I realized while you were gone. You don't love me, Cage, except as a friend. What you love is Penton, and you'll always have a home here."

Thank God he'd been turned so many years that he couldn't cry anymore, or he might sob like an infant. Instead, he kept his eyes on one particular loose thread of carpet and said, "I want that."

And if he was to have it, to have Penton the way he wanted it, he had to fight for it. They all had to fight. They'd given Matthias Ludlam and the Tribunal too much power. Everyone who loved Penton so much, including himself, was so afraid of losing it that they were destroying it with their own fear. Doing Matthias and Frank's work for them.

A stirring in the hallway was followed by a soft knock at the suite door. Cage and Melissa exchanged a smile before he got up to answer.

Aidan stood in the corridor, dressed in black combat pants and a long-sleeved T-shirt—Cage didn't think he'd ever seen him quite so casual. He looked at Cage, looked past him at Melissa, then back at Cage. "Anything I need to know?"

Cage glanced back at Melissa, who shrugged and nodded. "Right. We were just setting to rest the mad rumor that we were destined to be Penton's next vampire super-couple. Sad to say you'll have to look elsewhere."

Aidan grinned, which lifted about two centuries of stress off his face. "Mirren's rounding up everyone in the old mill to start training at nine, so you have a couple of hours. I want everyone fed before training. One of you feeds from Nik and one from Mark. You pick."

He set off down the hall, where Cage saw Krys waiting. Aidan turned back. "We're about the same size, Cage—come by the house and get some clothes. You show up looking like that and Mirren will make your life a misery."

Right.

❦ CHAPTER 17 ❦

A s soon as Nik had dropped him off, seen that he'd made it into the house, and then driven away to find his little shifter friend, Mark made sure no one else was in his house and, only then, allowed himself the luxury of a loud groan. If you kept your self-pity to yourself, it didn't qualify as wallowing.

"You have a minor concussion," Krys had told him. "And you're just going to have to work through the back pain."

Easy for her to say. She wasn't the one walking around with the equivalent of a raw, exposed nerve that burned and throbbed with every move as if someone had scraped sandpaper across it. His back pain had company: his head pounded with its own miserable rhythm.

He reached in his pocket and studied the amber plastic bottle of prescription-strength ibuprofen Krys had given him. Wouldn't hurt him to take his moose-sized dose fifteen minutes early. If it burned through the lining of his stomach, well, what the hell. One more malady wouldn't make that much difference.

He shuffled to the kitchen and ferreted a bottle of water from its hiding spot behind containers of leftovers from the Chow House. As the only human in a houseful of vampires with no interest in solid food, and not much of a cook even in the best of health, Mark had qualified for Glory's version of Meals on Wheels. She'd drop anything left over from the Chow House each day when she went home to meet Mirren when he rose from daysleep.

Speaking of which, Mark had about an hour before Aidan arrived for feeding—he usually took some private time with Krys before coming back from the lieutenants' daysleep spaces. Mark probably could have weaseled out of feeding for one more day, but Penton was too short on humans for him to play martyr—especially with Max gone indefinitely, the new shifter girl not a viable feeder because of some weird reaction Mirren had at her bonding, and Robbie just plain gone.

Long story short, Penton needed its few humans to pull their weight, and he wouldn't let Penton down. He would, however, rest until Aidan arrived, and hope his back would recuperate from his too-busy day.

Mark shook out two white pills, tossed them toward the back of his throat, and swallowed them with about half of the water. He screwed the white plastic top back on the bottle and took it to his bedroom.

Speaking of wallowing, his sheets looked like a pig had rolled around in them, just as he'd left them this morning. If Melissa were here, she'd have his bed looking neat and straight in the time it would take him to figure out which way to turn the untucked sheet.

But she wasn't here, so he might as well suck it up and try to make it habitable, or sleepable.

Then he saw it. On the dresser, next to the wallet he rarely carried anymore unless he was going to be driving outside Penton, sat another amber plastic bottle, about half the height of the ibuprofen. Maybe Krys and Aidan had stopped by just after daysleep, and she'd had pity on him and left him something a little stronger. *She wouldn't have that much pity.* Mark stared at the label on the bottle, shivering as chills ran along his arms and into his fingers. He set it back on the dresser as if it might grow teeth and bite him. Krys wouldn't leave a full bottle of oxy for him to find. She'd dole it out a half pill at a time and deliver it with a stern warning.

Hell, what was he thinking? She wouldn't put an oxycodone tablet anywhere near him unless he were shrieking in pain. Even then, she'd have to think about it.

When he reached for it again, his fingers shook so violently that they knocked the bottle on its side. The sound of plastic hitting wood and of pills dancing merrily inside their amber cage sounded so loud he half expected to hear an echo.

Dosage: 80 mg. Strongest they make. Ironically, bright-yellow warning labels plastered the sides of the bottle. Addiction; respiratory distress; do not mix with alcohol or other medicines without checking with your doctor or pharmacist; do not operate machinery. It was the opioid script, so that after you got good and hooked, the drug manufacturers could claim innocence: you'd been warned.

If he had the sense God gave a billy goat, he'd march right into the bathroom and flush these babies into the local groundwater system. He wouldn't stand here mesmerized at the sight of the thing that had set him on the road to ruin.

Or the road to Aidan and Melissa. How could he truly hate the thing that had led him to the two people he loved most?

He'd flush them. He couldn't let Aidan down. Mel. Krys. Any of them.

"Mark? You here?"

He wrested his gaze from the bottle in his hand to the doorway. "Mel?"

He should tell her about the drugs. Let her help him figure out who put them here.

First, he'd see what she wanted. No point in dragging her into it if she was here to start a fight, after all, or discuss the terms of divorce now that she'd had a chance to get used to the idea. Not that he was sure he could go through with it; he'd accepted that he was always going to love her. But he did want her to be happy.

He jerked out the top dresser drawer and tucked the bottle underneath his socks. *I'm not hiding it. I'm getting it out of sight until I have time to figure out the right person to tell.* He got the drawer closed a split-second before she appeared in the door from the hallway.

"How's your back?"

Funny, he hadn't given it a second's thought as long as that bottle of pills was in his hand. Maybe he should just walk around with them: therapy by association. "It's better, but I probably over-did it today. I guess you came to talk about the divorce."

He was so preoccupied with walking to the bed and sitting down with as little wincing and groaning as possible that he didn't realize for a moment that she hadn't answered. Once he'd planted his butt on the mattress, he looked up at her and saw the tears.

"Is that really what you want, Mark?" She wiped her cheeks with a very human-looking flash of annoyance. "If it is, then we can talk about it. But not before I apologize."

God, he wasn't sure he could handle another tortured conversation. "Why are you here, Mel? Aidan will be by in a few minutes. It's dinner time for vampires, as I guess you know."

She had been standing in the doorway as if afraid to get close, but now she stepped inside the bedroom and closed the door behind her. "Aidan's not coming—he's waiting until the late feeding tonight and moving Britta to a new guy, Grayson, who came in from Atlanta today. Will and Randa recruited him. They're switching around the schedule since Max is gone . . . and Robbie."

That made no sense. "Why switch Britta?"

"You knew Matthias escaped?"

Melissa pulled the heavy wooden chair from beside the closet and parked it in front of him so they'd be facing each other. Only when she sat down and rested her hands on her knees did Mark notice what she was wearing: a loose pair of gray sweatpants and what looked like a tank top under her oversized sweater.

What she'd said finally sank in, and Mark felt the room tilt beneath him. *Not again. Oh dear God, not again. Haven't we been through enough?*

"No, tell me." He closed his eyes and listened as she shared what she knew, which was virtually nothing. Nobody knew where the old bastard was, or what he was up to.

"Until we know where Matthias is and what the Tribunal's up to," Melissa said, flicking a piece of lint off her pants, "they want the original Penton people sticking close together. Britta's not a target—she hasn't been here long enough—but you are, and I am."

Mark knew he had a concussion, but something still didn't compute here. "What does that have to do with feeding schedules?"

"I . . ." Melissa twisted her hands in her lap. "I wanted to see if you'd accept me in her place." At his dumbfounded look, she talked faster. "Aidan said I could go to you or to Nik, that Ranger guy, but Mark, I want to try . . ." She took a deep breath. "I've made such a mess of everything . . ."

She finally ran out of steam and her hands fell still.

"What happened? Cage got tired of you?"

As soon as the words were out, Mark wished like hell he could reel them back in and choke himself on him. He'd aimed them to hurt, and they'd hit their target. She looked at the floor, and when she spoke again, her voice was soft and subdued. "I was never with Cage. Never. I was so confused when I was first turned, and he seemed safe. I just let you both think . . ."

The heart of Mark's inner loser, the one who wallowed in self-pity and played at being the angry victim, beat erratically. "What are you saying, Mel?"

She looked up at him, her jaw set. "That I lied when I said I didn't remember our love. That I lied when I said I didn't want to feed from you because I was afraid I'd hurt you. I remember it all. I remember us. I've wanted you"—she closed her eyes—"so badly."

The loser's heart took off like a jackrabbit who knew the fox was closing in. "Then why? Why not tell me that three fucking months ago? You enjoyed watching me beg?"

"I haven't enjoyed anything since I've been turned. Especially seeing you hurt." She'd started regaining a little of the fire he loved so much. "But I kept hearing you say . . ." She shook her head. "Never mind."

Oh no, she wasn't clamming up now and leaving him with the blame. "You kept hearing me say what, Melissa?"

She smiled. "Remember when we went on our last date night, before things got so bad?"

He remembered, all right. The theater had still been there, before it burned. Old Clyde's barbecue place—he was the only original Penton resident who stayed when the vamps moved in—hadn't been bombed. None of them knew what kind of shit was coming their way. It was nine months ago. A lifetime ago.

"We ate at Clyde's, then walked down the street to the theater and watched that *Twilight* movie," he said, and laughed. "We made jokes about the sparkling vampires and how pissed off Mirren would be if he sparkled."

Then they'd gone home and made love. It had been the last perfect night he could remember.

"That was when Krys and Aidan were fighting their feelings for each other, when Krys was so scared and Aidan was in total denial," Melissa said, her voice so soft he had to strain to hear. "You said you'd never want to be mated to a vampire, that it wasn't worth the things you'd have to give up."

Mark's inner loser rolled over and gasped for air. He seemed to realize he was dying, and in his place sprang up a man Mark had thought dead—the hopeful man. The one who knew who he was and where he belonged.

"Mel, I was just talking out of my ass. I didn't mean . . ." *Shit.* "You were avoiding me because you thought once I came to my senses I wouldn't want you?"

Her smile was genuine. It was heartbreaking. It was the most beautiful thing he'd seen in months. "When you put it like that it seems pretty stupid, huh?"

He tried to get up and cross the fourteen inches to get to her, just two small steps. His back seized up on him halfway and he stumbled.

She caught him, eased her arms around him, and before he knew it they were hugging, her body achingly familiar against his. He'd missed her smell, her skin, the feel of her breasts pressing against his chest. None of that had changed.

Goddamned back. "I want to see if you know how to kiss with fangs, but I've gotta sit down."

She helped ease him onto the bed, and this time when she plumped up the pillows and tugged his sheets and quilt back into place, he didn't try to stop her. And when she climbed on the bed and lowered her mouth to his, he didn't try to stop that, either. Her mouth molded to his, and when she scraped a fang across his lip and drew blood, he laughed at her horrified expression.

"If you were too good at kissing with those things, I'd worry about who you've been practicing on." He grinned at her. "You're terrible at it."

She laughed, and instead of finding the sight of the delicate fangs unsettling, Mark found them sexy as sin.

Still, this felt like a sudden change. "Mel, we need to take this slow." What he didn't add was that he didn't trust her not to change her mind; she'd been jerking him around for three months, after all, and he couldn't go through it again. "Cage is back. What does that mean?"

She sat up and settled next to him, hugging her legs to her chest. "It was pretty funny—last night was the first time I've really had a chance to talk to him since he got back. I went in ready to let him down gently and tell him there was no future for us, only to find out he'd wanted to tell me the same thing."

Mark looked for any sign she was glossing things over or holding something back, but she met his probing look without flinching. She'd never been a good liar, and he doubted that had changed just because she was a vampire. Although she'd certainly lied well enough to push him away all these months, and he'd obviously been willing to believe her.

"Plus, I think Cage is interested in Penton's newest wildlife— that shape-shifter."

"Robin?" He tried to imagine the fiery little woman he'd met at the site of the fire being with the cold-as-ice Cage Reynolds, and couldn't do it. "Talk about an odd couple. And speaking of odd"— he pointed at her pants—"what's with the track pants? You started jogging in your spare time?"

She laughed. "Hardly. But Mirren's going to help me learn to defend myself—not like for Omega team work but just basic skills." She stretched out alongside him and propped on one elbow. "I'm tired of being afraid, and the only way I can get unafraid is to learn how to take care of myself. Go ahead. Tell me I'm nuts."

He thought it was a great idea. "Do it. If I can get this back healed up again, I'll be right there with you. We don't need to learn how to be killers, but we do need to learn how not to be victims. When are you training?"

"No set schedule—the lieutenants are meeting first. And, um . . ." She blushed, and he enjoyed the sight. After she'd been turned awhile longer, she wouldn't have enough human left in her for the pink to fill her cheeks. "I'm supposed to . . . you know." She tapped a finger on one of her fangs. "The word *feed* sounds so . . . impersonal."

"It's okay. I want you to."

She took a deep breath before reaching out to grasp his arm.

He pulled it back. "Not like that." He rolled his head to the side, baring his neck to her. No one had ever fed from his neck; he'd thought it too intimate and he'd always been a feeder, not a familiar.

"Are you sure? I've never done this."

"Aidan never fed from you this way? I mean, you were his fam a long time before he met Krys. I always figured you . . . you know." He turned back toward her. He'd always wanted to ask her but feared getting the outraged expression she had on her face now.

"Seriously? No way. You're my first."

He liked that. He also liked when she maneuvered to sit astride him, giving him a hard-on that ignored his insistence that they take it slow. It only knew want. It only knew now.

She laughed and moved on him just enough to give him some delicious friction.

He groaned. "Damn, woman. Did you miss that memo about taking things slow?"

"Yep, missed it totally." She lowered her mouth to his and kissed him, a soft brush of lips, sans fangs. She nicked him a little when she moved her mouth along his jawline, and sighed when she touched her tongue to the cut.

"You know how teenage guys don't last long in the foreplay department?" she asked.

"I'll have you know that I . . . ah." She sucked his earlobe into her mouth, and he felt the scrape of a fang, then the rush of the vampire mojo.

Melissa raised her head, and Mark wished he could keep the image in his mind forever. Her hazel eyes had lost focus, her breathing had grown heavier, her lips parted. She looked like a woman who'd just been fucked within an inch of her life, and still had energy to spare. "I wasn't talking about you; I was talking about me."

"What do y—"

She lowered her head and bit, a sharp knife-edge of pain followed by the sensation of floating, like a cocaine buzz and an orgasm unfurling in his body simultaneously. Who the fuck needed drugs?

With every pull at his throat, another wave of pleasure washed over him, and when she reached down and began stroking him while she fed, he thought if he were to die tonight, he could die happy.

Or not so much. "Oh man, that's harsh."

She'd pulled away and snuggled against him. "I'd finish that off, but you really don't want these inexperienced fangs down there. My hands are pretty talented, though."

Which she was proving to him. "Uh-huh."

Eloquent, but it's all he could manage.

"Plus, I don't think your back could handle what I'm going to do to you once you decide we don't have to take it slow." She gave him a hard squeeze to prove her point.

Damn back. It felt okay right now, although he was overstimulated in other areas.

Except the image of the amber bottle came back to him, and he knew he was one oxy high from ruining whatever it was they'd begun tonight.

"Wait, Mel." She began nuzzling at his neck again. "Seriously. Wait."

Something in his voice must have sounded different, because she rolled off him and sat up. "What's wrong? Your back?"

If only. "Go to the dresser, open the top right-hand drawer and look under the socks."

She smiled until she saw his expression, then got up and padded to the dresser. He was glad her back was turned so he couldn't see her face when she found the bottle. He heard it rattle, and then the long silence began.

She was wondering if he'd stolen them. How many he'd taken. He couldn't blame her; it had been his pattern, after all, so he steeled himself for her anger.

When she turned around, though, she looked confused. "You haven't taken any of these, or I would've been able to tell when I fed." She studied the bottle. "It's a generic prescription label, too. Krys wouldn't have given you oxy—where did they come from?"

Struggling with the gravity that wanted him to remain on his back, he used his arms to push himself into a sitting position. The back twinges were fainter; maybe the vampire high had staved it off for a while. "I found it sitting on the dresser when I got in tonight. I'd been over at the Chow House with Nik Dimitrou. I know it didn't come from Krys. She had to think hard about giving me freaking ibuprofen."

Melissa returned to sit on the bed. "You think someone deliberately set them there who knew your history and wanted to get you hooked again?" She rolled the bottle in her hand, shook it, examined it again. "Anybody have keys to this house except you and Aidan and Krys?"

They looked at each other as one answer dawned: Britta.

Without a word, Mark got up, slipped into his shoes, and followed Melissa toward the front door. They didn't need to discuss what came next: they had to talk to Aidan.

❧CHAPTER 18❧

Nik hadn't been this tired in recent memory. He'd been worse off after slogging through waist-deep mud and muck during Ranger School survival training. His muscles had hurt worse after his last tour of duty in Afghanistan when his unit got pinned in their mountain outpost for forty-eight hours. But after the having the lining of his lungs seared, keeping vampire hours, keeping human hours, and now approaching vampire hours again? Something had to give.

Robin had fared better—not just because she was a shifter and had better physical tolerance, as much as it annoyed him to admit that, but because she was a professional napper. Leave the woman in silence for more than a minute, and she'd be asleep.

Tonight, though, she was nowhere to be found, and if he were a betting man, he'd wager a paycheck she was soaring somewhere high above Penton. Flying relaxed her, cleared her head, helped her think. He'd also wager a paycheck she was thinking—at least a bit—about Cage Reynolds.

And about the three chunks of blue glass. He'd found them on his bed, no note or anything. She'd be too cautious to leave his drawing lying around. He decided to take a nap before picking them up and using his Touch, however, because training time would be coming up soon and he'd be back on the vampire clock.

He'd spent the afternoon running Mark Calvert around town to tend to Penton business. The town might be in ruins, but it still had utility bills to pay; a burned house whose electricity needed shutting off; and a couple of small work crews of humans to check on, making slow progress hauling off the rubble of what had been, a year ago, a thriving little vampire-human community. He'd even taken Mark to pick up the mail; everyone kept post office boxes in the nearest town, LaFayette, ten miles down a road to nowhere.

Nik used the back of his hand to shove the glass pieces aside and stretched out on the brown-and-green patchwork quilt. The longer he lay there with his eyes closed, the stronger the pull grew to pick the damned things up.

Shit. He rolled over and looked at them, steeled his mind for whatever might be headed its way, and wrapped his fingers around the largest chunk, grasping it in his fist. An image flashed behind his closed eyelids: a canine—the one in his drawing, but it wasn't a wolf. Smaller, maybe a coyote, with a yellowish coat and cream underbelly. What made it stand out was its muzzle, not carrying the bottle but coated in blood. Blood dripped from its mouth, colored its bared teeth red. He didn't just see it; he felt it. It was hungry, but more than that it was angry. So, so angry.

He released the chunk of glass onto the bed and waited for his mind to clear before picking up the second. Where the first one had been the size of a large marble, this one was more like a button. From it came only the vision of a soundless explosion followed by a rush of flame, the image of a smoke-filled room, the struggle to breathe, the urgency of escape.

Nik tossed that one off the edge of the bed in his frenzy to get rid of it, and he lay panting for a minute, waiting for his heart to find its normal rhythm, for his brain to remind his skittering nerve endings that it was a memory, and not even his memory. He was safe. He would not burn. Whoever, or whatever, had been with this glass in the fire hadn't been so sure.

One piece of glass remained, and he prayed he'd either learn more or get no images at all. Drained of energy, he slid his hand along the quilt, its texture soothing to his fingertips, its fabric bringing only a brief glimpse of Glory's sweetness and nothing more.

Okay, last one. He raised his fingers and dragged the piece of glass to him, groaning and curling into a fetal position as its sensations hit him. *God, make it stop. The burning sensation, the thirst. The horrible, horrible thirst because nothing will go down, nothing will cool the veins and arteries as they dry up, empty out, refill with acid. He had to stop it, had to stop, had to stop, had to—*

"Nik!"

Someone pried his fingers open, and as suddenly as the mental assault had begun, it ended. His mind cleared, and all he could do was curl up tighter and let the tears come.

"Bloody hell, do I need to call Krys? Do you need a doctor?" The bed dipped as someone sat down, and Nik opened his eyes to see Cage, mumbling and fumbling with his cell phone.

"Don't call Krys. Give me a minute."

Cage looked at him, brows drawn together. "Hang on, then."

He disappeared and came back in a couple of minutes with a washcloth. "Here, you have a nosebleed." He shoved the cold, saturated piece of green terry cloth into Nik's hands and reached behind him to erect a mountain of pillows. "Move back and elevate your head, pinch the bridge of your nose. It'll help slow it down."

Nik had been down nosebleed highway before, and he did as Cage suggested. The cloth was cool against his nose and upper lip, and he closed his eyes and finally began to relax. It was done, but he didn't know what the hell to make of what he'd seen.

It was easy to say what he hadn't seen: a face, an identity.

When he opened his eyes, Cage was studying the pieces of glass. "Where'd these come from?"

"Your bedroom at the burned house, I think." Nik took a final dab at his nose, found no red smears on the washcloth, and set it aside. "Robin and I went through the house today, and we think that's where it started."

"So I was the target?"

Nik shrugged. "Maybe, or maybe it's coincidence."

"My room's in the center of the hallway, so that's not likely."

Nik agreed. "Go in Robin's room and see if there are any drawings lying around—she likes to stick stuff under her pillows. It's what I got from the house, before she found the pieces of glass."

Cage got up and headed for the door but stopped halfway.

Nik smiled. "Don't worry, she's not here. Probably out flying around somewhere."

"Right. That does make it simpler." Cage disappeared, and Nik heard him in the room next to his, walking around.

He returned holding Nik's sketch pad and flipped through it. "You're quite the good artist."

"Look at the last one in the pad." The coyote whose skin he'd inhabited briefly.

"A wolf? No, too small. Another dog, or is it a jackal?"

"Jackal, I think, or coyote." Nik watched Cage as he processed the meaning of it, his frown deepening. He looked at the piece of blue glass in his palm and back at the drawing. "Can shifters take on more than one form?"

Nik groaned. "God, I hope not. But there could be two different shifters hanging around."

"Fuck. How can strange jaguars and jackals be running around Penton without us seeing them? A bloody jackal ran in my house? Why didn't that useless piece of dogflesh Barnabas bark or something?" He jerked out the leather cord tying his hair back and ran his hands through his hair. "Well, maybe we can get some answers."

"Maybe Robin can come up with some theories. I haven't known her all that long, but her pattern seems to be that when she flies a long time she's either after somebody or thinking through a problem."

Cage quirked an eyebrow. "After somebody as in a criminal?"

Me and my big mouth. Nik knew about Robin's little vigilante program to reform domestic abusers, but that wasn't his story to tell, and even he didn't know why she did it except that it had something to do with why she was on the run from her family in Texas.

"Yeah, you know, like this guy in Houston that did the bombing last month—she tracked him all over eastern Texas and western Louisiana."

"Right." Cage pursed his lips and gave Nik a perceptive look. The man saw too much, and Nik's hesitation in answering gave him away. "Anyway, I had Hannah in mind, for answers. I came here hoping to feed, but I don't think you're up to that. Maybe you could meet Hannah, though. Talk to her."

Nik sat up, pleased that the room spun only a few seconds before coming to a halt. "I'd like to meet her, actually. Other than my dad, who wouldn't talk about it and advised me to wear gloves all the time, I have never met another person with psychic abilities. Tell me about her—and I'm okay for feeding. I know you guys are short on feeders."

Cage stood up. "We'll see—Hannah needs it more than me. I'll fill you in before we walk over. She's at Aidan's house."

For the next few minutes, Nik heard the capsule version of Hannah's story, most of which he'd already learned from the colonel's dossier. What hadn't been there were the more recent events—mostly that her familiars, an adult couple who were feeders as well as parental figures, had been killed by Matthias in his siege of Penton. How she'd been withdrawn since then.

"I thought she was pulling out of it when Max settled in here—she liked him, although I have no idea why because he's a total arsewipe," Cage said. "She had Max and she had the bloody dog. Now that Max is gone, she hasn't spoken to anyone. I thought she might talk to you if you spoke to her about your abilities."

"She has visions of the future, right?"

Cage nodded. "They aren't like yours, where they're tied to touching a person or object. They just come to her in pieces. I'd hoped to work with her eventually to see if we could figure out how to let her access them when she wanted and avoid them when she didn't. But things got too crazy too fast."

While they'd been standing on the porch and talking, Penton had slowly come to life around them. The vampires were out and about, and Nik saw the blonde vampire he'd run into the night of the fire, Shawn, leave the house two doors down—halfway between Mirren's house and the burned-out hulk of his own. She was accompanied by a young, dark-haired woman. She waved when she saw Nik and Cage.

"You met Shawn the night of the fire, right?"

Nik nodded. "I think she inherited me as a feeder, or the other woman, Britta—not sure which."

Cage laughed. "It'll be more pleasant than with me, no doubt."

"Yeah, about that." Nik liked the Brit and all, but he really didn't want to get a hard-on from having the guy suck on his forearm. That was fucking warped. Maybe that effect had been exaggerated. All he'd done with Mirren was relax. "Am I gonna, you know . . . uh . . ."

"Want to fuck me?" Cage smiled. "No, I don't think so. And if you do, keep it to yourself, right?"

"No problem." Nik never would've believed it, but shifters were downright simple compared to vampires. Blood. Sunlight. Silver reduced their strength. At least Robin just sprouted feathers and flew around.

They walked across the street and up the steps. Cage unlocked the door and led the way to the room Hannah had taken in the front.

He knocked, but there was no answer, so he tried the doorknob and opened it.

Someone had tried to make the room cheerful. Exotic flowers sat in a bright blue vase in the corner, and colorful pillows had been tossed on chairs and on the bed.

"Where—" Nik had started to ask where Hannah was, but Cage put a hand on his arm and jerked his head toward the corner.

God, she was tiny. He knew she'd been turned at twelve and that on some level she was still twelve, but he'd expected her to look more vampirish. She was smaller than Robin and looked like a little kid.

Cage patted him on the back and stepped back into the hallway, leaving Nik alone with the girl. She sat wedged into the corner, a big, wrinkled mass of reddish-brown fur filling her lap.

Nik walked over and sat cross-legged on the floor facing her. "Is this Barnabas?"

She nodded and ran a small hand over the dog's head and down the length of a floppy ear. Bloodshot eyes opened and looked at her adoringly.

"He loves you. Look at that expression."

She cocked her head and scratched under Barnabas's chin before looking up. Her jet-black eyes widened, and her mouth opened to form a small O.

"You're the one. The one who's like me."

Nik nodded. "My name is Nik—Nikolas. I'm sort of like you. I can see things in the past, where you see the future, right?"

Hannah smiled, and the difference it made in her face was remarkable—and horrifying. She looked even more like a little kid. Nik was glad Aidan had killed the monster who stole her childhood and the life she should've had. "Maybe we can work together and learn to use our gifts better. I could use some help."

To Nik's dismay, she began to cry. He thought vampires couldn't cry. Maybe the rule book got thrown out on a technicality if the vampire was a kid.

"Hey, it's okay." He patted her shoulder awkwardly, and when he got no hint of images, leaned over and hugged her. To his surprise, she moved the grunting, protesting Barnabas out of her lap and threw her arms around Nik's neck.

He picked her up, took her to the bed, and just held her for a while. Maybe he *could* help her. Since joining forces with the shapeshifters and now the vamps, he'd done nothing but wonder what contribution he could make as a human. He didn't have supernatural powers. He couldn't pick up tall buildings with a single thrust. He didn't own a cape.

"We can work together if we make it," she whispered. "Cage can help us if he makes it."

A chill stole across Nik's shoulder blades at her whispered words. "What's going to happen, Hannah?"

Her arms tightened around his neck so fiercely that he worried she might cut off circulation to his carotid and he'd end up unconscious on the floor.

"I don't know," she said in a voice both childish and much, much too old. "But I keep seeing horrible things. Monsters. Animals."

Nik's chill deepened. "What kind of animals have you seen? Did you see them in visions, or did you see them in Penton?"

She pulled away from him and studied his face. "Both. I saw a black lion in my head and a coyote in the house before the fire. I remember seeing coyotes from my human life, but I have never seen a black lion. Barnabas was afraid, and he hid under the bed in the empty room. I went to get him, and that's when the fire started. It got big so fast, and I was afraid."

"Have you seen the coyote anywhere else, or the lion?" No point in going into the whole black-jaguar spiel.

"Only in my head." She looked down. "Both of them are so angry and so hungry, but they can't eat."

He'd felt some of that rage and hunger in his own head when he'd held the glass. "Why can't they eat, sweetie? Why are they angry?"

"I don't know." She shook her head, and then threw her arms around him again. "I don't know."

❧CHAPTER 19❧

Matthias thought he knew starvation. He'd dropped at least fifty pounds off his frame since the pandemic vaccine had put vampires at the bottom of the food chain, and only twenty pounds of the loss looked good on him.

When he'd been arrested in Aidan Murphy's old clinic office in Penton and jailed in his own dungeon, his tormenters had intentionally kept him on the edge of starvation.

It had been nothing like this. He wanted blood. He also wanted food. Solid food.

For the first time in more than seventy years, he daydreamed of the things he ate during his human life. He had loved a fatty slab of prime rib swimming in its juices; a baked potato with butter, chives, and an extra dollop of sour cream on the side; bread warm from the oven, its outer shell crusty and flaky, its insides soft and tender.

He thought of ice cream in summer, hot chocolate in winter. Of clambakes and sweet, smoky Virginia hams.

He must be in hell. Forget pitchforks and His Satanic Majesty's Secret Service, or whatever else attracted people's beliefs. Hunger was the worst.

Wolfgang, dutiful toady of Frank Greisser, still brought a plastic bag of unvaccinated blood every night, handing it to him while another toady stood behind him with a gun at the ready. Wolfie even managed to look sincere when he left, apologizing just before the lock clicked shut and Matthias again was a prisoner.

It was almost feeding time now, and Matthias paced his room in restless angles and circles. Surely his feed would take the edge off this insane hunger.

He breathed a sigh of relief at the sound of movement in the hallway. A part of him always feared that the day would come when Frank felt he'd outlived his usefulness. The man wouldn't hesitate to have him killed; of that, Matthias had no doubt. The Slayer had nothing on Frank Greisser when it came to death with dispassion.

The lock clicked, and Matthias turned to greet Wolfie, anxious to feed. Confusion set in quickly, however, when the armed toady came in first, followed by Wolfgang not holding a bag of red nourishment, but pushing a stainless-steel service cart.

On top was spread a fine white linen tablecloth and service for one, the plate covered with a stainless-steel domed lid polished to a sheen that reflected a fun-house version of the room around it, including Matthias himself.

"What kind of joke is this?" Only was it? He had been craving food, more so every day. The hunger was devouring him.

"I thought you might be hungry," Wolfgang said, bowing his head in a no-doubt-sarcastic show of respect. "There is also a bag of unvaccinated blood on the shelf beneath the main tray."

Matthias reached out and lifted the dome, thinking about that old movie where Bette Davis the sadist fed Joan Crawford a similarly displayed rat.

But beneath the dome, the tasteful white dinner plate held not rat but roasted chicken, its skin crisped to a golden brown, juices seeping from beneath it onto the plate next to the baked potato of his dreams. Butter pooled in its center, and a tiny glass dish of sour cream sat beside it. A separate basket held rolls, and another glass bowl, pats of pale yellow butter.

His mouth watered. Actually salivated as he looked at the food. He paid no attention to Wolfie or his armed friend. He barely felt the prick of the needle into the side of his neck, at least not until the horrible burning sensation began again, so sudden and overwhelming he dropped to his hands and knees.

He burned as if his blood had turned to acid and was eating away at every blood vessel, every muscle, every bone, until it seemed inevitable that he'd eventually melt into one big pool of liquefied skin and smoking ash.

The room went gray, and his arms gave way. Rolling onto his side, he was dimly aware of feet moving away from him, the door opening and then closing.

He didn't know how much time had passed before awareness began to seep back in. The burning sensation dwindled down to a raw memory, and the hunger returned.

Sitting up, he looked around the room, frantic until he saw it. They'd left the tray.

Matthias climbed to his feet, staggering like a drunken man toward the steel dome, fearful even now that he'd lift it and find a rat, or worse. But the chicken was there, and the smell of roasted meat and thyme and basil hit him like a slap. Could whatever they were giving him, the shots, possibly enable him to eat food again? What the hell was it?

His hand trembled, and he flexed his fingers to calm it before reaching out to pull a delicate web of roasted skin off one chicken leg. He held it to his nose, basked in the aroma; it didn't make him sick or even disinterested. His mouth watered, his taste buds roared to life, and he stuck it in his mouth.

It was glorious. He chewed it, his teeth out of practice and feeling awkwardly big. He swallowed, and the sensation of something solid passing through his digestive system was alien to him.

He waited to see what would happen. He'd tried to eat after turning vampire—all vampires did, whether they admitted it or not. And they could eat for a few days after being turned. But when the thirst set in, the thirst for blood, all other taste failed to appeal.

Until now.

He'd been planning to rip off Frank Greisser's balls and force him to eat them when he got out of here—but instead, he might buy the man a cigar and a steak cooked medium well.

Matthias pulled the tray to the nearest chair and polished off the rest of the chicken, and then the potato. He finished with bread and butter, best of all. He felt full. He was satisfied.

Humans, of course, had systems equipped to eliminate waste; how would that work for a vampire?

He settled back in the room's armchair, watching German-language television and not understanding a word. Until he got the answer to his digestive question.

The pain propelled him from the chair and he again hit the floor on hands and knees, crawling toward the bathroom, which he had treated as a closet. He'd been allowed to retrieve some things from his New York estate, and he was horrified when the next agonizing spasm revisited his glorious baked potato inside his favorite Italian leather loafers.

❧CHAPTER 20❧

In the old Southern Mills's biggest workroom, Mirren heaved the last remaining table into the wall, then picked it up and smashed it against the concrete floor until it lay in kindling sticks.

"Feel better?"

"Fuck no." He glared at Aidan, who glared back at him. "Should I?"

"Save your energy. We're gonna need it."

If only he knew how to use it. Mirren parked his ass on the concrete and leaned against the wall, trying to make sense of the latest Penton disaster—a stupid, cheap flyer posted all over town during daylight hours. Only Glory had kept the fallout from being worse.

That pile of flyers on the floor provided proof—like they needed any at this point—that Penton was under attack.

Except the attackers were ghosts, smoke, invisible, and Mirren didn't know how the fuck to fight them. Or how to go after them when he didn't know who or what they were.

"The others will be here soon, so we need a strategy." Aidan hopped on one of the big wooden thread spools they'd left in the room, his boot-clad feet dangling off the sides. He'd abandoned his business clothing for jeans and a sweater, and his hair was growing out again—he looked like Aidan, in other words.

Before Glory had arrived at 8:00 p.m. with flyers in hand, Mirren had almost finished equipping the room with punching bags, weights, cycles—basic gym equipment that Will had bought in Columbus and had shipped to their storage space yesterday. Nik had helped Mark pick it up.

There was also a lot of not-so-basic equipment: silver-laced rope, blades, kukri knives, bullets. For a week, Mirren had pulled his best human workers off debris cleanup and had them shoring up the walls and ceiling of the mill, the only space big enough to convert into training space until they got the training center finished. *If* they got it finished. The mill wasn't luxurious or high-tech, but it would work.

If they only knew who they were fighting.

"What strategy can we have if we don't know what the fuck we're up against?" Mirren scrubbed his hands over his face, hating the helpless feeling.

"Everybody coming tonight needs to know everything. We need any and all ideas. Agreed?" Aidan's phone buzzed and he sent a quick text. "Cage and Nik are on their way. Robin's AWOL."

"Figures. She'll be here if it suits her, and if it doesn't, she'll be gone. We can't count on that damned shifter."

"Then it's your loss." Robin stood in the open doorway, wearing impossibly tight jeans, an impossibly tight black-and-white-striped shirt (or at least Mirren thought it was black), and a navel ring.

"Seriously?" He climbed to his feet and stalked around her. God, the woman was built like a matchstick. "You thought you could train in that getup? On a dance floor, maybe."

"Oh, stick a fork in it." Robin punched Mirren in the stomach on her way to sit next to Aidan on the wooden spool, and he'd be damned before he let on that it hurt. He kept underestimating her strength.

Mark and Melissa came in next, together for a change, and Mirren looked at Aidan, brows raised. They hadn't been invited; maybe Melissa had misunderstood that her training would be separate.

Aidan shook his head. "You guys aren't supposed to train with us tonight. Or is something wrong?"

Mirren would place bets on the latter. Mark walked with the stiff gait of a man trying to coddle an injured back, but Melissa looked ready to spit nails.

"We needed to talk to the lieutenants," Mark said, looking around and finally spotting a folding chair off to one side of the sparring mats. Melissa saw it, too, dragged it over, and massaged his shoulders when he sat down.

"You two back together?" Robin asked. "Looks like it. Good."

"That's none of your business," Melissa snapped.

Mirren closed his eyes and shook his head. They had no time for a Cage Reynolds–induced catfight. "Whoever's fucking which person and whoever isn't fucking anybody—put a lid on it, all of you. We've got bigger problems."

"We have at least one you don't know about," Melissa said.

Well, wasn't that just fucking good news?

"Nik and I do as well," Robin said. "He's on his way, but he's been talking to Hannah."

Better and better. Mirren felt the beginnings of another table-smashing itch.

"Wait until the others get here before we start sharing news." Aidan said. "No point in having to repeat it."

But when Nik and Cage arrived, Hannah wasn't with them.

"She wouldn't leave the house," Cage said, going to lean on the wooden spool next to Robin. "But at least she's talking—well, she's talking to Nik. We'll fill her in afterward."

"I'll do it when I go back so she can feed," Nik said. "I promised to stay with her until daysleep."

Hannah talking was at least one piece of good news. Mirren had been afraid she was spiraling into some dark place they might never get her out of. If Zorba could get her back, he'd more than earned his keep.

"That's all of us then." Aidan went to close the door and lock it. "Mirren and I will fill in Glory and Krys afterward. I put Fen, Shawn, and Britta on patrol tonight, along with some of the other scathe members. But we lost five more today—four vampires, one human."

"The only good news about that is that it puts us at twenty-one vamps and, thanks to the new human that got in yesterday, ten feeders," Mirren added. "So we can cut all but one of the feeders back to two each. I'll work out the schedule before daysleep."

Robin cleared her throat. "I can take the leftover. I'm not poisonous."

"You are poisonous." Mirren was getting tired of everything being a production with this shifter. She took too much work. "Stay away from fangs. Period."

"If we need you we'll try it, and I appreciate your willingness to be a feeder," Aidan told her. It softened the fury she'd been directing at Mirren. "Two isn't bad, and the new guy has offered to take the spare."

"What is that?" Cage edged around Aidan, walked toward the nearest mat, and leaned over to look at the stack of flyers. "Bloody hell."

He snatched it up and read it, turned it over, and then handed it to Robin. "Tell me that's not real."

"Who is it?" Robin held the flyer up so Nik could see it without touching it.

"It's Will." Mirren took another flyer off the mat. On it was a photograph blown up to fill most of the page, showing a man at the end of a torture as brutal as any Mirren had inflicted in his Slayer days—and that was saying something.

The man was clearly Will Ludlam, strapped naked to a chair and beaten black and bloody. His legs were ribbons of torn flesh. One eye appeared to have been gouged out. At least two fingers had been cut off, leaving bloody stumps.

Robin read: "'One of Penton's leaders is dead. Who will be next?'" She held the flyer at an angle so the light would hit it differently. "It's a Photoshop job, I think. The head's a little too big for the body—they don't belong to the same person. And I think some kind of filter was applied on his face to make it look so beat up."

Silence. Robin looked up and seemed surprised to find everyone staring at her—even Nik. "What? Gadget's been teaching me how to retouch photos."

Aidan held up a hand. "Good thing to know—it might have saved us some angst. Yes, it's a fake. I talked to Will and both he and Randa are fine. They're in Columbus, getting ready for Rob's funeral tomorrow. The colonel's flying in there tonight. I told them not to come back until after the Tribunal vote. I think things are just going to keep getting uglier until that's behind us."

In Mirren's opinion, Aidan was naive if he thought becoming a member of the Tribunal would solve their problems. On the other hand, at least it offered some hope, which had been in short supply around there.

"Where'd the flyer come from?" Robin asked.

"I hoped maybe Nik could tell us." Mirren handed the flyer to Nik, who took it reluctantly and walked over to a corner of the room where he could get away from everyone. Except the damned shifter, who followed him.

"Glory found the flyer tacked to an electrical pole outside the clinic," Mirren said. "She tore it down and was on her way to bring it to me when she started seeing them all over town—on every surface that was still standing. Too many people had seen it."

Aidan nodded. "The damage was done. The ones who left called me not five minutes after I talked to Will. Even after they found out it was fake, they still wanted to leave. I can't blame them."

"Whoever did this is a fucking coward." Mirren kicked at one of the mats, sending it sliding across the floor in a flurry of dust. "How do we fight it?"

He'd engaged in every kind of battle imaginable, or so he thought. He'd met men armed with battle-axes and swords; he'd fought wearing chain mail of his own construction. He'd used fangs and his own brute strength to tear opponents' limbs from their bodies. He'd beheaded, stabbed, shot, burned, poisoned. But he couldn't fight what he couldn't see—and that just pissed him off.

"It's classic psychological warfare," Cage said, sitting on one of the mats. "The Germans used it a lot in World War II, and so did the Brits and the Yanks. It's effective from a victim standpoint because there's no way to fight it except to let people know what's happening and hope they have the courage and patience to stick it out. It's effective from the enemy's standpoint because there's little risk. Well, normally."

Aidan had been nodding while Cage talked. "Suggestions?"

Cage shrugged. "I'd say we call a meeting of everyone in town, tell them exactly what's going on, and warn them not to believe what they hear or see unless it's coming from one of us."

"I agree." Aidan looked at Mark. "Do you feel up to organizing the meeting for tomorrow just after daysleep? It'll take us that long to get the word out. We can have it here."

"Will do." Mark looked up at Melissa, who nodded. "There's something else you need to know."

Mirren walked to the nearest wall and leaned against it, arms crossed. He so didn't want to hear one more piece of fucking bad news.

In halting speech, Mark laid out the scenario: finding the drugs, being tempted by the drugs, deciding he could do without the drugs. While he talked, Melissa stood behind him with a hand on his shoulder.

"So whoever did this knows your background well enough to know your particular poison." Mirren didn't like this one bit. "Whoever did it also has access to controlled drugs. And, most serious of all, whoever did it has access to Aidan's house."

"Britta." Aidan's voice was flat. "I have a key, as do Mark, Krys, Hannah, and Britta. Cage got one tonight. That's it." He jumped off the spool and started pacing. "My instincts about people are usually good, and I would've sworn she was with us."

"She's history." Mirren pushed off the wall. "And don't defend her, A. There's no one else it could be."

"Yeah, there is." Nik had returned from communing with the spirits, but the man looked like the spirits had beaten the hell out of him. His nose was even bleeding.

"I'm gonna call Krys—I don't like the looks of that." Aidan dug out his cell phone.

"She's not the only doctor in town." Robin looked at Cage. "Don't psychiatrists have to go to medical school?"

Cage was already getting to his feet. "It's been a right long while, but we've already treated the nosebleed once today. I'd suggest you not use those skills of yours for a bit."

"Tell me about it." Nik held the hem of his sweater up to his nose with one hand and pinched the bridge of his nose with the other.

"What could you tell?" Mirren returned to his spot against the wall, hoping like hell Zorba had learned something helpful and not more confusing.

"I couldn't get anything from the flyer—sorry." He tossed it back on the mat with the other copies. "Just Glory, pulling it down. A few faces looking at it with enough agony for me to know they didn't put the damned thing up."

"So what did you mean about Britta not being the only one who could've done it?"

Nik sat on one of the mats and lay on his back, his voice muffled and strained through the pinched nose and sweater. "Just that unless you've looked at all the access points—doors, windows, attic—there's no way to be sure someone came in with a key. Also, we have two unaccounted-for shifters in Penton."

Aidan had been pacing while Nik talked, but he stopped so fast his own momentum almost toppled him over. "Two? Not just the jaguar?"

"Robin can tell you."

Cage had found a first-aid kit in the corner and handed Nik a portable bag of dry ice, which Nik applied to his nose while Robin talked. Mirren had to admit, the Ranger and the shifter—this shifter, anyway—were proving useful. They'd be more useful if Robin weren't a pain in the ass—but then, from what Mirren knew of eagles, they weren't exactly possessed of warm, fuzzy personalities, either.

"So we have a coyote shifter who walks right into the house where Hannah's hanging out with Barnabas, sets a fire, and nobody sees him." Mirren shook his head. "How is that possible? How can two shifters be here without us knowing?"

"Easy." Robin sat on the mat next to Nik, pulled the ice pack from his nose, and leaned over to look. "It's stopped bleeding and you're getting frostbite. What I mean is, these woods around here are full of animals, so how hard would it be for this guy to shift, fill a bottle with accelerant, then slip in as a coyote? He shifts back, sets the fire, then shifts again to leave. He'd use up a lot of energy and be weak afterward from shifting that many times, but it's doable."

"Or." Cage took Aidan's former seat atop the wooden spool. "They're both among our remaining humans. I think we need to isolate and question all of them."

"Then even more of them will leave." Aidan resumed his pacing. "But we keep watch on them, all of them. And this doesn't let Britta off the hook. I want to go through the comm-house and find out if there's any sign of forced entry. Nik, you up to helping with that?"

Zorba had sat up and climbed to his feet. "Yeah, I'm good."

"Okay, we're going back to the house." Mark stood up and tried to stretch his back. "Britta's supposed to drop by before midnight to feed. What's the plan with her?"

Mirren would like to plan her death, and if they found out she'd planted those drugs, nothing Aidan could say would change his mind. "Don't mention the drugs. See if she asks any questions. Call me when she leaves. I want to know every word she says."

"She'll know he hasn't taken any from feeding." Melissa followed Mark toward the door. "It's how I knew he was clean."

Mirren exchanged a raised eyebrow with Aidan as the door closed behind them. Guess they were back together. Another sliver of good news among the bad. True love will win out, and all that shit.

"Nik and Robin—find a schedule you can live with, especially for the next week." Aidan filled them in on the Tribunal's upcoming vote as he gathered his own stuff to leave. "When I take Meg's seat, I'll be in a position to really pull together allies without sneaking around behind Frank Greisser's back. But in the meantime, I need you on day duty and also available part of the evening to meet with us. Mark tries to sleep about midnight until sunrise, and I suggest you make yourself get in that habit."

Speaking of treacherous assholes, Mirren had his own theories. "This flyer business sounds more like Frank Greisser than Matthias."

"Absolutely." Aidan nodded. "A war of attrition is exactly Frank's style. Matthias wouldn't have the patience for it. I also think Frank has Matthias hidden, and probably has plans to use him if he hasn't already. But if he's counting on Matthias for loyalty, he's looking in the wrong direction.

"The question is not whether Frank is working with Matthias." Aidan paused in the doorway on his way out. "The bigger question is: how long before he loses control of Matthias?"

❧CHAPTER 21❧

First, Robin thought Mirren would never leave. Then Cage got up as if to follow him out.

Not happening. She had other plans.

Cage Reynolds was going to be hers tonight. Just tonight. She wanted him, and that itch had to be scratched so she could move on and forget about it.

The obstacles had been cleared. Curvy old Melissa had returned to her husband, where she should've been all along. Fen Patrick was off patrolling. Cage had no pressing business of which she was aware.

Besides, if she waited until Cage stopped worrying about Penton long enough to focus on her, she'd be old and her feathers bedraggled.

Robin didn't like to wait. Never had. *Our eagle cousins might be predators, but we're not.* That had been her parents' mantra, nice old hippy-dippy shifters that they were. And where had it gotten them? Where had being the passive and gentle women they'd raised their daughters to be ever gotten her and Wren? Wren was ruined, and Robin had to live the life of a rover.

No, if she'd learned anything in life, it was that sometimes, only predatory behavior got you what you needed. Getting Cage off his Superman cape–wearing, heroic ass called for predatory skills. And she knew just how to get him moving.

"Let's spar."

Cage squatted in the corner, dumping all the first-aid supplies back in the kit where he'd found the cold pack. He swiveled to look at her. "Tonight? Tempting though it might be, love, I'm patrolling."

Or so he thought. "Have fun, then."

She waited, muscles taut, nerves alive with possibility. He set the first-aid kit aside and grabbed a jacket—distressed brown leather. Sweet. Where had he gotten clothes? She'd been so caught up in the drama of tonight's revelations, and in arguing with her favorite fanged Scotsman, that she hadn't noticed how damned good he looked. Jeans worn light in all the right places, his normal old boots, a dark golden-brown sweater almost the same color as that silky hair. The ponytail had to go. She wanted her hands in that hair.

And those boots had a strap around the ankle that would suit her needs.

He looked down at her and smiled. "Right, then. I'm off. You're staying here?"

"Yeah, just gonna hang out awhile." Said the spider to the fly.

As soon as the fly got within reach, she shot out a hand, slipped her fingers in the strap of his left boot, and jerked it toward her.

Oof. "Bloody hell."

A less experienced fighter would have hit the concrete floor with all his weight on his right shoulder, but Cage knew how to land. He'd broken the fall with his hands and pushed himself immediately into a seated position. His eyes grew to the size of moss-green quarters as they looked at her, then down at her hand and the fingers still looped through the strap on his boot. "What the fuck are you doing?"

"Getting your attention."

His eyes grew a shade lighter as he raised his gaze to hers. A smile lifted one side of his mouth. "You have my attention. Question is, what are you going to do with it?" His voice had morphed from outrage to purr, and a shiver ran down her spine. She hadn't expected him to play so quickly and didn't want to just have a quickie on the concrete floor. This needed to play out slowly. She wanted to savor it.

She released his boot and climbed to her feet. "I want to spar. Come on. Bet you can't throw me. I took down Mirren, so you're gonna be easy-peasy."

Cage gave her a slow smile and began to stand. The pendant lighting they'd had installed in the work space arced golden gleams off his hair. Slowly, he snaked out a hand and wrapped his fingers all the way around her ankle. And stopped.

She tugged, but his grip might as well have been a vise. His eyes had lightened another shade, and their gazes met. His expression was downright . . . predatory.

Robin's heart sped up, and he felt it, judging by the widening smile.

Maybe, just maybe, she'd met her match. And she wasn't ready for that to hap—

He jerked her leg toward him, and she went down hard on her back; only the padded mat saved her. He still had hold of her ankle and used it to pull her toward him. "I think there are many ways to spar, love, so let's try a bit of mattress wrestling. You've wanted this from the beginning, admit it."

Only on her terms, not his. She relaxed her right leg and Cage's grasp loosened; when she shot out her left leg and slammed her foot into his shoulder, he had to release her to break his own backward momentum. Advantage: eagle. "So sorry. Did you hit your head on the concrete?"

He wiped his hand across his temple, and the fingers came away bloody. Which reminded her . . .

Robin slipped the tiny pocketknife from her pocket and flicked it open, waving it in the air to make sure he saw it.

"Robin." His voice held a warning. "Don't test me."

She drew the knife across the base of her throat, just an inch-long cut where her clavicle met her sternum. It wasn't a silver blade, nor was it very sharp, nor was the cut deep. But it made a little trickle of blood she'd barely registered before Cage lunged, pinning her to the mat, his heavy weight on top of her.

"Taste me, Cage."

He wanted to; she could see it. His eyes had lightened even more, as silvery as they were green. His breathing had turned ragged, and he'd fixated on her neck. The blood tickled as it seeped out and ran toward her shoulder. She whispered, "Do it."

"Damn you, little bird." He dropped his mouth to the edge of her shirt, nearest her shoulder, and the swipe of his tongue was pure silk as it traced the line of blood back to the cut. He groaned as he took a light pull on the cut, or at least Robin thought he did. The sensation when Mirren had bonded her felt nothing like this. That had been a burst of power, where this was power and sex and thunder and lightning all rolled into one, coming in waves and settling into her core.

"Touch me."

Cage raised his head, his lips stained from her blood, eyes unfocused, breath ragged. "What?"

She ran her fingers down his arm until she reached his hand, then pulled it to rest between her thighs. "Touch me. Please."

"We can't do this." Cage sat up, jerked the cord out of his hair to let it spill free, and threw it across the floor.

Robin took a deep breath, her brain finally engaging again. "What just happened?" Had she begged him to touch her? She didn't beg. Ever.

He looked up at her with his silvery eyes, running the edge of his tongue along the edge of his bloodstained lips, and she knew she could lose herself in him and it would be okay. Because he'd always bring her back to herself in the end. She could lose herself but not be lost.

It was the scariest fucking thought she'd ever had.

"Have you ever heard about the mating of Mirren and Glory?"

Robin thumped herself in the head, because he couldn't really have asked that question. "We just backed away from the edge of the best-sex-of-our-lives cliff because you want to talk about *Mirren Kincaid?*" No wonder the Americans had kicked the Brits' asses in the Revolution; those people had serious emotional issues.

Cage grinned. "We haven't backed so far off that cliff we can't return to it, sweetheart."

He got up, walked to the door of the mill, and flipped both dead bolts. When he got to the edge of her mat, he dropped on all fours again and crawled toward her, looking sexy and predatory and hungry, and by God that was her role. She flipped him on his back with a hard shove and sat on his stomach, digging her knees into the mat on either side of his waist to hold him in place.

"Well, isn't this an interesting position? I rather like it." He molded a big hand around each of her thighs and shoved her back until she could feel the hard ridge of him pressed against her. As badly as she wanted not to let him know it got to her, she had to move against him. Just a few times, rocking back and forth, the friction of their clothing adding to the heat until she—

He flipped her again, and she let out a long, shuddering breath. Damn it. So close. "Asshole."

He continued as if nothing had interrupted. "So Mirren and Glory had this incredible chemistry, or so the story goes, and she was his familiar. But one day, they got rather carried away and fed and fucked all at the same time, and a funny thing happens to vampires in such a situation."

Okay, maybe he did have a point in his rambling. "What kind of funny thing?" Because it sounded pretty damn sexy—or it would if it were she and Cage and not the big old hulking Scotsman.

"It's called a bond-mating ritual in the vampire world." He wedged a knee between her legs and rolled on top of her again, lowering his mouth to her neck, creating the most delicious scrape of fang against her skin but not biting. He stopped with his mouth just above her ear and whispered, "It's a lifelong bond. Literally until death you do part."

"What?" Robin shoved him away, and he fell back on the mat, laughing.

"I thought that would get your attention, since you're all about getting attention tonight." He had a silly laugh, almost a giggle. It was the first time she'd heard it; she would've remembered. Yeah, it was sexy coming from him.

"So did that qualify as feeding? I mean there has to be more to it than that."

He smiled up at her, and there was nothing silly about his chuckle or the dark undercurrent of need in his eyes. "No, that wasn't a true feeding. Actually, creating a mating bond requires a blood exchange, so you'd have to taste me as well as the feeding and fucking."

"Then we're not in danger of repeating history?"

"No, because I'm not going to feed from you, as badly as I want to. Just that taste . . ." His eyes lightened at the memory, which corresponded with the tightening Robin felt in her gut. He'd felt the magic as strongly as she had. "I don't know what it would do to us, a full feeding, and we have to be able to move fast if anything happens."

When something happened. There was no doubt in Robin's mind that events were escalating.

She crawled toward him and stretched out on top of him, her arms slipping beneath his so she could prop on her elbows. "You aren't feeding from me, and I don't plan to bite you, at least not hard enough to draw blood. That leaves one option on the table."

His hands rested on her waist for only a second before he slid one hand between them and touched her. Finally touched her where she'd needed him all night. She'd thought the sensation had passed, but the barest pressure of his fingers and the need for him roared to life inside her.

"The look on your face right now is something I will dream about," he murmured, rolling them over again and jerking her shirt over her head. "And these. I've already dreamt of these."

His mouth latched onto one breast, sucking so hard she thought she might die of pleasure or her nipple might come off, and she didn't really care which as long as he didn't stop. He released it with a gasp and looked at his handiwork. "Beautiful, red. Too much?"

She couldn't speak, just shook her head. "Then I should make the other one match, yes?"

She nodded. "Uh-huh."

God, what a talented mouth. Robin threw her head back and just felt. Gave her brain permission to vacate the premises, as she began to slowly rock against him. Clothes, damn it. Too many clothes.

Cage released her breast with a pop. "Nicely matched now."

"Take off your fucking sweater." She clawed at the fabric, tugging it up, up, until he finally grasped it and jerked it over his head while she moved to the buttons on her jeans.

"Stand up. I want to see you." Cage lifted her off him, leaving her little choice but to stand. He shook back that glorious hair and kept his gaze pinned to hers as he finished unbuttoning the jeans, sliding them down her hips, latching his fingers onto her panties along the way.

Only when they got far enough for her to step out of them did he lower his gaze. She heard his breath hitch, followed by a soft curse.

"I shave it, just in case you think shifters don't have hair down south," she said, loving the way his eyes caressed her, and she adjusted her stance with her legs farther apart to accommodate his exploring fingers. "It also makes me feel . . . oh . . ."

He replaced his fingers with his mouth, sucking hard on her clit the way he'd caught her breasts. Robin cried out when her knees gave way, but he wrapped his arms around her and lowered her to the mat, never stopping his assault with lips and tongue and fingers until she wasn't sure what was moving where, only that it was building and building and she heard herself cry out with a primitive plea that bypassed her brain entirely.

And then he stopped. Blew warm air on her clit until she shivered and ached. God, how she ached for him.

Emptiness, then cool air. "Damn it, you can't . . ." She propped up on her elbows and stopped breathing at the sight of him, the hard planes of his body in the gentle play of the lights, and his own jeans on the floor next to hers. His cock was long and ready for her, and she liked that at least a little of the blood fueling that hard-on had come from her. He was every bit as beautiful as she'd imagined.

"Can't what, love? Can't do this?" He dropped to his knees and shoved her legs apart, lowering his mouth to her again until she was aching for him—again. "Or maybe this." He raised his head and turned it to kiss her inner thigh, and then she felt a sting of pain as he bit, took one quick draw of blood, and sent her off the edge of that cliff. He slid his mouth up the length of her body as the shudders sent her dizzy and spinning.

Her breathing returned to normal, but she was still shivering when he whispered her name. "Robin, look at me." She opened her eyes and lifted her head. He was poised over her left breast, her nipple still a rosy red from his attention. He licked his tongue slowly over it, circled it, and she saw the fangs just before he bit on the soft underside. This time she didn't even feel pain, just the drowning, heaving ocean of mindless pleasure.

She came with a great, frenzied call to the heavens and before she was done, he was inside her, filling her as surely as she knew he would, not being gentle or cautious as she feared he would, but grinding her into the mat with every thrust.

And when he came, it was his turn to cry out to whatever being had given them this moment of beauty and joy in the middle of their disintegrating world.

❧CHAPTER 22❧

If Nik had come barreling into Robin's bedroom at the comm-house thirty seconds later, Cage might at least have been wearing trousers. As it was, he had to treat the human to the scenic view while holding his jeans—well, technically Aidan's jeans—in one hand while holding his finger over his lips with the other.

Nik looked at Robin, rolled his eyes, threw up his hands, and stomped back into the hallway.

By the time Cage joined him in the living room a couple minutes later, Nik had collapsed on the sofa, black shaggy hair askew, clearly in a temper.

"Sorry about that." Cage patted his pockets, looking for his cell phone. Next hiding spot he checked was the end table, and then the coffee table that had been knocked aside when he and Robin got started on round two of the sexual Olympics—or was it round three?—on the sofa.

"Looking for this?" Nik held up the small black phone. "It was on the floor in the hall. Which I know because it started ringing a half hour ago. Apparently, one of the vampire lieutenants isn't where he's supposed to be and it's a half hour until dawn. No one's seen him since ten o'clock last night."

Like he was in any danger of missing sunrise? "We don't exactly catnap, you know." Cage stuck the phone in his pocket. "I'm not likely to forget such a momentous event, which takes place daily, by the way. Haven't missed one in seventy-five years. I'll make it with five minutes to spare." Though he had to admit—but only to himself—that time had gotten away from him and he'd have to hurry more than he'd like.

"Yeah, well, expect a lecture from Mirren when you get there. He's in a temper."

"I hate to break it to you, but he's always in a temper."

"Whatever."

Mirren wasn't the only one in a temper, and Cage had to wonder if his being with Robin might bother Nik more than he'd thought it would. After all, Nik was a friend she occasionally had sex with. For Cage's part, while that fact hadn't bothered him yesterday, it now bothered him a lot. A whole lot.

He needed to bring the subject into the open. "Look, about Robin. We—"

Nik waved him off. "Robin's my friend. Nothing you can do will change that. If you make her happy, go for it. You both deserve it. I'm just enjoying a hangover from using the Touch too much yesterday, first going through the burned house and then with the flyer. I need to sleep it off, which is hard to do with insomnia."

Cage started to tell him to sleep all he wanted because Robin should be plenty tired and sleeping late herself. He thought better of it. "Need anything before I leave?"

Nik waved a hand in the air, which Cage interpreted as a negative, so he let himself out the back door and set off in a straight, speedy clip for the Quik Mart. No time to lay false trails this morning; if a killer jaguar was stalking him—or a coyote—he couldn't do much about it.

Mirren waited in the hallway, much as Nik had anticipated. "Where the fuck have you been?"

"Laying about." And inside and around and, hell, maybe upside down.

"Well, keep your phone on you next time you"—Mirren reached out and held out the bottom of the brown sweater Cage wore, which now had a big hole in it—"go laying about. Hell, you didn't feed from her, did you?"

Cage grinned. "And end up accidentally mated? Hell no. I like to forge my own way, and I hear that's been done already, mate."

"Fuck you, Reynolds. Here's a new path for you to forge." Mirren shoved a forearm against Cage's sternum and stalked back toward his room.

Cage hit the floor hard and got up rubbing his ass. The look on Mirren's face had been worth every ounce of pain.

He entered his daysleep thinking of soft kisses and hard, pounding flesh, and he came out of it worrying. What had he been thinking, locking himself away a whole night when the world could be on the verge of coming down around their heads? He'd come back to Penton to protect it and find a home, not let Rome burn while he fiddled away in the old mill with a woman.

An amazing woman, admittedly—but Robin Ashton did not have a role in his game plan. Maybe after all of this was over he'd revise that plan, but not now. She was too big a distraction.

He spotted her when he entered the mill for the town meeting, sitting next to Nik on the big wooden spool. He gave them a casual wave and moved to where Aidan and Krys sat, but not before he noticed Robin's narrowing eyes and lowering brows. She wasn't going to make it easy to step away.

They'd either lost more people or some had stayed away—probably the latter. Cage counted fifteen vampires, including himself; eight humans, including Nik Dimitrou; and one known shifter, Robin. Fen had come in early, and Shawn had slipped in right before Mirren and Glory. Of Britta Eriksen, there was no sign. If she were innocent and realized they suspected her of being a plant, missing this meeting was bad form indeed. If she were guilty, well, it made her look guiltier. He'd never said two words to the woman, so he didn't know enough to form an opinion.

Perhaps if he'd spend more time learning Penton's new players and less time learning his way around one sexy little woman, he might remedy that.

When everyone had found seats, either in the chairs Mark and Melissa had brought in with Nik's help, or on the mats, Aidan walked into the middle of the group. Off to one side, Mirren leaned against the wall near the door like Earth's biggest sentinel.

Silence fell immediately when Aidan held up the flyer. "First off, in case you haven't heard, this is a fake. Somebody took a photo of Will, put it on another body using computer software, and made it look as if he'd been tortured. I talked to him this morning, and he and Randa are fine. They should be back in Penton in about a week."

He talked about psychological warfare and even asked Cage to elaborate.

"Remember the stories from World War II about Tokyo Rose?" A few nodded—several of the vampires had already been turned at that time, but likely most of the older ones had paid little attention to the war unless they lived in a place where fighting would impact their feeding. "Well, Tokyo Rose wasn't a single person, but was the pseudonym, if you will, for a group of Japanese women who had an English-language radio show broadcast throughout Europe and the Pacific. Tokyo Rose would report so-called news about the war, and the soldiers and Navy men and flyers would listen to it. The reports were mostly false, and the whole point was to destroy the morale of the Allied troops."

Fen spoke up. "Say you're right about this being psychological warfare. How do we know the reports are false? I mean, after the fact, sure. But once you see something like that flyer, isn't the damage already done?"

"You have to assume that it's a lie," Aidan said. "Anything you see like this, or anything you hear, come and talk to me or Mirren or Cage. During daylight hours, those of you who aren't in day-sleep, talk to Nik or Robin over there—they're our newest Omega team members. If we don't know the answer, give us time to find out before you make a rash decision. Another week, and I think things will improve."

One of the human fams, a guy named Rusty who'd been in town before everything went to hell, stood up. "Aidan, what about Matthias Ludlam? I heard he was out?"

Hell. Cage watched eyes widen and people lean over to whisper to each other. Aidan had been able to keep the news about Matthias quiet until now, which made him wonder who spilled it to Rusty. Still, maybe it was for the best that people knew. They'd either leave or they wouldn't.

"He escaped, but no one has seen or heard from him," Aidan said. "All I can tell you is that we're doing our best to keep everyone safe, but be on your guard. Travel in pairs. Don't take off without letting someone know where you're going. Keep your cell phones charged and within reach."

Aidan paced around for a full minute, and everyone fell quiet, waiting to see what was next. "Okay, look. I'm just going to ask.

Has anyone seen a strange animal around town or in the woods outside town?"

"Stranger than that ugly bloodhound of Hannah's?" Rusty asked, which got a chuckle even from Aidan. That was one ugly dog, Cage had to admit, but Barnabas had probably kept Hannah sane.

"I'm particularly looking for info about a coyote or a black big cat, like a jaguar."

Well, that brought the silence again. Finally, a scathe member from Florida stood up. "I saw a big black cat last week, but I just thought it was cool. I grew up not far from here, and there were always rumors that there were bobcats and black panthers in this area. I just thought maybe it was one of them, venturing out of the woods because there are so few people around here now."

"Where was it?" Aidan asked. "What was it doing?"

"It was kind of funny, because it was slinking out of that greenhouse that you used to keep over by your house on Mill Trace—not far from the collapsed end of the clinic."

Yeah, Cage knew exactly where it was. That greenhouse had a door into a tunnel that led to the suite of rooms beneath the clinic itself. The tunnel had collapsed after he'd used it to help Melissa escape Matthias earlier this summer, but it was possible someone could've dug enough debris out to stay in one of the rooms. There was no electricity, but portable lighting was easy to buy.

"Thanks, Joy," Aidan said. "Anyone else?"

While a discussion about the size and coloring of jaguars ensued, Cage saw Aidan look over at Mirren and give a slight nod. Then the big guy crooked a finger at Cage and walked outside.

Good. Cage was tired of talking, and it looked like a trip to the tunnel was in his future. On his way out, he looked back and expected to find Robin watching him. She wasn't, and that annoyed him more than it should have.

It took Mirren and Cage ten minutes to walk to the old neighborhood on Trace Way, stopping at the comm-house first to get a couple of high-powered flashlights. Before all the shit began with Matthias Ludlam's first attack on Penton last January, Aidan had lived here near the end of a cul-de-sac, with Mark and Melissa next door. Now, both houses lay in burned rubble and ruin, but the glass greenhouse that stretched from the house to the edge of Aidan's property remained intact.

The plants inside should by all rights have been dead, but a few hardy green ones dotted the greenhouse shelves.

"The tunnel was still clear up through that first suite last time I was in here," Mirren said, walking toward the back corner where the trapdoor lay beneath a layer of artificial turf and a pile of flowerpots. "I was with Glory, and it was just before Matthias had his big show downtown that sent us into the Omega facility. So you've been here since then—is that part still open?"

"I'm not sure." The steel-framed room at the foot of the ladder had still been clear, and he tried to remember whether or not the cave-in had blocked the tunnel altogether. The memories were fuzzy, though. He'd been shot, trying to get Melissa to safety, and had been pretty certain he was about to die.

They shone their flashlights over the stuff piled on top of the trapdoor. "If it's been moved recently, whoever moved it did a good job of camouflaging it." Cage knelt and studied the edges of the turf. The dirt around it didn't look as if it had been disturbed, but it wouldn't be that hard to lift the whole thing up—especially for a shape-shifter.

"So, in your *dealings* with Robin, did you ever get around to asking her if she could, I don't know, smell another shifter?" Mirren began studying the dirt floor of the greenhouse, probably looking for footprints—or paw prints. "I mean if she ran into Mr. Coyote or Mr. Jaguar in human form, would she know?"

That had been one of the few coherent conversations he and Robin *had* managed to work into their busy evening. "In my *dealings* with Robin, we did talk about that. She says sometimes yes, sometimes no. I think it's like us with other vampires. An older, savvier vamp can scent out another vamp whereas a younger one, or one who's too self-absorbed to pay attention to what's around him? Probably not."

"That's a fucking lot of help." Mirren walked to the corner and pulled the turf mat aside, revealing the trapdoor. He pulled a small ring of keys from his pocket but pulled on the door's metal ring before trying any of them. The hatch top lifted off easily. "Wasn't locked." He trained his flashlight beam into the hole. "Nothing looks out of place."

Cage had already decided that, short of a life-threatening emergency, he wasn't going down there. He'd managed before only out of sheer desperation. Melissa had to be gotten out of Matthias's clutches, and working through the tunnel had been the only way to do it. Plus, his gunshot wound had helped to distract him from any claustrophobic panic. Today, Mirren would have to shoot him to get him down there.

"You going, or am I?" Mirren planted his hands on his hips and gave Cage a look that probably meant *I'm a lot bigger than you and it would be easier for you to crawl down in that hole.*

"Go ahead, knock yourself out." Cage stepped back and pretended to examine the blackened remains of a hibiscus.

Mirren grumbled a few names in his direction and climbed down the ladder, his glaring gray eyes the last thing Cage saw.

"Come down here." The voice might as well have come from hell itself, but the tone brooked no argument. Cage took a deep breath and lowered himself into the bowels of the earth. Somehow the daysleep spaces never felt underground, so it was easy to psych himself out.

Once he reached the bottom, he realized it wasn't so bad. Inside the steel-lined room at the bottom of the ladder, he could still look up and see stars and open sky. The narrow, low-ceilinged tunnel might be another story.

His breath grew labored the second he stepped into the entry room and his view of the open trapdoor was obscured. He would not hyperventilate in front of the Slayer, by God, if he had to stick his fangs into his own lip to distract himself.

Not necessary, as it turned out. The blood scent hit him the instant he got two feet from the tunnel entrance. "What the hell *is* it?"

"Dunno, but it's the blood of a vampire. I thought we better go in together." Mirren's uncharacteristic caution was in itself worthy of panic.

Mirren grasped the wheel that opened the steel door into the tunnel. Whoever had been behind that door had bled. A lot. Recently.

He looked back. "You ready?"

Cage nodded. "Sure." Hell no, he wasn't ready.

Mirren wrenched open the door to the tunnel, and the blood stench hit them like a physical blast. Cage lost his balance and had to lean propped against the wall a few heartbeats to make sure he could stay upright. Even Mirren had to pause and catch his breath.

"Okay, let's see what we're dealing with."

Cage followed him through the door and for several long seconds they stood side by side, silent, trying to understand what lay before them.

Two long wooden beams, probably taken from the collapsed tunnel beyond them, had been erected in an X shape and nailed to the wall.

Pinned to the St. Andrew's cross with long silver knives that had been used to pierce her hands, shoulders, thighs, and ankles as if she were a butterfly being attached to a board, was a woman. Those wounds had bled, but most of the blood appeared to have come from her chest, which had been splayed open. The front of her clothing was drenched with blood, and it had formed large dark pools on the concrete floor.

Her head hung forward, dark hair obscuring her face.

"Holy fuck." Mirren looked at Cage as if asking permission to touch her. Cage nodded. They had to see, God forbid, if she was anyone they knew.

Mirren stepped beside her, placed two fingers beneath her chin, and raised her head. He flinched. "Fuck me. She's still alive."

They still hadn't gotten a good look at her. Holding his flashlight with his left hand and directing the beam at her face, Cage reached out with his right and brushed her hair aside.

Fear shot from his scalp to his boots. "Britta?"

❦ CHAPTER 23 ❧

W hat's eating you? Or should I say who?"

Nik grabbed Robin's hand on their way out of the mill and tucked it into the crook of his elbow as if they were prom dates. He hated seeing her unhappy, so whatever Cage had done, the vampire better undo.

"Where'd Cage and Mirren go again?" Robin pulled out her cell phone and checked the time. "It's almost two a.m. Let's see if they're still there."

So completely not what he had in mind. "You heard Mirren. We need to be on shifter watch during daylight hours—so, you know, sleep?" He was so tired he could probably zonk out standing barefoot on the cracked and broken pavement of the mill's parking lot.

"I'll sleep when I'm dead." They'd almost reached the steps to Mirren and Glory's comm-house, but Robin stopped and pulled him back toward the street, where his SUV sat beneath the streetlamp. "C'mon. At least drive me by there, wherever it is. Then we'll sleep. It'll be relaxing."

"What are we, in junior high? You want me to drive you past your boyfriend's house and see if he's home?"

Nik did know where they'd gone, though. Mark had given him the grand tour of the Penton-That-Was on their errand-filled afternoon, one of the highlights of which was the street where Aidan, Mark, and Melissa used to live, and the greenhouse where Aidan grew night-blooming plants to keep him connected to the soil and to life.

Oh, what the hell. She'd brought up the subject, and now his curiosity was aroused. It wouldn't hurt to drive by there. If Mirren shot them for intruding, at least then he'd get some rest. Unless he died.

"They've been gone for two hours, so chances are we'll have missed them," Nik pointed out, climbing into the SUV. "You had to have a snack. Then you had to play with the punching bags."

"Blah blah blah. Just drive."

He headed north, hoping he'd recognize the location of the turnoff in the dark. The juice had been cut off to everything north of the clinic. "So, what was it like? Did Cage do it?"

Robin stared at him, a slow grin lighting up her face like one of those dimmer switches being turned up to illuminate a room. "You want sex details? Why Niko, I'm shocked."

He'd taken a sip of water from a bottle he'd swiped out of the mill gym's mini fridge; he choked on it when he realized what she thought he'd asked. By the time he got the coughing under control, Robin had spilled out everywhere she and Reynolds had done it. "Damn, Robin. Shut the hell up. I'll never be able to touch one of those gym mats again without a can of Lysol. Shit."

"Hey, you asked." She laughed, and the sound was so infectious he couldn't help chuckling himself.

"I meant *feeding*. I wondered if he fed from you after Mirren said not to. Holy Mother of God, I didn't want to hear the rest of that. Glory's *sofa*? If Mirren finds out you and Reynolds fucked on his sofa, you are both going to be roadkill."

"He won't know unless you tell him." Robin smiled. "I like Cage."

He glanced over at her. "*Like* like? Or *love* like?"

She didn't answer, and at first he thought she'd fallen asleep. In which case he was turning this rig around and going to bed.

"It's not that simple with shifters, you know."

Nik had always wondered about Robin's family and what her life had been like before she'd moved to New Orleans. It was as if she'd sprung fully grown and fully formed into her lower French Quarter third-story flat, not far from his family home. He was curious but respected her enough to avoid being nosy.

"You know if you ever want to talk about your life before, I'm here, right? No pressure. Just if you ever want to."

Her voice was soft. "I know."

The case in Houston they'd just finished had involved a wolf shifter who'd basically been sold by her parents into an arranged marriage. Robin had been even more infuriated by it than the rest of the team, and she was impatient with the woman for not going against her family sooner. It had made Nik wonder what the eagle-shifter culture was like. He'd done some research into the wild raptors, the golden eagles. They mated for life. They spent most of their lives in a fairly small area. They were expert trackers and hunters.

Yet here was little Robin, an expert tracker, but one who was ready to hit the road and go wherever it took her, keeping people at arm's length. So who knew? She'd tell him when she wanted, and not a second before. He had to respect that.

"Where are we going again? A greenhouse? Why would a vampire have a greenhouse?"

"It was Aidan's. The way I heard it, he was a farmer back in Ireland, and this was a way he could still work the land. And greenhouses hold sunlight, so I think it helped him stay in touch with who he was before he was turned."

He drove slowly once they'd passed the clinic, and he made a right onto Mill Trace Lane. "It should be up here on the right. I think we missed Cage, though. The whole street looks dark and empty." In fact, if he hadn't known the greenhouse was there, they wouldn't have found it. This far in the country, dark meant *really* dark.

"You got a flashlight? Let's look around as long as we're here."

Nik's inner voice, which he usually heard in the form of his grandfather Costa, told him this was probably a bad idea, but he pulled over and killed the truck. "I have flashlights in the hatch, in the toolbox."

"Always prepared." Robin hopped out, and by the time he got to the hatch, she was holding out the largest flashlight and had the other tucked under her arm. "Okay, where is this greenhouse?" She looked around and zeroed in on what looked to Nik like a big black blank. "Never mind. I see it."

"You see it? I don't see it." He squinted into the night, but if not for the flashlight he wouldn't have been able to see an inch in front of his nose.

"I'm a raptor shifter, remember? We're night hunters."

Great, something else about which to feel inferior. Nik followed her through the overgrown side yard, scanning the ground for debris so he wouldn't trip over it and add that embarrassment to a collection that had begun when Robin had doubled his bench-press maximum in her first Ranger School workout.

"Wait." He knelt and traced the flashlight beam over the area he'd just passed. "There's a wet trail here."

Robin squatted next to it, reached out, and scrubbed a fingertip over the grass. She lifted it into the beam of his flashlight. "Blood, and it's fresh." She lifted it to her nose. "It's vampire, not human."

"How can you tell?"

While they talked, they'd been following the path of blood drops and ended up at the greenhouse. "It doesn't have that iron scent like human blood; it's richer, or meatier or something. I don't know—I just had that one little freakout sip from Mirren. I just know it smelled different."

"The scent seems stronger in here." Nik led the way into the greenhouse, which before the Penton siege had probably been a beautiful place. Most of the plants were long dead.

"And strongest back here." Robin knelt and dragged aside a turf mat that had been pulled over a trapdoor of some kind.

"I think we should wait—"

She'd already pulled open the hatch, so no point in finishing that sentence. All he could do was follow her into the bowels of the earth and try to ignore Pop Costa's dire warnings.

By the time he reached the bottom of the ladder, she'd disappeared into a doorway that branched off to the side through a heavy steel air-lock-type door. *Damn it, Robin.* He stepped through the blood-spattered doorway and swung the arc of his flashlight up and onto something that surely to God was a torture rack straight out of one of Dante's inner circles of hell.

"Look." Robin had knelt again, and he followed her gaze with the flashlight beam. A silver knife lay on the floor. "I'm not touching it. I think it's silver and not steel."

Shifters could touch silver without danger, but a silver-inflicted wound, unless superficial, would kill them. Even if Nik did feel physically inferior sometimes, being human was much simpler.

"Leave it there, Robin. We'll let Mirren and Cage come back for it if they need to see it." Then again, damn it, he liked these Penton people. Didn't he have an obligation to help them if he could? "No, on second thought, I want to use the Touch on that knife."

"No." Robin took her shoe and shoved the knife away from him. "You've had two nosebleeds today, and I know that means you're overdoing it. You don't know what the long-term effects are, Niko. I'll wrap it in something, and you can do it tomorrow if you feel like it."

He knew better than to argue with that tone, but it didn't mean he had to do what she said. "Sure, okay. Maybe there's something over there in that rubble to wrap it in. Fabric, or plastic sheeting."

"I'll look." She walked over to the head of the collapsed tunnel. "This thing led all the way into the clinic subsuites, didn't it? It must have taken them forever to build all this."

While she dug in the debris and chattered about the brilliance of the Penton infrastructure, he took a deep breath and walked to where the knife lay. As soon as he wrapped his hand around it, the burning pain hit him. Like when he'd held the glass, only stronger. Such rage, and such pain.

He dropped to his knees and held the knife with both hands, willing not just the emotions to come, but the images. Finally, they filled his mind, vivid images in bright, nightmare-inducing color.

Britta, pinned to the St. Anthony's cross by knives.

A jaguar, lapping up the blood at her feet.

Fen Patrick, with blood on his chin.

Then it was all gone, and Robin was holding his head in her lap and talking in a nonstop, soft drone. "Nik, you idiot. You beautiful, sweet idiot."

He tried twice before choking out the words. "Get me out of here, Robin. Help me. It's bad this time." He'd never reached out for the images before; he'd always let them come to him. Good to know he could summon them if he tried; bad to know it could kill him.

She tried to pull him to his feet, but he couldn't stay upright. Finally, she pulled his right arm around her slim shoulders and lifted his weight. "You're gonna have to climb out. I can't carry you up the ladder, but I can push you from behind. Think you can hang on?"

"Or die trying." He'd try to climb to the stars if it would give him one fresh breath of air, away from the smell of death and the vision of Britta Eriksen hanging on that cross.

Each rung of the metal drop ladder was harder to heft himself onto than the one before it, but when his head finally cleared the opening of the hatch, he gulped enough fresh air to give him the energy to finish the climb. He collapsed on the floor of the greenhouse and waited while Robin closed up the hatch and replaced the turf mat.

"I've gotta see Aidan now." He tried to get up but couldn't. "Gimme a minute." He closed his eyes and waited. His equilibrium would come back. It just took a while, and Robin was right. He'd overdone it.

He was moving and realized Robin was mostly carrying him toward the SUV.

Then he was in the passenger seat, the truck was bumping along the road, and Robin was talking as if from a long distance.

Then he awoke, and the sun was out, and he was naked, and Robin was curled up beside him.

Everything was a blur except for the most important things: Fen Patrick. The jaguar. Britta.

He sat up, waiting for the dizziness to pass, and was pleased that it did. He scrambled on the nightstand for his watch. Shit. It was almost noon, and there was no way to reach Aidan or Mirren until dusk. The only good part? Fen Patrick couldn't be creating havoc during daysleep.

"You okay?" Robin sat up, her hair stuck in about forty directions, her mouth stretched wide in a yawn.

"Thanks for taking care of me last night." He leaned over and kissed her cheek. "Think you can help me do some sleuthing today, before the vampires wake up?"

"Coffee, shower, coffee, more coffee, then sleuthing." She crawled off the bed and shuffled toward the door. Nik stood, monitored his balance, and walked to the mirror to check out his face. He'd been covered in blood, that much he did remember. Another nosebleed, plus he'd grasped that knife pretty hard. He held out his hands; shallow cuts made horizontal swaths across both palms where he'd held onto the blade. Nothing serious, but Robin must've had a big cleanup job.

Could Britta have lived? Was Fen the source of the rage and the hunger? Who was the coyote, and was Fen working with him?

All he'd done was get more questions and no answers. But at least they had a place to start, and Cage needed to tell Aidan everything he could about Fen Patrick.

᪥CHAPTER 24᪥

Matthias had always prided himself on his appearance. He'd enjoyed the finest things his wealth had afforded him since graduating from being a human attorney serving the privileged class, to one of the vampire elite, heavily involved in the Tribunal's investments and well-compensated for it, both in what they paid him and what he took.

Tailored suits, silk ties, and Italian leather filled his closets. His salt-and-pepper hair had always been stylishly cut—whatever the style du jour happened to be.

Now, he looked in the mirror at a stranger whose hair fell out in clumps when he tried to comb it. Who found clothing itchy and hot, as if ants crawled across his skin wherever it touched him.

Who was always so very, very hungry.

Wolfgang no longer came to his room but sent a silent guard not unlike the one who'd tended his cell in Virginia. He always brought a bag of blood and a plate of food. Beautifully prepared food. Always a succulent roasted meat with potatoes and vegetables and bread. A dessert—the Austrians knew how to make pastries to make a grown man weep.

Especially a man who was starving but whose body rejected any food he ate.

A man who had to drink blood to stay alive but whose body found it nauseating.

So when the doorknob jangled, the lock turned, and he looked up to see Frank Greisser striding in with his fine jacket and polished shoes and healthy good looks, Matthias knew there was someone on this earth he now hated as much as the Penton Five. And he knew if he got a chance, and if he were as patient and cunning as his captor, he would kill Herr Greisser.

After making sure Matthias had seen the armed guards in the hallway, Frank closed the door and came to a stop before the chair in which Matthias sat, looking him over. "You appear unwell, my friend. But I have news that will make you feel better."

"If you told me the entire town of Penton and everyone in it were dead, their blood running in the streets and their heads on pikes around the town square, it would *not* make me feel better." Matthias rose and was glad to see Frank take a step back. "What the fuck have you been giving me in those injections?"

Frank cocked his head and looked Matthias over again. "How have they made you feel?"

"Like death itself." Matthias walked to the table and held up his bag of blood. "I need this to live, yet it sickens me." He lifted the dome of his tray to reveal a beautifully browned duck with a citrus glaze. "I crave this, its aroma taunts me, and yet I can't eat it."

He threw the shiny dome at Frank's smirking face. "So I repeat: what the hell is in those injections?"

Frank looked at the floor, and when his gaze fell on Matthias again, it was . . . excited. The man was mad.

"What if I told you that with one more injection, you will be able to eat again. And more, Matthias. You will be able to walk in sunlight."

Matthias sat in his chair again, stunned. He'd pinned the hopes for his future on a madman. "We are vampires, Frank. We don't eat food. We don't walk in sunlight."

"But what if after a series of simple injections and some temporary discomfort, we could be more? Have our immortality and strength, and yet be able to live among humans? Get our nourishment in whatever form we like—from the vein or from the plate? No longer worry about vaccinated blood? Aidan Murphy and his soldiers can't offer our people a way to survive this pandemic vaccine crisis, but with this, the Tribunal can."

Matthias didn't know how to respond to such a ridiculous speech, so he didn't. He only knew he wasn't going to accept another syringe full of Frank's magic potion.

Frank walked to the table and picked up the bag of blood. "Did you realize you'd been feeding on vaccinated blood for the past two days?"

A chill stole across Matthias's shoulder blades, turning his skin ice-cold. "That isn't possible."

And yet he couldn't help but think about his feeding for the past couple of days. The bags themselves had been opaque instead of clear; he'd attributed the change to the supplier. The blood had tasted more metallic, but he'd blamed the difference on his changing appetite.

If what Frank said were true . . .

"What have you done, Frank?"

With growing wonder, he listened.

❦ CHAPTER 25 ❦

Robin followed Nik into the community house Fen had called home since recuperating from the fire. He shared the space with Shawn and three other scathe members. Originally they'd thought Hannah might move there, but she'd latched onto Nik, and he didn't seem to mind, so it was easier for her to stay at Mirren's.

"Don't you feel kind of criminal doing this?" She watched as Nik picked the back-door lock with a deft hand, popping the dead bolt as if it were made of tin foil.

"Not in extenuating circumstances, which these are." Nik eased the door open. "Only vampires are living in this comm-house, so we've got a good couple of hours to look around."

The house was nothing like Chez Kincaid. The furnishings were similar, but the warmth was absent. Robin had always hated that bit about the "woman's touch," but maybe it was true. Glory had made that sterile house into a home; even Robin thought of it that way. Though some of the vampires who lived here were women, so maybe it was the *human* touch.

"You know which room is his?"

"I'm guessing the one with no personal belongings. Whatever he had with him from Atlanta probably burned in the fire."

Robin had been thinking about that fire. "Fen's the one who got hurt. I mean, he was healed by the time he went through a day-sleep, but if he set the fire, why would he go in to rescue Hannah?"

Nik opened the middle room on the left and walked inside. "This is it. I recognize that hat." A red-and-blue Atlanta Braves cap sat atop the dresser; Robin had seen Fen wear it as well.

"As for your question, what better way to convince people you didn't set a fire than to get hurt trying to put it out?" Nik said. "Besides that, we figure Cage was the target, not Hannah. My bet is that if Cage were the one trapped, Fen wouldn't have gone in to save him."

"I guess. But there's something else that doesn't make sense."

Nik laughed. "There's a lot that doesn't make sense to me, but which thing in particular?"

"You saw the jaguar in your vision, along with Fen. Where does the coyote that set the fire come in? You think Fen's in league with two different shape-shifters?"

"Don't know. I've been thinking about that, too." Nik began pulling out dresser drawers, so Robin joined him. All were empty but one, and it had only a few clothes. "Okay, I'm girding my mental loins; get ready to haul me out of here."

He picked up each garment, careful to fold it back the way he'd found it. "Nothing. Fen hasn't been turned that long, and he's traveled a lot. He might have met some shifters during his merce-nary days, same way he met Cage."

What she really wondered was if Fen was *still* a mercenary. It might be worth a lot of money for a vampire to infiltrate his old buddy's lair and sabotage it, maybe even kill someone who was getting too close to the truth.

They spent the next hour searching Fen's room and going back through the burned house as well, trying to find anything they'd missed.

"We still have an hour until dusk." Robin waited while Nik popped the back-door lock back into place. "Maybe we don't start with asking questions about Fen. Maybe we start with Britta. Maybe we talk to Mark." At least Mark was human and therefore, theoretically at least, awake.

It took a fruitless trip to Aidan's house, a call to the clinic where Mark kept an office, and a drive around town, but they finally spotted Mark's small sedan parked in front of the Chow House.

"Great, I'm hungry." Robin had been wanting to come here, but this was her first chance. There always seemed to be crises to handle, psychics to rescue, vampires to seduce. Good times. But she'd had enough of Glory's leftovers to figure the fresh-made thing had to be even better.

Glory was packing up leftovers behind the counter when they entered. "Hey guys, you're in time to grab some of this before I send it home with Mark. Most of it's still hot."

"Whatcha got?" Robin looked over the red-and-white cardboard boxes, each with the name of the contents written on top in black ink. "How about the lasagna. Is it good?"

Glory laughed. "Well, I think so. Here." She handed her a heavy container the size of half a shoebox. "Eat whatever you want. And there are all kinds of sandwiches and some tortilla soup left."

Robin glanced around to locate Nik and was glad to see he'd joined Mark at the table in the corner. "You're meeting Mirren when he wakes, right? What's it like being, you know, tied to vampire hours?"

Glory leaned on the counter, grinning at Robin with a knowing expression she didn't much like. Big old Mirren was a big old gossip. At least the woman seemed to read Robin's mood, because she cleared her throat and offered no editorial comments to go along with the grin.

"It was hard at first because I wanted to stay up when he was up, and sleep when he was daysleeping, but it just wasn't practical. First, who sleeps that long? I'd wander around the daysleep space, talking to myself for hours, bored out of my skull. And I missed seeing the sun, feeling it on my skin. I mean, I'm sorry he can't enjoy it, but I can. Not gonna feel guilty about that. Besides, he says he can smell it on my skin and he likes that."

TMI. Robin didn't want to think about Mirren Kincaid's nose getting anywhere near her skin; she doubted that would ever happen unless her knuckle happened to collide with his face. Which, on second thought, might not be so far-fetched.

"Cage is a good guy." Glory raised an eyebrow, probably waiting to see if Robin was going to tell her to fuck off. But she was such a nice woman, Robin couldn't help but forgive the fact that she never stopped talking. "Melissa wouldn't have survived if he hadn't rescued her from Matthias. Maybe none of us would've survived because, eventually, if he tortured her enough, Mel might have slipped up and told him something he could've used to find us."

Yeah, yeah, Robin had heard about the great rescue. "Cage has that whole Superman thing down, all right. He wants to save everybody." Maybe she needed to have Nik tie her to a railroad trestle so he'd come running to rescue her for a change.

Where the hell had that thought come from? She wanted to be the predator. Since when had she started daydreaming about being prey?

"Well, if he has a savior complex, think of it this way." Glory finished packing up the boxes and grabbed her purse from behind the counter. "You like the guy, and if he didn't have that savior complex, he might be a different guy—one you didn't like."

By the time Robin devised a comeback, Glory had already gotten in her car and driven back toward the house. "I just want him to save me," she whispered, and then looked around to make sure no one had heard her.

Damn, but she was acting too much like a girl. She needed to fucking get over herself.

She grabbed the container of lasagna and a plastic fork and sat at the corner table next to Mark and across from Nik. She'd stuffed the second forkful of food into her mouth before she realized the tension level between the two men rested somewhere in the ozone.

"What happ'n?" She might not have the best manners in the world, but her mom had taught her not to talk with her mouth full. Sometimes she forgot.

Nik leaned back and scanned the big dining room, which was empty except for the three of them. "All that blood in the tunnel below the greenhouse? It was Britta's. Cage and Mirren found her."

Suddenly, the pasta covered in thick red tomato sauce didn't look so appealing. "She's dead?"

Mark shook his head. "No, but having your guts ripped open with a silver knife's a hard thing to heal, even for a vampire. Krys is keeping her in one of the rooms at the clinic that's still usable." He drummed his fingers on the table. "They locked her in her room, and I understand it. I just have a hard time believing she's in on any of this. The more I think about it, the more sure I am that she didn't leave those drugs for me."

Robin thought of how easily Nik had gotten in the back door of the house they'd just scoped out. It made the possibility that someone had broken into the house more real, which meant Britta might not be guilty at all—just a victim. Maybe a scapegoat.

"You got to know her pretty well?" she asked Mark. Britta had been feeding from him for a while, and although Robin still hadn't had the experience of a real feeding, she'd felt enough to know it had to make two people close.

"Yeah." Mark took a sip of beer. "She's a good kid. She got turned when she was twenty, about four or five years ago, and heard about Penton from some people in Atlanta—or heard about Aidan, rather."

"Is she friends with Fen Patrick?" Robin asked, wrinkling her nose at Nik giving her *the look*. It translated as *information on Fen Patrick isn't on Mark's need-to-know list.*

"Not in a good way." Mark smiled. "He kept coming on to her, and she thought he was a sleazebucket. Why? What does he have to do with it?"

"Nothing—just thought I'd seen them together," Robin said.

Nik pulled Robin's lasagna container across the table, and she handed him the plastic fork. He needed the nourishment. Using his Touch so often had given him a thin, strained look.

"She came in at the same time as the blonde, right?" Robin asked. "Shawn something?"

"Yeah, Shawn Nicholls, and . . . speak of the devil." Mark forced a smile to his face. Robin looked up to see Shawn coming in, then leaned her head sideways to read Nik's watch across the table. It was only 6:32 p.m. The vampire must've jumped out of her coffin and sprinted over here.

"Hey, guys, mind if I join you?" She pulled out the chair next to Nik, not waiting for a response, and leaned over to look on the plate. "Lasagna. I've heard Glory really knows how to cook."

Robin started to suggest she take a box home with her and head out now, but she gritted her teeth instead. Hard to talk through gritted teeth. She really needed to develop better manners, or so Nik kept telling her. Besides, he liked Shawn. He was cracking a joke. He was making eye contact. He was batting those long dreamboat, Greek-playboy eyelashes at her. The woman would be a puddle of horny vampire in no time.

He could do better. Robin would tell him later.

"Could I interest any of you in a feed?" Shawn looked hopefully from Nik to Mark and back to Nik. He'd lost enough blood the last two days to feed a hundred vampires, so that wasn't happening.

"Sure," Nik said. "Let's do it."

Let's do it? Who was this flirting cad, and what had he done with her best friend?

"Maybe you can speak Greek to me." Shawn had that kitten thing down.

Speak Greek? Oh, please. Nik had been born in New Orleans. He knew enough Greek to pronounce *souvlaki* correctly at a restaurant. She was not feeling the love for Shawn Nicholls.

Robin ignored Mark's smirk and sat with her arms crossed, showing great restraint when Shawn bumped shoulders with Nik and reached out to cover his hand with hers.

Nik flinched. Not an outright startled jump, but a definite flinch. He met Robin's gaze and frowned, jerking his head slightly toward Shawn the Oblivious, who was chattering about some restaurant she visited while doing a study-abroad program in Athens.

Nik interrupted Shawn but gave her a quick, reassuring smile. "Mark, can you give Robin a ride back to the house? I think Shawn and I are going somewhere more private."

Robin didn't like this one bit. Something was wrong.

Nik followed Shawn out but looked back at Robin before closing the door behind them. This look, she didn't know how to interpret.

Mark finished off his beer and turned to her. "You ready to go, or you want to find something else to eat?"

"I'll eat when I get back to the house." She pushed her chair back and stood up. Maybe Nik's look meant she needed to get hold of the lieutenants as soon as they surfaced for the evening and see if they could figure out what the whole Fen Patrick and jaguar thing meant. "I need to talk to Cage."

❦CHAPTER 26❦

Cage couldn't wait to get his hands on Fen Patrick. The bloody sonofabitch would wish he'd died back in Nicaragua or that his transition to vampire had been unsuccessful and his maker had left his dead, bloodless body in an alley.

Cage didn't approve of torture; he'd been on the receiving end of it in Paris, and Fen knew that. He knew it was something Cage could never do, nor would Cage expect it of anyone claiming to be his friend. Fen probably considered Cage's willingness to give him the benefit of a doubt to be his insurance policy.

Robin watched him from across the living room of Mirren's community house. She looked worried. He struggled between going to allay her fears and rampaging into the night to find his traitorous, backstabbing acquaintance—but he finally chose peace, for whatever time he could steal it.

When he sat on the floor next to her, she wrapped her arms around his waist and rested her head against his shoulder. His anger didn't dissipate, but he did take a deep breath and appreciate the comfort she offered. Who'd have thought his fierce little bird would turn out to have such a big heart?

Aidan sat at the end of the sofa, one leg jostling up and down in a nervous twitch. Mirren sat in the adjacent chair, on the phone, filling in Will and Randa about the latest developments.

But first, Robin had told them about her and Nik's fishing expedition at the tunnel. Cage didn't know what it meant—the images of the jaguar and of Fen and of that poor woman who had yet to regain consciousness. Guilty or innocent, nobody deserved to be brutalized in that way. Krys, Melissa, and Glory were with her now, trying to figure out how to help.

But he knew this: should it turn out that Fen Patrick had anything to do with what had been going on in Penton, he would kill the man. If it took the rest of his long vampire days, he would see him dead.

"This isn't your fault—you told them from the beginning that you didn't really trust him." Robin's voice was whisper soft.

"She's right," Aidan said, and Cage stifled a small smile at Robin's surprised expression. From a whisper to a scream, all sound was the same to a vampire. "You had no way of knowing he was up to something. Hell, we still don't know. We just need some answers."

Cage shook his head. "I knew that I never trusted him when he was human, mostly because he was cunning and treacherous and good at his job. And I know that becoming a vampire doesn't make a lamb out of a lion—or a jaguar."

Aidan shrugged. "All I know is, we—" He turned to Mirren with a frown as the big guy finished his phone call and slammed the phone onto the end table. "What's wrong? Is it Will?"

Thunderclouds had nothing on Mirren's expression. "Will's fine, but seems we haven't been keeping up with the news."

Cage rarely watched the news anymore. Over a long life, another war or another feud or another deadlocked American political system seemed like just so much empty drama. "What happened?"

"Ten bombings, scattered around the country in ten cities." He got up and began pacing. "Only one thing in common—all the buildings housed new blood banks containing unvaccinated donations. The media hasn't put that piece of it together yet, but they probably will. The colonel figured it out and just briefed Will and Randa."

Bloody hell. "How many blood banks had been set up?"

"That was it; they took out every goddamned one of them." Aidan's voice was hard and as cold as a fierce London winter. "Wiped out all the progress we'd made so far in a matter of seconds."

Shit. Cage knew it had taken a virtual act of Congress to get those blood banks opened to begin with. The CDC didn't see the need; not enough people had been allergic to the vaccine; blood supplies could be segregated within existing blood banks with less expense; blah blah blah.

"The likelihood of getting them started again anytime soon is nil." Cage shifted to put an arm around Robin, who'd fallen asleep. Insomnia, he'd noticed, was not a problem for her. "The only way we can get them going again is to do it through private clinics, if that's even possible."

Aidan leaned forward and propped his elbows on his knees. "The only reason we haven't had the problems the UK is having— the protests and threats to reveal the existence of vampires to the public—is that our people knew those blood banks were about to become operational. We were two weeks away. I don't know what will happen once word gets out."

"A shitstorm," Mirren said. "And you know Frank Greisser will get the word out immediately."

Aidan stood up and looked at his watch. "I'm going to set up a conference call with Meg Lindstrom and Edward and our other Tribunal allies and try to get the colonel in on it before it gets any later. Where's Nik?"

Cage didn't have a clue, but Robin sat up, apparently wide awake. Sneaky little bird.

"He's with Shawn, doing . . . something. Feeding, maybe." She shrugged and laughed, but Cage sensed an undercurrent of worry. "I know he wanted to talk to you guys tonight. He can describe the images of Fen better than I was able to."

"Go and make your call, A. I'll stay here with Glory and see if Nik shows up. Robin, why don't you and Cage do some patrols tonight and see if you can locate Mr. Patrick."

Cage nodded, and Robin was already on her feet and halfway to the door. "Can we kill him if we find him?"

Mirren and Cage exchanged glances. "No idea," Cage mouthed to him. She could be joking, or she could have a knife with Fen's name carved into it hiding inside her boot.

"Don't kill him," Mirren shouted after her, then pointed a finger at Cage. "Keep her in line."

Yeah, bloody good luck with that.

They walked the long block to the mill in silence, but as they crossed the street, Robin grabbed his wrist. "Wait."

She was looking toward the woods visible to the left of the mill, the edge illuminated by the one working parking-lot light.

He kept his voice low. "What did you see?"

"Flash of light color. I think it was the coyote."

Cage reached inside his jacket and pulled out the small automatic Mirren had given him his first night back in town. It didn't have the kick of a big Smith & Wesson, but it was a lot more portable. And it was plenty big enough to maim a coyote if he got a good shot. Not kill it, though. This wily coyote, they wanted to have a conversation with.

They walked silently toward the mill, watching the wooded areas without being obvious about it. No point in letting the coyote, if it was still out there, know it had been spotted. For all it knew, they were going back for more sex on the gym mats. If only that were true.

They'd stopped near the front entrance of the mill when Cage heard something. A rustling sound from behind the mill. He and Robin looked at each other, and in a split instant, he had to decide whether or not they were suitable partners. They hadn't trained together. He didn't know her skill set, nor did she know his. They should've been finding that out instead of fucking.

They'd have to find out on the fly. He pointed to her and to the right side of the mill, then to himself and the left side. She nodded, reached inside her right boot, and pulled out a small pistol—a Ruger, by the looks of it. And she handled it like she knew how to use it. He'd revisit that particular sexy image once this was over. He hoped.

They each set off. Cage looked over his shoulder every few steps to make sure she was okay, but she was moving faster and out of view before he'd cleared half the side of the building. *Focus, dickfor-brains.* He kept the weapon poised and stayed in the shadows until he reached the corner nearest the woods and then crouched to listen.

For a few seconds, there was nothing. Then another crackle, maybe a stick breaking. Another rustle. A low-pitched growl.

He moved faster and reached the back of the building at the same time as Robin. She was focused on the woods, and they walked toward the sounds together, he with his weapon scanning to the left, she to the right.

Another shuffling noise, and then a sound that was most definitely not a coyote, unless they'd grown male voices and learned to say *fuck you.*

"That was Nik," Robin murmured, taking off at a run. Cage stayed behind her, willing to let her take point. She and Nik were partners, so he'd take his cues from her on how to proceed. Part of being a good tactician, after all, was knowing when to lead and when to fall back.

She held an arm out and Cage stopped. They listened again, and the silence dragged on for what seemed like minutes but was likely only seconds.

Another curse, and more scrambling to their left, so they set off again. Finally, they reached the edge of a clearing and halted. In front of them, a bloody, ragged Nik sat on a bed of thick brown straw, his left arm latched around the neck of a struggling, snapping coyote. In his right hand was his pistol, pointed right at Robin.

"I can't see worth shit out here, so identify yourselves or you're fucking dead."

Before Cage could shove her out of the way, Robin spoke. "It's me, Niko. Me and Cage. Cage, say something."

"Right. Uh, it's Cage."

At the sound of his voice, the coyote's struggles increased, and it snapped back with such a lunge it caught Nik's ear in its teeth. When he tried to pull his head away, the beast locked its jaws. They rolled so that even with his vampire night vision—better than a human's but probably not as good as a shifter's—Cage couldn't get a clear shot.

Finally, the coyote broke loose and raced into the woods, leaving Nik panting on the ground, his neck covered in blood.

"Your ear!" Robin ran to him and knelt, ripping off her shirt and balling it up to press against the wound.

"Call Mirren and stay with Nik. I'm going after the coyote." Cage didn't wait for a response, racing into the tree line where the coyote had disappeared. It had enough of Nik's blood on it—not to mention his earlobe—that tracking it was simple, even in the dark and with it moving at a run.

Moving due west. Cage calculated his own speed and knew he could outrun a coyote, so he angled away until he thought he might be ahead of it. He stopped, crouched, and waited.

Only it wasn't a coyote that ran out of the woods, headed straight for him, and it wasn't Fen Patrick.

The naked woman racing through the dense pine forest, covered in blood, was Shawn Nicholls.

CHAPTER 27

Nik couldn't get his Ranger training out of his head. *Don't be a hero*, their unit leader would tell them before a mission. *Don't be a martyr. Don't be a Lone Ranger. Don't be a cowboy. Don't go in without backup.*

He'd broken every one of those *don'ts* in the last few hours, and he was paying for it. Only his stubborn male pride kept him from giving in to Robin's pleas to let her carry him back to Mirren's. He'd be damned if he went before the biggest alpha male on God's green earth in the arms of a ninety-eight-pound woman, no matter what she could or couldn't turn into.

"Just let me c—"

"Robin, I'm not giving on this, so shut it."

"Stupid boy." They hobbled the longest block in the world, from the mill to Mirren's house, with his left arm over her shoulder and her right arm around his waist. "Are you sure it was her? How do you know? And what happened back at the restaurant?"

Her being Shawn. "Let's get to Mirren's first. I can't go through it twice, and hello—I'm bleeding like a sieve."

She stayed blissfully silent the rest of the walk and didn't even laugh at him when she had to mostly drag him up the steps; both feet left the ground simultaneously at least twice. At that point, Mirren spotted them and took over. He just picked Nik up without asking.

Another embarrassing moment in the life of Rangers versus Others. "Down," he said. "I can walk."

"Shut the fuck up, Dimitrou."

Couldn't argue with that. By the time Mirren got him to his bedroom, Glory had spread out a white sheet over the bed and had water running in the bathroom. She rolled up her sleeves and worked with Robin to get his shirt off and his cuts and bites cleaned and bandaged. Finally, Krys bustled in wielding a rolling suitcase and a big needle. Better and better.

"Gotta stitch up the ear." She numbed the area and worked quickly. Either that or Nik had fallen asleep or fainted like a girl. At any rate, she was there, and then she was done, and then she was gone. Only Robin remained, stretched out next to him, watching him with sharp eyes, her eyebrows drawn together.

"Hey." Why did everyone who'd been injured sound like a four-pack-a-day chain smoker?

She smiled and patted his shoulder, one of the few body parts that didn't hurt. "Hey, you stupid boy. I gotta go and get Mirren. He wanted to know as soon as you woke up. You know he still calls you Zorba behind your back?"

"What? Wait." He tried to sit up. Once, twice, third time was the charm. "Well, Zorba doesn't want to talk to him flat on my back. Help me get into the living room."

Robin narrowed her eyes—her usual precursor to arguing—but finally nodded. Maybe Cage was having a good influence, bringing out her kinder, gentler side. Nik and the vampire were probably the only ones who'd ever seen it. "Heard from Cage?"

She hovered nearby until she was sure he could stand on his own. "Not yet. I'm worried."

"He can take care of himself. You'll see." Except he was up against something for which none of them had prepared. Something none of them could understand, because it shouldn't exist.

They made their way to the living room. Mirren was in his usual chair, with Glory on his lap getting a little PDA time. As soon as she saw them, she jumped up and cleared a spot on the sofa nearest Mirren.

Only when he was settled did Nik take a full breath. He'd been focusing all of his energy on staying upright.

"Talk."

A man of few words, Mirren. "Bottom line or from the start?"

"Both."

"Shawn Nicholls is our coyote." Nik held his hands up and winced as a cut threatened to reopen. "I know, I know, not possible. I don't know how, but it's true. Cage is after her now."

"Holy fuck." Mirren sat back, his frown etched so deeply into his face that it might never come out. Glory, wide eyed on the floor next to him, didn't even seem to notice his use of the F-word. If any situation called for an F-word, this was it.

"You gonna call Aidan? I'm not sure Niko can go through this twice." Robin, the guardian angel his friend Kell called "Razorblade Robin," held up her smartphone.

"He's on his way to Atlanta, to deal with the fallout of these blood-bank bombings," Mirren said. "I'll fill him in before daysleep. Maybe he can check around while he's there and see if anyone else has heard of something like this. It's the damnedest thing I've heard in a while. Now, let's start at the beginning."

Nik took a deep breath and began to talk, picking up the story from his and Robin's trip to talk to Mark at the Chow House. "Shawn was flirting, you know, wanting to feed from me." She wanted to fuck him, too, but no point in adding that since it didn't happen. "She put her hand on mine, and I got a flash of memory from her. Nothing to do with our sabotage at that point, just a flash of her in a restaurant from before she was turned."

"But you don't get images from vampires." Robin sat next to him and was fiddling with the edge of an afghan. "Or you haven't before."

"Exactly. That's what made me think something was off about her. So I agreed to let her feed and went back to her place, hoping to get more images. I didn't want to bring her in here, where Glory might be, in case things went south."

Up to that point, his plan had worked like a charm—although he wouldn't mention how her feeding had aroused him or the fact that he was so hard and aching that he let her jack him off while she finished. "I was getting ready to leave when she hugged me, and that's when I saw a flash of a coyote and a fire. I knew then she either witnessed it, or she set it.

"I followed her but lost her when she passed the tree line into the woods behind the mill. By the time I found her, she'd shifted, and I ended up wrestling the coyote." He looked down at his bites and scratches and bruises. "I think she won."

Mirren had been doodling on a notebook while Nik talked, but now he looked up. "Did you actually see her shift?"

Nik shook his head. "No, but she was there, and then the coyote was there. It didn't run away, like a real coyote would. She turned and attacked. That plus the images . . . it's right. I feel it."

He thought of all the lore Robin had shared about shifters. Only two shifters of the same species could produce healthy shifter children. Shifters couldn't have kids with shifters of other species or with humans.

The only way to get a hybrid was for a shifter to bite a human multiple times—usually three—and the results were usually freakish. Some shifter had made his own Shawn Frankenstein. "I know it sounds crazy, but I swear my gut tells me it's true. What I don't understand is why."

"I think we're about to get some answers," Mirren said, propelling himself from his chair and striding toward the door.

Robin was on her feet as well, and Nik and Glory exchanged exasperated glances. "I don't hear anything," Robin muttered.

Neither did Nik, but a few seconds after Mirren opened the front door, Cage strode in hauling Shawn behind him on a leash—in her human form. She was wearing his shirt, or so Nik assumed since she wore a man's shirt that came almost to her knees and Cage was bare chested. Her arms had been bound behind her with duct tape, and Cage appeared to have fashioned a leash and collar out of the heavy tape as well. He tossed the handle of the leash—the cardboard roll of tape—at Mirren.

"She's all yours, mate. I'm done." He collapsed on the other side of Robin. "What a nightmare. She's a woman, then she's a bloody jackal, then she's a woman again. And she fucking bites."

Yeah, well, Nik knew a thing or two about that. She'd eaten his earlobe.

With no pretense at kindness, Mirren dragged Shawn into the middle of the living room and dropped the makeshift leash. The tape roll swung gently in front of her legs.

The silence was long and uncomfortable. Mirren asked no questions, just sat back down in his chair and stared at her. When he first released her, she'd looked from one of them to the other, a stubborn, defiant gleam in her eye. The longer the silence lasted, the more that gleam died until she finally seemed to realize her position and dropped to her knees.

Nik almost felt sorry for her. Almost.

"Please don't kill me." She repeated it, rocking back and forth, looking mostly at the floor but up at Mirren occasionally. Back and forth. Back and forth. And only begging Mirren; the rest of them had ceased to exist. Even the younger vampires had heard stories of the Slayer, Nik supposed. He'd been quite the terror in his day.

Next to him, Cage wrapped his arms around Robin, and she relaxed against him, her hand looking impossibly small resting on his thigh. She looked worried but also content in the moment.

He wanted that for her. Now, if he could just find it for himself. Although at the rate he was going, he might not live long enough to worry about it.

Shawn continued to rock on her knees, but Mirren finally had enough. "I won't kill you." His voice was low, and if "deadly" had a sound, Mirren had captured it. "That'll be Aidan's decision. He usually takes my advice."

No more rocking. Shawn had frozen in place, her gaze fixed on Mirren.

"What I will advise him to do depends on the next few minutes. You can tell me exactly what the fuck is going on. If I believe you, I'll recommend he wipe your memories and send you somewhere way the hell away from Penton."

Nik didn't believe that for a second, but it sounded good. It sounded like a lifeline thrown to a drowning coyote.

"Or," Mirren said with exaggerated slowness, which made his faint Scottish accent more pronounced. "Or you can tell me lies, and if I know they're lies, I'll recommend that you be killed. Your final choice is to say nothing, in which case I'll recommend you be killed so fucking slow you'll beg me to finish you off. Maybe you'd like to go the way your friend Britta suffered."

Finally, Shawn reacted. "Britta's missing. Do you know where she is?"

Mirren studied her with such intensity even Nik wanted to squirm, but Shawn didn't so much as twitch. Nik thought she was telling the truth, which meant if she was indeed both vampire and shifter, Fen Patrick was very likely their jaguar.

"Britta is alive, for now." Mirren still had that blank, cold expression on his face that had probably put the fear of the sword into many opponents over his long lifetime. Nik hoped he'd never see it directed his way. "She was brutalized—crucified with silver, her guts laid open—at the hands of your accomplice."

Shawn had been standing on her knees, but at the word *accomplice*, she crumpled. "There's another one? Oh my God, who is it?"

"Another what?" Mirren asked. Such an agreeable, calm voice. *Deadly.* "Say the words, and remember the options I gave for your future."

"Another abomination." She hung her head. "It's what I am."

"You are both vampire and shape-shifter. How is that possible?"

Nik knew the instant Shawn decided to talk. Her shoulders drooped inside the billowy fabric of Cage's shirt. Her fingers, clutched into such tight fists the knuckles had whitened, relaxed at her sides. Sitting back on her heels at Mirren's feet, with her head down, she looked like exactly what she was: a supplicant, making confession to the high priest who would decide her fate, whether penance and forgiveness or death.

She began talking without another prompt. Now that her decision was made, the words seemed to come easily, and Nik listened with horrified fascination at a glimpse into a world so corrupt he found it hard to imagine it existed in tandem with his own.

She never knew her contact's name, only that he'd found out she was a shifter who'd racked up enough gambling debt to be vulnerable. He made her an offer, and she took it.

"Coyotes are loners; we don't travel in packs or even keep in touch with our families, so I didn't have anyone to go to. And he did a great sales job." She shook her head. "I was so stupid. God. All I could see was the picture he painted. I'd be immortal, and I'd be rich. I'd be able to walk in sunlight like a shifter but have the strength and longevity of a vampire. In return, all I had to do was come here, take orders." She took a deep breath. "It didn't quite work that way."

"No shit," Robin said. She'd crawled in Cage's lap, and they held each other, listening, the horror in their faces mirroring the others. Glory was crying—whether for Shawn or for the sorry state of affairs in general, Nik wasn't sure. Shawn had been selfish and stupid, but she was paying for it.

"Did you start the fire?" Nik knew the answer to that question but wanted to gauge her response.

"Yes. A bottle of some flammable liquid was left for me; my contact said to take it to Cage's room, open it, light it, and get the hell out." She stared at the floor. "I didn't know Hannah was in there. I swear."

"I notice you didn't worry if I was anywhere in the house." Cage's face had shown a little pity, but that was gone.

"And the construction site—did you sabotage that?"

This time, she looked surprised. "N-no. I wouldn't even know how to sabotage a construction site."

Nik believed her. If Fen Patrick had worked in third-world countries doing dirty mercenary jobs, he probably would know how to weaken a brick wall.

"The only other thing I did was leave the drugs for Mark Calvert. I knew Britta would be blamed for it."

Mirren again: "Did you ever see your contact?"

"No, and his number never showed up as a recall option. I had to wait to hear from him." Shawn paused. "He had an accent, though. German, maybe?"

"Fucking Frank Greisser," Cage muttered.

Mirren looked at him and gave a single nod. "Tell us how they changed you, and what you can and can't do."

"Wait." Glory pulled a spare chair from against the wall and dragged it to a spot in the room that was more conversation spot than interrogation spot. She held out a hand to Shawn. "Up you go."

Shawn looked at Mirren, who gave another slight nod. Nik had never seen him not give Glory her way, although he was glad Shawn was cooperating. If she hadn't, he wasn't sure even Glory's plea for mercy would carry much weight.

The unexpected kindness finally broke through Shawn's resigned calm, and she cried for a few minutes before taking a deep breath. Mirren and Cage just stared at her, while Nik and Robin both had to look away.

"Once I agreed to do it, a vampire came to me. I never knew his name. He was young, handsome, and when he began feeding from me I thought I'd gone to heaven. I'd never been fed from before. He said it was . . . powerful, feeding from a shifter."

Mirren blinked at that, and Nik figured that's what he'd had a taste of when he bonded Robin. Shawn had taken him halfway to heaven earlier tonight, and while he hoped he'd turn her down if the opportunity arose again, he couldn't make any guarantees.

On the other hand, he could probably find a female vampire who'd deliver the same results without his losing an ear.

But that thought brought up an interesting question. "If Shawn is bonded to Will, why didn't he know she was being disloyal and warn us?"

"Will's been out of range since long before the fire," Cage said, and then turned back to Shawn. "How were you turned?"

"He turned me the usual way, I guess," Shawn said. "He drained me to the point of death, and then began to feed me his blood until my body changed enough to accept it. I was sick for months before I started to level off to what's become normal."

She turned back to Mirren. "To answer your other questions, I can't go out in sunlight anymore," she said. "I can't eat solid food, yet I'm so damned hungry all the time. I smell it, I crave it, but if I eat it, my body rejects it. Blood's the only thing that keeps me alive, but I hate it. Seems like I'm always starving and always sick and always angry."

"Even when you're a coyote you can't go in the sun or eat?" Robin leaned forward.

Shawn shook her head. "No. It's kind of the worst of both worlds. I don't know how another person might react . . . Wait, you said there's another one like me here? A shifter turned vampire?"

Mirren raised his gaze to meet Cage's. "Find Fen Patrick. Now."

❧CHAPTER 28❧

Robin was surprised to see Nik still up when she and Cage returned from their failed mission to find Fen. They'd run into Mirren as he hauled Shawn, still with duct tape in place, to the silver-lined room down in the old Omega facility. It was their most secure site. Afterward he planned to meet Glory at the lieutenants' daysleep space.

She'd expected to have the living room all to Cage and herself, but there Nik sat, wide awake at 3:00 a.m.

"You should be asleep." She did her mother-hen thing that always annoyed him, feeling his forehead with the back of her hand. His bandages still looked good except the wound on his ear had bled through.

The thing that really worried her—whether Nik had taken in enough shifter DNA through his bites to turn hybrid—was something that Nik hadn't considered yet. She didn't plan to mention it unless he did, but she'd sure as hell be keeping an eye on him.

Cage came from the kitchen with three glasses and a bottle of Mirren's private stock of scotch that he kept under the sink. So sue her, she'd snooped. She grinned at him. "Does our host know you found his secret stash?"

Cage smiled but not very convincingly. "Do I care?"

"Brave words, big man."

Her attempts to cheer him up hadn't been successful all evening. Not when he'd first learned the suspicions about Fen. Not when they'd scoured all of Penton trying to find him and had come up empty. Especially not when they'd revisited the space under the greenhouse, although it had surprised her to learn how claustrophobic he was.

Nik had sucked down his scotch way too fast but had finally stretched out on the sofa, so she propped a hip on the arm of Cage's chair, hoping he'd invite her to join him. He finally snaked an arm around her waist and pulled her onto his lap. Who'd ever have guessed her stuffy British vampire was a snuggler? A good one.

"Can I ask you something?"

He'd been resting his cheek against her hair, stroking her leg, lost in thought. Now, he pulled back and gave her half of her favorite old cocky smile. "It worries me that you're asking permission. You usually don't."

"It's something I figure you won't want to answer."

He laughed and kissed her forehead. "Ask away. I reserve the right to plead the . . . whichever amendment to the US Constitution protects me from incriminating myself."

"The fifth."

"Right."

She settled back against his chest. "You're this really together guy, you know? Calm. Steady. Know how to handle yourself."

"You make me sound like a fucking cocker spaniel."

"I'm serious." She elbowed him in the ribs. "So where'd the claustrophobia come from? And those scars on your legs."

"Those are big questions, love."

She didn't blame him. There were things she didn't want to talk about, either. Maybe, if this all ended and they could see what they had together, they'd both open up. And if they didn't, she was okay with that. She'd never been a happily-ever-after girl; she wasn't even sure she believed in that capital-L Love for herself. She'd always been grateful for the small moments of happiness in her life, and Cage gave her that without knowing it.

They sat in silence awhile; Robin thought she could sit like this forever.

"I was turned vampire during the war." Cage's voice was soft, whether from not wanting to wake Nik or because he was so lost in the past, Robin wasn't sure. She kept her mouth shut, something most people didn't realize she knew how to do. She could listen when she wanted to.

"I was a psychiatrist, had a practice in London that was disrupted by war. When war's over, people have time to sort out their problems; when war's in progress, no one has time. So I signed up."

"The British Army?"

He chuckled. "Oh no, that would have been too safe, wouldn't it? I was SOE—the equivalent of today's black operatives, I suppose, working directly under Churchill. We were placed undercover in occupied territory. Don't know how many of us there were—we weren't encouraged to fraternize. I was airdropped into occupied France and worked as a radio operator for the resistance. There were about six agents in my unit."

She didn't find it hard to imagine him in that kind of environment—loving the excitement of the subterfuge, the intellectual chess match of outwitting the enemy. Until things went wrong.

Her breath caught. Claustrophobia. Scars. "You were caught."

He didn't answer for a while. "The Gestapo found us—I don't know how. We were taken to Fresnes, a prison south of Paris where the SOE captives were held. I was locked up for a year."

Cage's voice had grown monotone, as if the only way he could tell the story was to withdraw from it. She wanted to stop him; she never should have asked him to tell this. But she remained silent.

"All of us were tortured. The only time I left my solitary cell during that time was to visit the interrogation chamber. Later I learned others fared worse than I—teeth and nails pulled out one at a time. Public hanging by piano wire to make death as slow and humiliating as possible. Water torture—modern warfare has invented nothing new. I had a guard who enjoyed knives and carving neat, tidy lines into skin."

Robin tried to imagine what he'd been through, how he survived, but her little life had been so tame compared to his. Filled with its own torture, but not like this. "How did you escape?"

He smiled. "One of the guards took a fancy to me, I suppose. We were being transferred to a prison camp in Germany, herded onto a cattle car in the middle of the night, and he pulled me aside and dragged me into a shed behind the train depot. I was weak and thin. I thought he was going to shoot me and actually hoped he would. Instead, he turned me."

They sat a while longer. It seemed insufficient, but she meant it: "Thank you for trusting me with that."

"Aren't you sorry you asked? At any rate, that's my sad, woeful tale of how I get rather undone in tight spaces."

And why the sight of Britta, tortured, had probably haunted him.

Robin shifted in his lap until she sat facing him, her knees wedged between his thighs and the chair arms. She ran her fingertips over the lines of his face, the long lashes that rested on his cheeks when he closed his eyes to feel her touch, the straight nose, full lower lip, stubble more blond than brown.

She thanked him the only way she knew how—with a soft, sweet kiss. Which didn't stay sweet or soft for long as she lost herself in the sweet tangle of tongues, and his big hands roving up her back.

"I swear to God if you're going to have more hot monkey sex, don't come anywhere near this sofa or I'm telling Mirren. And give me a minute to leave the room."

Robin collapsed against Cage's chest, laughing. "Niko, you voyeur."

"So not true. Cage has nothing I want to see."

She kissed Cage again, a kiss she hoped was full of promise, and got to her feet. She tossed him a throw pillow and pointed at his lap. "Might want to hide that."

He groaned and put the pillow over his face instead. "You are evil."

She did the mama-hen thing with Nik again. He didn't seem to have a fever, which was good. Of course, Krys had pumped him full of antibiotics when she stitched up his ear.

"Help me sit up."

Robin went behind the sofa, reached over, and pulled Nik upright by grasping his shoulders. "You want me to help you to your room?"

"No, I want to talk."

"We're consenting adults, Niko." Robin sat on the sofa next to him and gave him her most innocent smile. He didn't return it. "Oh, serious talk."

"I remember you telling me shape-shifters are born and not turned like vampires, right?"

She nodded, pretty sure her boy had figured out the thing that most worried her.

"When we had that case in Houston, we were told three bites from the same species would turn a human into some monster-hybrid. Or was it three bites from the same shifter?"

"Same shifter." Robin looked at Cage, whose stricken expression told her this was all news to him, and he grasped the horrific possibilities.

"I have five bites. Six if you count the fact that she ate half of my ear. What's going to happen to me?"

Robin didn't have an answer, and that was answer enough for Nik. "Shit. If I turn into some freak like we saw in Houston, you end it if I don't have the guts."

"Nik, don't talk like that." She wouldn't kill him. Couldn't. Ever.

He reached out and grasped her wrist, pulling her to him. "Promise me, Robin. I don't want to live like that."

"It will be done," Cage said. "I'd feel the same way. But don't ask Robin to do it. It would kill her. Ask me."

Nik nodded. "Consider yourself asked."

"Done."

Well, wasn't male bonding just too sweet? Robin fought back tears. If she lost Nik, she didn't care what fate Mirren recommended for Shawn Nicholls. Robin would kill her.

"But don't write your own obituary yet," Cage said, getting up to pour himself another scotch. "We're not dealing with an ordinary shifter. From her description of what she could and couldn't do, Shawn had more vampire traits than shifter after her turn. And vampire bites won't turn you into anything except maybe a blood whore."

"What's a blood whore?" So many things about the vampire world that Robin didn't know.

"A human who gets addicted to the high from being fed on by a vampire. There are always a group of them hanging around wherever there's an active vampire population."

She didn't like the sound of that, and she didn't want Cage feeding from anyone else. Oh, Nik was okay because she knew neither of them found it comfortable. But not another woman. She would have to trick him into feeding from her somehow.

Every girl needed a project.

"So how will I know?" Nik asked. "You keep checking for fever. If I have a fever does it mean anything?"

Robin's biggest job was going to be keeping Nik preoccupied, so he wouldn't obsess. "If you have a fever, it means you have an infection," she said slowly. "Cage is right—Shawn is more vampire than shifter now. If"—she held up a finger—"and I mean *if* you've been changed, the first thing you're going to notice is your hair. It might change color or fall out or turn straight. Shawn's hair is about the color of a coyote, so my guess is your hair would start changing color."

Nik looked like he'd swallowed a raw eel. "Have you ever seen a Greek man with blond hair?"

"Give me a break. You're from New Orleans. The closest you've been to Greece is that island where they make Tabasco sauce."

"It's not an island; it's a salt dome."

"If you two don't mind." Cage shook his head. "Have you ever heard of anything like this, Robin? What would happen, for instance, if instead of turning a shifter into a vampire, they tried to hybridize a vampire into a shifter?"

She couldn't imagine any outcome where that would be a good thing. "I don't know, but it sounds like somebody's doing really fucked-up science experiments, and I've gotta wonder why."

❧ CHAPTER 29 ❧

Matthias drove with the window rolled down all the way, relishing the cool night air on his fevered cheeks. He hated the South, but tonight even the godforsaken pine-scented mountains of south-central Georgia smelled like freedom.

The trip had gone more smoothly than expected, even though Frank's grand promises of walking in daylight and eating food hadn't panned out. At least Matthias could live on vaccinated blood, even though it tasted like shit.

Oh, he was still angry. He was still starving. The aromas of food still spurred the hunger to rage and beckon, making his fury more bitter. But his strength was returning a little more each day, and he'd adapt. He'd always been good at adapting.

And once he took care of tonight's order from Frank, delivering the deathblow to Penton, he'd return to Europe and show Frank Greisser how effectively one of his genetically enhanced monsters could kill.

Matthias had arrived in Atlanta at dawn and spent daysleep in a space arranged by the oh-so-clever Herr Greisser, who had a rental car waiting for him at dusk.

In the trunk was a high-powered sniper rifle and directions to a private range where he could get used to the feel of the weapon, gather his strength, and wait for tomorrow night's phone call that all the plans were in place.

The fine people of Penton wouldn't know what hit them.

❦CHAPTER 30❧

One look at Aidan's face, and Mirren knew more shit was about to rain all over their heads. The man had gotten back from Atlanta with only a half hour to spare before daysleep, barely enough to be filled in on the situation with Shawn and Fen.

As usual, Aidan blamed himself for not figuring out what was going on. Like anyone could have foreseen what that sick freak Frank Greisser was up to. They didn't have proof he was behind these genetically impaired abominations, as Shawn had called herself, but Mirren knew it as well as he knew his own name.

Matthias Ludlam, as it turned out, seemed to be the least of their worries. Though whether or not he was involved in this mess was anyone's guess. For all they knew, he could be the mad scientist doing these experiments under Frank's orders.

The sun had set less than fifteen minutes ago—they hadn't even left the lieutenants' quarters yet—and here Aidan was, in Mirren's room, with that restless, angry expression he got when major shit had gone down.

How much could possibly have happened in fifteen minutes?

"Go ahead and tell me. Glory's going to help Krys with Britta tonight." Britta, whom they'd apparently all misjudged, was still unconscious, but Krys hoped they could wake her up tonight and ask her some questions. Like if she had any clue where Fen Patrick might be hiding.

"We wait on Cage; he's coming." Aidan placed his cell phone on the coffee table in the suite's sitting area, parked his ass on one of the armchairs, and stewed.

It had to be bad.

Cage arrived less than a minute later, and Glory left the three of them alone. Mirren glimpsed Krys in the hallway waiting for her, looking scared as hell, so she'd probably fill his mate in on whatever had happened.

Three days until Aidan joined the Tribunal. Three fucking days, and Mirren wasn't sure they were going to survive it. Rob Thomas was dead, Frank Greisser was creating monsters in the basement, Hannah had withdrawn into her shell after saying death was coming to Penton, a mutant shifter-vampire was locked in a silver-lined room in the Omega facility, and now . . . something else.

"Better sit down." Aidan pointed to his cell phone. "I'm putting it on speaker. You can listen to the six messages I had waiting when I woke from daysleep. The first is from Meg Lindstrom's familiar, Gary."

Aidan, I have to be quick. Someone was waiting for Meg when she rose tonight. She's . . . she's dead. I'm hiding upstairs in her closet, but they know I'm in the house. Two men. No idea where—

The call ended with shouts, a plea for mercy, gunfire, and silence.

Aidan reached out to hit the next "Play" button. "This one is from Caroline Pressman."

Shit. Mirren had a sinking suspicion as to where this was going. From the way Cage had clenched the arm of the chair, so did he.

The voice on the message was a whisper.

Mr. Murphy, this is Edward Simmons's business manager, Caroline. Edward was killed in a car bomb just after sunset last evening, and his staff has gone into hiding. He'd left instructions to contact you if anything happened to him and to pass the word to Cage Reynolds.

Cage flinched and looked at the floor.

The next three were the same. Canada, Japan, Australia. Along with the UK and the US, they made up the five biggest blocs supporting Aidan—all with leaders who'd been assassinated just after rising. It was Meg Lindstrom's seat Aidan was due to take in three days.

They sat in silence for several minutes, trying to comprehend what had happened. Mirren didn't like the Tribunal. Its members caused as many problems as they solved, and the organization was rife with corruption—and yet some of them were good people who genuinely had the best interests of the vampire population at heart.

Five of the best were dead.

"You said there were six messages." Cage's voice was subdued; Edward Simmons had not only been his scathe leader in London, he'd been his friend. Chances were good that if Cage hadn't come back to Penton, he'd be dead alongside Edward or in hiding.

"This one doesn't need an introduction." Aidan pressed the "Play" arrow on his phone again.

Frank Greisser here. Mr. Murphy, you've no doubt heard the tragic news about some of our most-valued colleagues. Such a sad situation. As you were set to take Ms. Lindstrom's place in a few days, please be in Atlanta this evening for an emergency strategy meeting. The bar at the Marriott downtown, at ten p.m., please.

Aidan picked up the phone, reset it, and stuck it in his pocket. "I'll be leaving in forty-five minutes. Cage, I'd like you to go with me."

He had to be joking. Mirren leaned forward, getting in his face. "No fucking way you're going to that meeting. It's a setup, and you know it."

"You're right. I do know it's a setup, and I don't have any delusions about talking strategy. We're beyond that. I'm going to take Frank Greisser out. The Tribunal's beyond saving as long as he's in power."

Mirren didn't like it. "If you're going after Greisser, then there's no way I'm staying here."

Aidan gave him that pigheaded Irish-farmer expression that made Mirren want to throttle him. Once the man got that look on his face, he'd made up his mind and wouldn't back down. But Mirren could be stubborn, too. "Reynolds can stay here, and I'll go with you. I want Greisser as much as you do."

"Won't work." Cage said. "I don't have the loyalty of the people here the way you do. If you and Aidan are both away, and God forbid something happens here—Fen shows up and burns something down or hangs up posters, or worse—Penton's dead. Everyone will leave. Mirren, if you're out and about where people can see you, they won't panic."

"I'm not the master of this scathe." Mirren pushed himself off the sofa and prowled around the seating area. "I didn't ask for it. I don't want it."

"Don't fight me on this, Mirren." Aidan's voice held a warning, and Mirren didn't hear that tone often. When he did, he always listened. He respected Aidan too much, and owed him too much, not to.

But he didn't have to like it.

He took a deep breath and nodded. "What's your plan?"

"We go armed, and we play it by ear."

Damn it all to hell and back. "That's not a plan, A. That's a fucking suicide mission."

Aidan ignored him. "In the meantime, you work with Robin on patrols. Nik needs to recuperate. If you find Fen Patrick, don't kill him. If I'm not able to get to Frank tonight, we might need him."

Mirren glanced over at Cage, who couldn't hear Patrick's name without looking as if his head might explode. He could empathize.

"Of course," Aidan said, "if you want to make him suffer a little on Cage's behalf, feel free."

Now that, Mirren would enjoy.

❦CHAPTER 31❧

For all his claptrap about finding a home in Penton and set-tling down, Cage loved the feeling he got before a mission. His senses sharpened, filtering through every pedestrian they passed on the streets of Atlanta. Every tinted back window of every lim-ousine got a moment of his attention. Each cab, bus, cyclist. All the scents, sounds, rhythms.

On the drive from Penton in Aidan's sedan, they'd talked strat-egy. Possible scenarios. Trying to anticipate the unexpected. They were as prepared as they could be on virtually no notice.

In case anything looked amiss on the drive toward Peachtree, Cage had the Smith & Wesson in his right hand, the smaller auto-matic on his lap. This wasn't like the frustration of trying to chase down ghosts in Penton, which had been wearing them all down. They had a target, or targets. They might not know what he or she looked like. They might not know if Frank's minions would be shifter or vampire or some fucked-up combination. But whoever it was, if it could be shot, it could die.

If it turned out to be Fen Patrick, all the better.

Cage hated uncertainty, hated not being able to identify his enemy. If it hadn't been for Robin, he'd have gone mad this past week. She'd distracted him, amused him, exasperated him, shocked him, and somehow burrowed under the hard shell of his heart to a place he hadn't known was still alive.

And all in a single week. She'd been an unexpected gift, his little bird. He didn't know what the future held for them. He was at heart still in love with the adrenaline rush, as was she. They both had secrets, although he'd certainly spilled some of his major ones last night.

But it didn't matter what lay ahead. He hoped they could face it together, but if his years of lonely wandering had taught him anything, it was that happiness, for whatever time one could claim it, was to be treasured.

For now, however, the time for thinking of happiness had passed. He wrapped his thoughts of Robin in a neatly tied package and tucked it away in a part of his brain to be taken out and enjoyed later, when there was time for reminiscence and reflection.

For now, there was an enemy to deal with and a man he wanted, above all else, to keep safe.

"Think Greisser will even be in town, or if that was a ruse to get you in place for the setup?" Cage leaned forward and scanned the bag of a pale woman crossing in front of the car at the red light. Possibly vampire, but absorbed in her own thoughts, not alert enough to be an assassin or even a spy.

Not that an assassin would be vampire. Frank Greisser had money and power at his disposal; he could hire anyone. In fact, he was likely to go with a human. Less risk, and disposable.

"Doubt it." Aidan turned right at the light and continued their slow progress through streets dense with restaurant patrons, tourists, and shoppers. "He's probably not even in the country—I couldn't track that call back. Will might have been able if he'd been here, but there wasn't time. Greisser knows that Meg's people will rally eventually. He just wants to make sure it's not me they rally around."

Cage had been thinking the same thing. In Greisser's shoes, he'd want Aidan taken out at the earliest opportunity and the news spread as quickly as possible. And the way to catch him at his most vulnerable was to get him out of Penton.

They'd be expecting Mirren to be his backup, however, which gave Aidan and Cage an advantage. If they were looking for a six-foot-eight, three-hundred-pound Scotsman, they might not notice the Everyman with the .45-caliber weapon skulking in the shadows.

In a perfect world, anyway. Not that a boil on the arse of vampiredom like Greisser would exist in a perfect world.

Finally, they arrived within sight of the Mirage, a towering mirrored rectangle overlooking a forest of shorter towering circles and squares. Cage had scoped out the floor plan on his phone during the drive. It had three lobby levels; the one they'd be approaching from the street was the middle level. Above the second level, the rooms rose around an open atrium fifty-two stories tall.

Lots of places for a sniper to hide, in other words. Way too many.

"Here's our spot." They'd decided that Cage would get out of the car two blocks down and walk into the hotel, assessing as much as he could. Aidan would enter on the second level from a neighboring hotel that was linked via a skywalk.

Aidan pulled a small device from his pocket. "Got your headset?"

"Roger." Wasn't that what all the Yanks said? "Who was Roger anyway?"

Aidan grinned. "I don't know, but if we live through tonight, I'll research it."

They'd gotten the headsets from Nik and Robin, it being a popular means of communication among Ranger types, apparently. The earpieces were small, undetectable except at close range, and even then, looked like a regular cell-phone set except they were tuned to the same frequency.

Not quite as convenient as psychic communication between master vampires, but it would have to do.

"Right, then. You're going to circle until I give you the go? Then I'll shadow you from the skywalk entrance."

"Roger." They exchanged smiles filled with all the things guys didn't say to other guys, and Cage exited onto the street, crossing quickly to the sidewalk and walking toward the hotel. If they'd had time, he could have dyed his hair a few shades darker. He and Aidan were of similar size and build; he even wore the man's clothes. He would've been a useful decoy.

Cage suspected Greisser had set this meeting time carefully, though. He'd know how long the drive from Penton to Atlanta would take, and he had given Aidan virtually no time to prepare. He just wished to hell they had a clue as to what the old bastard had in mind. Why stage a setup in a hotel in the most crowded part of an overcrowded city? At the same time, it had to be a setup—in what world would Frank have any kind of "strategic discussions" with Aidan?

Either Greisser underestimated Aidan's intelligence, which Cage doubted, or he planned some public spectacle that would force Aidan to travel to an isolated area or even outside the city— somewhere Aidan would never go without incentive.

Cage reached the hotel's curved drive, which was lined with taxis and hotel customers loading and unloading baggage from personal vehicles. He maintained a steady but slow gait, scanning the vehicles, the people, the bags. The .45 rested in a shoulder holster under his jacket. In his right jacket pocket, he clutched the semi-automatic with the safety within easy reach. Just a normal bloke, heading back to his hotel after dinner with a couple of firearms.

Inside the hotel entrance, he noticed an alcove to the left of the doorway with an automated teller machine, so he parked there, pressing buttons while eyeing the wide rectangular lobby. He slipped on the headset and pressed the activation button. "I'm inside. Clean thus far."

"Got it. Stay in touch and be careful."

A pair of escalators rose in the part of the lobby nearest the entrance; farther back stood an elevator tower, with glass-encased lifts rising up and down floors at a speed that made Cage a bit queasy. A glass lift was not in his plans.

The trick, Cage realized as he studied a dark-suited man standing near the far escalator, would be telling any of Frank's people from hotel security. Getting arrested while traipsing around a crowded hotel lobby with two guns and several pockets of ammo clips was also not in his plans.

Finally, he stepped out of the alcove and entered the main lobby, circling the outside areas before hopping the escalator to the second level. As he rode up, he knelt and pretended to fiddle with his boot; it made him a smaller target. A third thing not in his plans was dying tonight; watching Robin fly had made it to his bucket list, and it was a sight he hadn't yet enjoyed.

The open atrium towered above him, surrounded by fifty-two sets of hallway balconies behind whose rails untold sharpshooters could crouch. *Don't get paranoid, Reynolds.* Next to the elevator tower on this level was one of those clubby bars where young professionals gathered after hours, flirting and swapping business tips around tall tables with no chairs or on low-slung ottomans scattered in tasteful groupings.

Two of the young professionals, however, looked a bit too professional. They were looking around at everything but each other, not talking. One had a bottle of water in front of him; the other, nothing.

"Spotted a couple of possibilities," Cage said softly. "Hang tight."

The guys looked nervous; they also looked human. "No fangs," he said.

"Have they spotted you?" came Aidan's voice through the headset.

"Not yet . . . yep, they have me. Moving."

Water Bottle Guy punched his buddy on the arm, and they both turned toward Cage, but before they moved, Cage had ducked into a darkly carpeted corridor lined with meeting room doors.

Not the sharpest guys in the world.

"Status?" Aidan's voice was muffled by traffic noise.

"Number One is making a phone call. Finding backup, maybe."

"They're not trying to find you?"

Cage frowned. They hadn't tried to find him, actually. They'd spotted him, jumped up, and then made a phone call. "No, and I'm not liking—"

A muffled boom sounded from the lower lobby, and Cage instinctively crouched. Frick was still on the phone, but Frack spoke into a headset not dissimilar to Cage's. Another boom, and the odor of smoke reached him, and people began to scream. "Bloody hell, they've set off a bomb. First-level lobby."

"Meet me at the front of the adjacent hotel. Wait—shit. Hang on."

While Cage slipped down the hallway and found the corridor that led to the skywalk, he listened to Aidan's side of a phone conversation. It was pretty easy to guess at the other half.

"Frank, yes, I got your message, if you mean a bomb at the Mirage. What do you think that'll get you?"

Aidan sounded much calmer than Cage would have.

"You twisted bastard. So you'll set off a bigger bomb if I don't show up at your little party?"

Cage had guessed right; Frank was using innocent humans as motivation to get Aidan to walk into a trap.

"And if— *Shit!*"

Damn it. Cage couldn't worry about drawing attention to himself; Aidan's last words had ended in a gunshot and a screech of tires.

He raced along the glassed-in skywalk, looking below at the street, where crowds of people were huddled, smoke pouring from the lobby entrance to the Mirage.

The Gravier Hotel looked exactly like the Mirage, so as soon as he exited the skywalk, he headed for the street side of the second level. Sure enough, escalators.

Thank God it was late enough for most of the shops and boutiques on this level to be closed. Cage was able to run down the escalator, realizing only when a dark-suited guy pulled his jacket back to reveal a shoulder holster that he might be mistaken for a bomber hurrying away from the scene. The real bombers, as far as he knew, were having a leisurely phone conversation in the neighboring hotel.

"Just a moment, sir. I need to ask you to wait a minute. You're in an awfully big hurry."

Cage shrugged, treating the guy to a fangless, charming smile. The man wore a Gravier Hotel name tag that read Douglas Banks.

"So sorry, Mr. . . . Banks, is it? I'm late for a business dinner. Is there a problem?"

"Are you a guest here at the Gravier, sir?"

Terribly polite, these hotel security guys. But he didn't have time for a chat. He held out his hand to shake. "Frank Greisser, sir. I'm visiting from Vienna—lovely city you have."

He made eye contact with the soon-to-be-confused Doug Banks, who made the mistake of looking back. In seconds, his eyes grew unfocused and his jaw slackened.

"Sorry, mate. Must run. Remember the name Greisser. Vienna." Cage pulled his hand back and left the enthralled Mr. Banks to stand aimlessly behind. Handy vampire trick, enthrallment.

Cage paused at the street entrance, trying to figure out which way to go. If Aidan had a chance to get away, he hoped he'd take it. Cage could make his way back to Penton. If Aidan had been hit by that gunshot, he'd be somewhere in this area.

Scanning the street for any sign of a dark-blue BMW, Cage began walking toward the nearest corner.

The sedan arrived from behind and came to a fast stop, and Aidan reached over to open the passenger door. "In!"

Cage dived for the seat, pulling the door closed after Aidan had already begun to drive.

"You all right?" He didn't see any bullet holes or blood, but the driver's side backseat window was broken.

"Yeah, I saw the shooter in time to speed up—they played us on that one."

Cage had come to the same conclusion. Greisser's hitmen must have been briefed on everyone in Penton who might show up, figuring Aidan wouldn't go in first but would be nearby.

"What's next?"

"Get the hell out of Atlanta, first. Then we'll regroup."

Cage's heart slowly returned to its normal rhythm, and his muscles felt heavy after releasing their adrenaline. "Take a back route from town. Stay off I-85 as long as you can."

Aidan drove awhile in silence, but Cage could tell he was fuming.

Finally, he blew. "What kind of sick freak bombs a hotel full of innocent people just to coerce me into an ambush? Does he think I'm a fucking idiot?"

"No, he thinks you're a decent man, and to guys like him, decent equals weak. Please don't tell me you're going."

"Hell no." Aidan drove through a less-than-savory area of the city.

Ironic if they escaped the big bad vampire and got offed by a street gang. "Good, because otherwise I'd be forced to bash you over the head, and you know I don't drive."

Aidan tried to smile but failed. "Frank won't waste too much time. He'll probably set off another bomb, but the authorities might find it before it detonates. Once I don't show, he won't bother with another one. He'll probably set up one of his flunkies as the bomber, so the case will be closed."

Cage nodded. "And then the guy will die in a jail-cell brawl or from a sudden suicide."

They drove in silence until they got to a major road that would take them back to the interstate.

"I want you to drive for a while." Aidan pulled off in a fast-food parking lot and put the car in park.

"Uh, no, you really don't. I haven't driven a car since a full tank of petrol cost twenty pence." Okay, call him a chicken. But automobiles had changed a lot, and it was dark.

"We need to get back to Penton now, and I also need to make some calls. I particularly want to check on Edward's people, tell them to lay low and stay hidden until we can regroup or at least decide what to do."

At the mention of Edward, Cage grumbled and opened the car door. Low blow. How could he refuse to drive a fucking car when the whole world was coming down on their heads?

"Fine, but don't blame me if we end up in a lake or something."

Aidan guided him through the complexities of gear shifting, which he was relieved to see amounted basically to forward and backward and stopping and accelerating. Once he got the feel for it, it was rather exhilarating.

"We're on the interstate now, Cage. You can go faster than forty miles an hour."

Right. He watched, fascinated, as the speedometer rose to fifty, then sixty. This was bloody amazing. Seventy.

"That's probably fast enough, hotshot."

"Right." He dropped it to sixty-five and kept it there while Aidan first called Krys to reassure her that he was alive and headed home.

Cage wondered what Robin would do if he called her. He suspected she would say something to the tune of, "Why are you bothering me?" Which would be quite the letdown after hearing Aidan's soft reassurances and promises.

He ended the call. "Krys says Robin has called her at least six times since we left, asking about you. Didn't ask about me at all."

It was dark in the car, but Cage could tell Aidan was smiling. So was he. What a sap.

Another ninety minutes or so, and they should be home.

Home was Penton. Home, he realized with some surprise, also was Robin.

"Hey." Aidan leaned forward. "Slow down. What's that?"

Cage eased his foot off the accelerator, letting the car coast a few feet before cautiously putting his foot on the brake. He'd been doing so well at driving; he refused to skid out at the sight of a little orange dunce cap or two in the road.

"I don't like this—there's no construction visible." Aidan's voice was tense. "Floor it. Go as fast as you can and let's get past it."

"Right." Cage pressed his foot on the accelerator and as soon as the car started rolling, he stomped the pedal. The back end of the car skidded a bit, the tires squealed, but by God they were—

A white light flashed from the side of the road. Before Cage could register what it might be, flying blood and glass filled the air around him. The world turned in a rapid roll.

The world fell to black.

❦CHAPTER 32❧

Matthias checked his watch for the fourth time in ten minutes. He'd gotten the call at Frank's safe house at half past 9:00 p.m. and had been sitting on the side of the interstate ever since.

The plan was so simple it was brilliant. A few orange construction cones in the roadway, moved from a site several miles back. Murphy would slow down, Matthias would take aim, and—boom—no more Penton. With Murphy dead, they'd scatter like rats. If Matthias was lucky, he'd be able to take out Cage Reynolds as well.

In fact, he might shoot Reynolds first. Murphy would lose control of the car, and Matthias would be able to make him suffer. Die more slowly. Pay for the humiliation of taking William away from his father. Pay for taking Matthias's life away from him.

It was off script, but he liked it. The Austrian megalomaniac would never know the difference, and by God, Matthias deserved a reward after what Frank Greisser had put him through.

All he had to do was wait for a dark-blue sedan.

❦CHAPTER 33❦

Robin slipped her phone back in her pocket and ran to catch up with Mirren. Damn, but that vampire could cover some ground with those long legs.

"Cage is fine. That was Krys, and they're on their way back."

Mirren looked at her and squinted. "So I have to assume Aidan's fine as well? Or did you ask about him? You didn't the other five times you called her."

Robin's face heated, and she was thankful it was dark so he wouldn't see her all red and embarrassed. She might have called six times, but who was counting?

"I don't have to see you blush. I can smell it when the blood gets that close to the surface of your skin."

"Ewwwww." Jeez, but vampires were creepy sons of bitches. "Do you want to know what happened, or do you want to keep grossing me out?"

"Talk."

Monosyllabic ass. They'd been sneaking around Penton for the past four hours on little eagle feet, and Mirren wasn't the best conversationalist. He sucked at it, in fact. And when he told her she talked "even more than Gloriana but not as interesting," she'd talked more just to spite him.

Not that it had been completely boring. They'd run across two vampabonds—she liked that word—coming into town. Neither of them put up much of a fuss; once they got a look at the not-so-gentle giant, they moved along quickly enough.

"Wait."

She stopped and looked around. They were in downtown Penton, or what was left of it, near the Baptist church. Nik had told her that the original entrance to the Omega underground hiding place lay in the floor of the church sanctuary, and that Matthias had thrown a grenade down it.

She hoped she'd get the chance to meet that vampire one day. He was an abuser of the first order, by all accounts, and she hated nothing worse than a bully. They were cowards with big sticks, nothing more.

A flash of white moved behind the church building, and she tapped Mirren's arm and pointed. He nodded, and they set out toward it. Cage would've split the direction with her; Mirren just plowed ahead and expected her to follow. As she trailed the grump, she reflected on the way Cage had treated her the night they caught Shawn. He had trusted her to carry her weight, just as she'd trusted him to follow Shawn while she tended to Nik. Somehow, they'd expanded their repertoire to include respect. Which, in the long run, probably lasted longer than lust. Not that they'd run out of that by any means. The man was still going to feed from her.

Mirren cleared the back corner of the church and kept going, slowing only when two guys stepped out of the shadow of the hardware-store alley. They weren't thin. In fact, she couldn't be positive, but she didn't think they were even vampires.

"You assholes better head north and keep going."

Nice, Mirren. Make friends first. "You're shifters," she said. "What kind?"

The one nearest her frowned, but the other guy—a tall blond—looked surprised. "What are *you?*"

His shorter, darker companion gave her an uncomfortably thorough once-over. "Gotta be a shrimp. Popcorn shrimp at that."

"Funny." She'd claw their eyes out with her shrimplike talons. "Who're you working for?"

"That would be me, love."

She got only half-turned before the heat of a silver blade pressed against her throat. "Hiya, Fen Patrick. Funny, we've been looking for you."

She hoped Mirren was in a fighting mood, because she couldn't do a lot unless she got free of the silver blade.

Mirren seemed to have his hands full, though. He'd broken Blondie's arm with one good crack; he was wailing and rolling around on the ground like a baby. Brownie had a gun.

She was on her own. "So, Fen. How does it feel being one of the vampire science experiments? How's that walking in sunlight thing working out for you?" The knife pressed harder, but she'd heard his intake of breath, felt his heart jackhammer up. "Eaten any good meals lately, big cat?"

"Who the fuck talked?" He released his grasp just enough for her to drop down and wriggle free.

"Your partner." An image of Britta Eriksen flashed through her mind. She hadn't seen her hanging, but she'd seen that bloody wooden X, and it still pissed her off. "Tell me this—why did you kill Britta?"

She wasn't dead, of course, but it might surprise him enough to talk. "The bitch followed me and saw me shift." He took a step closer. "I might not be able to eat like a human anymore, but I do still enjoy the taste of raw meat. You're scrawny, but it might be fun to gnaw on Cage Reynolds's leftovers."

Okay, that was it. She'd had enough of fun banter with the frankendouche.

"Well, you might as well start here." She monitored Mirren's standoff with Brownie, who'd lost his gun and shifted into some kind of smaller cat with tufted ears. The big guy was having trouble shooting him while he was riding around on Mirren's back, hanging on by his claws. That looked well in hand.

Robin grasped the hem of her sweater and tugged it off, shivering slightly as the cool air hit her bare breasts and pebbled her nipples.

Fen's gaze dropped, and his grip on the knife loosened. Stupid, predictable boy.

She moved slowly to unbutton her borrowed, rolled-up jeans, sensing his skin heating. He licked his lips, which was totally gross. And now the coup de grace—her shaved surprise.

His intake of breath was audible. "I always said Reynolds had good taste."

Yeah, well, Fen would never taste anything of hers. He moved closer but not fast enough.

"Let me give you a better view," she said, putting a little purr in her voice as she climbed atop a Dumpster at the edge of the alley. She could shift from the ground, but this would be easier.

She spread her legs for his approving view. Arms raised, she closed her eyes, felt the breeze, and leapt, shifting midair.

"Fucking bird."

She sank long, golden talons into his shoulder, and before he could shake her off, used the sharp, downward-curved end of her beak to tear open a gash in his head. When he stabbed at her with the silver, she had to fly, soaring into the colder air above, circling, watching to see where she was most needed.

Mirren's big-ass gun echoed through downtown, and Robin circled again. The little kitty was down, and if she knew her vampire, he had silver bullets.

Blondie had crawled off somewhere to mend his broken arm, and Fen seemed to have come to the same conclusion about the bullets. He shifted, and his big cat was a dark blur that raced out the back of the alley and toward the woods north of town.

She circled again and prepared to follow, but Mirren had sat down on the pavement, clutching his head. What was up with that?

Robin settled to the ground and took a few steps toward him. She'd make sure he was all right, then she'd hunt down Fen like the prey he was.

Mirren rolled to his side, gasping for breath, so Robin shifted back. "What's wrong? Where are you hurt?"

She slipped back into her sweater and pants and ran to him, looking for any sign of injury. Damn it, she didn't see anything.

"Mirren, talk to me. Where are you hurt?"

He groaned and rolled to his back, and Robin heard music. She didn't think choirs of heavenly angels sang country music, so she patted around on his pockets and finally dug out his cell phone. Krys, thank God.

"Something's wrong with Mirren." She waited for Krys to say something. "Krys?"

"Robin? It's Nik. Something's wrong with Krys, too, and Glory. Where are you?"

She filled him in as quickly as possible. "He's rolling around on the ground."

"Bring him to Aidan's house now. Glory says . . . never mind, it's too complicated. Can you get him here?"

She looked down at the biggest man she'd ever seen in her life. She bet he weighed four-hundred pounds. "I'll get him there."

At least she finally knew her physical limits, and they cut off somewhere short of Mirren Kincaid. She tried lifting him, pulling his arm over her shoulders and hefting him to his feet, and even a poor attempt at a fireman's carry.

Finally, she slapped the shit out of him. It seemed to bring him around a little. "You are going to get up, and you are going to walk—do you hear me? Glory is sick. Glory needs you."

If Mirren had a weakness, it was his wife, or mate, or whatever they called themselves.

Her ploy worked. It took a few false starts, but he managed to roll to his knees and then, with her help, rise to his feet. "Come on." She helped as best she could, but given their size difference, it wasn't much. The trip took forever, and her role mostly consisted of tilting him to the right when he began listing left and pushing him to the left when he veered right.

Finally, Aidan's house was in sight, and as soon as he saw them, Nik came limping out to help.

"Careful or you'll open up all your cuts again; he's a moose," she panted. "What's going on?"

They slowly maneuvered Mirren inside and let him collapse on the sofa. Glory sat cross-legged on the floor, crying. Krys . . . "What happened to Krys?"

At first Robin thought she was dead, but then she had a seizure of some kind. "Nik, what's going on?"

He sat on the floor next to Krys and smoothed back her hair. "I'm not sure. It has something to do with the vampire bonds."

Glory had managed to climb on the sofa, and although her face was tight with pain, she had Mirren's head in her lap, stroking his forehead, his cheeks. She looked up. "Everyone in Penton is bonded to Aidan or Mirren, and Mirren's bonded to Aidan. The tie of a bond-mate is closest of all. They share strength. One is hurt and pulls strength from another in order to live."

Robin closed her eyes and prayed for the patience she rarely had. "Speak English, for God's sake. What does she mean?"

Nik apparently understood vampire crap better than she did. "It means Aidan is hurt, and he's unconsciously pulling strength from all of them. I've got a splitting headache, too, but I don't think I've been bonded long enough."

"Hurt how? Hurt how badly?"

Nik looked down at Krys, who trembled with an occasional spasm but had fallen still otherwise. Her breathing was shallow. "I think he might be dying."

Robin's heart froze, and fear skittered up her spin. *Where was Cage?*

The crunch near Cage's left ear was impossibly loud. He didn't hear things during daysleep. What would he hear during daysleep?

"You damn fools won't even let me have the pleasure of shooting you, either one of you."

Cage wanted to open his eyes, see the source of that voice. He'd heard it before, but why was he hearing it during daysleep?

"Guess I better make sure. Here's that goddamned sonofabitch Aidan Murphy. This one's for seducing my son away from the life he was meant to have."

A gunshot echoed, and Cage's eyes shot open. The wreck. Matthias.

Why couldn't he see?

He didn't dare move but rolled his eyes from side to side, then up, then down, focusing in on a sliver of light from the vicinity of his feet.

"And this is for stealing my freedom and putting me in a position to be a victim of that motherfucking Frank Greisser."

Another shot.

Fuck fuck fuck. He was shooting Aidan. Why can't I see? Why can't I move my arms?

I'm trapped. The chill of an ice cube rolling across his skull signaled the onset of panic. He automatically began the litany he'd learned from his own psychiatric textbooks. *I'm not going to die. I'm not trapped forever. It's just temporary. Think about Aidan. Think about the Queen. Think about the sonofabitch who's out there shooting your friend.*

He opened his eyes again and studied the sliver of light. Something moved, casting a shadow. He was pinned under something, probably part of the car. His legs were free.

"And Cage Fucking Reynolds. You weren't supposed to be driving, you backstabbing bastard. But you got yours anyway, didn't you? You deserve a little payback, so here's for suckering me in, earning my trust, and then turning on me."

Cage heard the gun before the pain registered, and it took every ounce of strength he could muster to grit his teeth and not move. The only chance he had of surviving, to save himself and save Aidan if it wasn't too late, was to outlast this madman who'd just shot a fucking hole through his exposed leg.

"And here's for that big, shit-eating grin on your face when you told me all about my death sentence."

Cage had screwed his eyes shut, tensed his jaw, knowing it was coming, but the second blast hit bone and he wanted to die. But he didn't make a sound. Didn't twitch.

Not until he heard the sound of a match striking and the smell of sulfur and gasoline, an engine rev, tires squealing on pavement, and silence.

A curl of smoke reached him beneath whatever lay on top of him. If he didn't move, he was going to die out here.

Cage gathered every ounce of strength he could into his shoulders and pushed his arms straight up. Metal, and it moved. With a great heave, it shifted, and cool air hit him like a caress. The smoke was thicker now; he had to find Aidan.

He struggled to sit up, shoving the crumpled hood of the car away from him and looking for the fire. It had fizzled but still smoked. He had time—but even if the fire didn't get them, it would only be a matter of time before a motorist saw them and stopped.

He had to find Aidan.

In the shock of it all, Cage had forgotten about his legs until he tried to stand and fell with all the grace of an orangutan. Both legs felt as if they were on fire below the knee. When he sat up again, he saw blood-covered denim on the front of both legs, six inches or so above his ankles. At least Matthias had given him matching gunshot wounds, the old bastard.

He could crawl, though. Crawling was good.

Rolling to his knees, he hung his head and waited for a wave of dizziness to pass. Blood. He scented blood, and a lot of it. Thank God for safety glass that broke into nuggets instead of shards. It still dug into his hands and knees as he inched toward the strongest blood scent, but at least it didn't shred him to ribbons.

Finally, he spotted a boot, a leg.

Holy fuck, Aidan had to be dead. Nobody could survive such a head wound. Even a vampire had limitations. His face was covered in blood; a bullet wound to his right temple was the worst of it, maybe crushing the bone around the eye.

Cage rolled to his side as another wave of dizziness hit him, sending the world into a sickening spin, He wanted nothing more than to sleep. To take out the package he'd wrapped memories of his little bird inside of, to remember it, enjoy it. Dream about it.

Stupid vampire, she'd say if she saw him now. *Aidan's your friend. Suck it up and help him if you can.*

Somehow he pushed himself up on hands and knees again and crawled to Aidan.

"Aidan, can you hear me?" *Of course, he can't hear you, bloody fool. He's dead.*

Robin wouldn't let it drop. *Be sure, vampire. And even if he's gone, don't leave him out here for the sun to find him, or humans. Take him home to Krys. Take him home to Penton.*

"You're right, little bird." He raised his right hand, waited a second to see if he could stay on his knees without both hands to support him, and he could. He reached out with tentative fingers that left a white trail through the blood covering Aidan's neck and closed his eyes, praying to whatever God might hear him that there would be a pulse.

There. See, vampire? The fluttering thump against his fingertips was faint, but Aidan was alive.

Cage thought he could drag them both into the stand of trees that filled the median near where the car had overturned—at least if he rested every few inches. After a couple of feet, he had to stop and rest. The ache in his legs set the tone for the rest of his body. Of course, the old bastard had used silver bullets. They'd need to be dug out. Later.

Groaning, he threw an arm around Aidan's chest, hooked it under his arms and tugged. After a while, time meant nothing, and Cage's mind was empty but for the need to slide one knee forward, then the other, pull Aidan with him, then repeat.

Finally, the rough pavement under the bloody heels of his palms hit cool grass. Wet grass. He wished he could roll in its soothing chill. At least he could rest his cheek against it for a moment. They were off the road.

Just for a moment, he could sleep.

CHAPTER 35

Y ou tell me."
        Robin shook Glory hard enough that Nik pulled her
away. "Don't push her. Mirren being sick is making her sick. She's
doing the best she can."

Damn it, she didn't care. She pushed Nik away and got on
her knees in front of Glory, who cradled a half-conscious Mirren
against her and rocked and cried. Robin wanted the chance to do
that for Cage.

"Where were they when Aidan called Krys? You were here.
Where were they?"

Glory swallowed hard. "I'm trying to remember. Aidan called
just after eleven p.m., and they were on I-85 just leaving Atlanta.
I think that's right." She winced and pressed a hand against her
temple.

"And how long after that before Krys started getting sick?"
From what garbled mess she'd been able to interpret, Krys had
the tightest bond with Aidan, so it made sense she'd be the first
one to feel it if he were hurt. Robin still had trouble believing all

that bond-mate stuff, but something was making them sick. "How long, Glory?"

"An hour maybe, or forty-five minutes. About that."

Robin patted Glory's knee and got up, edging past Nik. He grabbed her arm. "What are you going to do?"

"I'm going to find them. And don't try to stop me."

Nik followed her into the bedroom. "I'm not stopping you. I'm going with you."

Robin grabbed the pouch she wore around her leg when she shifted, stuck her cell phone inside, and strapped it around her ankle. Around her neck she tied a little genius thing of her own invention, a scarf that would unroll large enough to serve as a dress—just in case she had to make nice with some humans.

"I can go faster without you." God, that sounded harsh. She looked up at Nik and whispered, "I have to find him."

He smiled. "I know. Okay, then. I'm going to start driving. When you find them, call me and I'll find you. If they're outside, we've gotta get them in before dawn."

She wrapped her arms around him, taking comfort in his warmth and the fact that he never, ever doubted her. "I love you, Niko."

"Good thing. You need me."

She couldn't argue with him on that one. "Yeah, you right." They laughed at the New Orleans-ism.

"How's Krys?" Robin looked across the hall, where they'd put Krys on Nik's bed. Both Mark and Melissa were sick, too, and Britta was in the subspace below Aidan's house. What a fucked-up mess vampires were.

"Still the same. In a human, I'd say she was in a coma. I don't know what the vampire equivalent of that is. And hey"—Nik squeezed her shoulder—"be careful. We don't know who's still out there."

Yeah, Fen Patrick, for one.

On her way out, Robin noticed the small packet of cigars on her nightstand—she'd refused to let Cage smoke one in the house. She picked them up and tucked them into the pouch with her phone. He could smoke them all he wanted if he'd just be okay. Please let him be okay.

You've gone a little off track in your life to be bargaining with God, little bird. She shook her head. He was talking to her, and he wasn't even here.

She kissed Nik good-bye, took a final look at Mirren—a slab of pale marble, still and silent—and knew she had to save Cage and Aidan both if there was any way to do it. Somehow, in only a week, she'd come to love these people. Vampires. Whatever.

She undressed on the porch, shook her shoulders loose, and shifted, taking off northeast. The night was clear and cool, and there were no headwinds to fight. She'd alternate flying at about thirty miles per hour until she got a good burst of air, then she'd glide at a hundred twenty.

Staying over the tree line, she kept the interstate in her sights, diving low when she thought she saw a gleam of metal or glass.

Near the Georgia-Alabama state line, she saw it—what was left of Aidan's car, overturned in the wide median near a stand of trees next to a steep drop-off. Glass littered the highway, and she saw a big rig slow down to take a look as it passed. The driver sped up and kept going, but chances were good he'd report it—if someone hadn't already. She had to find them.

She circled the area, looking for a landing spot where she could be away from sight of the highway, and that's when she saw it—a dark spot in the side of a low mountain, less than a mile from the wreck. A cave. If they were alive, she might be able to take them there until Nik could reach them.

Better not plan too far ahead, little bird.

Robin chose a spot on the other side of the stand of trees to shift, out of sight of both sides of the interstate highway, quickly untying the scarf and wrapping it around her in case the state police showed up. She'd have to do enough fast talking in that case without trying to do it naked.

The broken safety glass glittered in the moonlight and crunched under her bare feet without cutting her, and it seemed wrong that it should look so pretty, like crystals or diamonds. There was no one in the car. No bodies nearby.

But there was blood. And where there was blood, there was a trail. The predatory part of her liked the scent of it, wanted it.

The human part of her used it to find them, following a smear barely visible on the pavement, across two lanes and onto the grass. Just outside the tree line, she saw them and froze. They were so still, so pale in the moonlight. Cage was on his belly with an arm draped across Aidan's stomach. Aidan's face. That beautiful face . . .

You have to forget who we are, little bird. Follow your training.

She knelt beside Aidan and felt for a pulse, breathing a sigh of thanks when she found one, thready and fast but at least he was alive for now. What happened to all those bonded to him if he died? She didn't want to know, not yet.

Carefully, she turned Cage over, again feeling for a pulse. She closed her eyes in silent thanks when she felt it, and that it was strong. He was in better shape than Aidan.

Now, to get them hidden before anyone arrived. Her instinct was to take Cage first, but she knew that wasn't what he'd want.

Aidan had to make it to ensure the others did and to ensure Penton did.

She slipped her hands beneath Aidan's knees and back and lifted. Her spine protested, and her shoulders, but she managed to stand. *Piece of cake, Robin.*

"I'll be back, vampire." She stayed in the cover of the trees while another truck passed, going toward Atlanta, then hurried across the highway as fast as she could carrying a couple of hundred pounds of vampire. Her bare feet slid on the wet straw and leaves, and twice she fell, twisting to cushion Aidan's head against her so it wouldn't hit the ground. She didn't need to add to the damage that had already been done.

Finally, she reached the cave, panting for breath, sharp pain stabbing through her lungs and against her ribcage. Bad thing about caves—reaching them on foot always required an uphill climb.

Robin left Aidan near the mouth of the cave, and since she'd already approached God, unsure he'd remember her or want to hear from her if he did, she pushed her luck and prayed there weren't wildcats or bears in the cave who'd make a tasty snack of Aidan while she was gone.

By the time she reached the bottom of the hill and crossed the highway to Cage, a shrill siren of some vehicle coming up fast carried through the night. She hoisted Cage up and took off at a sloppy, off-kilter lope. "Sorry, no time to be gentle, vampire."

She made it into the tree line just as the first flashing light crested the hill to the east, toward Penton. She'd had to sit down to catch her breath anyway, so she stayed put, watching through the pine boughs as a state police cruiser stopped and two officers walked around the wreckage. "Wonder what they'll think happened to the driver?"

She didn't wait to find out but managed to get Cage up and start moving again, relieved to see Aidan still where she'd left him. Pulling her cell phone from its pouch, she checked the time. Damn it, they'd be pushing it to get them to Penton before dawn, but they'd try.

Nik answered on the first ring and was all business in his questions: location, landmarks, condition of the patients, presence of police. He'd gone into Ranger mode, and a good thing. Her emotions had ridden one too many roller coasters already tonight.

Now, they waited, she and her still, silent companions, their blood looking black in the soft moonlight. Which gave her an idea . . .

Robin crawled to where Aidan lay, and wouldn't Cage be proud that she stifled her need to take care of him first and instead went to his friend? She remembered the night of the bonding, when Aidan had flicked that little blade across his wrist. He'd pulled the knife from his right pocket.

His pants were stiff with dried blood, but she'd touched worse. One would be an awfully sorry bird of prey if one got queasy over blood. Spiders? Another matter altogether.

She found the knife and, touching the blade to her forearm, made a small incision. She massaged the skin around the cut to get the blood flowing and held her wrist to Aidan's mouth. Damn it. His face was so bloody that she couldn't tell what was going in and what was already there.

Cage's head injury was in the back, so she crawled over to him. "I told you you'd feed from me one day, vampire. Make it today. Please."

She had to cut again—shifters healed fast, and a cut that small wouldn't last long. The new incision needed to be twice as big, so she gritted her teeth and dug the knife in deeper and dragged it across an extra inch of skin.

Stretching out alongside Cage, she held her arm over his mouth, but the blood dripped on his face. "Damn it." She sat up, thinking. *Idiot bird. Feed it to him.* She swiped her left forefinger through the blood, gathering as much on her fingertip as she could, and slipped her finger between his lips. Again. Again. Again.

"Cage Reynolds, we are going to do this until Nik gets here, so you might as well get used to it."

Robin made another cut, another swipe, another finger between his lips. Once more. She pulled her hand away, but quicker than any movement she could track, he had grasped her wrist. "Cage?"

His eyes remained closed, but his grip was forged in iron. She reached out with the knife and made another cut, this time in the arm he was holding.

Cage pulled it to him so frantically that Robin toppled over, and he bit hard. The fangs hurt like hell going in, but then she forgot all about it as every neuron in her brain's pleasure center went on overload. She let herself sink to the ground next to him, letting each pull of his mouth take her deeper, so deep.

"Well, isn't this cozy?"

Robin yelped and tried to sit up, but Cage had her arm imprisoned with both hands, still feeding. "Who are you?"

A young guy, early twenties at the oldest, had come from the woods on the other side of the hill from the wreck. He was blond, flashed a lot of dimples, and had eyes that had lightened to a tawny gold. Vampire. But whose side was he on?

"Good God, Will, leave me in the ditch next time why don't you?" A red-haired woman walked up behind him and smacked him in the head.

It finally hit her, who they must be. "You're Will and Randa?"

Will cocked his head. "Intros later, little shifter. Where's Aidan?"

"I see him." Randa ran past them and knelt next to him. "Oh my God. Will, I don't know. You've gotten sicker the closer we've gotten to him, and I see why. We've got to get him to Penton."

"Jesus." Will knelt next to Aidan, and if vampires could cry, Will would be sobbing. His lip was trembling when he looked up. "Who did this? Who the hell did this?"

Will asked the question of Robin, but it was Cage who answered. "Your father."

❧CHAPTER 36❧

Cage felt like hell. His legs hurt from where Nik had dug the bullets out —without anesthesia — just before daysleep the morning Will and Randa brought them home. He thought he might have cried, but he couldn't remember for sure. The back of his head throbbed from what Nik said was probably a concussion.

He was the luckiest sonofabitch on earth. Two nights after he'd been sure death was imminent, he was lying here in his bed in the lieutenants' quarters with his guardian angel beside him. He rolled over, trying not to groan aloud, and looked at her—really looked at Robin Ashton, without the mouth and the attitude that made her seem twice her size. Without those dark-brown eyes glaring or dancing or heating up, her long lashes were more delicate and sensuous. Her nose turned up slightly, and her impossible auburn hair stuck in every conceivable direction. It might be the sexiest thing he'd ever seen.

He had no right to be this content, and part of him wished they could stay like this forever. Here in their little cocoon, making love, making each other laugh, fighting. Because he wasn't sure he wanted to know the answers to the questions that were already bombarding his mind. About Aidan. Krys. Melissa. Mirren. All of them. What the future held for Penton.

Robin moaned and opened her eyes a crack, then all the way. "You're awake. I mean really awake. The last couple of nights you were . . ."

"Pretty stupid, I imagine." He leaned over and kissed her, then kissed her again. "I do remember some things quite well. I believe I fed from you."

She grinned. "And I do believe you made me feed from you, sort of."

He planted a kiss on her neck, where he'd definitely be feeding from her again at a near-future date. "And then I think we fucked, just before twilight."

"Oh, we definitely did that. Twice, I think."

He leaned over and took one small, perfect breast in his mouth, then the other. "You realize you're stuck with me for good, right?"

She squinted at him, reached over and thumped him on the head. "Don't think that gives you a free ride to be an asshat."

He laughed and lay back.

"I need to tell you about my family."

Cage rolled over and pulled her to him. "It doesn't matter, unless you've got a husband stashed away somewhere."

"I don't have a husband." Robin sat up and wrapped her arms around her knees. "You really don't want to know?"

Cage reached out and took her hand. "I want to know whatever you want to tell me. When you're ready, I'll be ready to listen. Until then, it doesn't matter. We're what matters."

She lay back down with her back to him, and he held his breath, waiting to see if she'd continue. He wouldn't press her, but he desperately wanted to understand her.

"My sister Wren is two years younger than me." Her voice was muffled and had fallen into a soft, Southern twang different from her usual sharply clipped accent. "We lived south of Dallas in a town where there were lots of eagle shifters, and she fell in love with this guy, Kevin, who was the nephew of our Goia."

She stopped, and Cage rolled over and pulled her into his arms, holding her, thinking about the strong protective streak she'd shown over Nik and over him. "Things went badly with him?"

She shifted her head slightly, which he interpreted as a nod. "He beat her. Belittled her. She became this scared, anxious person I didn't know anymore."

He waited, willing her to go on. When she spoke again, her voice was strained, filled with pain. "I killed him, Cage. I went to their house to try to talk Wren into leaving him, and she was unconscious. Covered with blood on the floor of their kitchen. He was sitting in the fucking recliner watching a football game while she bled on the floor."

"You were just protecting her, love. That's what you do." Cage pulled her against him more tightly and let her cry for a long time. When her body stopped shaking from the force of her sobs, he asked the question whose answer had made Robin the woman he'd come to love.

"What happened? With your family? With your Goia?"

Robin rolled onto her back, so she could look at him. "Wren hates me. She defends the bastard, even now. The Goia demanded payment in kind: my life for his son's." The tears had started again.

"But what about your parents?" The sister's reaction didn't surprise him; victims of abuse were indoctrinated to blame themselves and not their abuser. That much hadn't changed from his human days.

"I broke their hearts." Robin had stopped crying and now looked simply sad. "If they defended me, they lost their place in our community. It meant too much to them, so I slipped away. They're duty bound to turn me in if they find me, so I stay on the move."

Cage brushed his fingertips across her cheek and kissed her forehead. "No one will ever find you here, little bird." And if they did, whether it was family or Goia or a posse of eagles, they'd have to go through him to touch her.

She pulled away from him, and the old fire had returned to her brown eyes. "Penton has to survive. Aidan's improving, but we don't know if Krys will wake up, or Britta. We have unfinished business if we're going to make this a safe home for all of us."

He nodded. He'd been thinking the same thing. Now that he was back on his feet and Nik had recuperated enough to drive, they needed to find Matthias. And then he wanted Fen Patrick and the dickhead who'd set all this in motion, Frank Greisser.

"Nik can help us," Robin said.

He hated to ask the guy to use the Touch when he'd barely recovered from his run-in with Shawn. "Nik needs some recovery time, love."

Oh yeah, she was definitely back to normal; her jaw was clenched, and her eyes had narrowed. "Nik doesn't need recovery time; he needs a chance to help. He's just waiting for you to give him the go-ahead."

Which was all well and good, but he wasn't in charge. "It's not my call to make."

She kissed his shoulder, then slapped it. "Aidan's out of commission, and until he's back on his feet, that means Mirren's running on low batteries. Which, in turn, means that you and Will are in charge."

Well, shit. "That is quite a frightening scenario, then. Two half-lame vampires with bossy women by their sides."

"Exactly. So move it."

First, Cage needed to talk to Will, who'd also been feeling peaked since getting in close proximity to Aidan; their theory was that Cage's steady diet of shifter blood was somehow making him invulnerable to the bonding energy leach—yet another reason to appreciate Robin.

He held Robin until she finally fell asleep, then walked down the hallway to find Will sitting with Aidan and Krys, whose room in the lieutenants' quarters had become a makeshift hospital bay. Aidan had awakened a couple of times, briefly. Krys hadn't stirred. She was still breathing, though, and where there was breath, there was hope.

"He wake up?" Cage propped against the wall next to the bed. Aidan's head was heavily bandaged; the rest of his injuries had healed like a vampire should—fast and clean.

Will shook his head. "Not yet." They remained quiet a few moments as Cage tried to figure out how to broach the subject of Matthias.

"I need to ask you something." Cage stared at the floor. He didn't think he could ask permission to chase down a friend's father and look his friend in the eye while doing so.

"When you find him, kill him," Will said. "Aidan is my family. Randa. You. Mirren. He gave up that right a long time ago."

"You're sure?"

"No."

Cage and Will looked at each other, then at the bed where Aidan lay, his one visible eye open and almost pure white. "No?" Cage wasn't sure if the man knew what he was responding to. "You find him, hold him. But don't kill him. He's mine."

❧EPILOGUE❧

Two Months Later, Outside Lexington, Virginia

Movement from above. Unfamiliar voices. His dreams always began this way. A different time, a different man, the same dream.

A shaft of light would pierce the darkness from above. Heavy boots would descend the steps. The gleam of a sharpened sword would rivet his attention until his gaze rose to the face of the man who bore it. The Slayer, Mirren Kincaid. The man who'd come to kill him.

In this new version of the dream, Matthias Ludlam begged Kincaid to kill him quickly, to end the damnable hunger that was eating him alive from the inside out. To end the need to feed on what disgusted and sickened him.

To erase the memories of his final humiliation, when Cage Reynolds—him, always him—had tracked him down in suburban Atlanta and brought him back here, to his own house, to sit. Awaiting what, he didn't know. He would've sworn the cocky Brit was as dead as the Irish farmer whose boots he licked, but somehow, he'd survived.

Frank Greisser wouldn't help Matthias now. He'd disavowed any knowledge of Matthias or his whereabouts, Reynolds had gloated. Frank had heard Matthias was performing unspeakable experiments on other vampires; in fact, the newly reformed Tribunal would welcome news on the whereabouts of the despicable Herr Ludlam.

Matthias hadn't counted the days of his imprisonment this time. It could be November or January or June. It didn't matter. All of time centered now on the door at the top of the stairs, where a turn of the knob sent down that shaft of light. A hand flipped the switch and the resulting glow illuminated the dark shadows of his cell.

Matthias stood and squinted at the boots descending. They belonged, as in his dream, to Mirren Kincaid. The man seemed even more massive now, looking through the bars of the cell where he himself had once been locked up.

"You're looking pretty sad, Matthias." Kincaid quirked one side of his mouth. "What happened to your hair?"

Matthias flinched. It had fallen out except for a few white tufts. He'd never known what type of shifter DNA he'd been injected with, for which he hoped Frank Greisser rotted in hell with his perverted plan of finding a way for vampires to drink vaccinated blood.

Hope flickered to life. He'd wondered why they kept him alive, why Reynolds and his human Army friends hadn't just taken him out when they found him. Maybe there was time for a deal.

"I can give you Frank Greisser." Matthias realized he still had a card to play, and it was a big one. "I can tell you whatever you want to know about what he's been up to."

"Can you now?" Kincaid, the insolent lout, walked to the staircase and called to whoever was above. "I think Matthias wants to talk business."

Who was up there? Reynolds, probably. He, like Kincaid, was a mercenary at heart. They'd both be willing to bargain.

And sure enough, Reynolds came down the steps, as haughty and arrogant as ever.

"I told Kincaid, I can give you Greisser." Matthias hated the pleading sound in his voice but couldn't control it. "He's the one with the power, and the only way you're going to change the way the Tribunal is handling things is to get rid of him."

Reynolds grinned. "You're talking to the wrong guys, Matthias. Mirren and I don't make the rules where Penton is concerned."

Then who? "William?" He didn't know whether to be elated or frightened. His son was a mystery to him, always had been.

"No, Will wanted to be here, but he's having surgery on those legs you mangled with your little grenade-tossing stunt," Reynolds said. "The person we pledge fealty to is the one we've always followed."

"Murphy's dead." They were playing games with him now. "So you'd do well to take my offer if you have any hope of getting Frank out of power."

They just looked at him for a moment, amused and arrogant, and then Reynolds pulled a set of keys from his pocket and unlocked the door to Matthias's cell. He didn't move at first, not sure what game they were playing.

Finally, he stepped out the cell. Funny how once the silver bars were behind him, the room looked brighter, the world more hopeful. "Does this mean you're ready to talk?"

"I am." The voice came from the top of the stairs. It had a faint Irish lilt. It was the voice of a dead man.

Holy mother of God. Matthias had never been a religious man, even in his human life, but he felt the heavens and all its angels must be laughing at this cosmic joke.

"I killed you," he whispered to the newcomer, who walked down the stairs and came to stand in front of him. "I saw you die."

"You gave it a good shot." Murphy was thinner. A ragged scar, still red and unhealed, zagged from his right eyebrow to his ear. He wore a patch over his right eye, but his left eye was pale and cold and unyielding.

"I can help you get Greisser." His voice sounded wild and desperate, even to himself. "I'm a victim, too. He turned me into . . . this." He grasped a tuft of white hair and pulled. Half of it came out in his hand.

"I will get Greisser in due time, Matthias." Murphy took a step closer, and Matthias swallowed hard, noticing for the first time the curved silver blade of the knife in Murphy's right hand. "I will get him without your help."

"I still have contacts on the Tribunal. I can convince them to support you." Matthias looked down and said the word he'd always said in his dream: "Please."

"We're declaring war on the Tribunal," Aidan said. "We'll fight on their terms, on their turf, whatever it takes. You, however, won't be there to see it."

Matthias looked down as Murphy raised the silver blade, the overhead light glinting off its surface.

In the old dream, Matthias had met his final moments not with brave defiance but with humiliation, pleading for mercy from the man whose life he'd tried to destroy.

The dream had always reached the same end: his executioner would smile, and the blade would fall.

Aidan Murphy smiled.

More from Susannah Sandlin

Read on for a sample chapter of *Lovely, Dark, and Deep*, the first book in a new romantic suspense series by Susannah Sandlin.

❧ CHAPTER 1 ❧

Gillian tripped on the threshold of the ICU doorway, attracting a small flurry of alarmed nurses. By the time she assured them she was a habitual klutz and not a terrorist or the crazed lunatic family member of a patient, she'd eaten up a considerable chunk of the paltry half hour set aside in the evening for visitors.

Not that Viv knew she was here. Gillian tugged the heavy wooden chair closer to the bed, using her thumb to stuff a tuft of padding back into the ripped mint-green vinyl seat. For the first few seconds, she tried to comprehend the beeping machines and wires and IVs holding her best friend together.

Not just her friend. Vivian Ortiz was her neighbor and mother figure, dispenser of wisdom and light beer and home remedies to get rid of fire ants. She was also the only other woman Gillian knew who was crazy enough to live in a single-wide trailer at the edge of a wildlife reserve in hurricane country.

They'd been separated at birth, only in different generations, Viv always said.

Gillian took her friend's hand, which looked naked and frail minus its normal assortment of oversized rings, most purchased from one of those TV shopping channels Viv was addicted to. Tears pressed heavily against the backs of Gillian's eyes. Vivian was warm and full of life, not hot and dry like this husk of skin.

She whispered the question the sheriff's deputy couldn't answer: "What the hell happened?"

Viv couldn't answer, either. She could only lie there, her eyes closed, dark lashes resting on her cheeks, her warm olive skin pale against the sterile white sheets under fluorescent lighting. An automobile accident, the deputy had told Gillian after finding her phone number in Viv's purse and tracking her down. Viv had plowed into a tree not a mile from her trailer, scattering groceries across Highway 24 near the old Rosewood Baptist Church. A one-car accident, the officer said, but a blinding rain had been coming down about the time it happened.

Vivian was the slowest, most cautious driver Gillian had ever met. They laughed about it, about how Viv said if God meant people to go fast, he wouldn't have invented middle-aged women and old men. About how, especially if one of Florida's afternoon storms was in full force, Vivian's car could be outrun by a slow-moving gator.

A bell sounded from somewhere near the two monitors sitting on the desk outside the glassed-off cubicles, announcing the end of the day's last visitation period.

A nurse in green scrubs waved at Gillian and pointed toward the door, ready to spend her evening hovering over the monitors, watching to see if Viv or the person in the other cubicle, so old and wrinkled Gillian couldn't even determine a gender, might need transferring from the county's little hospital here in Williston to Ocala or even Gainesville. Waiting to see which patient's condition descended from stable to critical, or rose from serious to stable. These categories didn't mean much when held up beside a pale face, closed eyes, shallow breathing, and hot, dry hands.

Gillian stopped in the hallway and dug in her pocket for quarters to plug in the soda machine, giving a startled jump at the buzz of her phone vibrating in her jeans pocket. She didn't recognize the area code, and the screen read "Private Caller." Since she was the only licensed nuisance-gator trapper in the county, "on call" was a constant state unless she found another trapper to cover for her. Alligators couldn't care less that Labor Day weekend was imminent or that Viv was hurt.

She sat in one of the three plastic chairs in the waiting area and scrambled in her shoulder bag for a pen and pad in case she needed to write down an address, then hit the "Talk" button. "Campbell."

"Is this the Gillian Campbell who was on the *Noonday Chat* show a few days ago?" The man spoke with a deep baritone that had a Southern twang—not a twang from the Deep South or from Louisiana, but maybe Texas or Oklahoma. *Jeez-Louise*, she hoped he wasn't some whacked-out stalker.

"Yes, it is. Can I help you?" His answer to that question would determine whether she ended the call or kept listening.

"I want to talk to you about that ruby cross, the one your ancestor lost."

Gillian laughed. "Look, that's just a family legend, and what I said on the show is all I know about it. Sorry I can't help you."

"Oh, you'll help me, honey."

Honey? She might be a state employee with a responsibility to be polite to the public, but she didn't have to listen to sexist cowboy stalkers. "I assure you, I can't help. Good night, sir, and please don't call again."

It had to be the damned Campbell curse. As long as she could remember, her grandparents and parents—and now Gillian herself—had blamed old Duncan Campbell and his thieving ways for anything that went amiss, from a hangnail to a creepy phone call.

The phone buzzed again before she reached her car, again from "Private Caller." "Forget it," she muttered, unlocking the door of her seven-year-old Jeep and tossing her bag on the passenger seat. Another buzz told her the jerk had left a message. Private Caller needed to get a life.

She stared at the phone a moment, knowing she should just erase the message, but curiosity trumped common sense. She jabbed at the screen and turned up the volume. "As I was trying to explain before you cut me off, Ms. Campbell, I represent someone with a keen interest in acquiring the ruby cross you talked about in your little TV interview."

The voice paused so long Gillian had her finger poised over the "Erase" button when he spoke again. "That car accident your friend Ms. Ortiz had? I hope it got your attention. I'll call back at ten p.m., and honey, this time I suggest you answer."

Silence weighed heavily as adrenaline raced through Gillian's system. She used her elbow to lock the driver's side door, then leaned across the seats to lock the others. Was he here somewhere, watching?

Her fingers trembled as she retrieved the list of recent calls on the phone, and she stared stupidly at "Private Caller." Surely it was a sick prank. Maybe the guy worked at the hospital. Maybe he'd watched that silly television interview and recognized her when she came in to visit Viv. Maybe he was watching her now, from a window or from the deep shadows the hospital's single outdoor light didn't reach.

The afternoon's storm had moved out quickly, as storms in Florida usually did, but a dense layer of clouds remained to blot out the moon and stars. The parking lot of the small hospital was nearly deserted, and the drive from Williston back to Gillian's trailer halfway to the coast was over dark, two-lane roads through dense forest. If experience proved true, there would be no other traffic.

You're being an idiot. All the same, she double-checked the Jeep's door locks before shoving the key into the ignition and turning it. She'd grab a snack from the convenience store down the street, drive home, and watch the Home Shopping Network or QVC in Viv's honor. She'd not let a crackpot phone call ruin her day. If he called again, she'd contact the county sheriff's office.

At the Stop-N-Go near the high school, she parked in front of the entrance, unable to shake the willies. She shouldn't let a call like that creep her out, but she couldn't quiet the nagging voice that told her to get a hotel room at the Sleep Inn down the street. Spend the night here where there were people around and drive the twenty miles home in the daylight, when people would have their RVs on the roads, heading for a long weekend at the beach.

Two other cars sat in the Stop-N-Go lot. One had a foursome of teenagers hanging around outside it, laughing and drinking beer and flirting. The other was empty and probably belonged to the store clerk. Taking a deep breath, Gillian got out of the car and waved at the kids as she walked into the store and looked around for the ATM.

"Over in the back corner." The clerk squinted through orange-framed cat-eye glasses almost the same color as the thinning hair that floated in tufts around her head. "It's been tore up, but we finally got 'er fixed today."

"Thanks." Gillian eventually spotted the machine, half-hidden by a display of Pop-Tarts, and swiped her debit card through the machine's reader.

Terrific. *Transaction Declined; Please Contact Financial Institution.*

"Damn you and your curse, Duncan Campbell. Give me just one freaking break." She tried again, with the same results.

Obviously, the ATM wasn't fixed after all. She walked down the aisle of junk food and finally settled on a bag of tortilla chips, taking it to the counter along with a jar of her favorite chunky salsa. She'd eat it in Viv's honor while TV shopping for the biggest, most garish ring she could find. Viv would love it.

She handed her debit card to the clerk. "Sorry, the machine's still not working."

"It's those dang kids. Prob'ly tore it up already." The woman rang up the chips and salsa, then stared at the register screen, shaking her head. "Sorry, but your card's been declined. You wanna pay cash or put the stuff back? Don't feel bad about it; happens all the time."

The store clerk continued to pop gum while she talked, a skill Gillian figured she'd been honing for years. At least she didn't look judgmentally at the customer with the rumpled T-shirt and jeans, not to mention the droopy ponytail, whose bank had declined her five-dollar purchase of junk food.

The woman might not be judgmental, but the exchange didn't stop Gillian's face from heating with embarrassment. She'd gotten paid yesterday and had used the card to buy gas this morning, so what was up with her bank? She fished her wallet out of her bag and said a prayer of thanks when she found four one-dollar bills and some quarters jammed into the zippered coin compartment.

On the bright side, at least she knew not to stop at the Sleep Inn. If she stayed in Williston tonight, the only "sleeping in" she'd be doing would be in her vehicle, which settled that internal debate. She'd be driving home.

Back in the cocoon of the Jeep, she locked the doors and stared at the phone. It was almost ten o'clock, and she had to decide whether or not to answer the crackpot's call—and she was pretty sure he would call. If nothing else, he sounded like a persistent crackpot.

When the ringtone sounded, right on time, she took a deep breath and relaxed her shoulders before answering. "All right, who are you? What is it you want?" No point in pretending she didn't know it was him.

"Who I work for doesn't matter, lady. What matters is that the individual who employs me is serious and has a lot of reach."

Reach?

"Meaning what? He runs innocent women off the road because he wants some ancient relic that probably doesn't exist?"

"Oh, it exists, or you better hope it does." The man paused, and Gillian thought she heard the sound of a radio or television in the background, something with a canned laugh track. It only made the conversation more surreal. "Kinda humiliating to have your debit card turned down, wasn't it?"

The thread of fear that had stretched taut through Gillian all evening finally snapped, and she fought the urge to crawl under the floorboard and hide. Who the hell were these people? Where were they hiding? Watching.

Her spine tingled as if a line of ants were marching down it. "What do you want from me?"

She needed to get to the Williston PD. Find out how to trace private numbers. Surely there had to be a way the police could do it.

"We want the Templars' cross. I thought I made that clear," the man said. "You have thirty days to find it and deliver it, and then you can have your life back. We might even give you a little something for your trouble."

A laugh escaped her before Gillian could stop it. Tex, as she'd come to think of him, was clearly insane, which didn't make him any less dangerous. "Thirty days. Are you serious?"

"Oh, I'm deathly serious, Ms. Campbell, and you'd do well to remember it."

Gillian's temper finally overrode her fear and, probably, her common sense. "Look, Tex. Here's a reality pill for you to swallow. First, that whole story about my ancestor and the Templars' cross? It's a family tall tale I remember hearing as a kid. There's no proof it's true. It's probably been exaggerated and embellished so many times over the generations that any bit of truth in it has been lost.

"Second, even if it were true, Duncan Campbell was lost in a freaking shipwreck in the sixteenth century.

"Third, even if I knew where the ship went down, how the hell would I go about finding something that's been on the bottom of the ocean for four hundred years?"

Her outburst was met with a long silence. Good. She'd made her point.

"That's why you have thirty days," the man finally said. "So I suggest you take a leave of absence from those alligators of yours and get busy."

Yeah, she'd get busy all right, with the police department and the phone company. "Here's what I suggest, both for you and who-ever you work for: go fuck yourselves. And you can quote me on that."

"That's what you want me to tell that sweet little Holly Bryant?"

Gillian froze, and a layer of gauze seemed to pad the space between her and the world around her. The laughter of the teenagers in the parking lot grew tinny and muffled. Colors faded and dulled. Her own voice came out reedy and thin. "Wh-what?"

"You heard me. Surely after what happened five years ago, you don't want to be responsible for the death of another little kid, do you? Your niece is what, three years old now? Sweet little thing, too. One of my associates saw her down in Lauderdale today—sent me a photo, in fact, from the Rainbow Road Preschool."

"You wouldn't." No one could be fanatical enough to hurt a child, especially over something this stupid. She wanted to scream, to rant, to cry out at the heavens, but her mouth had grown so dry she could barely swallow. Only one strained syllable came out. "Please."

"Good. Finally, I think we understand each other. I'll call in the morning with instructions." Tex's voice became obscenely cheerful. "This phone can't be traced, so don't bother. Talk to the police, and you'll find our retribution fast and ugly.

"And if you talk to that little niece of yours, you tell her the pink dress she wore to day care today—the one with the kittens on the front? That was real, real cute."

❦ ACKNOWLEDGMENTS ❧

As always, I owe a great big "thank-you" to agent Marlene Stringer, who gives new meaning to the phrase "works tirelessly." Thanks to JoVon Sotak and the awesome team at Montlake Romance for the faith and the hard work—you guys are the best! Special thanks to alpha reader Dianne, who dispenses good advice in a gentle way (even though she still doesn't read paranormals); Debbie, who is always asking, "Got anything new for me to read?"; and my friends in the Auburn Writers Circle—Julia, Larry, Mike, Pete, Robin, and Shawn—who are not only fine writers but also can always make me laugh.

℘ABOUT THE AUTHOR℘

Studio 16, 2013

Susannah Sandlin is a native of Winfield, Alabama, and has worked as a writer and editor in educational publishing in Alabama, Illinois, Texas, California, and Louisiana. She currently lives in Auburn, Alabama, with two rescue dogs named after professional wrestlers (it was a phase). She has a no-longer-secret passion for Cajun and French-Canadian music and reality TV, and is on the hunt for a long-haul ice road trucker who also saves nuisance gators. Susannah is also the author of the award-winning Penton Legacy paranormal romance series: *Redemption*, *Absolution*, and *Omega*; the spinoff paranormal romance, *Storm Force*; and The Collectors, a romantic suspense series beginning with *Lovey, Dark, and Deep*. As Suzanne Johnson, she writes the Sentinels of New Orleans urban fantasy series.